the dark between

Also by Sonia Gensler

The Revenant

Ghostlight

the dark between

SONIA GENSLER

EMBER

Text copyright © 2013 by Sonia Gensler
Cover photographs copyright © 2013 by Emily Soto (girl on left), Valentino Sani for Trevillion Images (girl on right), and Shutterstock (background)

All rights reserved. Published in the United States by Ember, an imprint of Random House Children's Books, a division of Penguin Random House LLC, New York. Originally published in hardcover in the United States by Alfred A. Knopf, an imprint of Random House Children's Books, New York, in 2013.

Ember and the E colophon are registered trademarks of Penguin Random House LLC.

Visit us on the Web! randomhouseteens.com

Educators and librarians, for a variety of teaching tools, visit us at RHTeachersLibrarians.com

The Library of Congress has cataloged the hardcover edition of this work as follows:
Gensler, Sonia.
The dark between / Sonia Gensler. — 1st ed.
p. cm.
Summary: Three teenagers in Victorian era Cambridge spend the summer at a local college and soon discover that their hosts, the Metaphysical Society, may be conducting sinister experiments in an attempt to communicate with the dead.
ISBN 978-0-375-86702-6 (trade) — ISBN 978-0-375-96702-3 (lib. bdg.) — ISBN 978-0-375-89733-7 (ebook)
[1. Experiments—Fiction. 2. Dead—Fiction. 3. Cambridge (England)—History—19th century—Fiction. 4. Great Britain—History—Victoria, 1837–1901—Fiction.] I. Title.
PZ7.G29177Dar 2013 [Fic]—dc23 2012036208

ISBN 978-0-375-86140-6 (pbk.)

Printed in the United States of America
10 9 8 7 6 5 4 3 2 1
First Ember Edition 2015

For L. K. Madigan, who lives on in our hearts

the dark between

chapter 1

When Kate Poole was twelve, her body had folded easily into the medium's throne. Her limbs had been shorter, her joints more elastic. In those days she stayed cool and supple while waiting for the hymns to end.

Now, two years later, she was a leggy foal contorted in the womb, straining for freedom and the first breath of life. Perspiration soaked her chemise, and her limbs twitched and tingled.

After an eternity of singing, Mrs. Martineau's voice rose to a crescendo. In response, the sitters sang more passionately. Kate reached back to slowly lift the hinged panel, inhaled a lovely breath of fresh air, and pushed her head and arms out of the hidden compartment. Once her hands found the thick support bar on the back of the medium's chair, she slid her legs out and pulled herself up to a low crouch.

"Hand in Hand with Angels" drew to a close and the great chair creaked as Mrs. Martineau's body began to convulse. The sudden movement quieted the singers to a low hum. When the room fell silent, Mrs. Martineau spoke in her singsong trance voice.

"Dear friends, my spirit guide beckons. Do not be afraid. She wishes to show herself."

Kate heard the rustling of fabric as the sitters leaned forward. This was what they had come to see, after all. She clung to the back of the chair, bouncing gently on the balls of her tingling feet.

"The spirit will walk among you," continued the medium. "Do not be alarmed if you feel her touch. She reaches for the souls of your loved ones. She intends you no harm."

Kate rolled her eyes. The audience *loved* to feel the spirit touch—the gentlemen, especially. Some of them liked to feel back, and there wasn't much Kate could do to stop them. All part of the show, as Mrs. Martineau would say.

The medium shuddered rhythmically, rising off her seat a few inches as she did so. In response, Kate slowly rose behind Mrs. Martineau's head, hidden by the vast hood of the woman's white cloak. After another spell of twitching, Mrs. Martineau moaned dramatically and collapsed onto the table. At the same moment Kate stood at her full height behind the chair.

The audience gasped. They always did, even when they had come many times before.

Kate was a ghastly sight in the dim light sputtering from the gas fixtures—she knew this because Mrs. Martineau had once brought a mirror to the parlor so she could see her reflection in the near darkness. When Kate had looked in the glass and seen her thin frame draped in a shimmering, transparent shroud, her mouth fell open. The vision was perfectly ghoulish.

The next bit was her favorite. She pulled the shroud to her shoulders, revealing her face.

More than one lady cried out. A gentleman cleared his throat. Again there was a rustling of fabric as people shifted in their seats. Kate well knew how her brown eyes, rimmed with kohl, appeared as gaping holes against the unnatural paleness of her face. In that moment she didn't care that the luminous powder wrecked her skin, or that the wig made her scalp itch and sweat. Nor did it shame her that the costume—a gauzy wrap draped over the merest of underpinnings—left her exposed and shivering. In the dim light of the parlor, she was a wraith from a horror tale.

And she held them all under her spell.

Kate arched her back and began the slow movements of the spirit dance. The ladies rarely gave her trouble. They shivered at her touch and occasionally giggled when she sighed in their ears, but they never laid a hand on her. Once a lady had cried, "She reeks of onions!" and Mrs. Martineau had given Kate a good thumping when the sitters were gone. Thereafter she could take only bread and milk before the séances.

The gentlemen were altogether different. She could almost smell it on them—their longing to touch her. A few managed to keep their hands to themselves, but most had to claim a piece of her before she moved on. Some ran fingers through the long hair of her wig or stroked her bare arm; others probed underneath the shroud in a furtive search for her thighs. Though she'd long ago ceased to be shocked by their hot breath and wandering hands, she would never find it *pleasing* to be fondled by whiskery old fools. She often felt a powerful urge to pinch them back, but all she could do was step lightly away, sighing her sorrow as spirits were wont to do.

That night her dance lacked its usual elegance, for her right foot was still prickly and awkward. This sluggishness seemed to work to her advantage, however, for the men committed no worse acts than light pawing. The two gentlemen placed at the medium's left—attending for the first time that evening—did nothing at all. In fact, they barely looked her way as she floated past them.

Finally she returned to her place behind Mrs. Martineau. When the woman lifted her head from the table and sat up straight, Kate drew her arms together and crouched, as though melting into the darkness behind her. But just as she lifted the panel to the compartment, Mrs. Martineau spoke.

"My spirit guide has encountered a very powerful presence with us tonight. My friends, the spirit of Frederic Stanton has crossed the dark chasm to join us."

Frederic Stanton?

Kate dropped the panel, and the clatter echoed throughout the room.

"What the devil?"

She flinched at the exclamation. Robert Eliot was the medium's patron, and as such he always had the best seat at the table. The best angle for groping Kate, too. Missus would not be pleased that Kate's bumbling had so provoked him.

"This is utterly ridiculous," said a soft voice near her. She thought it must be one of the aloof gentlemen. "Mr. Wakeham," the man continued, "would you be so kind as to turn up the gas so everyone might see?"

"No!" bellowed Mrs. Martineau. "You will do great harm to the spirit!"

Roused by this sudden burst of anger, Kate lifted the panel again and thrust her feet into the compartment. A moment later a burst of gaslight brightened the room and a pair of hands seized her shoulders, pulling her to her feet.

"Here's the confederate, Thompson. Hiding in the chair, of all places."

Kate gasped as the wig was plucked from her head. She craned her neck to see whose hand gripped her upper arm. She did not know his name, but it was the younger of the two newcomers.

"I say," cried Eliot, puffing his broad chest. "You promised you would not disrupt the meeting." He directed his words to the grey-bearded fellow, her captor's companion.

Mrs. Martineau looked from the strangers to her patron. "Who is this man, Mr. Eliot?"

The bearded gentleman clasped his hands at his chest. "I beg your pardon, madam. I am Oliver Thompson. And Wakeham"—he gestured toward the man holding Kate—"is my colleague. We represent the Society for Metaphysical Research. Mr. Eliot encouraged us to attend tonight."

Mrs. Martineau's mouth twisted as she glanced at Mr. Eliot. "You invited *skeptics* here tonight?"

"They expressed an interest." Eliot's forehead gleamed with perspiration. "I've told them of your spirit manifestations, and they wished to observe. I meant to finally give them proof of the spirit's ability to communicate after death . . . but it's all gone horribly wrong."

"Thompson and I suspected fraud, Mrs. Martineau, and now we have exposed it for all to see," said Mr. Wakeham, his fingernails still cutting into Kate's shoulder.

"No, *you* have perpetrated a fraud, Mr. Wakeham!" cried Mrs. Martineau. "You and your colleague brought this girl here tonight. You planted her in an attempt to discredit me." The medium paused, her expression growing bolder as her favored sitters sputtered their outrage. She raised her hand to still their voices. "I sensed something was not quite right, but I could not put my finger on the source of the disturbance . . . until now."

Mr. Thompson lifted his hands. "This is ridiculous. Eliot, how can you countenance this woman's deception?"

"It seems the girl has tricked us all," said Eliot weakly.

Mrs. Martineau took a deep breath and looked calmly around the table. "Ladies and gentlemen—my dear friends—I have been deceived along with you. These men have tricked me and now they most certainly will slander me." She staggered back, eyelids fluttering. Mr. Eliot stepped to her side, offering his arm, and she smiled weakly at him before turning back to her audience. "I beg you all to leave me now. A dark presence has defiled our circle, and it will take some time for me to recover."

With a limp hand she beckoned her maid, who herded the sitters out. Mrs. Martineau sank back into her throne, eyes closed. Mr. Wakeham's grip finally eased, and Kate shrugged him off to step toward the medium.

Mr. Thompson sighed. "I think we're finished here. Shall we push on, Wakeham?"

"Take your little pawn with you, Mr. Thompson," called Mrs. Martineau softly.

What? Kate stared at her, but the woman did not open her eyes.

"Surely you are mistaken, dear lady," said Eliot, swabbing his forehead with a handkerchief. "This can't be the work of the Metaphysical Society."

"He's correct, of course. We've never seen the girl before." Mr. Wakeham's upper lip curled as he tossed the wig to Kate. "Eliot, I assume you're coming with us?"

"Ah, well . . ." The man shuffled his feet. "You two go on without me. I'll see you next week."

The instant the two gentlemen passed through the doorway, Mr. Eliot lurched toward Kate. "I believed in you," he said thickly, as if choked by emotion. "You seemed made of air—a creature from another world."

"If you thought me a creature of air, why'd you grope me every chance you got?"

She was pleased to see him wince at that.

After a moment he took a step closer, his eyes glistening.

"Did you . . ." He cleared his throat. "Have you come at Mrs. Martineau's bidding, as my colleagues suggested?"

Kate risked a glance at the medium. Only one eye was open, but it was trained on Kate and the message was clear. *Don't even try it.*

"I came on my own," Kate whispered.

Eliot's fists tightened. "You should be made to pay for your deceit."

"She's not worth the trouble, Robert," Mrs. Martineau whispered, still slumped in her chair.

"But she's done you great harm, so great that I should take her to the police this instant. Don't you mean to prosecute?"

"You are kind to take an interest, but I fear such action would only draw more dark spirits our way." Mrs. Martineau glanced briefly at Kate before closing her eyes again. "I will recover in time. When *she* leaves this house tonight, she will take the darkness with her, and eventually it will consume her."

Eliot nodded. "Wise words." He turned back to Kate, nostrils flaring. "If I see you again, girl, I *will* take you to the police." He moved a step closer. "Either that, or I'll deal with you myself."

Kate lifted her chin and stared back. With his clenched mouth and high color, he looked like an angry brat about to bellow. She longed to tell him so, but the insult stuck in her throat. She directed her gaze to the floor instead.

As soon as Eliot was gone, the medium's eyes snapped open. Her trembling and heavy breathing ceased, and she abruptly stood to close the door. Kate watched with numb detachment as the woman turned, the skirt of her delicate white dress flaring. In three steps Mrs. Martineau was upon her. "Fool!" A backhanded slap sent Kate reeling, and a moment later she was pinned against the wall.

"How could you be so careless? *Months* of effort to lure Eliot into my scheme, and in one night you've ruined it all."

Kate knew better than to struggle—the woman liked a tussle far too well. "You didn't wait long enough to call the spirit, ma'am. I wasn't ready."

"You were *clumsy,* idiot girl."

Kate kept her head down. "Why did you say my father's name?"

Mrs. Martineau grunted. "Your father?"

"The spirit you called. Frederic Stanton."

"I called on Stanton's spirit because the little detectives gave his name as one associated with the sitters. I'm sure it's no business of yours."

"Stanton is dead?"

"Yes, you thick-skulled creature! Frederic Stanton has been dead for years." She paused, and Kate glanced up to find the woman's eyes narrowed. "And I happen to know he had no living children."

"Not with his wife." Kate looked at the floor again.

"Have you lost your wits?" Mrs. Martineau shoved Kate's head against the wall. "Clearly you have. And now you've lost your situation as well. Your clumsiness has compromised my reputation, and the damage will be impossible to repair if you remain here. Pack your things and leave this house immediately. Take only the items you brought with you."

Kate blinked. "But where am I to go? You can't just kick me to the streets."

"I can and will. If you don't go, I'll get the police after you. See if they don't lock you up as a fraud." She paused, her face turning sly. "Or perhaps I *will* allow Mr. Eliot to discipline you. You're a frightful little criminal, after all. Shall I call for help?"

The glint in the woman's eyes forestalled further argument. "No, ma'am, I will go."

Mrs. Martineau released her and stepped away, a satisfied smirk on her face. Kate kept her back against the wall as the woman swept out of the parlor.

Kate dropped the wig to the floor. The shroud soon followed, and it took a powerful exertion of will not to trample them both. Rubbing her damp and throbbing head, she slipped out to the hall and dragged herself up two flights of stairs.

As she reached the attic floor, a shadow shifted near her door.

"Who's there?" she gasped.

"It's just me," the shadow replied, sounding more like a boy than a ghost.

"Christ, Billy! You shouldn't scare me like that."

She opened the door to the attic room and made her way to the washstand. Billy lit the lamp and sat on the small bed, watching in silence as she poured tepid water into the basin and scrubbed the white paste from her face, neck, and arms.

"You must have heard all that," Kate muttered as she dried herself.

"You've been sacked," said Billy sadly.

"Yeah." She sank onto the bed next to him. "What am I to do, Billy?"

He shrugged. "You hated working for Missus. Weren't you sick of parading about in your petticoat? And never able to come out in the daylight? Don't cry, Katie."

"I'm not crying." She wiped her nose with the back of her hand. "I *did* hate prancing for Missus, though it was a lark to scare those fools at the table." She turned to face him. "It's the time I spent with you and Tec in the kitchen, with Cook sneaking us morsels, that I'll miss."

"I'll miss it, too. You shouldn't worry, though. I'm working a new scheme, and it could bring enough to keep the two of us going for a while, at least until you find a better situation."

"You'd do that for me?"

He nodded. "Of course."

A rush of affection prompted Kate to kiss his cheek, and she giggled at the boyish fit of cringing that followed. "What's this?" She gently laid her finger on his jaw, tracing a bruise. "Has Martineau struck you?"

He shrugged her hand away. "She never touched me. It's nothing."

"This scheme, Billy—are you sure it's safe?"

"I'll be fine."

She bit her lip. For such a scrappy kid, he seemed fragile and hollow-eyed in the lamplight.

"Go to Tec's cottage," he said. "It's too late to go anywhere else. I'm workin' tonight, but I'll come by in the morning or thereabouts." His expression sobered. "If you don't see me tomorrow, you'll know someone's done me in."

"Don't say that! If the scheme is that dangerous, you shouldn't try it."

"I was only joking." Grinning, he reached down and pulled something out of his boot. "But take this, just in case." He held out a knife with a four-inch blade. The slick ebony handle shone in the lamplight. "I'd give you the sheath, but it's sewn into my boot. You'd better wrap the blade in something."

"Shouldn't *you* just keep it?" Kate shivered at the strangeness of an angel-haired child holding such a thing.

"I'd feel better if you had it," he said. "Give me something in return, and we'll swap back when I see you again."

"You don't trust me?"

"You might find a better situation and forget all about me. This way, I know we'll see each other again."

Kate's rigid spine softened at that. She looked about the room, considering her few possessions. "I don't have anything that's a match for such a blade."

"How 'bout your father's watch?"

She paused. "It doesn't work anymore."

"That's okay. It still might come in handy. You'll get it back; I promise."

Kate stared at him a moment, wondering at this request. But his wide eyes did not blink, so she knelt by the narrow bed and retrieved a muslin-wrapped parcel from under the mattress. She unfolded the cloth and gave him the watch.

As soon as it was in his hands, Billy opened it. His thin finger traced the inscription inside. "It'll do perfectly."

"So it's a fair trade . . . but only for now, right?"

"Right."

She took the knife from him and placed it on the bed. Billy politely looked away as she sucked in a great gasp of air and buttoned herself into the too-tight dress she'd worn the day she first knocked at the service entrance of Mrs. Martineau's house. The rest of her possessions—including the knife—fit easily into her mother's old sewing basket, which she clutched to her chest.

She turned to Billy, thinking to clutch him to her chest as well. "See you tomorrow," she muttered, chucking him on the chin instead. He grinned and blew out the lamp, melting into the darkness once more.

Kate stepped lightly down the stairs and through the corridor to the deserted kitchen. Without looking back, she opened the door and yielded herself to the damp embrace of night.

Chapter 2

A light rain fell as Kate picked her way over the slick cobblestones to the lair of the little detectives.

Their leader had long ago been christened Thomas, but those who knew him called him Tec, for he managed a group of vagrant boys who "detected" spirit clues for Mrs. Martineau. Though only sixteen, Tec ran his business as efficiently as any grown man. He taught his team to scan obituaries, search trash bins, and question staff for details on Martineau's clients, saving the cleverest boys for lock picking and stealthy home searches. All the detectives had sweet faces and enough schooling to know how to read, and were easily coaxed out at night with the promise of a meal, a few coins, and a safe place to sleep.

Kate knew Tec and his boys lived in a ramshackle cottage near Castle End, but she struggled to remember the details Billy had told her. It took ages of shuffling through side streets and peering in windows to actually find the place. She pounded on the door and slumped wearily against the building to wait. When Tec finally opened up, she smiled.

"Hello, Tec." The sight of him always warmed her.

He stared for a long moment. Then he glanced about before pulling her inside. "Missus will have my hide if she knows you've left the house to come here."

She brushed off his words with a wave of her hand, nodding at the two boys who sat by the potbellied stove. The room smelled of coal smoke, bacon, and dirty boy, but at least it was warm and dry on this damp August evening. She was safe now. Tec was kind—the most reliable person she knew. And though he must have known she fancied him, he'd never once tried to grope her like the old fools at Martineau's.

"Billy told me to come," she said. "Missus has sacked me."

"*Sacked* you? You must have done something awful if she done that."

"I stumbled, is all. One of the sitters—a new gentleman—grabbed me and held tight while his friend turned up the lights."

Tec clucked his tongue. "You're not much use to her now, I suppose. And she'll have to back off the game for a time." He glanced at the boys by the fire and lowered his voice. "Not good for us."

"You'll get more work once Missus gets a new scheme worked out. I'm at loose ends, though. Can I stay here tonight, Tec?"

"Course you can. We'll find you a space on the floor, and I'll lend you a quilt. But there's more boys coming in from their rounds tonight. May not get quiet for a while yet."

She nodded with a yawn and stood waiting as he tossed a ragged quilt in the corner, several paces from the stove. He glanced at her, eyes apologetic. "It's only proper not to jumble you up with the boys. And this way, you might not smell too bad in the morning."

"Ha," she said, yawning again. At his prompting, she placed her basket and hat next to the makeshift bed, kicked off her shoes, and sank to her knees. Tiny clouds of dust billowed up from the quilt, tickling her nostrils. She gave Tec a sidelong look.

"It's all I've got," he said.

She hadn't noticed before how his eyes were shadowed with weariness.

"It's fine, Tec. Just fine."

The boys came in throughout the evening, each announcing his arrival with a loud pounding on the door. Kate jerked awake each time, thinking Eliot was knocking down the attic door to punish her just as Missus had threatened. It was nearly impossible to fall back to sleep with her heart thumping, so she stared at the cobwebbed ceiling as Tec questioned the boys on their activities.

Doubts plagued her. What was she to do with herself? How would she keep fed and sheltered? She was lucky to have this dusty pallet for tonight, but in another day she might be sleeping on a street corner or curled up under a shop awning—at least until the angry proprietor brushed her away with his broom.

Finally she did fall asleep, but it was a heavy sort of slumber that dragged on her eyelids when she tried to blink herself awake the next morning.

Head aching, Kate rose to her feet and stumbled through the room, sidestepping various lumps of sleeping boy on her way to the window. She pulled back the curtain to find the sun perched high in the sky. It wasn't morning anymore. She turned back to the sleepers, stepping lightly around them and peering closely, but Billy was not among them.

Kate jumped when the front door opened.

Tec grinned at the sight of her. "Why so spooked?" he whispered, gentling the wild thumping of her heart. "It's just me with the pasties." As he lifted the large sack in his hand, the fragrance of onions and beef wafted toward her.

Her stomach rumbled in reply.

Tec glanced about the room before turning back to her. "The boys will wake once their noses catch a whiff of these. Come outside with me—the sun's shining and I've something to show you." He placed the sack on a chair, but not before taking two paper-wrapped pasties and placing one in each pocket.

It had been ages since she'd walked outside in the full light of day. Kate raised a hand over her eyes, blinking against the glare of the sun in the nearly cloudless sky. The street bustled with carts and wagons, the occasional bicycle speeding through the knots of traffic. She couldn't pause to look about, however, for Tec was making his way westward to a grassy area.

He paused at the foot of a hill and turned to face her, eyes twinkling.

She glanced beyond him. "It's Castle Mound, isn't it?"

"Have you never climbed to the top in the daylight?"

"Only at night with you and Billy. But that was forever ago."

"Thought as much. Let's have our pasties up there. The sun is nice today."

A memory scurried through her mind as they climbed the steep, snaking path to the top. That night the three of them had sat upon the hill—Kate shivering in terror at the prospect of Missus catching her out of the house—Tec had told them the mound was the remnant of a fortress built hundreds of years ago. She'd nearly forgotten to breathe as he pointed out stars and helped them trace the constellations. He was such a clever boy, so quick with a diverting tale. In truth, she'd stared at *him* more than the sky, her miserly little heart opening like a flower each time he smiled.

Today, however, the view of the city held her attention. As she sat in the overgrown grass, her cheeks tingling with the sun's warmth, Kate took in the alarming sprawl of Cambridge. So many rooftops, church spires, and college towers. She understood the small, dark confines of her former life—hard, but manageable. Now she had to contend with all *this*. It should have been exciting, but she felt a fist of fear clenching in her gut. How would she find her place?

Tec interrupted her thoughts as if he'd read them. "What will you do now, Kate?"

"I don't know. Can't think what's out there for a girl like me."

"Seems to me you'll have to go into service."

The fist in her stomach tightened again. "Service? You want me to work as a skivvy? I don't have a mind to scour pots or scrub floors."

"Perhaps a lady's maid, then. Or something in a shop? You've always talked proper, and your manners are decent when you try."

"I haven't any proper references, Tec." She stared down at the frayed hem of her dress, the holes in her boots. "I don't even have proper clothes. None would have me."

"Maybe if you brushed your hair . . ."

"Oh hush," she growled. "What I *need* is a new scheme." She smoothed her ragged plaits in silence before a thought struck her. "Could you use another detective?"

He frowned. "I can't see how that'd work. Especially now you've made a right mess of Martineau's scheme."

"She'll figure things out soon enough. And when she does, I could work the other side of the business. You know, cut my hair, wear trousers and a cap. Whatever it takes, I'll do it."

"Kate, you're nearly a young lady now. That game wouldn't

work for long, if it worked at all." He paused, his expression softening. "I'll consider it, though. Stay with us another night. Once I've talked with Martineau, I'll know better how we could use you."

Kate resisted the urge to fall upon him in relief. What would he do if she kissed *his* cheek? Would he put his arms around her and kiss her back? No, she was being foolish. He'd probably cringe just as Billy had.

Billy.

"Have you seen Billy?" she asked. "He said he'd be back this morning."

Tec shook his head. "That boy's not one for keeping to a schedule."

"Do you know where he went last night? After the séance?"

"I don't." He looked away. "Last I knew he was going to Summerfield College to do his sleuthing."

"The ladies' college? What's there to be sleuthed?"

"Fellow named Thompson lives there—one of Eliot's friends. Missus wanted the goods on all the sitters, but she seemed 'specially interested in those that knew Eliot."

The hairs on Kate's neck prickled. "Missus said Thompson was friends with my father." She searched her memory for the man's face, trying to recall whether his eyes were kind or cunning, but all she could conjure to mind was that old-fashioned beard. "What do you know about Thompson?"

"Not much at all. It were Billy tracking him down, not me."

Thompson. She had the queerest feeling about the man—like she'd forgotten something very important about him. After a moment of fruitless wondering, she sighed. "That Thompson fellow's ruined everything. If he's going to sweep into a medium's home and expose her lies, he should find new places for all those that's relying on her for a roof over their heads." Kate climbed to her feet with a groan and brushed the grass from her skirt.

Tec peered up at her, squinting into the sun. "What're you going to do?"

"I'm going to Summerfield."

He raised an eyebrow. "That's your new scheme? The college?"

"It's Thompson's fault I was sacked. He owes me, and I'll make sure he knows it."

He reached up and caught her hand. "Don't be hasty, now. What if he don't want to help you? What if he shuts the door in your face? It's Sunday, after all."

She bit her lip. "I'll figure something out."

"Come back with me." He squeezed her hand. "You need more sleep, for your brain is addled. I'll talk to Martineau later—no need to go bullying this Thompson chap yet. Besides, Billy may be back by now."

But Billy was not there. Nor did he appear that night.

When Tec returned from Mrs. Martineau's, he shook his head sadly. "She's thinking to pack up and start anew someplace else." He kept his voice low, clearly not wanting the younger ones to hear. "It ain't certain whether she's taking any of us with her. Perhaps you *should* try your luck with Thompson."

So the next afternoon Kate tidied herself as best she could and marched to the porter's lodge at Summerfield College. In contrast to the sooty spires of the men's colleges, the towered entrance to Summerfield was fresh and ladylike—four stories of coral brick with delicate white sash windows and a tunneled arch resembling a mouth gaping in surprise. The very sight of it made Kate fumble to straighten her hat and smooth the plaits she'd twice rebraided already.

An iron gate, wrought in a dizzying pattern of entwining leaves and flowers, protected the arched entrance. The tall center gates, which looked heavy enough to crush a horse, were flanked by two smaller gates. The one at the right stood open—though not in a welcoming way, thought Kate. Gathering her courage, she stepped through and addressed herself to the porter's window.

"Hallo?" she called, her voice breaking on the second syllable.

A man with greying hair came to the window, lowering his spectacles to frown at her. "May I help you?"

"I am here to see Mr. Thompson, please."

The man narrowed his eyes. "He's not in college."

"Might I come in and wait for him?"

"No, you cannot wait inside for Mr. Thompson," he replied with a snort. "He'll not see you. Go knock at the service entrance and see if the cook will spare you a bite. Otherwise, be off with you."

Kate's face flamed. "I'm not here for charity. I must speak with Mr. Thompson. He's done me a grave injustice," she added. "I'll not leave until he hears me out."

"Mr. Thompson is not here, you little chit. Now shove off before I send for a constable!"

Kate turned away, hot with frustration. A man stood a few paces off, satchel in hand. His eyes darted from her to the gate . . . and then back to her again. He was young and rather nice-looking, but with those fine clothes he clearly was a toff. She couldn't trust him. However, that didn't mean she couldn't *use* him.

She stepped toward him. "Did you hear how that man spoke to me? Do I seem a vagrant to you?"

"You don't *sound* like a vagrant," the young man allowed, removing his hat to reveal shiny light-brown hair. He didn't talk like a Cambridge scholar. He didn't even sound *English*. Irish, maybe? Surely the Irish were never so posh.

"Where are you from?" she asked.

"Boston." He stepped past her and gestured to the porter, who now stood just inside the gate. "I'm here to see Mr. Thompson as well. My name is Asher Beale. I'm the son of Mr. Thompson's colleague, Professor Harold Beale." He held out his hand.

The porter ignored the proffered hand, but respect softened his tone. "You can call me Jones, sir. As I was just telling the child"—he scowled at Kate—"Mr. and Mrs. Thompson are not in college at the moment. Best leave your card and call again tomorrow."

Kate drew nearer to the young man, taking cover in his shadow. "*I* can't leave and come back tomorrow. I've no place else to go, and I'm not spending another night sleeping on a cold floor with a pack of smelly boys." She swallowed hard against the panic bubbling in her throat. "It's Thompson's fault, and he's the one who should remedy this state of affairs."

The porter mouthed the word *remedy* in apparent wonderment—clearly he hadn't expected a rough girl to speak so well. Kate glanced at Asher Beale, noting that he also considered her with more interest.

"I'm happy to leave my card, Jones," he said. "But I do hope you would be so kind as to find someone to attend to Miss, er . . ." He looked to Kate for help.

"Poole," she offered gratefully. "Miss Kate Poole."

"Thank you." He turned back to the porter. "Miss Poole

clearly is not a vagrant and seems to be in some distress. It would be very gentlemanly of you to find someone who could speak with her."

Jones scratched his head. "This ain't exactly regular." He looked behind him and seemed to relent. "Young Miss Atherton—that's Mr. Thompson's niece—was wandering about the garden a short while ago." He stepped toward the green lawn beyond the archway. "I do believe I still see her," he said over his shoulder. "If you don't mind waiting a moment, I'll fetch her, though I can't say she'll have anything to do with either of you."

"Thank you, Jones." Once the man was out of hearing, Asher Beale turned to Kate. "Well, that's taken care of—it just took a gentleman to help him see sense."

She bristled at this boast. "I hope you're not expecting any favors in return."

"What do you mean?"

She cocked an eyebrow.

The young man's cheeks flamed. "I was only trying to help."

"Believe me, I had matters in hand," she said, pleased by his discomfort. "So don't expect me to swoon at your gentlemanly interventions."

chapter 3

Asher stared at the girl. *This* was his reward for arriving at Summerfield as directed? To be insulted by a waif in pigtails and a crooked hat? Her dress looked as though she'd outgrown it more than a year ago, but he'd politely overlooked that. In fact, he'd been downright chivalrous, and she'd repaid his kindness by accusing him of improper expectations.

"As I see it, you did *not* have matters in hand," he told her. "And I have better things to do than stand here and endure your insults." He fumbled in his waistcoat pocket for his card case. "If you'll just pass my card along to Jones, I'll be on my way."

She stared at the card without taking it. Of course, she'd probably never seen a gentleman's calling card in her life. Her nose wrinkled. Then she looked beyond him, through the gate.

"No need," she said. "The porter's coming, and he's got the girl with him."

Asher turned back to the archway. A young lady in a blue silk dress walked toward them, golden hair loose and falling down her back. It took some effort not to gape. She was a stunner, to be sure, but with a solemnity that brought to mind paintings of martyred saints and Madonnas. In her hands she held a curious brown box. A cross or crown he could imagine, but a camera? Too modern and peculiar for such a girl.

She smiled warmly, her eyes brightening at the sight of them. "I am Elsie Atherton. Jones said you were both very keen to see my uncle. He should be returning soon. In the meantime, would you join me in the garden?" She gestured toward the green space on the other side of the tunnel. "It would be my pleasure to show you the college."

The girl's voice was as lovely as her face. Soft and mellow, unlike that of the young harpy who walked next to him. Asher followed her away from the porter and into the college garden, where she paused by a tree to wave her hand at their surroundings. "Lovely, isn't it? Everything so new and the paint still fresh. Not at all the prison I feared." Her chin lowered. "The men's colleges are like mausoleums by comparison. Why, Summerfield Hall—the oldest building in the college—has stood here little more than twenty years. And the one we just came through? Built only eight years ago and recently fitted for electricity."

"It's very grand," Asher said, craning his neck to study the tower.

"Have you lived here long?" Kate asked.

"Oh no, I arrived only yesterday," Miss Atherton continued. "This is my first opportunity to explore the grounds. I meant to photograph the architecture, but . . ." She paused as a slow smile spread over her face. "Now I can practice my portrait work, if you don't object." Without waiting for a reply, she pointed away from the buildings. "Let's go this way."

Asher dragged his eyes away from Miss Atherton to survey the college garden, a meadow of tall grass dotted with trees and crisscrossed by dirt paths. Miss Atherton led them through an orchard of young fruit trees, plucking at the branches in a leisurely fashion. She stopped short when they encountered a structure at the end of the path—one designed in the same style and with the same brick as the other college buildings, but much smaller.

"A baby sister to the others," she breathed. "I wonder how it's used? I simply must take a photograph here." She gestured to him. "Mr. Beale, isn't it? Jones tells me you've come from America. Would you set your bag down and stand by the door, please? And you, Miss Poole—you must stand next to him."

Kate's face broke into a wide grin, and Asher felt his own mouth curving in response to her obvious delight. He doubted she'd ever had her photograph taken before. His heart softened toward her . . . just a bit.

Miss Atherton proceeded to open her portable camera and pull it wider, elongating it like a bellows and snapping it into place. She then held the camera at her waist, pointing the lens at them.

"Hold still," she said, her chin down as she looked through a square hole at the top of the camera. "Look straight ahead. And do try to smile. I can't abide a photograph full of grim faces."

Despite Miss Atherton's suggestion, Kate stood rigid next to him, nerves turning her smile to a grimace. Asher faced the camera, trying to smile more casually, but before he'd arranged his features the shutter clicked. With a sigh of satisfaction, Miss Atherton folded the lens back into the box once more.

"Now let's take a peek inside the building." She rattled the doorknob for a moment before turning away with a pout. "It's locked. I wonder what they keep in there—all the treasures of the college?"

"Probably just a storage shed," Asher said. "Maybe they've

locked the tools away lest the young ladies stumble upon them and hurt themselves."

Kate glared. "You must think young ladies have mashed peas for brains."

He opened his mouth, but a cutting retort would not come. The girl wouldn't have acknowledged it anyway, for she had shifted her gaze and was staring intently at Miss Atherton.

Asher turned to find the young lady in distress, her eyes closing tightly as she leaned against the door to steady herself. The camera tumbled from her hand and landed in the grass.

"No," Miss Atherton moaned. "Not now, not *now*!"

Kate clutched at the girl's hand. "Are you ill, miss?"

"I need my medicine," Miss Atherton said. "I've been a fool and left it behind."

"Where is your medicine?" Asher stepped forward and took her other hand. "We'll get it at once."

Her eyes widened. "Don't leave me!"

He took her by the shoulders, pulling her hand from Kate's grasp. "I won't leave you. Where is your medicine?"

Miss Atherton pressed fingers to her temple. "It's in my quilted bag," she gasped. "Jones will show you my room."

Asher turned to Kate. "Did you hear that? Go back to the porter and find her bag."

Kate stared at him, eyes wide with alarm.

"Miss Poole," he said more gently. "Please be as quick as you can."

The girl broke into a run toward the building just as Miss Atherton collapsed in his arms.

Asher had little regard for young ladies, having yet to encounter one who wasn't a hardened schemer, but a curious feeling of tenderness settled over him as he carried Elsie Atherton toward the college buildings. With her head resting against his chest, all that mattered was to have her peaceful and smiling again.

He set her down in the shade of an oak tree and sat next to her, cradling her head in his lap. His hands trembled as he smoothed the hair out of her eyes.

Soon enough Kate came barreling through the arch, her face sharp with anxiety, followed by a much slower Jones. Bag in hand, she threw herself to the ground next to Asher and rifled through Miss Atherton's possessions. She pulled out a bottle of brown glass and peered at the crisp white label. "Good God. It's Chlorodyne."

Asher did not recognize the name, but the girl's frown gave him pause. "Is it the only medicine in the bag?"

She poked through again. "Yes."

"Then open it and pour some in her mouth. I'll hold her."

Cradling Miss Atherton's head with one hand, he gently grasped her jaw with the other and pulled her mouth open. Kate leaned in and poured a thin stream of the liquid down her throat. Miss Atherton swallowed and coughed.

Asher turned to Kate. "Is that enough?"

Her face was solemn. "I know this medicine. You don't want to give her too much. Wait a minute and see how she does."

"Is everything all right?" Jones stood behind Kate, hunched over and wringing his hands.

Asher considered Miss Atherton. She no longer trembled, and her clenched jaw had softened. As her body relaxed, her breathing deepened into a steady rhythm.

"I think she's falling asleep," he whispered.

Kate sat back on the grass and sighed. Then she pushed the stopper into the medicine bottle and returned it to Miss Atherton's bag.

Asher nodded toward the bag. "What do you know about Chlorodyne?"

"My own mum used to take it. So much that she couldn't live without it."

"Did it help her?"

She frowned. "She's been dead for two years."

He hardly knew what to say. The girl was such an odd little creature—angry one moment and cringing like a wounded puppy the next. She unsettled him. It would be a relief to see the back of her.

"Oh dear," murmured Jones. "Here comes Mrs. Thompson."

Asher looked up to see a tall, thin woman in black gliding toward them. Her narrow face was grim as she knelt next to him.

"Did she have an attack?"

"She clutched her head as though it pained her, and then she began to shake," Asher said. "But she calmed down once she'd swallowed her medicine. She seems quite peaceful now."

Mrs. Thompson let her fingers rest on the girl's neck, feeling the pulse. Then she stroked the pale cheek before turning to him. "Whom do I thank for attending to her?"

"I am Asher Beale, ma'am. My father is Harold Beale."

Her stricken face broke into a smile. "Harold's son! How wonderful to meet you, even under such circumstances. Look, here's Oliver—he'll be so pleased."

A grey-haired man, stooped and frail, shuffled toward them with the aid of a cane. He did not kneel. "What's happened, my dear? Is she breathing?" His own breath came in gasps, and to Asher it seemed that even his long beard quivered.

Mrs. Thompson rose to her feet. "She had an attack, but her medicine brought it to a halt. She's resting now." She met

Asher's gaze. "It's something akin to epilepsy, as far as we can tell. We must make her more comfortable. Would it be too much to ask you to carry her?"

"Of course not," Asher said, shifting to his knees so he could gather her up. Miss Atherton slumped against his chest, breathing softly through her open mouth.

"I must speak to Mr. Thompson, please."

Asher turned to Kate, having forgotten for the moment that she was there. The girl's voice was a little too loud and had a nervous edge to it—clearly she was peeved at being overlooked.

Mrs. Thompson's expression hardened. "And who might you be?"

"I'm Kate Poole." The girl lifted her chin. "I've come to speak with Mr. Thompson about my lost situation."

Mr. Thompson's mouth opened, but he did not speak. He looked to his wife instead.

"And what would your lost situation have to do with my husband?"

"He's the cause of it, ma'am."

Asher expected Mr. Thompson to order the girl off the premises, for she was making a spectacle of impertinence in this moment of crisis. Instead the man merely stared at her.

"What can you mean?" Mr. Thompson finally asked, a catch to his voice.

"If you're a true gentleman, you'll hear what I have to say." The girl took a breath and stood a little straighter. "Especially since it pertains to your friend Frederic Stanton."

The man's jaw dropped, but he said nothing.

"Oliver?" His wife laid her hand on his arm.

"Well . . . I . . ."

Asher shifted uneasily, his shoulders aching. Mr. Thompson couldn't seem to *start* a proper sentence, let alone finish it, and

Kate merely stared back at him. If they didn't move soon, the girl might slide through his arms.

He cleared his throat. "Shall I carry your niece inside, sir?"

Mr. Thompson turned to him and seemed to collect himself. "If you would be so kind, yes. I would be more than happy to speak to Miss Poole in my study . . . once we get Elsie settled. Helena, will you lead the way?"

Relieved, Asher held Miss Atherton's body close as Mrs. Thompson guided them all toward the grand arch of the tower.

Chapter 4

Elsie sighed contentedly.

She always felt safe in his arms. Snuggled against the warmth of his body, she hardly felt the small jolts as they moved from step to step on the staircase. When he finally settled her upon the bed, she struggled to open her eyes, fighting the black wave of sleep that threatened to engulf her again. She wanted to thank him before she gave in to the darkness. She wanted to tell him she loved him, to feel his lips on hers. With great effort she opened one eye.

The man standing above her was a stranger—a boy, rather, with light-brown hair and a smattering of freckles over his nose. It wasn't him. *He* was gone. She sobbed and turned into the pillow.

The dose of Chlorodyne soon swept away her sorrow, replacing it with happier memories of *him*—chestnut hair ruffled by the breeze, the familiar crooked smile, his expert hand guiding hers as she applied paint to canvas. She was forever attempting to paint the grotto by the lake, the only place she could be alone with him. The only place she was free.

Photography was easier—for her, more natural. She imagined framing the same scene through her camera lens and felt him standing behind her, his chest pressed against her upper back as his hands steadied her own. She heard the shutter click, and her skin prickled as his fingers stroked the inside of her wrist before moving along her arm, coming to rest at her waist. Warm lips brushed her cheek as she turned to face him. . . .

Chapter 5

At first Kate had imagined the school's great arch as a battlement to ward off invaders, with Jones the porter acting as sentinel, but it turned out Mr. Thompson actually *lived* in the forbidding building. She'd barely had a chance to look about when she'd dashed in to get Miss Atherton's bag. Now she let her eyes linger. Having been Mrs. Martineau's prisoner for two years, she was eager to see what sort of house honest people might keep.

With Asher Beale and the old lady attending to Miss Atherton, Kate found herself alone with Mr. Thompson. Mr. *Oliver* Thompson. She could have kicked herself for being so thick-skulled. Her father's watch had been inscribed TO DEAR FRIEND AND PUPIL F. STANTON FROM O. THOMPSON. Mrs. Martineau had been right after all—the two *were* great friends. Had Billy known of this connection when he'd asked for her watch? If so, what had he meant to do with it? She regretted not having the watch with her now. It might have proven useful in her wrangling with Thompson.

She studied him out of the corner of her eye. His beard was biblical and his body withered, but his eyes were clear and stern behind the spectacles. He crooked a beckoning finger.

Kate followed him to the doorway of a study stocked with books—more books than she'd ever seen in one room. Leather-bound volumes of various sizes lined the shelves, just visible behind the ones stacked in front of them. Others were piled on the floor. Several more teetered precariously in untidy stacks upon the desk. Covering the books, furniture, and any spare patch of floor were hundreds of papers.

Mr. Thompson cleared a trail to a wide upholstered chair and transferred its contents—more books—to the floor. "My wife is extremely tidy, but she knew I was set in my ways when she married me," he said casually. "She lets me keep this room as I like, and thus I am always shifting books and papers when I have visitors." He gestured at the chair. "Please have a seat."

She had expected him to be pompous and rude, to have it out with her in the foyer, if not the alley behind the building. But he was treating her like a guest.

She didn't like it. Didn't trust it. She must keep her wits about her in the face of such politeness, even if her heart hammered wildly.

He leaned against his desk, not seeming to care that he crumpled a stack of papers and sent books sliding. "Now," he said briskly, "what's this about your lost situation? And what does it have to do with Frederic Stanton?"

She slumped, suddenly at a loss. When she'd imagined this conversation, she'd cast herself as the angry, injured party. How best to launch into her story now?

"I suppose you don't recognize me," she said lamely.

Mr. Thompson leaned forward to peer at her, lifting his spectacles briefly before placing them back on his nose. "There's something familiar about you, but I can't quite place it."

"I was the spirit at Mrs. Martineau's séance Saturday night."

His eyes widened. "Ah."

"She sacked me and I have no place to go." Anger roiled anew in her belly. "It's your fault, you see. You interfered, and now I shall have to beg on the streets."

"You have no family?"

"Mum's been dead two years. She never told me of her people."

"And your father?"

"I only just learned he's dead." She took a breath. "My father was Frederic Stanton."

Mr. Thompson went pale and gripped the edge of the desk, a reaction that sent her heart thudding again. Tears scratched behind her eyes, but she couldn't lose her calm in front of this man. Instead she fixed her gaze upon him, willing her heartbeat to slow.

He took a handkerchief out of his pocket to mop his brow. "As far as I knew, Frederic had no children, but there's no denying you have the look of him. Perhaps that's what seemed familiar about you." He thrust the cloth back in his pocket and spoke gently. "Would you please share more details? I confess to being deeply curious."

"My father . . . *knew* . . . my mother before he married."

Mr. Thompson grimaced slightly, nodding his understanding. "Go on."

"He thought her too common to wed, or at least that's what she told me. He didn't abandon her, though. He gave her an allowance and paid my tuition at a proper day school. I didn't know him well, but he was kind when I did see him. Three years ago the money stopped and my mother took ill." Kate paused, feeling her face crumple. "Mum died a year later."

A heavy silence followed. Kate wiped her nose on the inside of her sleeve. When she glanced at Mr. Thompson, she saw a glistening in his eyes, and it made her own prickle again. "I never knew my father had died. Perhaps Mum didn't know, either. Sir, please tell me when it happened."

He did not hesitate. "He died three years ago, on the first of June."

"How?"

Mr. Thompson shook his head. "Oh, it was a terrible thing. A very shocking and mysterious death." He paused, clearly uncomfortable. "I'm certain it was an accident," he finally said. "A tragic accident."

"But I must know."

He stared at the bookcase behind her. "It was an accident, and that is all I shall say. I hate to dwell upon it. He was a great man, a dear friend, and though three years have passed I've still not accustomed myself to the loss." His shoulders softened and he turned to her with a smile. "Let us instead discuss your predicament."

Kate straightened her back, prepared for battle. But before she could open her mouth, he spoke again.

"You needn't look so fierce. I wish to help you, especially now that I know you to be the daughter of a dear friend. I am horrified at the very thought of you participating in a fraud in order to keep fed and housed. You must stay here for a time, at least until Mrs. Thompson and I find a better alternative."

Kate breathed out, the battle fury rushing from her body along with the air in her lungs. A small voice in the back of her mind advised suspicion. She couldn't trust the people she *knew* to do right by her, much less strangers. But she was deflated by weariness and worry.

"We shall put you to work, of course," he continued. "Mrs. Thompson does not hold to the notion that ladies should be leisurely." He looked past her, his eyes brightening. "I may have an idea. Stay there, if you would. I must broach this to my wife before I say anything further."

There it is, she thought as he shuffled from the room. *I shall be carrying chamber pots and scrubbing floors.* But what else could she do? She had no place to go.

Besides that, she knew the man was keeping secrets from her. There was more to the story of her father's death—Thompson's inability to meet her gaze had told her that much. Secrets, once discovered, could prove quite useful. Kate longed to know what Thompson was hiding, and the only way to do that was to stay at Summerfield College.

She would become a little detective herself.

❊ ❊ ❊ ❊ ❊

Asher's room was on the top floor of the arched building, known in the college as the Gatehouse. According to Mrs. Thompson, the ground floor was given to the porter's lodge and tutoring rooms. A suite of private rooms for the Thompsons took up the second floor. Above that were lodging rooms for students, and this was where Miss Atherton stayed. It was also where Mrs. Thompson had placed Kate for the time being, though Asher couldn't imagine why they would offer to house that strange, uncivilized creature. His room was on the west side of the very top floor, with a handsome window looking out over the college garden. As most of the Summerfield students had departed for the long holiday, he had the floor to himself. It was cramped and stuffy, but he waved off Mrs. Thompson's apologies and expressed great satisfaction, particularly with the pleasant breeze that ruffled the curtains when he opened the window.

Asher dressed carefully for supper, brushing his jacket and

recombing his hair several times before he felt prepared to face Miss Atherton at the table.

But when he made his way to the sitting room, she was nowhere to be seen. Mrs. Thompson greeted him from the settee; next to her Mr. Thompson smiled. Asher raised an eyebrow at the sight of Kate Poole sitting stiffly in a nearby chair, wearing the same undersized dress as before. She stared back at him until he lowered his gaze.

"It's just us four this evening, I'm afraid," said Mrs. Thompson. "Our niece is still sleeping—apparently this often happens when she takes her medication. She was already quite fatigued from her journey here, poor child." She shrugged. "Ordinarily the college is full of students, and they take turns joining us for supper. It's always merry during term. Things are quieter in the summer."

"Of course," Asher said. "I wonder . . . has Miss Atherton suffered from this condition all her life?"

Mrs. Thompson's gaze dropped to the hands in her lap. "Since she was a child of twelve, I'm afraid. It's been a severe trial for the family. Her parents are abroad for the next several months, and my sister thought it best that Elsie not attempt such a journey." When she glanced again at Asher, her expression was curiously blank. "That's why she's at Summerfield, and we are very pleased to have her."

She stood then and led them to the dining room, where an apple-cheeked girl named Millie stood ready to serve them. The offerings were merely decent. Asher had been less than impressed by English cuisine since he'd arrived at his uncle's house, and this food continued the tradition, tasting downright institutional in its seasoning and preparation. It didn't seem to bother Kate Poole, however, for she attacked each dish with relish.

"I can't tell you how nice it is to have you here, Asher," said Mrs. Thompson. "We count your father among our dearest friends. How is he?"

"He's fine, thank you," Asher replied automatically.

"I do believe you had just begun to toddle last time Harold was in England. He certainly hated to leave you behind." She leaned forward as though to scrutinize him. "Now you must be nearly eighteen?"

"I am seventeen, ma'am."

"Wonderful! So is Elsie. I know the two of you will grow very fond of each other."

Asher fought to keep his expression neutral.

"And how long do you plan to stay in Cambridge, my boy?" Mr. Thompson asked. "We hope it's a good long visit."

The man's eyes twinkled with this remark. Did he know?

"I'm not certain, sir. I'd planned to tour Cambridge and Oxford—and perhaps the Continent, if my uncle's generosity continues. I've come here from his home in Rye, you know."

"But you must be going back to the States in the fall," said Mrs. Thompson. "Your father once wrote to us of your intention to study at Harvard."

They *didn't* know, then.

"I won't be studying at Harvard this fall. My father and I had a falling-out, and he's packed me off to England for as long as my uncle will have me."

"Oh dear," murmured Mrs. Thompson.

"In fact," Asher continued, "I'd thought I might enroll at one of your universities. Perhaps even Cambridge."

"One does not enroll at Cambridge—or Oxford, for that matter." Mr. Thompson's tone was gentle. "One applies to an individual college, and each college has its own entrance examination."

Asher straightened in his seat. "I'm hardly daunted by entrance exams."

"Nor should you be, my boy, but I'm afraid you've missed your opening for the Michaelmas term—the examinations for next year will be held in December."

Asher winced. "Oh . . . I see."

"You might consider this good news, actually. Most young men going up to Cambridge are a bit older than you, and this delay would allow you some seasoning, not to mention plenty of time to be coached in the exam subjects." Mr. Thompson nodded encouragingly. "Please don't take offense at the suggestion—even our top boys at Eton and Harrow need coaching beforehand."

"Of course," Asher said dully. He might have learned all this if he'd explained his plans more fully to his uncle. Now he would have to return to the man's house and trespass on his hospitality for much longer than he'd intended. His uncle was a very private man, and the house in Rye was too isolated. His father had known exactly what he was doing when he sent Asher to England.

"Harold never mentioned your interest in an English education," Thompson continued. "What subject would you read?"

"Read, sir?"

"He means to ask what subject you wish to *study*," said Mrs. Thompson quickly. "Americans don't use *read* the same way we do, Oliver."

Asher swallowed a groan. Lately, every distinguished greybeard he encountered seemed preoccupied with his plans for the future. What would he study, what would he *make* of himself? His friends were following in their fathers' footsteps, but Asher attributed that to lack of imagination. When he thought of his father and uncle—men who scribbled at their desks for a living—he knew he could not do the same. "I may very well go into law," he finally blurted, having never considered the notion prior to this evening. "I don't wish to be an academic, if you'll pardon my saying so."

Mr. Thompson smiled. "So no interest in experimental psychology?"

"My father's field? Absolutely not." Asher shuddered. "I can't think of anything I'm *less* likely to do."

Mr. Thompson glanced at his wife before continuing. "Nevertheless, the prospect of your studying at Cambridge pleases me greatly. Your legal training must be done in America, of course, but a thorough study of history or classics would provide a solid foundation. I do hope you'll give serious consideration to Trinity College."

The conversation turned to matters concerning Summerfield, and soon it became apparent that it was Mrs. Thompson, not her husband, who was the true principal of the college. At first this amused Asher. What a fearsome number of females living and working without male supervision! But as he listened to her report on the day-to-day running of the institution, he grasped the daunting nature of the task, and how capable she must be to undertake it. Her husband was a lecturer, and it seemed that he enjoyed this role and was favored by his students, but Mrs. Thompson was the authority figure of the pair. It didn't take long for Asher to realize that *she* made the difficult decisions, managed the budget, and enforced the rules.

"Our latest project, and one we must finish before the new term begins, is our move into the new library." Mrs. Thompson's eyes gleamed with pride. "The old library was a single room, filled to the rafters with books. Now we shall have an entire building—and a beautiful one at that—to house our old books and new bequests, with room to spare for growth in the collection."

Asher noticed Mrs. Thompson raising a thoughtful eyebrow at the Poole girl, but Kate was too fixed upon emptying her plate to be aware of it. He had a sinking feeling that in glancing at the girl Mrs. Thompson was considering yet *another* project. If this proved true, Miss Poole might be vexing him awhile longer.

Asher was free to leave, of course. He'd fulfilled his obligation by calling on the Thompsons, and it wouldn't be difficult to excuse himself from a longer visit and depart in the morning.

And yet . . . it would be nice to see Miss Atherton once more, to speak with her when she was feeling better. Surely this was only polite. How could he take his leave without wishing her well?

Chapter 6

Elsie woke the next morning to a familiar prickling sensation. Something flickered at the corner of her eye, but when she turned toward the movement nothing was there. She took her full dose, allowing the Chlorodyne's thick, peppery sweetness to coat her tongue, and waited for the prickling to subside. When it did, she brushed and pinned her hair, then dressed as quickly as she could with arms that grew heavier by the minute. Finally she made her way down the stairs.

As soon as she saw the strangers sitting at the breakfast table, she remembered.

They know now. They've seen it.

The boy smiled at her from across the table and then looked away. The girl blushed. Of course they were embarrassed to face her after yesterday's horrible display. How silly she'd been! So happy to see new people, *young* people who knew nothing of her condition. She should have taken more care. But she'd felt better since arriving at Summerfield—lighter, more clearheaded. Their arrival seemed to herald a new start, an opportunity for society rather than grim isolation.

Now she knew nothing had changed.

She greeted her aunt and uncle, adopting a polite smile before taking her seat.

Her aunt broke the silence. "You look very well this morning, Elsie. How do you feel?"

I feel as though four pairs of eyes are boring into me.

Elsie reached for the teapot and poured. She concentrated upon the pot, and her hand did not shake overmuch. "I am feeling a little better this morning, thank you."

"You remember our guests, of course. Asher Beale has agreed to stay with us for a time, and Miss Poole will be helping with our move to the new library."

Aunt Helena was only trying to be pleasant and helpful, so Elsie nodded despite her horror that the two young people would be staying on. "How lovely." As she inclined her head at each of the newcomers, she wondered how long before she caught them staring or heard their cruel whispers. When she took a sip of tea, her hand was not quite so steady as before.

She ate her toast, feeling it scratch her throat as she swallowed but not really tasting it. Her uncle was inquiring about young Mr. Beale's plan for the day. She remembered that the boy had carried her up the stairs and placed her in bed. Had she shamed herself by clinging to him? Her brain was foggy with the dose, but somehow she thought she might have. She looked away from him as he spoke, turning instead to the other stranger. The girl kept her eyes on her plate, not eating the food so much as inhaling it. She was a skinny thing and yet bursting out of the shabby dress she wore.

Elsie took a long swallow of tea and stared through the window at the garden. She was not meant to be at Summerfield, sequestered within its walls among strangers. This was not the place to start over, for the old malady would always be with her.

Nor was she meant to return home to Peverel Place.

A bold thought brought a flutter to her heart. She must find *him* in London. He had promised he would take care of her. She would find him and together they would lose themselves to London. In such a large city, no one would find them.

⊠ ⊠ ⊠ ⊠ ⊠

Kate hadn't felt full since . . . well, since before she could remember. Her belly strained against her lacings—not an entirely comfortable feeling, yet at the same time it was strange and wonderful to have food pressed upon her rather than doled out in minute portions. She'd assumed the thin bodies of Mr. and Mrs. Thompson were an indication of severe economy in the kitchen, but this was not so. What they could not eat they insisted be taken by the others at the table.

Both Asher Beale and the golden Miss Atherton had frowned and sighed over the food on the sideboard. Perhaps that was the fashionable response to such abundance. If so, Kate would not dream of striving for fashionable status. She would gladly eat until her dress ripped at the seams—a humiliation not far off, given the size of the garment.

It wasn't just the food that made her giddy. It was the small bed in the well-ventilated room—certainly more cozy than the dusty corner of a crowded cottage. It was the hot soak in the large porcelain tub—much preferred to a cold splash in a basin. It was the freedom to wander in the sunlight during the day. Most of all, it was the fact that she would *not* be hauling chamber pots and scrubbing floors. Instead she would be working with two Summerfield students to move the library collection into its new building. Mrs. Thompson thought the work would take at least two weeks, perhaps longer.

It was a gift. A little breathing space before she must fend for herself again. For that she was grateful.

But she couldn't let this sudden upswing in fortune derail her from her purpose. She needed a more permanent situation, and instinct told her that a new scheme might reveal itself when she learned more about her father. If nothing else, she would discover whom he'd married and where she lived. She harbored no fantasies of being welcomed into the lady's home and heart. The lady might, however, find her a comfortable situation far away in order to avoid further scandal. And if Kate were to confront her father's widow, she would need to be well armed with information.

What better place to find information than a library?

"Oh no," said Mrs. Thompson, interrupting her thoughts.

Kate looked up to find the woman peering intently at the *Cambridge Daily News*.

"I warned you not to read the local rag this morning." Mr. Thompson spoke from behind *The Times*.

"It's just so horrible. I'd prefer not to see Summerfield linked to it in print."

Kate set down her spoon and looked around the table. Miss Atherton had excused herself earlier, and now young Mr. Beale stared at his plate as though deeply pained by the sight of cold eggs. Why didn't he ask about this horrible thing? Didn't he feel a similar sense of dread to hear Mrs. Thompson's exclamations?

"Excuse me, ma'am," Kate finally said. "What is so horrible?"

Mrs. Thompson set the paper down. "Oh, it's nothing to do with us. A few days ago the body of a vagrant was discovered at the Corpus College cricket grounds—quite near here. The police can't even put a name to the poor creature." She shook her head sadly. "He must have wandered over here from Castle Street. One hears of drunkards and beggars congregating in that area."

Kate's spine tingled at the mention of Castle Street. In her mind she saw Billy, his pale, translucent skin turned chalky by death.

"Was it a boy?" she asked.

Mrs. Thompson frowned. "Hmmm?"

"The *body*." Kate fought to contain her impatience. "Was it a boy?"

"No. It was an elderly man, weakened by drink and hard living." She stared at Kate. "What has you so agitated, Miss Poole?"

"Nothing." Kate's shoulders sank in relief. "I know some boys on Castle End, is all. But they take good care of each other," she said quickly. "They'll be fine, I'm sure."

"I do hope so," said Mrs. Thompson, her eyes troubled.

Once breakfast was cleared, Kate followed Mrs. Thompson to Summerfield Hall, the oldest building in the college. The lady walked briskly, but as Kate was mostly made of legs, she managed to keep pace.

Mrs. Thompson paused before the door of the hall and glanced down at Kate. "I fear your dress may not hold together much longer."

Kate blushed. "When Mrs. Martineau sacked me, she took back the few clothes she'd given me. I came to her in this very dress."

Mrs. Thompson's expression did not change. "I will search out something more suitable later today. I hope you can manage basic sewing, because you'll be hemming tonight."

They entered the former library in Summerfield Hall to find two young ladies scanning the room with forlorn faces. Though not as untidy as Mr. Thompson's study, the room contained shelves of books piled in front of other books, and more piled on the floor. Several opened crates cluttered the remaining floor space, catching the ladies' skirts as they threaded their way between them.

"Good morning, Miss Freeman and Miss Barrett," Mrs. Thompson said. "I have brought Kate Poole to assist you with the move." She paused, turning to Kate. "The plan is to organize the books first and then transport them in batches, so as not to re-create this chaos in our new library. The task will involve unpacking the new bequests"—she gestured at the crates—"which will need to be labeled, inventoried, and placed with the previous acquisitions. Miss Freeman and Miss Barrett will show you what to do. I must return to my office to wrestle with the college accounts." She nodded at the three of them and, lifting her skirts high to clear the books, swept out of the room.

Freeman and Barrett were not overly friendly, but as Kate was unaccustomed to warmth, this did not concern her. She spent the morning pulling books from boxes and reading out the titles so that Freeman could enter them in a ledger. The books then went to Barrett, who marked the spines with letters and numbers. When finished, Barrett then put them in the appropriate stack for later transport.

At midday the two ladies went home to dine—like most students, they did not live in college during the summer holiday—and Kate went to the Gatehouse kitchen for as much mutton stew as she could swallow. The cook beamed to see her appetite, for the summers left her short of eager mouths to feed. Kate decided the only thing that could have improved the meal would have been Billy and Tec sharing it with her, just like the old days in Mrs. Martineau's kitchen.

Was Billy safe at Tec's now? She must contrive a way to visit Castle End without the Thompsons knowing.

She returned to Summerfield Hall before the others, which gave her time to poke about the room. Against the far wall she found the library's collection of bound newspapers, heavy volumes stacked haphazardly. They would take time to sort. With some searching, however, she might locate her father's obituary. Billy had once told her that obituaries provided a gold mine of information to mediums looking to hoodwink their sitters.

And perhaps, Kate thought, with some luck they also might provide useful details to daughters needing to know more about dead fathers.

chapter 7

Elsie kept to her room, claiming a headache as excuse for not joining Aunt Helena at the luncheon table. She had much work to do, and it must be done quietly.

First, she retrieved a sober grey dress and fresh underclothes from the wardrobe, all of which she laid out on her traveling trunk for the next morning. Then she pulled her largest drawstring bag from the top drawer. Not much room, but it was all she could allow herself. Everything else must be left behind. One day she might have fine clothes again, when London society recognized his talent, but finery mattered little in comparison to her love for him. For now they could make the most of a simple life.

Elsie opened her jewelry chest and spilled the contents upon the bed. She fished out the sovereigns, along with a crumpled ten-pound note, and placed them in her smaller coin purse. Then she divided the fine jewelry from the paste and cut glass. The diamond necklace and earrings were gifts from her father, presented on the occasion of her sixteenth birthday. The emerald ring and bracelet were bequests from a favorite great-aunt.

She gathered these and a few other valuable items and tied them all within a fine linen handkerchief.

Each piece would have to be sold, but she didn't care.

The coin purse and pouch of jewels went into her bag, along with her necessary toiletries, three clean handkerchiefs, and a spare pair of gloves. She retrieved a sealed bottle of Chlorodyne from her drawer and placed it in the bag. Two bottles remained, but including them would weight her bag overmuch. More could be obtained in London, of course. Elsie had never purchased her own medicine, but she was certain he would know how to procure it.

She stared longingly at the side table, where her camera sat. Though it was compact, it was still too large to fit in her bag. She must travel light—it would not do to leave the house clutching all her favorite things.

But . . .

The camera case had a strap, didn't it? She could wear it crossed over her body and still hold her bag. She lifted the strap over her shoulder as an experiment. Yes, she could manage quite well. The familiar feel of the camera at her side only strengthened her resolve.

With everything sorted and tidied away, one problem remained. How could she leave the house without attracting attention? Sneaking out before dawn wouldn't work, for she'd never get past the locks on the iron gate without somehow stealing a key—impossible in a household overseen by Aunt Helena.

The plan required more subtlety than that. And subtle planning was not something at which she excelled.

Elsie took a breath and concentrated, approaching the matter from a different angle. She knew from the servants that a horse-drawn tram carried passengers back and forth from the station to Christ's College. She also knew there was an 11:00

train to London, for she'd studied the timetables at King's Cross when changing trains from Essex. She merely needed to know where and when to catch the tram. The young housemaid—Millie was her name—would be able to tell her and probably wouldn't suspect a thing. She was sweet and rather dim.

The problem of how to leave the house still remained.

Her outing must seem ordinary and innocent. The skinny Poole girl was occupied each day, as was Millie. She couldn't slip away from her aunt or uncle even if they agreed to go out with her. She counted through each member of the household once more. Was anyone left? Only Asher Beale, and he'd be no help at all.

On second thought, however—

A knock at the door startled her. She tucked the drawstring bag under the bed and lay back against the pillow.

"Come in."

Her aunt opened the door. In her arms she carried a bundle of material. "How's your head, dear?"

Elsie touched her forehead with the back of her hand. "It's improving, I think."

"Good." Her aunt walked in and sat upon the chair near the bed. She gazed steadily at Elsie before finally clearing her throat.

Here it comes, thought Elsie.

"Your mother didn't explain in detail why you needed to come to Summerfield, but I gather it had something to do with your art tutor."

Elsie looked away.

"You had . . . an infatuation with him?"

"I *loved* him," Elsie whispered after a moment.

"And he returned your affection?"

"Yes."

"Then we must determine one thing if you are to remain here at Summerfield. Is it possible you are with child?"

Elsie blushed, not so much at the boldness of the question but at the memories it evoked. She'd allowed him liberties, and together they'd done wonderful, shameful things that would make her mother faint and her father unlock the gun cabinet. She almost wished she *were* carrying his child—a link to him that could not fade like memory.

"I am *not* with child."

"Good."

Elsie risked a glance at her. Aunt Helena did not appear sickened or scornful. Rather, she simply looked relieved . . . and oddly hopeful.

"My sister intended your visit to be temporary, but I do urge you to consider staying longer, perhaps as a student of Summerfield College?"

Elsie flushed with embarrassment. "I'm not clever, Aunt."

"Nonsense. You haven't applied yourself. And I've never approved of your father's refusal to give your education the same attention he gave to that of his sons. Such an absurdly outdated attitude toward female intellect."

Elsie sighed. "My episodes unsettle him, I think. After Mother insisted I take the dose, which always makes me slow and sleepy, he just assumed I was dull-witted."

"That is unfortunate," Aunt Helena said softly.

Elsie hardly knew what to say. She simply didn't care anymore what her father or mother thought. Soon she would be in London, and her parents wouldn't suffer the agonies of their loss very long.

"I didn't mean to upset you, my dear," her aunt said briskly. "I really only stopped by to see how you were feeling, and to show you these." She shook out the material bundled in her arms. One hand held a plain white blouse, the other a brown skirt. "Young Miss Poole's dress is in a terrible state, so I thought we might take in this old skirt and blouse. Do you think they are too plain?"

"The girl is certain to be glad of them."

Aunt Helena nodded thoughtfully and refolded the garments. "Might you have something that would suit her, Elsie? Something a little nicer for evening functions? I don't wish her to feel like a servant. You have many dresses, I know. There must be one you don't favor so much anymore."

"I'm sure I have something, Aunt."

When her aunt closed the door behind her, Elsie glanced at the wardrobe full of dresses she would never see again. Once she was gone, the girl could have them all.

❖ ❖ ❖ ❖ ❖

Asher had risen from the breakfast table in low spirits, for his plans had come to nothing. He'd imagined Miss Atherton joining him on his tour of Cambridge—she'd only just arrived herself, hadn't she? Together they could pore over his *Baedeker's Great Britain* and search out the most revered colleges and historic sites. He'd lain awake half the night plotting it out.

But Miss Atherton had been cold and distant throughout breakfast, rising to excuse herself long before everyone else had finished eating. Asher had stood quickly, banging his knee on the table as he did so. *Look at me before you go,* he'd thought. *Just one glance.*

But she'd never turned his way.

The revised plan involved drowning his sorrows at a public house. Asher had even peered into a promising establishment by the river, but its dark, low-ceilinged interior, the air thick with smoke and laughter, made him feel very young and very

American. So instead he wandered along King's Parade to Trinity Street.

Having studied his *Baedeker's* the night before, he recognized King's, Clare, and Caius Colleges. He dutifully admired their handsome facades and garden courts, the ornate chapels with their marble floors and medieval sarcophagi. All this luxury made such a contrast to the Puritan plainness of Harvard.

This had drawn him to Cambridge in the first place—the medieval grandeur of the men's colleges. He'd had no desire to visit Summerfield. An upstart college for spinsterly bluestockings was the furthest thing from his notion of a worthwhile social call, not to mention the fact that a notorious spook chaser resided there.

But his uncle had insisted he pay a visit to Oliver Thompson.

"I don't share my brother's fascination for metaphysical research," Francis Beale had said. "I'd much prefer that phantasms stay in the realm of fiction. However, Oliver Thompson was a Trinity Fellow and remains one of the most learned men I've ever met. Both he and your father would be offended if you did not make yourself known to him while in Cambridge. In fact, Thompson is likely to ask you to stay with him at Summerfield College."

If only that damnable Poole girl hadn't ambushed him at the gate, he could have presented his card and left it at that.

He turned back to *Baedeker's* with a sigh, determined to salvage something worthwhile out of this Cambridge visit. As the morning dragged on, however, he found himself walking past buildings that ordinarily would have made him pause. The medieval walls, gardens, and chapels of each college were blurring together so that he could no longer tell them apart. His senses were overwhelmed, and he was starving.

He purchased a meat pie from a street vendor and sat on a

bench near Saint Michael's Church. The pie filled the gnawing void in his stomach, fortifying him to cross the road and take in the grandeur of Trinity College. This was where Oliver Thompson had taken his degree, as had greater minds like Newton and Bacon. Asher stared at the gate for some time, craning his neck to admire the tall, crenellated towers. Above the heavy wooden doors was a statue of the college's founder, Henry VIII. What might one have found in his own town of Cambridge, Massachusetts, when King Henry held the throne of England? Meadows and trees?

Nothing so grand as this.

He passed through the gate to the Great Court and gaped at its dimensions. As he visited each spot recommended by Baedeker, he paid special attention to the gleaming woodwork in the Tudor chapel, the portraits in the dining hall, and the view of the River Cam from the Wren Library.

He crossed the river, leaving the ornate buildings behind. Beyond the bridge an avenue of linden trees curved over him like the vaulted ceiling of a cathedral. The branches trembled in the breeze, offering fleeting wafts of a heady fragrance. Asher didn't consider himself religious, but in that moment something tugged at his heart—a spiritual ache, if one could call it that.

On either side of the avenue lay a meadow. He veered off the path, avoiding the bees that buzzed through the low-hanging branches, and stepped into the grass. No one tried to stop him. After several paces he paused, looked around, and sank down. If he lay on his back, no one would see him. He placed his hands behind his head and stared at the clouds. Birds trilled in the trees, but otherwise it was peaceful. One might forget that this wide green space stood at the center of a busy town.

"This could be mine," he said aloud, closing his eyes.

When he woke—an hour later, according to his watch—he

knew it didn't matter that Elsie refused to smile at him, that the Thompsons were eccentric, or that his father might actually be proud of him for reaching so high as Trinity College, Cambridge.

He needed to be part of this place. It had called to him somehow, and he planned to stay and listen.

After such an epiphany, Asher could only be pleased that Elsie Atherton *did* smile at him upon his return to Summerfield. She greeted him quite warmly, in fact, and met his gaze more than once during supper.

As the five of them settled in the sitting room afterward, he noted an unusual animation to her expression. That morning she'd been cold and remote. Now, however, her eyes shone brightly. She did not fidget—nothing so unladylike as that— but when he looked up from his book to steal a glance at her, she seemed attuned to the atmosphere rather than withdrawn from it. He forced himself to look away, feigning indifference.

"I hope you weren't expecting to have port and cigars in the dining room, Asher," said Mr. Thompson. "I suppose it's what most gentlemen do, but I've always preferred to stay near my wife when in my own home." He and Mrs. Thompson shared a smile.

"Of course, sir," Asher mumbled, embarrassed by the display of affection, modest though it was. He turned back to his book, but minutes later he found he'd read the same sentence three times without comprehending it. A sigh broke the silence, and Asher raised his head to find Elsie's eyes on him.

"You know, I would so enjoy a visit to the Fitzwilliam Museum," she said airily.

Mrs. Thompson looked up from her sewing. "How nice, my dear. They have many treasures."

"I was thinking of visiting tomorrow, in fact."

Asher noted the furrow on Mrs. Thompson's brow. Even Kate, who'd been ripping seams on a brown skirt, looked up with interest.

"If you would wait until Saturday, Elsie, we could all go together," Mrs. Thompson said. "I'm afraid your uncle and I have too many engagements tomorrow, and Miss Poole has her duties in the library. You ought not go alone."

Elsie sighed again. "It's just that I am feeling much better and would like to see more of the town. All I've seen so far are the buildings and garden of Summerfield."

Asher chanced a look at her and felt his face grow hot as she boldly returned his gaze. She smiled and turned back to her aunt. "Might Mr. Beale be allowed to accompany me?"

Mrs. Thompson looked at her husband. "I'm not sure that would be—"

"Would be what, Aunt?" Elsie's expression was all innocence. Asher dragged his eyes from her to look at Mrs. Thompson.

"A young lady accompanied by a young man who is not her brother?" Mrs. Thompson shook her head. "It's not the done thing."

Her husband set his book down. "Is it really so terrible, Helena? Surely it isn't any worse than two *cousins* visiting a museum together."

"But they are *not* cousins, dear husband."

"And yet we know and trust his father so well, they might as well be. I've never known you to be this old-fashioned! They are merely going to a museum."

"What would my sister say?" Mrs. Thompson arched an eyebrow for emphasis.

"I'm sorry, my dear," Mr. Thompson said, "but your sister is a fusspot. I did not agree to have your niece here so that she could be locked within our walls until we have a spare moment to chaperone her outings."

"I suppose it would be nice for our guest to have company as he explores all that Cambridge has to offer," Mrs. Thompson relented, looking at Asher.

He smiled in reply.

"It's settled, then," said Mr. Thompson, opening his book once more. "That is, I assume it is amenable to Mr. Beale?"

"Of course, sir." Asher knew better than to meet Miss Atherton's gaze. Nor would he glance at Kate Poole, for he could almost sense the sly look she must be giving him. Instead he pretended to study his book most carefully, all the while rehearsing the clever things he would say to Miss Atherton the next day.

Chapter 8

"**M**iss Poole, I have an early appointment this morning and must let you into the library before Miss Freeman and Miss Barrett arrive. Does this suit you?"

Kate glanced at Mrs. Thompson over her teacup. "You trust me with the books? All alone?"

"I highly doubt you would run away with them." Mrs. Thompson's eyes gleamed with amusement. "They are of little value to anyone but scholars. Furthermore, I'm certain there's nothing in our collection that would be inappropriate for a young lady to read."

A young lady? Kate squirmed with pleasure to be termed such. "Of course, ma'am. I will unpack books until the lady scholars arrive."

As she entered the building, it occurred to her that no one had ordered the unpacking to commence *immediately*. With that in mind, the first thing she did once Mrs. Thompson left her alone was to survey the stacks of periodicals.

The Summerfield newspaper collection consisted of bound volumes of two London papers dating back to 1880. She also found stacks of unbound copies of the local paper, but they were sloppily folded and mostly out of order. It would take ages to get them all sorted. She turned back to the stacks of London papers. *The Daily News* appeared to be a smaller publication, quicker to search, so she pulled out the appropriate volume and paged her way to June 1, 1898.

No mention of Frederic Stanton.

She found nothing listed in the following day's paper, either. In fact, she didn't find his name in the obituaries until the June 7 edition.

> *STANTON. — June 1, at Brighton, F. Stanton, late Fellow of Trinity College, Cambridge, age 43.*

Kate stared at the words until they blurred on the page. How could that be all? She chewed her lip for a moment, then returned to the stacks of bound periodicals. The only other choice was *The Times,* and these copies were bound in wide volumes with bright red covers. She scanned the spines and heaved the appropriate volume to the floor next to *The Daily News.* This time she knew better than to expect the obituary to be printed the very day her father died. She turned pages quickly, and her heart leapt when she found a full paragraph.

> *We regret to announce the sudden death, by misadventure, of Mr. Frederic Stanton, joint secretary of the Metaphysical Research Society. Mr. Stanton, who was born in 1855, was the son of the Rev. Trevor Stanton, late Rector of Marylebone. He received his education at Trinity College, Cambridge, of which college he became a Fellow, after taking his degree in Classics in 1878. Mr. Stanton was the principal author of* The Metaphysical Mind. *He died alone at the Avalon Hotel, Brighton, whither he had gone for a night on business.*

"Misadventure?" Kate whispered.

What did that mean? She read the paragraph again. Her father had been secretary to the Metaphysical Research Society. The name sounded vaguely familiar. Had she heard it mentioned at Mrs. Martineau's? If so, the Society must have something to do with spirits and hauntings.

But that made no sense. Her mother had often told her, very proudly indeed, that Frederic Stanton was a serious scholar and gentleman. How could he have been involved in Martineau's world of séances and spirit apparitions? How could he have written a book on the subject? None of it was real.

She studied both entries again. Her father had been thirty-two years old when she was born, still a Fellow at Trinity. Fellows *were* allowed to marry, but Kate had to admit that her mother, a woman without education or refinement, could only have harmed his career prospects. Still, he hadn't abandoned them. They had lived comfortably enough, and Kate had vague memories of his visits. She knew that he'd towered over her when he stood at the door, and those few times when he held her on his lap, his wide brown eyes had seemed sad. The visits had stopped when he'd married, but the money had continued.

Until his death by *misadventure*.

Such an ominous word. It brought to mind darker words such as *murder* and *mayhem*. When she found the word in the dictionary, she was almost disappointed to find it merely meant *mishap*—an accident, just as Mr. Thompson had said.

She studied the title of his book again. *The Metaphysical Mind*. It sounded preposterous, but at that moment the book was the only remaining source of information on her father.

She glanced about the room at the jumbled stacks of books. Could she be so lucky?

Asher's rehearsed charm failed him the next morning when he saw Elsie Atherton. Dressed in somber grey and an imposing hat, with her camera strapped across her body, she seemed more handsome than ever. The light still gleamed in her eyes, and her tapping foot communicated a desire to be on her way.

"Do you plan to take photographs at the museum?" he asked, gesturing at the camera.

"Mostly likely not. Perhaps we'll have an opportunity on our return walk?"

When she tilted her head and grinned, all thoughts of the camera vanished from his mind.

Why did she have this effect on him? Her beauty disarmed him, of course, but it was her air of mystery that captivated him even more. She carried secrets about her, and yet he sensed nothing dark or cunning. Her secrets were worth knowing, and they waited for the proper man to discover them. Were others repulsed by her illness? The very thought filled him with indignation. Her ailment was no fault of her own. She merely required a steadying hand from time to time, someone to keep her safe.

The morning was bright and cool, which made for a pleasant walk. He'd intended to offer his arm, but Miss Atherton kept enough distance between them that he couldn't do so without being awkward. Her hands were occupied, anyway, for she held a parasol in one and clutched her bag with the other.

He gestured toward the parasol. "Might I hold that for you, Miss Atherton?"

"Have you need of it, Mr. Beale? Are you sensitive to the sun?"

She was teasing him. Perhaps he should have been pleased

by her casual manner—surely that meant she was comfortable with him—but instead he felt terribly young.

Fortunately, there were plenty of sights to distract him. It was a busy morning in Cambridge town as the butcher's traps and corn wagons made their noisy way to the market. Asher did his best to strike up conversation by noting the fierce glare of one butcher's pony or a pretty view of the river. Miss Atherton murmured agreement without pausing to study what he pointed out. She walked rather quickly, in fact—so quickly that they arrived at the museum in ten minutes. He had to admire how the exertion made her cheeks flush so prettily. He paid the admission and gestured for her to go ahead of him. She surprised him by holding her ground.

"Mr. Beale, would you mind waiting for me in the West Gallery?" She glanced meaningfully in the direction of the ladies' powder room.

"Of course," he said quickly. "Do take your time. I shall be well occupied."

Her cheeks flushed pink. "You are too kind."

Charmed again by her modesty, Asher stepped lightly up the stairs to the gallery. He took a catalog from the attendant, intending to use his time alone to review the descriptions of the paintings. He would share the most interesting details with Miss Atherton when she returned, for he wished to be convincing as a man of learning and artistic appreciation.

Asher studied the paintings and contrived brief commentaries for each, but still Miss Atherton did not return. His own mother took forever to primp in the powder room, yet even *she* was quicker than this. He'd thought Miss Atherton's flushed cheeks indicated exertion, but perhaps she was suffering from a fever? Yet what could he do but wait? He forced himself to make another survey of the paintings before checking his watch again. She had been in the powder room for twenty minutes.

He walked down the stairs to the entrance hall, thinking to procure a female attendant to politely check on Miss Atherton. He suggested this to the ticket seller, a young man with slick pale hair and a blank expression.

"Are you speaking of the lady who accompanied you earlier, sir?"

"Yes, the lady in grey. I paid her admission."

"Well, sir, that lady left the museum more than fifteen minutes ago. She seemed in a hurry."

Astonishment clutched at Asher's throat, bringing a fit of coughing. With great effort he steadied himself. "Do you know where she was going?"

"No sir, I didn't think it polite to ask."

Asher looked about the hall and raised his hands in despair. "But I am responsible for her! How could she just disappear?"

The man shrugged.

Asher stalked away and applied his anger to the door, shoving it open. He looked up and down the street but did not see the dove-colored feathers of Miss Atherton's hat among the people who milled about the shops. Had she returned to the college? Perhaps she truly was sick. Or worse yet, she'd had another epileptic spell.

Assuming a gentler expression, he turned back to the ticket seller. "Did you happen to see which way the lady turned as she left the building?"

The man thought for a moment. "I do believe she turned right, sir."

So she hadn't returned to the college.

Asher walked down Trumpington Street, peering in windows in case she'd entered a shop, but she was not to be found.

When he reached Lensfield Road he stared at the large hotel at the corner. He didn't think she'd go into such a building alone. Perhaps she'd walked to Coe Fen, for she did seem to enjoy a green space. But why leave so abruptly? Had he offended her in some way? He glanced at the hotel again. A boy sat on the steps, counting the coins in his hat.

"You there," he called out. "Did you see a lady in a grey dress walk past here twenty minutes ago?"

The boy tilted his head as though trying to remember. "I dunno."

"Yes or no?"

The boy shook his hat. The coins inside tinkled suggestively.

"You want money?"

The only reply he received was a blank stare.

"You'd better not be wasting my time." Asher reached into his pockets and dropped a few coins in the hat. "Well?"

The boy looked at the offering. "Sir, the lady offered me more'n that to keep my mouth shut."

The answer came as a blow. "You actually spoke to her?"

"I dunno."

This time Asher pulled a note from his pocket and tossed it into the hat. "That should be enough. Now speak up—I'm very concerned for the lady."

"Well, when you put it that way I don't mind sharing a few details with a concerned young gentleman." The boy gestured for Asher to sit next to him. "Now," he said in a low, confidential tone, "the lady did come by, and she did speak to me. In fact, she asked if I'd seen the tram. She was afraid she'd missed it."

"What tram is that?"

"The one that runs from Christ's College to the railway station." He pointed toward the cross street. "It creeps along

Regent and I has a good view of it from here. I see a great deal whiles I wait to help gentlemen like you with their bags."

Asher thought for a moment. "So you think she was heading to the railway station?"

"She didn't say, sir, but I can't think why else she'd take that tram. There's an eleven o'clock to London that's very popular with our patrons."

"Eleven, you say?" Asher looked at his watch. "Do you think I could make it in time by foot?"

"You'd have to take it at a gallop, sir, though I suppose 'tis possible—"

But Asher had leapt off the steps before the boy could finish.

Chapter 9

Elsie secured a seat to herself by spreading out her belongings and casting a sour stare at anyone who dared look her way. Alas, there was no escape from the noise and stench. Children squawked and wailed until her temples throbbed and she longed for a drop of the dose.

Before her accident she'd traveled often with her family, and in those days she always looked forward to riding the train. She loved how the lushly upholstered walls and seats, the curtained windows and gaslight sconces, transformed the compartment into a miniature sitting room. When her brothers allowed her the window seat, she sat mesmerized as the sheep-speckled countryside rolled past.

Until today, however, she had never traveled third class.

To pass the time she checked and rechecked the contents of her bag, jumping in her seat when the guard banged through the carriage door and called for tickets. She retrieved hers and returned the bulging bag to the seat.

The man stared as he reached for her ticket. His yellowish-white whiskers hung from either side of his mouth like the tusks of a walrus. "Is everything all right, miss?"

"Yes, of course." She averted her gaze.

After an eternity of fumbling with the ticket, he handed it back and moved on. Her bag had tipped over, so she pulled it and the camera into her lap and clasped their comforting bulk to ease the trembling in her hands.

An hour later she breathed a sigh of relief as the train finally rumbled into King's Cross Station. Leaving her parasol behind—*he* would think it gaudy—she pushed her way through the horde that spilled out of the crowded carriage. It didn't occur to her to be afraid of the station. She dissolved into a nervous wreck in the schoolroom or at social gatherings, always hating the inevitable moment when all eyes were upon her, but teeming train stations did not fluster her in the least. Blending into a crowd was liberating.

Elsie fought the tide of third-class passengers to find the porters, knowing they would cluster near the first-class cars. She caught the eye of one young man in uniform and, offering her most dazzling smile, asked him to direct her to the nearest cabstand. He readily obliged, but his cheerful sincerity deflated when she failed to pass him a coin.

She little cared whom she offended, for she was too eager for the first glimpse of *him*. Elsie had no doubt he would be at the museum. He had loved to recount the days before he came to Peverel Place, when he'd spent his hours sketching and painting in the galleries. Before her father had sent him away, he'd told her she would find him there, should she come to London.

She jostled through the crowds, undaunted by stiff shoulders and aggressive elbows, until finally she made her way to the street. The sky was low and dark—the air choked with coal smoke even in August—but at least it did not rain. For a moment she considered walking the distance to the museum. She'd save herself a shilling, and her path lay through residential neighborhoods. Yet she dreaded the prospect of appearing to him as a sooty and bedraggled mess, so instead she joined the queue for the next hansom cab. Once seated, bag and camera case clutched in her lap, she shouted the destination to the driver through the trapdoor. The driver's whip cracked, and she steeled herself as the horse leapt into a brisk trot. She hardly noticed the scenery as the cab sped along Euston Road. Rather, she passed the time imagining his expression when he recognized her.

When they turned the corner onto Great Russell Street, the grand columns of the British Museum rose up before her. The cab jerked to a halt. Elsie helped herself down and paid the shilling, stepping carefully around the clumps of manure. She took the steps quickly and breezed through the vestibule with little thought for propriety. Ignoring the manuscript room to her right—he would not care for that—she turned left into the Roman Gallery and paused to scan the room.

He was not there.

She glanced all around, panic tightening her throat until her gaze moved beyond the gallery to the Graeco-Roman room, where a young man stood before an easel. It was *him,* she was certain. She recognized the auburn waves of his hair, too long for fashion but lovely to run her hands through when she cradled his head in her lap. Elsie looked down at her hands, willing them to stop their silly shaking, and lurched forward to greet him.

She gasped when she crashed into the very solid form of a gentleman rushing in the opposite direction through the gallery.

"I do beg your pardon, miss."

She reared back to look up at him, shaken by the sudden contact. He was a handsome young man with dark hair, but that wasn't what made her stare. No, it was the light that suddenly shimmered around his head that mesmerized her. She stared stupidly as the tremors began.

He peered at her. "Miss, are you well?"

Never had it come upon her this quickly. The orb about his head shimmered and danced, and her own head began to throb. She tore her gaze away and fumbled in her bag for the dose, afraid it was already too late.

"My medicine," she cried. "I'm going to be . . . very ill."

The brown bottle was not there.

The young man grasped her upper arms as she staggered against him. She vaguely heard him calling for help as the darkness began to pull at her, sucking her through a ghastly tunnel. She closed her eyes and prayed for calm.

Finally the dreadful pulling sensation ceased. A sudden cold chilled her. She opened her eyes to find a woman walking toward her from the darkness, her pale face drooping with sorrow.

Elsie moaned, for she knew the woman was dead.

❈ ❈ ❈ ❈ ❈

Asher had kept his eyes on the grey feathers of Miss Atherton's hat as he followed the other passengers off the train. But when he passed her seat, the bright yellow of her folded parasol caught his eye. In her haste, she'd left it behind. As he retrieved it, he saw the white label against the dark fabric of the seat. Her medicine lay there—the bottle of Chlorodyne that had soothed her convulsions the first day he'd met her.

He stared . . . until he felt an impatient shoulder pressing into him. He plucked the bottle from the seat, ignoring the grumbling behind him.

On the platform he watched from a safe distance as Miss Atherton spoke with a cheerful young porter. Once she moved on, he offered the porter several coins to share the details of the conversation. It was easy enough to watch as she hired a cab and then to do the same himself. Clearly she was preoccupied, for she never turned to look behind her.

Once he reached the museum he followed only a few paces behind. He had no choice, for she was nearly running up the steps. He didn't want to lose her in the building's labyrinthine galleries.

What did she mean to do? Whom did she wish to see? He quickened his pace, determined to confront her. Just as he drew near, however, Miss Atherton collided with a tall young gentleman. Asher's heart quickened as she crumpled against the man. Another seizure? The bottle felt heavy in his pocket. If he offered assistance, she would know that he'd followed her all the way from Cambridge. She would think him strange. Certainly she would be offended. And yet—

She was in agony. Asher clenched his fists as her body trembled and her eyes rolled back. The young man had eased her to the ground, and while many had left the room in undisguised dismay, a few had circled to offer words of encouragement. How strange would it seem for him to step forward and pour medicine into the girl's mouth?

Damn his pride! He couldn't hold his vanity dearer than Elsie's health.

He pulled the bottle from his pocket, but as he joined the circle surrounding the young man and the girl, Elsie's convulsions ceased. For a moment, all was quiet.

Then her eyes opened. Her expression was strange—her eyes vacant and icy blue. She shivered and moaned, but her eyes remained open. The intensity of her gaze made Asher think she looked at something, or *someone*—yet her eyes were fixed on the ceiling. Then her moaning ceased, and to him she seemed to be listening.

The man patted her cheek. "Miss, are you feeling better?"

Elsie did not answer, nor did she blink.

Asher was certain the medicine would not help her now. She was breathing normally, no longer convulsing. Yet somehow she was not entirely conscious.

Another young man gathered his folded easel and backed away. As he brushed past, he kept his eyes on the floor. Asher curled his lip at the man's long hair, his lack of a proper jacket. *An artist.* No doubt he was rushing off to sketch Elsie for some hideous scene of a writhing mystic.

Elsie sat up with a harsh gasp. One lady squealed in alarm. Asher watched, his body frozen, as Elsie's eyes fixed upon the gentleman who held her. She clutched the man's arm so tightly her knuckles whitened.

"She's with you . . . always watching," she gasped to him. "She is so very sad. She begs you to know how sorry she is."

Her words—intimate and thick with yearning—made Asher feel slightly sick, as though he were spying. The dreamy, detached Elsie was gone, and in her place was something mystical and rather frightening—a Grecian oracle offering a divine message.

The recipient of this message opened his mouth but seemed unable to speak.

All around the onlookers whispered.

Finally, Asher stepped forward to kneel by Elsie. He dropped the parasol and reached for her hand, gently prying it from the man's arm.

"Elsie?"

She turned. Her eyes widened in recognition before they filled with tears. "Oh, Asher."

The young gentleman cleared his throat. "Do you know this lady?"

"I do," Asher replied, not taking his eyes from Elsie's face. He squeezed her hand. "Do you feel well enough to stand? Should I get you some water?"

Elsie shook her head, prompting a tear to spill down her cheek.

Asher turned back to the gentleman. "You may rely on me to see her home safely."

The young man searched his face, his grey eyes thoughtful. "May I know your name?"

"I am Asher Beale . . . of Boston."

"Beale?" His eyes brightened. "Are you . . . could you possibly be a relation of Harold Beale?"

Asher flinched. "I am his son."

"What good fortune! I've met your father and have followed his work with great interest." He pulled a watch from his pocket and frowned at it. "I am late for a meeting, but I'm certain I can trust this young lady to the care of Harold Beale's son."

Asher nodded, then turned back to Elsie. She stared as the young gentleman rose to his feet and attempted to brush the creases from his trousers. Her eyes were wide and more deeply blue than he'd remembered.

The gentleman gave Elsie a last lingering look before turning to go. With his departure the crowd broke up, the curious show having reached its conclusion. Asher helped Elsie to her feet and tried not to frown when she refused to meet his gaze. Instead she looked after the gentleman who'd held her.

Asher had not thought to ask for the man's name.

chapter 10

As Freeman and Barrett prepared to leave for luncheon, Kate lingered near the back of the room, aligning the corners of an unruly stack of books. Freeman pinned a straw hat to her head before turning a disdainful eye toward her.

"Don't tarry too long, Poole. I'm not sure I like the idea of you here alone."

"Mrs. Thompson doesn't mind," Kate murmured.

"Well, *I* do. When you're finished with that, go on to the kitchen. And don't bring any of Cook's treats back here. Food attracts mice. And you know what mice do."

"They nibble books and leave nasty little presents," Kate recited obediently, trying not to grimace.

"Exactly," said Freeman. Satisfied, she nodded toward Barrett and the two ladies made their way to the door.

"Silly prigs," Kate hissed under her breath. She went to the window and watched them until they were out of sight. Her stomach gurgled plaintively, but she could not have her lunch just yet. The shelves waited.

For the past day and a half, they'd worked on cataloging and moving the new acquisitions. The older books still remained on the shelves. She had only a vague idea what the numbers and letters on the spines meant, but having deduced the subject matter from the titles, she moved from literature to mathematics before finding the area devoted to science.

She shifted slowly through each scientific discipline, scanning the titles. It took some searching, but finally she found her father's book tucked among those having to do with witchcraft, superstitions, hallucinations . . . even insanity. She cocked her head to read the titles, whispering the strange words in wonderment. What could her father have had to do with all *this*?

She gently pulled the heavy volume from the shelf and carried it to a table. Flipping to the title page, she ran a finger across her father's name—FREDERIC STANTON, MA, LATE FELLOW OF TRINITY COLLEGE, CAMBRIDGE—directly under the title. The words brought a strange flutter to her heart. The preface followed, but other than an acknowledgment to Mr. and Mrs. Thompson, it told her very little of interest.

A list of Metaphysical Society members followed the preface. At first glance Kate noted the Thompsons' names again, as well as that of Asher's father, Harold Beale. Farther down the list she found James Atherton, 3rd Baron Rolleston. Could he be Elsie's father? She turned back to the beginning, studying the list more thoroughly. The remaining names were unfamiliar, except one.

Robert Eliot.

Eliot was Mrs. Martineau's patron. He'd been the one to invite Mr. Thompson to the séance that exposed her. So Eliot didn't just enjoy a passing familiarity with Mr. Thompson? He was a *member* of the Metaphysical Society? She knew the man was wealthy and well educated—he'd reminded Mrs. Martineau of that more than once—but he did not seem of the same class as Oliver Thompson. How could someone who dallied with mediums, who pawed spirit apparitions with greedy hands, move in the same circles as a gentle soul like Mr. Thompson?

Kate turned back to the book, frowning in confusion over the chapter summaries. *Thought-transference. Telepathy. Telepathic Hallucinations.* What did these terms mean? As far as she could tell, there was no mention of ghosts or séances. Perhaps she'd been wrong about the nature of the Metaphysical Society.

She continued to flip pages, disappointment weighing heavily on her shoulders. What had she expected? It was a scholarly book, not a memoir. Still, she scanned the chapters, looking for some glimpse into her father's mind. The word *phantasm* appeared again and again—a more scientific word for ghost, perhaps? She'd always felt clever in school, but now the words on the page bounced off her brain. She simply could not absorb any sense from them.

She flipped back to the introduction and focused harder, searching for something her brain could latch onto. In its final paragraph, the words *main thesis* caught her eye. Surely *this* would help clarify matters.

> *Experiment proves that telepathy—the transference of thoughts and feelings from one mind to another—is a fact of Nature. Testimony proves that phantasms (impressions, voices, or visions) of persons undergoing some crisis— especially death—are perceived by their friends and relatives with a frequency that mere chance cannot explain. These phantasms, then, whatever else they may be, are instances of the action of one mind on another.*

"The action of one mind on another," murmured Kate. Was the Metaphysical Society arguing for the ability of a dead person's mind to act on that of a living person? The language was scholarly, but the underlying notion was similar to what Mrs. Martineau used to dupe her sitters.

Just as she was about to close the volume in disgust, it fell open at a folded piece of paper. Someone had tucked a clipping of newsprint between the book's pages. Kate unfolded it to find a cutting from the *Brighton Gazette*, dated June 28, 1898.

She chewed her lip nervously as she read:

> *On Monday afternoon, Mr. Emerson Bell, the Deputy Borough Coroner, held an inquest at the Brighton Town Hall, on the body of Frederic Stanton, aged 43, a gentleman of independent means, who was found dead in bed at the Avalon Hotel, Brighton, earlier this month.*

The next several sentences detailed how Frederic Stanton had arrived at the hotel in good health on June 1 but did not appear for breakfast the following morning. Nor did he answer when a maid knocked at the door. After several attempts to rouse their guest, the hotel staff was forced to break down the door. Kate's heart thumped as she read the next sentences.

> *The deceased was discovered in bed, lying on his left side, already dead for several hours. He had a small sponge bag over the lower portion of his face, and near to the bed was a bottle containing clear fluid, supposed to be chloroform.*

She refolded the clipping and shut it within the book, barely resisting the urge to hurl it across the room. Tears pricked at her eyes.

Both her parents had met their ends as drug fiends?

❄ ❄ ❄ ❄ ❄

No matter where Elsie turned people stared, and their eyes were anything but warm with concern. Instead they reflected disgust, horror, and curiosity. Young ladies were not supposed to make such public displays. Shaking, convulsing, and crying out—why, it was almost obscene. At least that's what Mother had once said to Father when Elsie was just outside their bed-chamber and could hear every word of their distraught conversation.

She numbly took her parasol from Asher and followed him out of the British Museum, allowing him to help her into a cab. His hand at her elbow was steady, reassuring. They would return to Cambridge now, and she knew there was no point in summoning enough energy to resist. She had nowhere to go even if she somehow could evade him.

"Do you feel better, Miss Atherton?"

Elsie flinched at the gentle concern in his voice. "I do." She sat still for a moment, truly considering the question. "In fact, I feel quite well. Usually I fall asleep after an attack . . . and my head feels terribly muzzy when I wake."

"Last time this happened—or the last time *I* witnessed it, anyway—you took this." His hand touched hers, and she turned to him as he placed the bottle of Chlorodyne in her outstretched fingers.

"You found it."

"On your seat with the parasol. You must have been distracted."

She stared at him. "You followed me all the way from Cambridge on the same train? In the very same carriage?"

He nodded. "What I meant to say, however, was that you usually take your medication to stop the spell. This time was different. Without the medication, the convulsions ran their course."

She saw his cheeks color at those words, no doubt from his embarrassment at witnessing her distress. His handsome blue eyes, however, were earnest. He did not seem to look at her with disgust.

"Now my head feels perfectly clear," she said.

"That's something to ponder, don't you think?" His eyes brightened. "Miss Atherton, you spoke words during your . . ." He faltered, then took a deep breath. "May I be so bold as to ask what you saw?"

She thought of the pale woman, the vision of death reaching out to her. "I remember nothing," she lied, looking away. It was still too recent, too disturbing to contemplate, let alone share.

He came to mind instead. She'd been so close to freedom. As if recalling a dream, she vaguely remembered him standing a few paces away, his expression one of puzzlement . . . and then *revulsion*? Her heart shuddered at the memory. Was he just like her parents after all?

She took a breath and affected a light tone. "Did you happen to see a tall man with auburn hair, worn rather long, when I was indisposed?"

Asher did not answer immediately, and she could not bring herself to meet his gaze to see why he kept silent.

"Do you mean the one with the easel?" he finally asked. "The artist?"

Now it was her turn to blush. "Yes."

"He joined the crowd that formed around you, but then he hurried away. I thought him some opportunist gaining inspiration from your distress." His voice was heavy with disdain. "Why? Did you know him?"

She said nothing, looking out the window instead.

"Miss Atherton, were you *meeting* that man at the museum?"

"I'd rather not talk about it," she whispered.

All her efforts had come to nothing, her beautiful fantasy

having died a quick and miserable death. No cozy home in London, far from the forbidding frowns of her parents. No sanctuary where he could paint and she could experiment with photography. All of it lost because he couldn't bear the spectacle of her distress.

But why should she be surprised? Mother had warned her that men would find her attacks disgusting. If she'd had the sense to confirm that her medicine was still in her bag, she'd be with him now.

Wouldn't she?

For some reason, she struggled to form a clear image of his face in her mind. Instead she saw the gentleman who had caught her, his grey eyes widening as she sank against him. He had a noble face, and he'd held her so gently as she trembled in his arms. He did not wince in disgust, nor did he hasten to get away from her at the first sign of trouble. And though he'd clearly been rattled, he had stayed until her spell had passed—as a true gentleman would—even after she blurted the lady's words to him.

That ghastly lady of her vision . . . *she* had loved the gentleman, loved him quite desperately. And yet there'd been something wrong about this love. Elsie knew in her bones that the lady's death had not been natural. What tragedy had befallen the young pair? Elsie had been frightened during the vision, but now that it was over she was intrigued.

She turned to Asher. "The man who caught me—who was he?"

"He never introduced himself. I thought it strange at the time, as I gave him *my* name, but he seemed too much in a hurry to return the courtesy."

"He was quite gentlemanly, don't you think?"

Asher frowned, saying nothing.

"This will sound odd," she continued, "but I have a feeling we'll see him again."

Her statement was met with silence. Asher faced the window, not turning even when she openly stared at him. She noted his rigid jaw, the pursed lips, and imagined she could see the man he might become. He would be handsome, she thought—he already *was* handsome—but his beauty would be marred if he grew proud and pretentious . . . like her father and brothers.

He did not speak again, neither as he helped her from the cab nor as they made their way to the platform at King's Cross. He escorted her to the ladies' lounge, murmuring his intent to purchase return tickets to Cambridge. He shook his head when she fumbled in her bag for a sovereign, then turned away to leave her standing alone with flushed cheeks.

He'd arranged for opposing seats in the first-class carriage, but still Asher would not meet her gaze. Instead he unfolded *The Times* and raised it like a barrier between them.

She sat in silence for half an hour, her worries multiplying. She had no contingency plan for a return to Cambridge. How would they explain their extended absence? Perhaps Asher meant to expose her deceits. Elsie cleared her throat. "Mr. Beale, what do you plan to say to Mr. and Mrs. Thompson upon our return?"

Asher folded the paper with a heavy sigh. "Miss Atherton, I have attempted to restrain myself. I have not demanded that you explain why you tricked me into escorting you to the Fitzwilliam. Nor have I pressed you to tell me what you were thinking when you took the train to London. I won't ask again *whom* you were meeting at the British Museum. But now you ask me what I will say to Mr. and Mrs. Thompson when we return to Summerfield? *You* deceived me—why must *I* be the one to explain where we've been?"

She shrank against the seat. "I understand you are upset, but you were under no obligation to follow me. You might rather have minded your own business."

"The Thompsons trusted me to take care of you," he snapped. "You were under my protection, and therefore I had no choice but to follow you. Perhaps I should have stayed in Cambridge and left you to the mercy of strangers at the British Museum? If it weren't for me, you might be locked away in Bedlam by now!"

She took in his high color, his sneering lip, with familiar dread. It always came to this—the anger, frustration. The deep disappointment. She looked down at her hands. "I'm sorry," she said in a small, dull voice. "You were right to follow me . . . after what I did. I'm very grateful to you, of course."

She heard him exhale, sensed his shoulders softening ever so slightly.

"I'll tell the Thompsons something," he finally said. "They won't be angry once I come up with a proper reason for our delay." He leaned forward and lightly placed a hand on hers. "I only wish us to be friends, Elsie. I want you to trust me."

She nodded, smoothing away her tears with a gloved hand. Asher seemed to be waiting for her to respond, but no words came to mind—nothing remotely reassuring, anyway. After a moment he unfolded his paper and once again raised the barrier between them.

Really, what could she tell him? She'd only told one person what she'd seen during an episode . . . and that had ended terribly. Elsie swallowed against the lump that threatened to rise again in her throat. How could she explain to Asher how one careless confession had changed her life forever, separating her from society and transforming her into the dull and drowsy addict she was now?

chapter 11

Kate struggled with needle and thread under the best conditions, but it was nearly impossible to make a proper stitch with Mrs. Thompson pacing before the window. She hardly knew the lady, but even so she wondered at this crack in her composure.

"I can't imagine why they haven't yet returned," said Mrs. Thompson. "They can't have spent the entire day at the Fitzwilliam."

Her husband looked up from his book. "Come away from the window, my dear. Staring at Summerfield Walk won't bring them to our door any faster."

With a shake of her head Mrs. Thompson returned to her seat and picked up her sewing. "Did Mr. Beale happen to mention this morning when he and Elsie would be returning from the museum?"

It took Kate a moment to realize the question was directed at her. "Mention to *me*, ma'am? He rarely speaks to me."

The woman's eyes darted to the window. "It's just . . . they've been gone the entire day. I didn't think there was enough to occupy even the most devoted art historian for more than a few hours at the Fitzwilliam. The collection is not that extensive."

"I'm sure it's nothing to worry about, ma'am," Kate replied absently.

When Mrs. Thompson fell into silence again, Kate's thoughts returned to her father and the obituary clipping. The account of the inquest had ended rather abruptly with the jury verdict of "accidental death." Clearly, however, there'd been questions surrounding his death, for various doctors were called to testify. A medically inclined friend named Marshall argued that her father suffered from acute neuralgic pain and had only resorted to inhaling chloroform to relieve it. A long jury consultation followed.

Kate well knew why so many had been called to testify, and why the jury had taken a considerable amount of time to render a verdict. There was a possibility other than "accidental death" to consider—a possibility very familiar to Kate. The death could have been a suicide, just as her mother's was deemed to be.

Frederic Stanton had been a solemn man, to be sure. But her mother had often told her what a brilliant mind he possessed and how respected he was by his learned friends. Kate knew he came from a good family and had a very comfortable inheritance. If one was blessed with such an easy life, why end it so abruptly?

Her mother, on the other hand, had been a broken woman. When the money came regularly and Kate spent most of her time in school, her mother's fragile state hadn't been so obvious. But once the money stopped, and both of them were forced to work, she had suffered deeply and quite openly. She'd taken more Chlorodyne each day and died within a matter of months. It was Kate who found her facedown on the bed. Even if she lived a hundred years, she'd never erase the memory of her mother's wide-staring eyes and mottled skin when she turned her body over.

Kate shook her head. It made no difference whether or not her father had actually committed suicide. The *suggestion* was there in the obituary. That meant many of his friends and colleagues had considered the possibility, too. This was something she could take to her father's widow, a little piece of intelligence that she could embroider with more damning details, if she could harden her heart to do so. She was not so desperate . . . as yet.

And though she'd found the widow's name—Elizabeth Grove Stanton—how was she to find the lady herself? Earlier during lunch she'd risked a walk to Castle End, hoping to find Billy safe and smiling. Willing to answer the questions that plagued her. One of the young ones met her at the door, however, and told her Billy had not yet returned. She'd been so rattled during the walk back to Summerfield—wondering if Tec somehow blamed her for Billy's disappearance, worrying that Billy lay broken and bloody in a ditch—that she failed to fabricate a convincing excuse for being almost an hour late. Freeman's ire had lasted the entire afternoon.

Mrs. Thompson's voice jerked Kate from her thoughts.

"I suppose we should hold supper for them? But how long?"

Mr. Thompson turned a page of his book. "No need to worry about that for at least two hours."

"Perhaps what I should ask," Mrs. Thompson continued, her voice pitched noticeably higher, "is how long does one sit and wait for one's children to return before one contacts the police?"

Mr. Thompson looked up. "For heaven's sake, Helena—there's no cause for such speculations. I'm surprised at you! Even when there is reason for panic, you usually remain stoic, and at this point, *there is no reason for panic.* Please calm yourself, my dear."

Mr. Thompson returned his gaze to the book. Mrs. Thompson frowned at the bundle of sewing on her lap, but she did not pick up her needle. Kate could only stare at the window, thoroughly unsettled by the queer silence.

They all jumped at the clang of the doorbell.

❂ ❂ ❂ ❂ ❂

Asher felt a sinking in his gut when he saw the Thompsons. They each stood the moment he and Elsie entered the room, their eyes wide and mouths crimped. Only Kate remained seated, her expression curious rather than concerned. It occurred to him that she'd never looked at him with much interest before, and he wondered why that struck him now, when he was about to face an inquisition.

"And where have you been all this time, my boy?" asked Mr. Thompson.

The man's voice was steady, but the hand that gripped his cane was white-knuckled. Asher stepped forward, feeling much like a pupil brought before the kindly, long-suffering headmaster.

"Well, you see . . ."

He couldn't continue. He hadn't contrived a convincing story to start with, and now he struggled to recall the details. All the worry and anger over the girl beside him had muddled his brain. What a load of trouble she'd brought him! He turned to her, meaning to frown, but her pale-cheeked anxiety melted him once again. He blinked when she put a hand on his arm.

"No, it's all right, Mr. Beale. Let me explain." Elsie turned to the Thompsons. "It's my fault, you see. Mr. Beale was prepared to take the blame like a gentleman, but I can't allow it. The truth is, we did spend a considerable amount of time at the museum. And shortly after we left, I suggested we take a walk through Coe Fen and . . . well, while we were there I'm afraid I had an episode."

"Oh, my dear!" cried Mrs. Thompson, her stern expression dissolving. "Come sit at once."

Asher stared at her, torn between satisfaction that she had owned up to the blame and astonishment at her bald-faced lie. He sat across from her to better study her expression as she spoke.

"Mr. Beale helped administer my medication," Elsie said softly. "Before I lost consciousness, I begged him to wait until I'd recovered. I couldn't bear the thought of the entire town seeing him carry me back to the college."

"But . . . oh, I see what you mean," said Mrs. Thompson, glancing at her husband, who nodded slowly. "Though perhaps you might have sent someone for a doctor."

"The medicine worked," Asher said. "It was just a matter of waiting before she woke and could face the walk home." His mind worked furiously. "I propped her against a tree—she was quite comfortable and no one seemed to notice her distress."

"He didn't wish to leave me alone, you see," Elsie continued, "so there was no way to get word to you."

Mr. Thompson studied her. "Are you feeling better now?"

"A little groggy, Uncle, but relieved to be safely returned."

"Perhaps it's best that you stay home for the next few days," said Mrs. Thompson. "I confess, I never considered the possibility that you might have an attack in public. It's quite an inconvenience, isn't it? A bit more than an inconvenience, actually. I should have thought of it, but I was more concerned about . . ." Her eyes widened. "What if you hadn't had your medication?"

Asher forced himself not to look at the girl.

"I always have it with me, Aunt," she said.

He marveled at her steady voice.

Mrs. Thompson nodded. "I'm certain you both would like an opportunity to rest before supper. Elsie, why don't you go upstairs? Kate, would you accompany her and see if there's anything she needs?" She glanced at her husband. "Mr. Thompson and I wish to speak with Mr. Beale for a moment."

Elsie smiled demurely, giving him the briefest glance before she followed Kate out the door.

Asher felt the sinking sensation again. What if they interrogated him and later cross-referenced his answers with Elsie's? His father had often used this tactic to ferret out the truth. Asher would somehow have to convey his answers to Elsie. Perhaps a note tucked under her door—

"Asher," Mrs. Thompson said gently. "You needn't look so worried. We don't blame you for what happened today. It's just that Elsie's mother is very concerned about propriety. And I'm afraid she also feels some . . . *unease* . . . about the nature of Elsie's illness, particularly how it could be perceived by onlookers who know nothing of her condition."

Asher nodded, remembering the crowd that circled her at the museum.

"The poor girl has scarcely left the confines of her home for years. I'd hoped she might have a bit more freedom when she came here—a chance to see more of the world now that she's seventeen. And I still feel that way. But she'll need our protection in order to keep safe."

Mr. Thompson laid a hand on his wife's arm. "What my wife is trying to say is that we thank you for protecting Elsie today. It reassures us that someone we trust was with her during such a trying episode."

"Of course, sir."

"That's settled, then," said Mrs. Thompson, her smile faltering. "But there is something else."

Asher stiffened. "Yes?"

Mrs. Thompson reached into her skirt pocket and withdrew a sealed envelope. "Your father has been in touch. This telegram is for you." She handed it to him. "He's also written to us asking after you."

"How did he know I was here?"

Mr. Thompson straightened in his chair, his expression contrite. "We wired him as soon as you arrived."

Asher choked back an angry retort. The Thompsons were old friends with his father—surely it was a courtesy to contact him. So why did it feel like meddling? "No doubt he had terrible things to say about me."

Mrs. Thompson lifted an eyebrow. "He asked after your health and said that he wished to hear from you." She gazed at him searchingly. "Asher, is there any way we can help? Perhaps if we knew the nature of the trouble between you—"

"It was a difference of opinion, and I'm afraid there's *nothing* you can do to help," he said, taking a deep breath. "I do appreciate your concern, however."

"Just know we are here if you need us," said Mrs. Thompson, clasping her hands in her lap. "It's been an eventful day. Won't you take some rest before dinner?"

He'd spent less than three days with the Thompson family and already he was lying to them. And for what reason? First to protect a girl who'd deceived him, and just now to preserve his own pride. If he were smart he'd be on his way before he became further entangled.

Once in his room he threw the envelope on his desk. He couldn't really blame the Thompsons for their concern, but that didn't mean he would read the message. His father deserved no such courtesy.

Elsie was a different story. As he rehearsed the day's events in his head, he found it impossible to maintain his indignation toward her. She had lied, to be sure, but not merely to protect herself. She had covered for him as well.

In fact, she'd made him look like a hero.

Asher had hoped to meet Elsie's gaze over the supper table, to somehow channel the thoughts in her head by looking directly in her eyes. She had elected to retire early, however, and he had no choice but to focus his efforts on maintaining light conversation with the Thompsons.

Kate was no help. She hardly said anything, as usual. She did stare quite a bit, though—particularly at him. That night her gaze held more than curiosity. She seemed to be assessing him somehow, and he didn't like it one bit.

Everyone looked up when the front doorbell clanged. Mrs. Thompson turned to her husband. "Are you expecting someone, my dear?"

"Of course not."

They waited in silence, their forks suspended in the air, until Millie appeared in the doorway. When Mr. Thompson beckoned her, she murmured at his ear. He nodded solemnly, folding his napkin next to his plate before turning to his wife. "Please continue with supper. I'll see about this."

"See about what?" she asked, her brow wrinkled.

But either he did not hear her or he deliberately ignored the question. Before anyone could say another word, he was out of his chair and through the doorway.

"This is highly unusual, I must say," murmured Mrs. Thompson. "Such a strange day."

Asher noticed Kate staring at the doorway with a frown. Was she afraid? She'd seemed skittish from the moment he'd encountered her outside the gate, as though she were constantly looking behind her. Whom did she fear to find there?

The three of them sat at length in stilted silence, poking at the food on their plates, before Mr. Thompson finally hobbled back into the room. Asher studied the man's drawn face as he sat at the table without saying a word.

"Well?" Mrs. Thompson raised an eyebrow. "What was that about?"

"Perhaps we should discuss it later."

"Oh, Oliver," cried Mrs. Thompson, "don't be so mysterious! Who was at the door?"

"The police," he said quietly.

Asher kept his eyes on his plate. The police had somehow learned of Elsie's escape to London. Perhaps someone had reported her collapse at the museum, and had given details on *his* appearance, thinking him an abductor. He cast a covert glance at Mr. Thompson, dreading his hard gaze of condemnation.

But the man had returned to his supper.

"Oliver, what did the police want with you?"

"My dear, if you insist, I will tell you, though it's not a proper thing to discuss at the supper table." He paused for a sip of water. "The police have found a body, this time in Queens' Green."

"*Another* body?" asked Mrs. Thompson. "Was it an elderly man, like before?"

"No. It was a boy."

Kate's chin jerked up. "A boy? How old?"

Mr. Thompson turned to her, clearly perplexed. "Not even ten years of age. Why do you ask?"

The girl bit her lip. "Just curious," she mumbled.

"Why did the police come *here?*" Mrs. Thompson tapped the table. "Queens' Green is much farther than the cricket grounds. I don't see how they could connect this with Summerfield."

"I couldn't really say, my dear." Mr. Thompson did not meet her gaze. "Just routine, I'm sure."

"I well remember the tales of your days as a Trinity undergraduate. Think of those ill-behaved young fools who had the habit of luring street people into the college to drink themselves into a stupor for their entertainment. There was even a death once, wasn't there? Is this happening again? This time to a *child*, Oliver?"

Mr. Thompson turned to her, his face pale. "It's not even term time now. The students are gone. This is merely a coincidence."

A heavy silence fell over the table as the Thompsons stared silently at each other.

As if to bring an end to the matter, Mr. Thompson once more put his napkin on the table. "It has been a long day. I suggest we all retire early for the evening."

His wife nodded slowly, allowing him to help her to her feet. But rather than twine her arm around his as usual, she walked ahead of him through the dining room door. Asher moved to do the same but paused when a hand pressed his arm. He turned to find Kate looking up at him, her eyes dark and bold.

"What is it?" he asked.

"I must see that body." Her fingers tightened on his arm. "I may know who it is."

chapter 12

Elsie woke early the next morning, her eyelids lifting easily. When she sat up her head felt clear of its usual fog. She threw back the coverlet and walked to the window, parting the curtains to welcome the golden glow of early dawn.

When was the last time she'd woken before the sun had topped the horizon?

She turned away from the window and sat before the mirror. As she brushed out her hair she delighted in the tingling sensation on her scalp. Her cheeks were pink, her eyes bright. She left off brushing and stretched her arms wide, yawning a great gulp of air. Her body felt deliciously awake, just as it had when she was a young girl.

She glanced at the bottle of Chlorodyne that sat before the mirror. The prior evening she'd taken only a small sip before falling into bed. Her stomach knotted at the thought of sinking back into that dull drowsiness. What harm would come if today she skipped her dose entirely?

A vision of the ghastly woman flashed in her mind, prompting her to reach for the bottle. The feel of the cool glass reassured her. She ran her thumb along the edge of the stopper as she studied the label.

It had been a long time since a seizure had run its course. Nearly five years, in fact. She hadn't dwelled on those episodes in ages—the drug had dulled her memory—but now they came to mind in vivid detail.

On the first afternoon she'd been allowed outdoors following the accident, Elsie had celebrated her new freedom by sitting in the sun, weaving flowers into a wreath near the old well. Upon completing the dainty circlet, she'd placed it on her head and wandered closer to the well to admire the lichen that crept along its stone.

Suddenly the air had writhed and shimmered before her eyes. That first time had felt like falling into a hole or a dark dream. When she opened her eyes again all had vanished—the meadow, the well, and the trees. Elsie shivered in the darkness. A small figure emerged from the gloom, a girl whose long curls fanned away from her pale face. The skirt of her dress, wet and mud-stained, seemed to float around her slight body. When her mouth opened, words billowed out like fog.

"I only wanted to see myself," the girl breathed. "Mummy's going to be very angry about my dress."

That was all—a simple confession that framed a horrible truth—and then Elsie blinked and found herself back in the meadow.

She'd dismissed it as a nightmare, more unsettling than frightening. Not worth mentioning to anyone. A short time later, however, a gossiping young housemaid let slip that the vicar's niece had fallen into a Peverel well and drowned. As soon as the words were spoken, the maid clapped her hands over her mouth. "I weren't supposed to say anything, miss," she mumbled. "Her Ladyship said you was too delicate to hear of it, but maybe now that you're healed proper and out of bed, she won't mind you knowing?"

At first Elsie was too stunned to speak. Had she somehow *seen* the vicar's niece that day by the well? Was it a premonition . . . or an encounter with the dead?

"Exactly when did the poor child die?" she finally asked.

"Whilst you was recovering. You was sleeping most of the day and having the most peculiar nightmares, so Her Ladyship didn't want you to hear of the girl's death. She feared it would upset your rest. Oh, miss, you've gone so pale—have I upset you?"

Elsie dismissed the maid as calmly as she could and spent the morning puzzling over what she'd learned. Could such a vision, one in which a girl's hair and gown floated as though she were underwater, merely be a nightmare? It seemed too specific to be coincidence.

It was the second vision, a few months later, that truly terrified her. Sadly, it also proved her undoing as her mother's darling little girl. They had been packing away her grandmother's clothes and linens shortly after the old woman's death. Though Elsie had suffered a bout of gooseflesh as she folded the yellowed underclothes, she'd felt no hint of sorrow. The Dowager Lady Rolleston, widowed early and kind to no one but her son, had excelled at being unpleasant. It was no secret that only Elsie's father mourned her death. And that death had seemed to go on for an eternity—an extended cycle of relapses and last-minute rallies. Elsie had sighed with relief when Mother told her the old woman's struggle had finally ended.

That day, as she tidied the room so the maids could give it a proper airing, she glanced toward the handsome oak headboard of the bed and saw the air writhe and shimmer as it had that strange day in the meadow. Her knees buckled and she collapsed to the floor, hearing her mother's cry of surprise as if it came from a long distance. This hole gaped even deeper and darker than the first, and the figure that rose from the gloom was not a sweet-faced girl who merely looked lost. Instead it was the formidable apparition of her grandmother.

Only it was something else, too. The old woman's eyes were black, and a substance like ink stained her mouth, making it a dark pit in the middle of her face. She lifted a hand and beckoned her closer. Elsie's heart pounded, but she could not resist.

"You thought to be rid of me," the woman said, showing blackened teeth.

Elsie stared, unable to speak.

"Poison, you stupid girl! You thought to rid me with foul poison."

"What?"

"You gave that poison to me every day with a spoon," her grandmother spat, "and then you poured the entire bottle down my throat. But I'm still here, aren't I?"

The woman's hand reached out to clutch Elsie's wrist, her grasp cold as ice. Elsie looked down and saw her fingers darkening to the ink black of her grandmother's mouth. The black traveled through her veins as the chill snaked up her arm. She fell backward, drowning in darkness and bone-shivering cold.

She'd opened her eyes to see her mother's anxious face hovering over her.

"My dear!" Mother slapped her lightly. "Elsie, are you awake?"

Elsie had pushed the hand away. "Stop, Mother."

"Thank God! I've never seen you shake and moan like that. Your eyes were rolling back in your head!"

Elsie had rubbed her eyes to push away the image of her grandmother's dark gaze and blackened grimace. "I saw Grandmama. She spoke to me."

Mother frowned. "What?"

"Grandmama said . . ." Elsie's voice quieted to a whisper. "That I poisoned her!"

A flush of anger mottled her mother's neck and spread across her cheeks. "You never saw her. You never heard her say such a terrible thing." She gave Elsie another slap, and this time it stung. "Don't ever speak such lies again."

Elsie had lain awake most of that night, afraid to dream again of her grandmother. By the time the dawn light streamed through her window, she was certain none of it had been a dream—neither the girl by the well nor the vision of her grandmother. They were *real*, and yet they were dead.

She had little time to ponder it further, for later that morning her mother had taken her to a London doctor. With little prompting he'd dashed out a prescription and presented it to Lady Rolleston like a gift. After that Elsie's existence had devolved to a Chlorodyne haze, each day melting into the next with hardly anything to anchor her to waking life—nothing until *he* came to Peverel Place and put a camera in her hands.

For the first time the memory of his touch made her stomach convulse.

A dull pain began to thud behind Elsie's eyes, making her groan. Her clear head came at a price—pain and nausea, as well as the threat of another full-blown episode.

She opened the bottle and took her dose.

After that she dressed and pinned her hair, frowning slightly as the heaviness settled over her body. There was comfort, however, in its familiarity. With the drug she was calm and grounded. Thus protected, she finally turned her thoughts to her beautiful artist, for whom she'd been willing to risk everything. She remembered him at the museum as if in a staged photograph—"Portrait of the Artist Preparing His Canvas"—

and a wave of sorrow washed over her. The convulsions must have repelled him if he'd left the museum so abruptly. In his case, at least, her mother had been correct. How pathetic were the lengths she'd been willing to go to in order to be with him, when he couldn't even look at her during her fit. Perhaps he'd never truly loved her at all.

At least Asher hadn't abandoned her.

And the dark-haired gentleman who'd held her . . . Elsie's heart fluttered to remember him. He'd been quite tender in his attentions to her.

A curious rush of relief followed these thoughts. She needn't give up everything after all. Her treasures and comforts need not be abandoned for a life of poverty. She glanced at her camera and smiled. The light would be good this morning.

Perhaps the Poole girl could help her. After all, if Elsie were to continue on at Summerfield, she would need practice in making friends.

⊠ ⊠ ⊠ ⊠ ⊠

For once Kate was entirely without appetite. She tapped her toast against the plate as the others tucked into their own breakfasts. Asher avoided her gaze each time she risked a glance at him.

The previous night he'd stared at her as though she were a lunatic.

"Why would I want to go look at a dead body with you? The very idea is repulsive."

"I doubt they'd let me see it if I went alone. Aren't you at least curious to know if this dead boy is who I think it is?"

"It has nothing to do with me," he'd said.

He was my dear friend, she thought. *Doesn't that mean any-thing?* Judging by his scowl, she doubted it would. She'd taken a breath and switched tactics. "If we identify the body, it could help with the murder investigation. That would be rather heroic, don't you think?"

A flicker of interest had passed through his eyes. She let the idea hang in the air between them, resisting the urge to press him further.

"Ask me again tomorrow," he'd finally said. "I'm too tired to think right now."

Now she was biding her time until the Thompsons rose from the table. She would ask him then, and she would have to be persuasive.

All night horrid thoughts about Billy had plagued her. Where had he gone that night after the séance? Who would dare hurt him? The last time she'd seen Billy, his thin face peering out at her from the shadows of Mrs. Martineau's staircase, he'd assured her he'd be fine. Even then she'd had a feeling of dread.

The notion that he could be dead had flourished in her imagination, and now its hazy borders had hardened into certainty. But if she was so certain, why this powerful need to *see* the body? She stared at her toast, considering this. Seeing the body would bring an end to the matter. And it might help her to know *why* it happened, perhaps giving her some clue as to who would kill a small boy. What scheme had Billy been working? Did it arise from his work with Martineau and the little detectives? More specifically, did it have something to do with Mr. Thompson and her father? Billy was clever for his age, but sometimes too brash. Perhaps he'd crossed a line and angered his target. He may have uncovered a piece of information that someone wished to stay buried.

If only she hadn't taken the knife from him, he might have been able to protect himself. She shuddered at the thought of an adult—a burly man, she imagined—laying cruel hands on Billy. Knocking him down, wrapping his hands around the boy's throat. The body would be bruised and broken, and it might as well be her fault. She would have to steel herself.

"Aunt, I would like to take some photographs in the garden today," Elsie was saying. "I hoped you might allow Miss Poole the day off so she can assist me."

Kate studied Miss Atherton. She seemed very sleek and pink-cheeked. Obviously she knew nothing about the body found near the college. She'd gone to bed before supper, and no one had dared tell her this morning.

Kate turned back to Mrs. Thompson. "I really can't ignore my work in the library. Miss Freeman depends on me."

Mrs. Thompson sipped her tea as she considered Kate. "I'm pleased to see someone of your years taking an obligation so seriously. Why do you need her, Elsie?"

"I hoped to pose her for a portrait. I don't have enough practice with live models, you see. I'm imagining her as a character from a story, like the work of Julia Margaret Cameron."

Kate didn't know who this Cameron lady was, but she smiled behind her napkin in spite of herself. Miss Atherton wished to photograph her and her only. She couldn't deny it was terribly flattering. And yet . . . there was Billy to consider.

Mrs. Thompson was smiling, too. "Seems like a worthy project. You may use the darkroom in the Science Annex—that way we can all see the results of your endeavors. Why don't we compromise and say that Kate can have the morning to work with you?" She turned to Kate. "That is, if it suits you."

Kate nodded shyly, feeling a traitor to Billy. Somehow, though, she would manage to steal away before Freeman expected her at the library.

"I can help, too," said Asher, his eyes on Elsie.

"Sounds like a lovely plan," Mrs. Thompson said. "All I ask is that you don't leave the grounds today, Elsie. And send Kate to the library when you're finished. I will explain to Miss Freeman."

When Asher stood to the side, allowing the ladies to exit the dining room first, Kate trailed behind. Once they were alone she clutched his shirtsleeve and cocked an eyebrow.

He shook his head. "You heard what Mrs. Thompson said. We are not to leave the college grounds today."

"She doesn't want Miss Atherton to leave, but I'm quite certain you and I could slip out for half an hour. Mrs. Thompson need not know." She held his gaze. "And if you don't help me, I'll be forced to tell Miss Atherton about your face when she doesn't know you're staring at her."

"I don't stare at her." Asher frowned. "What are you saying about my face?"

"It reminds me of the wolf staring at Little Red Riding Hood."

"Not sure I follow," he muttered.

Kate grinned. "Ready to swallow her in one gulp."

chapter 13

Shamed by Kate Poole's threat, Asher kept to the background while Elsie posed the girl for a series of photographs. He'd taken a seat on a wooden bench, affecting boredom as Elsie brushed the girl's hair until it rippled softly down her back. It seemed to Asher that Kate's hair, glinting a deep auburn in the sunlight, sighed with relief to be free of its customary plaits. Elsie had dressed her in a loose-fitting white dress—some sort of night-gown, he thought—but it achieved the medieval look she'd sought for the portrait.

Asher had scoffed at the idea of photographing an awk-ward girl like Kate, but with her soft hair and flowing gown she wasn't quite so dreary a subject as he'd expected. Her face lost some of its sharpness when her hair hung loose by her cheeks. Her color had improved, too, and her skin looked smoother than when he'd first seen her.

Elsie, on the other hand—it took effort not to stare at her as she worked. For a girl who ordinarily moved as if walking through a dream, she was surprisingly precise with her cam-era. Her clear sense of purpose beguiled him, but at the same time he was intimidated by her expertise with the contraption. Afterward he offered to carry the camera and plate holder to the darkroom for her, but she declined. She hadn't met his gaze directly all morning.

As he watched her walk away, he sensed Kate at his elbow. He turned to find her smiling coyly. She looked almost pretty.

"My, what big eyes you have," she murmured.

He sighed. "Let's get this over with."

"Just allow me to dress—I'll be quick."

She *was* quick. In less than ten minutes she returned wearing an everyday white blouse and brown skirt, her hair restrained once more in plaits. Her hat was less crumpled than the first day he'd met her—perhaps Elsie had tended to it.

"I don't even know where we're going," he said.

"Regent Street, near Parker's Piece."

He stared at her blankly.

"It's not far. Just follow me."

They took the same route he and Elsie had taken the day before, but instead of turning at Trumpington, they continued on to Regent. The building, quite obvious with POLICE boldly chiseled into the stone arch above the door, stood on the west side of the road.

In that moment Asher imagined himself a police detective, or better yet a gentleman detective consulting with the police on a murder case. Surely that would be more interesting than a career spent in a dusty courtroom. He knew he was clever and had a good eye for details. He could become the sort of person who merely glanced at a dead body and knew exactly how the poor soul had died and why. He could be the American Sherlock Holmes—just as intuitive and logical, but not nearly so odd.

"All right," said Kate, clasping her hands. "There should be a constable at the front desk. Tell him you've heard about the murdered boy and you think we might be able to identify him."

"Why do *I* have to do everything?"

"You're male and you're posh. Don't you remember how Jones treated me at the Summerfield gate? He *listened* to you."

Subdued by her words, Asher opened the door, remembering just in time to let her go before him, and approached the young man hunched over the counter.

"Excuse me, constable?"

The man looked up. "Yeah?"

"We're, um . . . we're here about the body found last night in Queens' Green."

"Here to confess, eh?" The man's eyes sparkled with mischief. He hardly looked older than Asher.

"Of course not!" Asher took a breath and relaxed his clenched fists. "We think we may know who it is."

The constable straightened. "Well, I've only just come on duty. Last night would have been Sergeant Floyd—he'd be more help to you."

"Is he here?"

"No, he don't come in until after four." He looked around. "Truth is, we're a little short of staff right now."

Kate stepped forward. "All I want is to see the body. I don't have any questions for the sergeant."

His eyes widened. "You want to gawp at a corpse? We're not running a sideshow here, miss."

"I'm not here for entertainment. I fear it's my friend you've got back there. Couldn't you please just let me have a look?" she asked. "It won't take much of your time."

The young constable studied her for a moment. "I'd like to

help you, but it's contrary to the rules. I'd catch a great deal of trouble for letting a stranger off the street into the morgue."

"Perhaps we should go, Kate," Asher said quietly.

She turned bold eyes to him. "I think all the constable needs is a little encouragement."

"What?"

She rubbed her index finger and thumb together.

"I never suggested anything like that," the constable objected, and yet the gleam in his eyes was unmistakable.

Asher glanced back at Kate, fully prepared to end this farce with a cutting remark, but her expression choked the words in his throat. Her chin was up, but her eyes glistened with unshed tears.

Before coming to Cambridge he'd never bribed anyone in his life, but if this continued he'd be bankrupt by the end of the week. He reached into his pocket and pulled out a half crown. "Well, constable?"

The young man affected indecision for the briefest moment. Then he grinned. "Oh, why not—I'm bored as it is. But I can't be away from the desk for more than a moment."

"A moment is all I need," said Kate.

Pocketing the coin, the constable led them down a long corridor, past several offices, to a room at the far end of the building. When he opened the door, a sickening odor assailed Asher's nostrils. Was *that* the smell of a dead body? How was it possible to live your life working amid such a stench? Feeling lightheaded, he quickly drew a handkerchief from his pocket. After staring at it for a moment, he steadied himself and offered it to Kate.

She shook her head.

"Ah, it's just the one body. Coroner will come for it by the end of the day." The constable pointed to a table draped in cloth. "Just a small fry, I'm afraid." He pulled the cloth back to reveal a boy with pale hair and skin a deathly alabaster. The flesh of his face was sinking, and his jaw was darkened by a bruise . . . or perhaps decay. Asher glanced at Kate out of the corner of his eye. Though she stood straight, her face had lost all color.

"Is it your friend?" he asked.

"Yes," she whispered.

He braced himself to catch her, thinking she might fall to the floor in a faint, but somehow she held steady. After a moment she took a step closer, lifting the cloth to peer at the boy's hand before turning to the constable. "I see marks on his wrist, as though he were bound."

Asher stared at her, unsettled by such a coldly stated observation. Beside him the constable nodded absently.

"There's a bruise on his jaw, too, but he had that the last time I saw him," she continued. "How did he die?"

The constable snapped his fingers. "Now I remember hearing of this one. Dick said something about it just this morning." He took a deep breath and shook his head.

Asher waited in vain for him to continue. "Well? What did you hear?"

The constable's only response was another deep sigh.

Asher dug into his pocket again. "For pity's sake, this is the last coin I have."

"Well, I won't show you the entire body," the constable said, pocketing the money, "but from what I heard, there's no evidence of fatal trauma. No cuts or heavy bruising." He pulled the cloth to the boy's waist. "They did note these two marks."

Asher leaned in. Two red splotches stood out on the boy's sunken chest. "What are they?"

The constable shrugged. "Search me. They look a bit like burns, but nothing that would kill a boy. The only other thing I can say is, he wasn't outside for very long, 'cause there's no maggots. Someone kept him in a cool, sheltered place after he died. For a while, anyway." He turned to Kate. "You say you know who he is?"

"His name was Billy," she said quietly. "I'm afraid I don't know his surname. He might have been an orphan. He worked for . . . well, he did odd jobs around Castle End."

"That's not much to go on," the constable said.

"Did you find anything in his clothes?" Kate asked. "A gold watch, perhaps?"

He moved across the room to open a drawer. "No watch here. Why would a boy like this have a gold watch?"

"Because I lent it to him," Kate said, her expression forbidding.

"No doubt he sold it, or it was stolen," the constable said. "You said he was a Castle End boy, right? That other body—the old man—was from Castle End, too. Curious, ain't it?"

Kate didn't blink. "What will happen to the body?"

"Well, I ain't exactly certain." The constable frowned. "With no one to claim him, he'll likely find his rest in a pauper's grave at Mill Road. There's the inquest to get through yet, though that's not likely to take long."

Asher pulled a card from his pocket and handed it to the young man. "We are staying at Summerfield College. Would you contact me about burial when the coroner is done with him?"

Once out of the building, Asher paused to inhale the smells of the street. Even fresh pony droppings were a relief after that death reek. Kate stood rigidly next to him, her eyes dark against the pale of her skin.

He cleared his throat. "Are you . . . I mean, shall we go?"

Her only response was a curt nod.

As they made their way back to the college, Kate kept her head down. Her silence unsettled him. He'd offered money to that fool of a constable, not to mention his card, but she didn't seem at all grateful or inclined to explain. Why was she keeping him in the dark?

He did know one thing, however—the boy had been her friend. Perhaps she was struggling not to cry. A gentler approach might draw her out, but Asher wasn't accustomed to speaking in a soothing way to young ladies.

"May I know more about this poor friend of yours?" he finally asked.

Kate gave him a sidelong glance but said nothing.

"Miss Poole, I'm only curious. You went to a lot of trouble to see his body."

She sighed. "I thank you for your company—and your coins—today. You made things much easier than they otherwise would have been."

He nodded, somewhat mollified.

"There's not much more to say," she continued. "Billy's dead, and at the moment I've no idea who's responsible." She glanced at him again. "But you can be sure I'll find out."

Chapter 14

Elsie gently dropped the paper into the developing solution. The negative image from the glass plate blossomed quickly over the stiff paper, creating a positive image of Kate reaching for a rose, her head turned to the side and hair rippling over her shoulder.

"You've put her in a nightgown," her aunt had exclaimed.

"We're not leaving the grounds of the garden," she'd calmly replied. "Besides, you can't *see* anything. She's fully covered."

Aunt Helena merely rolled her eyes.

Elsie smiled as she immersed the photograph in fixing solution. She'd tried for something like Julia Margaret Cameron's *The Gardener's Daughter*—the virginal, innocent beauty of a girl contemplating a flower. In this photograph Kate seemed bored rather than enraptured, but it still worked well.

For the second image, she had moved the camera closer for a profile view of Kate standing by the vine-covered outer wall of the Thompson Building. Here she'd aimed to follow the style of Cameron's *Maud* or *Alethea*, with the subject's hair mingling with the greenery, her expression otherworldly. Kate's hair turned out beautifully, but Kate herself was stifling a giggle.

Elsie had to admit it was charming to see Kate smile, but there was nothing ethereal about her expression.

The third was the best of the lot. Kate stood in front of a young willow tree, a slender branch held before her face. The gentle morning light softened the girl's skin. Elsie had asked her to look directly into the camera, but the expression of challenge on Kate's face had been entirely her own idea. *Look at me,* her eyes said. *I know something you don't. I've seen things you haven't.* Elsie preferred this bold expression to the demure profile of the first two photographs.

She'd taken only three shots of Kate, but one plate remained. She studied it, trying to recall what it was. She'd not brought any undeveloped plates from Peverel Place. When she held it up to the amber light, she could make out two figures standing next to a large structure.

The last time she'd used her camera was . . . *Oh yes.* It was the photograph of Asher and Kate, taken near the small outbuilding at the far end of the garden. That was the day she'd had her seizure—the day her new acquaintances had witnessed just how strange she could be. What a warm welcome she'd given them.

She exposed the plate to paper and placed the latter in the developing solution. The image spread like a stain, revealing Asher, wide-eyed and smiling fatuously, standing next to a grimacing Kate. Elsie giggled. It was a crisply focused shot, but certainly not a flattering likeness of either of them.

A blur next to Kate caught Elsie's eye. She bent closer, scrutinizing the flaw, but the details were impossible to make out in the low light. She quickly lifted the print and placed it in the finishing solution, waiting the appropriate amount of time before she could risk exposing the image to bright light. Finally she switched on the electric lamp—such a marvel—and held the print near it.

It wasn't a flaw in the photograph. It was a blur, indeed, but the blur had human outlines. Squinting, she could just make out a small boy standing next to Kate. A small boy in a very grown-up jacket and hat. Had she double-exposed the plate? She couldn't see how, for she'd not encountered any children for months.

The closer she looked, the clearer the details became. Under the brim of his hat the boy's eyes were dark splotches. His mouth gaped in a silent cry.

Elsie dropped the photo with a shudder.

❈ ❈ ❈ ❈ ❈

Though she'd longed to run directly to Tec after that wretched visit to the police station, Kate barely had time to drop by the kitchen and stuff a piece of bread in her mouth before reporting to Freeman at the library. She couldn't afford to rouse the woman's ire anytime soon if she wanted to keep her situation, and thus she had no choice but to push her sorrow and frustration to the back of her mind. She threw herself into work for the rest of the day, heaving boxes and sorting through unruly stacks of books as if her life depended on it. Before she left to change for supper, Freeman nodded grudgingly.

"Good work, Poole."

The simple compliment didn't erase the horrors of the morning, but it was something.

When Kate finally sat down at the dining table, she couldn't help staring at Mr. and Mrs. Thompson. They looked to be dressed in their Sunday best. Mr. Thompson's suit, not nearly as shabby as his daily wear, had been carefully brushed, and his tiepin sparkled against the glossy red silk at his throat. His wife was dressed in her usual dark colors, but this particular fabric boasted sheen and a subtle stripe. Kate peered closer. The woman was wearing *earrings,* too.

"Is this a special occasion, Aunt?" asked Elsie brightly.

"We have a Society meeting tonight," Mrs. Thompson said. "Just a small gathering for the local members to plan the agenda for our London meeting Saturday after next."

A rash of goose bumps prickled Kate's arms. "Would this be the Metaphysical Society, ma'am?"

"Indeed," she murmured, not meeting Kate's gaze.

"What exactly do you do at these meetings?" blurted Kate. "I mean, I know about the Society. I just wondered . . ."

Mrs. Thompson smiled. "Don't worry, Kate. I'm glad to tell you. Usually we hear reports on recent findings and research. We might also discuss the latest publications on metaphysical subjects, and make plans for future meetings and conferences."

Recent research. Did that mean Mr. Thompson would be reporting on the frauds of Mrs. Martineau? Would they all laugh at Mr. Eliot for being duped into believing that a scrawny fourteen-year-old girl was a spirit apparition? The thought of Eliot's shocked silence, his plump lips tight with dismay, was deeply satisfying. But his shame was linked to hers, so Kate said nothing. She glanced out of the corner of her eye at Asher, who was frowning at his glass of wine.

Mrs. Thompson must also have noticed his expression, for her next words were directed at him. "I hope you don't mind keeping the girls company in our absence, Mr. Beale. We ask that you all stay in this building tonight. Certainly you must not venture outdoors, not with the recent disturbing incidents."

Her gaze quickly turned forbidding, and Kate nodded in compliance.

"Certainly, ma'am," Asher said.

Just as quickly Mrs. Thompson's expression turned affable again. "I know you three will have a lovely time together without the subduing influence of your elders. Of course Millie shall be at hand, should you need anything."

Kate stifled the urge to roll her eyes. By that she meant Millie's ears and eyes would be open, and her tongue ready to wag, should the three of them get up to any trouble.

"And you must not forget about our dinner party this weekend," continued Mrs. Thompson. "We intend to introduce Mr. Beale to our Trinity friends so that he might learn about the college, but we invite you young ladies to attend as well."

Kate nodded again, not certain what to say and noting that Elsie's smile lacked enthusiasm.

An hour later the three took their places in the sitting room. Asher stared at an unopened book in his lap while Elsie looked blankly in the direction of the window. Kate glanced at the clock and saw that it was only eight. She wasn't the least bit tired. It was still light out, for goodness' sake. Perhaps it was better to retire to her room than to sit in this frozen silence. And yet, if she sat alone in her room, her mind would turn to Billy.

"Miss Poole, isn't it about time you told us about your dead friend?"

Kate stiffened.

"What dead friend?" Elsie gasped.

"No one's told her, Poole," Asher said. "Why don't you explain? We could work through the evidence together."

"You know I don't wish to speak of it," Kate replied sharply.

"What *are* you two talking about?"

Asher closed his book. "She's been blackmailing me, Elsie, buying my compliance with threats of telling you that I stare at you when you're not looking. Well, of course I stare at you! You're a beautiful girl." He turned back to Kate, his cheeks spotted with color. "All right, you must spill it now. Start with the police calling for Mr. Thompson."

Bastard. And yet she was impressed by this sudden appearance of a backbone. After considering them both for a moment—they *did* seem genuinely concerned—she cleared her throat and recounted the details leading up to the police station visit.

Elsie's eyes widened. "This body was found in Queens' Green yesterday? Why did no one tell me?"

"You retired early . . . after your episode," said Asher.

Kate noted the strange look that passed between them. "When I heard it was a young boy," she continued, "I feared it was someone I knew. A friend of mine—Billy was his name—had been missing since Saturday night. So I asked Mr. Beale to accompany me to the police station to view the body, to confirm that it was my friend."

Elsie's brow furrowed. "You *looked* at the dead body?"

"She did," Asher said. "Most girls I know wouldn't have the stomach for it."

"I'm nothing like most girls."

"That much is becoming clear to me," he said quietly.

"Do go on, Kate," Elsie prompted.

"Billy was like a brother. We worked together for quite a long time." She paused, grappling for the right words. "I needed to be certain it was him. But I also wanted to know what happened to him. I thought if I saw the body, I would have some idea of how he died. I suppose neither of you has ever lost someone dear to you . . . at least, not in such a peculiar way." She clutched at her skirt to still the tremor in her hands. "It's like a pain in your gut, the wondering."

They stared at her.

"I understand," Elsie finally murmured.

"You say you worked with this boy," said Asher. "What do you mean? What sort of work?"

Kate looked to Elsie for help, but it was clear the girl would provide no cover. Her eager expression was eloquent—Elsie wished to hear the answer as much as Asher. "Well . . . we both worked for Mrs. Martineau. She's a medium, very popular with ladies and gentlemen of Spiritualist leanings. I heard once that she really did have psychic powers when she was younger. But since I've known her, she's relied on tricks and theatrics. She employs clever young boys from Castle End to search out clues on her patrons' dead loved ones. That's how she impresses them during her séances."

"And Billy was one of those boys?" asked Elsie.

"He was the best of the lot."

Asher leaned forward. "But what do *you* have to do with all this? You still haven't explained how you worked with this boy."

"When I was twelve and could no longer attend school, Mrs. Martineau hired me."

"To do what?"

Kate paused, steeling herself. "I performed during her séances . . . as her spirit apparition."

Asher snorted. "*Spirit* apparition? And Mr. Thompson found you out?" He shook his head. "I'd share this with my father if I had any interest in corresponding with him—yet another example of fraudulent Spiritualists."

Kate shot him a dark look. "Your father is a member of the Metaphysical Society, isn't he?"

Asher winced. "How did you know?"

"I've seen a list of members. Your father numbers among

them, as well as Mr. and Mrs. Thompson, and even"—she glanced at Elsie—"Baron Rolleston."

"My father?" Elsie gasped.

"Rolleston?" Asher frowned. "But your name is Atherton."

"Rolleston is his title," Elsie said absently. "His name is James Atherton. I just . . . it's difficult to believe he's a member."

"I'll show you the list later. If Baron Rolleston is not a member now, he was once." Kate paused before turning to Asher. "My own father was, too. Mr. Thompson shelters me because my father was Frederic Stanton."

Asher's mouth fell open. "I know that name. He was a friend to my family—Father even stayed at his house during one of his trips to England." He frowned. "But if you are Stanton's child, why is your name Poole?"

Kate hesitated. "I am Frederic Stanton's natural child," she said softly. "I was born before he married. As a matter of fact, he refused to marry my mother."

Elsie cast her eyes downward at this revelation. Asher merely stared.

"He supported us for a time," Kate continued. "When Mum died, I had to fend for myself." She looked away, not wanting to see their pity. "Do you know what this means? We are all children of Society members. Odd that we came together like this, don't you think?"

"I came here partly to escape all that metaphysical hokum," Asher said. "My father's made a damn fool of himself over it."

"After working with Mrs. Martineau," Kate said quickly, "I had plenty of doubts myself. I still don't understand precisely what the Metaphysical Society does. I thought Mr. Thompson came to the séance to expose Martineau as a fraud. But a book I found in the Summerfield library—the same one that listed our fathers and the Thompsons as members of the Society—devoted entire chapters to the belief that minds can communicate with each other without speech . . . even across great distances."

Asher sighed. "My father calls it thought-transference."

"Yes, that's it," she said. "The action of one mind on another, but not just between living people. It also meant communication between a living person and one who is about to die or has already passed on."

Elsie's face was pale. "Our fathers believed this?"

"That's what I don't understand," Kate said. "Are the members of the Metaphysical Society skeptics? Or believers?"

Asher stood abruptly and moved to the window. "My father is a Harvard scholar. He is renowned for his psychological research. But yes, he is a believer. In fact, he's trying to prove that some people have the ability to communicate with the dead. Personally I rather despise his methods of collecting data."

An awkward silence followed. Kate stared at the back of Asher's head, wondering at the anger that sharpened his tone. What exactly was behind this falling-out with his father? It had to be more than disdain for the man's beliefs.

"There are men of *learning* who believe in communication with the dead?" Elsie's voice was unsteady. "And my very own father may be one of them?"

Kate studied the girl as she clutched at the high neck of her blouse. "Elsie, are you all right?"

Elsie closed her eyes and took a deep breath. "What did your friend Billy look like?"

Kate flinched. "Pardon me?"

Elsie lifted her hand. "Wait, don't answer that. Let me ask it in a different way. Did Billy wear a handsome jacket—well cut for a child of his size—and a trilby hat?"

A hot dizziness came over Kate, and she nearly swayed in her seat. "How did you know? Had you met him before?"

Elsie shook her head. "I'd never even heard of him until now. And yet I think I've seen him."

Asher turned from the window. "How?"

Elsie looked from him to Kate, her face pale and pinched. "Wait here," she finally replied. "I'll show you."

chapter 15

Elsie paused on the staircase, the photograph clutched in one hand. How much was she willing to tell them? She'd known them a mere four days. And clearly, neither of them held much faith in visions of the afterlife.

But she had to show Kate this photograph. Once the girl saw it, *she* might believe.

The need to unburden herself was powerful. Secrets weighed heavily upon her, clinging to her like a second skin that itched to be sloughed away. And if the telling might actually *help* rather than harm, wouldn't that make the risk worthwhile?

What was the worst that could happen? Kate had no station, no power to expose Elsie, let alone have her sent to an institution. Asher came from a prominent family, but he was young. He was smitten, too—even she could see that. He wouldn't wish to hurt her. Neither of them had any connection to her family, so they shouldn't feel threatened by her revelation. In fact, they might help her to better understand it. They were both clever and clearheaded, and Elsie had been wandering alone in a fog for too long.

Thus reassured, she continued down the stairs. She would

show them the photograph. Then she would decide how far she wished to take matters.

They were both seated when she entered the room. Their silence unsettled her.

"I printed the photographs from this morning," Elsie said quietly. "They're in my bedroom—I'll show them to you later, if you like. But I also developed the photograph I took near the outbuilding. Do you remember? It was the day we first met."

"You wanted a photograph of me and Asher," said Kate.

"Yes," Asher said, "and afterwards you fell and . . ."

"I had a seizure," Elsie finished for him. "Keep that in mind—it is important." She handed the photograph to Kate. "Look at this and tell me if you notice anything odd."

She watched as Kate studied the print. After a moment the girl's eyes widened. "My God, I see it." Her hand trembled as she passed it to Asher.

He held the photograph near the lamplight, squinting. "I see a blur next to Kate, that's all."

Elsie held her breath, praying Asher would open his mind.

"But that blur has eyes, a mouth," Kate whispered. "It's wearing a hat."

Asher shook his head. "You see that because you're *looking* for it. Elsie already told you what to expect. I see a blur, or at most a double exposure."

"But I've taken no photographs of young children," Elsie said.

Kate frowned. "You said something about your seizure—that it was important. Why?"

Elsie sat down, panic tightening her throat. Was she really about to put this into words? She could barely breathe.

Kate lightly touched her arm. "Tell us, Elsie. Don't be afraid."

This is it. Now or never.

"Other than my mother, I've told no one of this." Elsie clasped her hands to keep them from shaking. "Mother could not accept it. In fact, I fear she despises me for it. I can't make *you* accept it, but I do ask that you keep what I tell you in confidence."

"Good Lord, this sounds dire," muttered Asher, but he looked uncomfortable rather than dismissive. She gave him a pleading glance and was reassured when his expression softened.

"Go on," said Kate.

Elsie took a breath and looked toward the window. "When I was twelve, I died."

She waited for that to sink in, not daring to look at their faces.

"I'm sorry," Kate said after a moment, "but what do you mean?"

"I was walking outdoors on a spring day." Elsie kept her eyes trained on the window. "The clouds were dark and heavy, and there were gorgeous rumbles of thunder. It seemed likely to storm, and in those days I enjoyed a walk in the rain, much to my mother's dismay." She paused, pained by the simple memories of childhood. "To make a long story short, I was struck by lightning."

"Oh, Elsie!"

Elsie turned, grateful for the concern in Kate's eyes. "I remember nothing of it, but I learned later that a stable boy saw it happen. He ran to me, thinking to help, but I wasn't breathing. So he picked me up and threw me over his shoulder. That's when I began to cough and cry. He carried me back to the house, practically running the whole way. My mother sent for the village doctor."

"What did the doctor say?" asked Kate.

"He hardly knew how to explain it. There certainly wasn't a treatment for such a thing. The lightning left no marks on my body—there were no wounds to heal—but I was very sluggish. My memory was cloudy. The doctor directed me to stay in bed until my strength and memories returned. It took weeks, but I did recover."

"A miracle," said Asher, his expression neutral.

"A miracle that I was alive, perhaps, but it soon became clear I wasn't the same girl. My mother chided me for turning inward when I used to be so lively. I had heart-pounding nightmares that I couldn't quite remember the next morning." Elsie paused to take a breath, unaccustomed to speaking so long without interruption. "One day, when I finally was allowed outdoors on my own, I had my first seizure. It was a mild one, but I didn't have any medication at that time, so the episode ran its course. And during the seizure . . . I had a strange vision."

Both Kate and Asher leaned in slightly.

"I saw a girl." She recounted her vision of the girl whose words billowed like fog, how she spoke of her mother's anger at her wet dress. "It seemed like a dream, but I assure you I was wide awake. It was as if I'd fallen into another world for a moment, and while there I encountered an inhabitant of that world."

"Do you think you suffered a brain injury?" The skepticism had returned to Asher's expression. "It may have been a hallucination."

"I considered that." Elsie related the housemaid's tale of the vicar's niece and her fall into the well. "She drowned when I was confined to my bed, so I knew nothing about it. Mother strictly forbade me knowing because she felt I was too vulnerable to hear such news."

"Were you terribly frightened when you saw the dead girl?" asked Kate.

Elsie thought for a moment. "No. The girl—the spirit, perhaps I should say—was merely confused. She didn't seem to know she was dead."

Asher's mouth tightened. "I'm sorry, but that sounds like typical Spiritualist claptrap—spirits who are trapped on this earthly plane, who must be guided toward the light. That sort of thing makes me ill."

Elsie met his gaze directly. She'd prepared herself for disbelief, skepticism, but not for this trace of venom in his voice. Something had set him dead against anything otherworldly—against anything that defied his notion of what was logical. Was it his father who'd so colored his perceptions? Or someone else? Whoever was responsible, she sensed pain behind his anger.

She took a breath and spoke gently. "Asher, I know next to nothing about Spiritualist beliefs. My father may have been—perhaps still is—a member of this Metaphysical Society, but *I* have lived a very sheltered life." She looked down. "I can only tell you what I saw. Do you wish me to continue? I'm trying to give you the background for what happened yesterday at the British Museum."

"The British?" Kate's brow wrinkled in confusion. "I thought you were at the Fitzwilliam and then Coe Fen."

Elsie glanced at Asher, who lifted a hand as though prompting her to continue.

"I will tell you about the British Museum, Kate. But first I want to explain . . . that is to say, I want you to understand why I take Chlorodyne." An image of her grandmother flashed in Elsie's mind, and she fought to still the trembling in her hands. "Not long after my encounter with the vicar's dead niece, my own grandmother died. She'd been living with us for at least a year and had battled illness the entire time. When my mother and I were packing her things, it happened again. One moment I was folding clothes, and the next I was convulsing. But this time my mother witnessed the episode . . . and the vision was much darker." She explained her grandmother's blackened mouth, the accusations of poisoning. "When I regained consciousness, I told Mother what I saw. She called me a liar. She . . . *struck* me. After that she sought to control my episodes with Chlorodyne."

"Good Lord," whispered Kate.

Asher's eyes were wide. "You accused your mother of poisoning your grandmother?"

"Of course not! I merely told her what Grandmama said. She said *I'd* poisoned her. I didn't know what she was talking about."

"Maybe your mother did," Asher said after a moment. "And that's why she was so angry. Maybe her next act was to silence you, like most guilty people do to those who have information on them."

"What do you mean?"

"I don't mean anything, Elsie. *I'm* certainly not accusing your mother of murder. It's ridiculous to even talk about it. I'm only saying that an *imaginative* sort of person might interpret your dream to mean that your grandmother's death wasn't natural."

Elsie bit her lip, wondering why men so often paired logic with condescension. "My *dream*? How can you call it that? Why would I dream something so specific . . . so horrible?"

He shrugged. "Maybe when your grandmother was living you saw something that you didn't understand. Later on, your dream worked it out for you in the form of a nightmare."

"It wasn't a nightmare," Elsie said, her voice shaking. "I know the difference between a dream and this sort of vision."

Asher looked pained. "Believe me, I've heard that before."

"Asher, please." Kate glared at him before turning back to Elsie. "Why do you think this image on your photograph is Billy? I mean, it certainly reminds me of him, but . . . what does it mean?"

"I don't know," Elsie said after a moment. "It's never happened before."

Asher narrowed his eyes. "And yet . . . forgive me if this sounds rude, but you want us to believe that your camera somehow captured the image of a ghost?"

Elsie looked away, wishing she'd burned the photo and left well enough alone.

"Don't worry about the photograph for now," Kate said quickly. "Why were you at the British Museum?"

Elsie hesitated. "It's difficult to explain."

Asher opened his mouth, but then closed it again. After a moment he nodded, and to Elsie his expression seemed vaguely contrite.

"The important thing is that I forgot my Chlorodyne and had another vision. I saw a young woman. She may have been beautiful when she was alive. She wasn't hostile like my grandmother—she didn't terrify me—but she was terribly sad. She said again and again that she was sorry." She tried to picture the woman's face. "I didn't recognize her, but she seemed to know the man who held me."

Kate's eyebrows shot upward. "A man *held* you?"

"This gentleman happened to be near when she had her episode," said Asher.

"No, I don't think it's that simple." Elsie paused to find the right words. "I believe he *caused* the seizure."

Asher leaned forward. "What do you mean, he caused it?"

"It was almost as though *he* were the haunted one, and I just happened to be in the way."

"So you're saying your seizures are triggered by proximity to spirits of the dead?" Asher looked thoughtful. "If that's possible, and I'm not saying such things are, it means Billy was dead on Monday."

Elsie nodded. "I suppose so. . . ."

Asher turned to Kate. "When did you last see him alive?"

"Saturday night."

"But how could Elsie see him—or photograph him, actually—on the grounds of Summerfield?" asked Asher. "I thought he lived and worked in Castle End."

Kate cleared her throat. "Billy had been gathering information on Mr. Thompson and my father for the Saturday séance. He'd been *inside* the college, trying to get details from the staff." She glanced at Elsie. "Does this mean he was murdered within the grounds of Summerfield?"

"Possibly," said Elsie slowly, shivering at the thought. "Though I hardly know how to make sense of it myself."

Asher lifted his hand. "I know Kate suspects it was murder, but there were no marks of deadly violence on the body. For all we know he may have died of exposure."

"Don't be ridiculous. It's summer," said Kate.

Asher shrugged. "The nights have been cool. It's easier to believe that than to believe in the existence of spirit visions."

Elsie stared at him. "What if I could prove it to you?"

"And how would you do that?"

"What if I *try* to reach out to this boy?" A knot formed in her stomach at the very thought of it. She'd never once initiated an episode—she didn't know if it was possible. "That way you'd have your proof, and Kate might gain more information about what happened to Billy."

Asher turned to Kate. "You think we're actually going to learn anything from this? You should know better after what you've seen . . . and *done.*"

"I'm not proud of what I've done," said Kate. "And there's no doubt Martineau was a cheat. But why would Elsie lie? What's the harm in letting her try?"

Asher sighed. "I'm not saying she's lying. I'm skeptical because . . ."

"Because you think I'm delusional," Elsie finished for him, gratified to see him flinch at her words.

"All right, then," he said. "We'll try it as a scientific experiment in which you prove you're not delusional. I'll even take a photograph, with your permission."

Elsie frowned at the thought of Asher's broad hands fumbling with her camera. "No, I don't think so."

"You don't trust me with it?"

"I want you watching the entire time. You're the skeptic, after all. Kate can work the camera."

"Really?" Kate beamed at her.

"Fine," Asher said. "But where should we conduct this experiment?"

"We should go back to that outbuilding on the edge of the garden where Elsie had her seizure," Kate said. "It may be that Billy . . . that *something* lingers there."

"That sounds like as good a place as any," said Asher. "When do we begin?"

"Tomorrow," said Elsie, her gut pitting with dread.

❖ ❖ ❖ ❖ ❖

Asher awoke the next morning with a headache.

He'd lain awake half the night, harassed by memories and doubts. Was he falling for the same swindle that had made a fool of his father? One that had made a fool of Asher, too, for that matter. A beautiful lady, educated and refined, who happened to have spirit visions. A young lady setting a trap for the next gullible Spiritualist . . . or the next young idiot with delusions of chivalry.

When would he finally erase Letty from his memory? He could hear her soft laugh, feel the pressure of her hand on his arm. But he also remembered the cunning curve of her mouth as Father whispered in her ear. These persistent memories made Asher hate himself all the more for not yet deadening his heart to the viper.

After nightmares of Father and his beautiful muse— whispering together, embracing—he'd woken in a sweat. Once his breathing finally calmed, he shook his head. It was old territory and he was weary of returning to it.

Nothing would come from their experiment today. No doubt Elsie would feel betrayed—a thoroughly illogical reaction, but just what he'd expect from a sensitive girl like her. It was best for her to face the truth. If she could put this nonsense behind her, perhaps she could be happy.

But Kate's words echoed in his mind. *Why would Elsie lie?*

He groaned. If Elsie was telling the truth and something *did* happen, if she saw a spirit and communicated with it, in a way that left no doubt of what she'd seen . . .

But that *wouldn't* happen. Not one shred of science proved the existence of an afterlife or of man's ability to communicate with the dead. For years he had watched his father attempt to collect such data, and the old fool had failed to gather anything more conclusive than anecdotal evidence—and that from a load of self-serving liars, no doubt.

He walked downstairs with his head pounding and a scowl on his face.

The others were already seated at the breakfast table. Mrs. Thompson smiled at him.

"I have another telegram for you, Asher."

His heart sank. *Father.* He took the offered envelope and stuffed it in his pocket without giving it a second glance.

"Aren't you going to read it?" Kate's expression was quizzical, but to Asher it also seemed vaguely challenging.

"I will later," he said stiffly.

The room fell silent—a noisy, uncomfortable sort of quiet.

"Such a beautiful morning," said Elsie, her tone so giddy it nearly rang false. "Perfect light for camera work."

Mrs. Thompson turned her sober gaze to the girl. "Another day of photography? But you already had Kate for the entire morning yesterday. That wasn't enough?"

"There are a few more poses I wish to stage, Aunt. I understand Kate is expected in the library. What if I helped in the afternoon to make up for her absence this morning?" She glanced at Asher.

"Er . . . I could help, too," he said quickly. "I mean, if that would make it easier to do without Kate this morning."

Mrs. Thompson gave them each a hard look before her mouth flattened into a tight smile. "This must be quite a project you've undertaken, Elsie. I confess I'm glad to see you all occupied in such an artistic pursuit." She glanced at Mr. Thompson, who nodded almost imperceptibly. "I'll tell Miss Freeman to expect you this afternoon."

"Thank you, Aunt." Elsie beamed. "I wish to take a

photograph by the outbuilding on the far reaches of the college gardens, perhaps using the doorway as a frame. But the door is locked. Might we borrow the key?"

"I'm not sure where that key would be." Mrs. Thompson turned to her husband. "Oliver?"

Mr. Thompson frowned. "Do you mean the old laboratory? The groundskeeper has a key, but he's off in the country visiting family at the moment. I used to have a spare. . . ." He trailed off, looking sharply at Elsie. "Must you get *inside* the lab? It's rather in disrepair—the building's not been used since we built the new Science Annex."

Asher noted the flush in Elsie's cheeks as she bowed her head contritely.

"It was just a thought, Uncle."

When the Thompsons finally rose to attend to their duties, Asher eagerly followed their example. Kate raised an eyebrow at him. Did she think he was looking forward to this test of Elsie's abilities? He just wished the entire business to be over with.

Elsie led the way to the old lab. Once there she set up her tripod, mounted the camera, and gave Kate a quick lesson in activating the shutter. Asher watched in silence, still annoyed to have been denied this privilege.

Kate peered through the lens. "When should I take the photograph? How will I know when you're seeing a spirit?"

Elsie frowned. "Good question. I'm not certain I'll be able to tell you." She turned to him. "What do you think, Asher?"

He thought back to her convulsions at the British Museum. After the initial seizure she'd gone deathly quiet and still. Then what happened? Had she opened her eyes? That was it—she'd appeared to be looking at someone or something. It had almost seemed that she was *listening*.

"Wait until she goes quiet and opens her eyes," he said to

Kate. "She'll still be in the trance, but I'm guessing that's when she experiences her vision."

Elsie rubbed her temple, frowning. "I purposely didn't take my medicine this morning, and my head is beginning to pound most dreadfully."

"Then we should get on with it," Kate said simply.

Asher crossed his arms. "What can I do?"

"Have an open mind," Elsie said.

Her direct gaze brought heat to his cheeks. He nodded slowly and shoved his hands back in his pockets.

Elsie made her way to where she'd stood the day of the photograph. She clasped her hands and closed her eyes. Asher turned to see Kate peering through the camera lens. With her head down the curve of her neck seemed almost swan-like.

He looked back at Elsie. She swallowed but did not open her eyes. Her pale cheeks and grimly clenched mouth softened his irritation. Another glance at Kate caught her watching him. She frowned, and they each turned back to Elsie.

But nothing was happening.

Asher watched in silence for several more minutes. He did not look at Kate again, but he heard her feet shuffling.

Finally Elsie moaned. Her head turned to the side, eyebrows arched. Next to him, Kate placed her hand on the shutter.

Asher held his breath as a curious sensation fluttered in his chest—a feeling strangely akin to hope.

Chapter 16

Kate watched through the camera lens as Elsie reached out, her fingers stretching as though they clutched for something that just eluded her grasp. After a moment, however, Elsie sighed and shook her head. Her eyes opened, and Kate knew this was not part of the trance Asher had described. Elsie's eyes were focused on the camera, and her mouth drooped.

"I'm sorry," she murmured.

Kate was surprised by her own disappointment. Had she expected Elsie to lift her head, much like Mrs. Martineau, and announce the arrival of a spirit presence? Had she really thought Billy might speak through the girl? She'd never believed in any of that during her time with the medium, but Elsie's story had made the possibility so vivid in her mind that it had been easy to push aside the shame of trapdoors and spirit dances.

Swallowing a sigh, Kate stepped back from the camera. "You saw nothing at all? You almost seemed to . . ."

"I felt that cold darkness just briefly. It seemed to cloud around me, but then it receded."

"Discouraging," said Asher.

"Not for *you*." Anger sharpened Elsie's tone. "I'm sure this is exactly what you expected to happen."

"Let's not waste time arguing," said Kate quickly. "Why not move along to where Billy was found?"

Elsie's brow furrowed. "My head aches." She rubbed her temples as she turned to Asher. "Where *was* he found?"

"Queens' Green," Asher said.

Elsie nodded. "That's not very far. Did my uncle say exactly where in Queens' Green? And who found him?"

Asher shook his head. "I don't remember. He seemed reluctant to speak about it—didn't he, Kate?"

Kate thought back to that night. "Yes, he did. And it seemed to bother Mrs. Thompson. She yammered on about Trinity students luring vagrants into drinking themselves to death. He brushed that off, but he couldn't—or *wouldn't*—explain why the police came to Summerfield. I wonder how they even knew to look for Billy? Did someone find his . . ." She faltered. "Did someone find him in Queens' Green and alert the police?"

Elsie turned to her. "Did you ask when you went to see the body?"

"I didn't think to," Kate said. "I was nervous."

Elsie's expression softened. "Of course you were." She massaged her temples a moment longer before dropping her hand. "I suppose we must stroll through the Green."

Asher glanced back at the Gatehouse. "Aren't we supposed to stay on Summerfield grounds?"

"That was the rule yesterday," Kate said. "We've been given no orders about leaving college grounds *today*."

She led them to the wide grassy space that lay along the River Cam behind Queens' College. Starting at Silver Street, Kate held Elsie's hand as the girl took cautious steps. Asher followed a few paces behind, carrying the camera. Together they continued along the Green until they reached the northern border of the college. At that point they turned and walked the opposite direction, this time nearer to Queen's Road. Kate released Elsie's hand when they reached Silver Street once again. "That's the end."

Elsie shook her head. "I felt nothing at all—not even the slightest chill."

Kate waited for Asher's inevitable cutting remark, but he merely frowned as though deep in thought. At least he had the grace not to look triumphant. She turned back to Elsie. "What do you think it means?"

Elsie glanced toward Summerfield Road, then back at Kate. "Perhaps Billy wasn't killed here."

"How could you know that?" asked Asher.

Elsie stiffened. "I don't *know* anything. I've only had these visions a few times—the Chlorodyne keeps them at bay—but each time the seizure has run its course I was standing in or near the place that person died."

Kate opened her mouth, but Asher spoke over her.

"What about your episode at the British Museum?" he pressed. "The spirit you saw—are you suggesting it was the ghost of someone who died in that very gallery? You said the young gentleman caused your seizure, but he seemed very much alive to me."

"When I bumped into him, I fell to the dark place," Elsie said. "As I already told you, I saw a woman. She spoke to me, and somehow I knew that she was giving me a message for the young man."

"My question still stands. Does that mean the spirit woman somehow died in the museum? That she haunts the place?"

"She wasn't haunting the museum!" Elsie raised her chin defiantly. "I think she may have been haunting the young man."

Asher shook his head. "This is exactly what I find so provoking about all of this—the complete absence of logic. Spirit visions are impossible to test because there's nothing predictable or measurable about them. Do spirits haunt people or places? Does one find them where they died, or where they lived? There is no logical pattern!"

Elsie started to speak but seemed to choke on the words.

Kate glared at Asher. "I think you've made your point."

"Ah, I'm the villain once again," he muttered. "How am I to be blamed for merely asking questions?"

"You're not the only one with questions," Elsie said in a small, tired voice. "I've been in a stupor for years with that hideous drug. I have no idea how to explain why I have these visions or why spirits behave as they do. I never asked for any of this!"

"That's the most common excuse for any medium whose 'gifts' are called into question," said Asher.

Elsie gasped. "Must you be such a brute?"

"Must you make it so easy?"

"That's enough," Kate said, noting the grey tinge to Elsie's skin, the perspiration that beaded her lip and brow. "Elsie needs her medication, and I must report to Freeman. But I'm not willing to give up just yet. Let's think on it tonight and perhaps try the old lab again later."

Elsie moved ahead, nearly stumbling as she hurried toward Summerfield and her bottle of Chlorodyne. Kate followed, wishing to keep up with Elsie even if it meant leaving Asher behind. Upon turning onto Summerfield Walk, however, she felt his hand on her arm.

"Shall I . . ." He cleared his throat. "I mean, do you still need me?"

"Please don't trouble yourself," Kate said crisply. She turned to see Elsie already nearing the Gatehouse. "Just leave the camera in the foyer, Asher."

She stepped quickly to join Elsie, and the two walked in silence until they reached the great iron gate of the college. Kate nodded politely as Jones let them through.

"Please don't ring the bell, Kate," Elsie whispered. "I don't want Millie to make a fuss."

"Then I shall help you up the stairs."

Elsie's brow furrowed, and for a moment Kate thought she might refuse. But then she held out her hands and Kate saw how they shook. "My aunt shouldn't see this. Perhaps you might help with my medicine?"

"Of course."

Kate opened the front door and, seeing the path to the staircase was clear, took Elsie by the arm and guided her upstairs. After softly closing Elsie's door, she led her to an upholstered chair and eased her into it.

"You're a good nursemaid," said Elsie.

"I tended to my mother before she died."

"Oh, I see. I'm terribly sorry."

Kate shrugged and turned to the vanity table, noting the delicate brushes and combs, the jeweled hairpins and the bottles of scent made of exquisitely cut glass. The room was sparingly furnished, but everything was orderly and sweet smelling. A fine lady's room. At the moment, however, the lady looked anything but fine. In fact, she grew paler by the minute. Kate scanned the table again, then turned to Elsie with eyebrows raised.

"In the drawer," Elsie whispered.

Kate opened the drawer and found two bottles of Chloro-dyne and a small collection of spoons. She chose the bottle with the broken seal and twisted the stopper free. "How much?"

Elsie paused, seeming to consider. "One—no, two spoon-fuls, please."

"Are you certain? You shouldn't take too much. I happen to know . . . well, I've heard of people dying after taking too much Chlorodyne."

"How dreadful." Elsie stared longingly at the bottle before lowering her gaze. "I suppose you're right. One spoonful will have to do."

Kate poured the medicine with a steady hand and placed the spoon in Elsie's mouth. After a moment Elsie leaned back and inhaled deeply. "Thank you," she whispered. Kate watched in silence, waiting to see the color come back to the girl's cheeks. Soon her breathing calmed and the trembling of her hands stilled. She opened her eyes.

"The headache is fading." Elsie took a deep breath and ex-haled slowly. "All these years I thought Mother made me take Chlorodyne so I wouldn't suffer the seizures. I always suspected she was embarrassed by my convulsions, but now I wonder if Asher was right." She turned to Kate. "Do *you* think she's been keeping me in a stupor all this time just to protect herself?"

Kate bit her lip. "I don't know her, Elsie. Do you think your mother capable of murder?"

"Maybe." She frowned. "I don't know."

"You do, don't you?"

Elsie's cheeks flooded with color. "Yes?"

Before Kate could press further Elsie turned away, raising a hand to hide a yawn. "I feel the heaviness settling over me now."

"Shall I help you to your bed?"

Elsie shook her head slowly. "Not just yet. I really don't want to be alone. I wanted to tell you . . . that I'm sorry we couldn't reach Billy today."

Kate sighed. "I was surprised by how much I wanted you to see him. I hate the thought of his spirit being troubled." She forced a smile. "And I'm sorry Asher was so rude. I hope he feels rotten about it now."

Elsie smiled. "He reminds me of my brothers. They never took me seriously, even before I ever had a seizure. Men never do."

"On the contrary—I'm certain most men must worship you."

Kate regretted the words as soon as they were spoken. They were too familiar, too passionate coming from a near stranger. But Elsie's smile didn't waver.

"Worship isn't the same as respect. Every man I've known has felt the need to think *for* me, but perhaps all ladies suffer that from the men they know. Well"—her smile broadened—"except for my aunt."

Kate laughed. "She does seem to wear the trousers in this house, if you don't mind my saying."

Elsie straightened in the chair, her expression suddenly imploring. "Kate, you *will* join us at dinner tomorrow night, won't you? The gathering with Uncle's Trinity friends?"

Kate imagined a finely dressed group seated at the dinner table, enjoying a good meal and lofty conversation. Then she tried to place herself at this same table, sharing in the conversation. She couldn't see it at all. A skinny girl in a made-over blouse and brown skirt whose formal education ended when she was eleven years old? A girl who'd helped perpetrate frauds on innocent people?

She shook her head. "I'm certain Mrs. Thompson invited me out of kindness, but the idea of an evening at table with learned people doesn't sit well with me."

"I would like to have you near," said Elsie. "I'd feel stronger that way, don't you see? Having a friend with me?"

Kate blushed. "Of course, if you wish it—"

"And I have a dress you could wear, if that's troubling you. I have more dresses than I know what to do with, and nothing would please me more than to share one with you. Pick one now, and we'll make adjustments tomorrow." Her eyelids fluttered as she stifled another yawn. "Surely Aunt Helena won't make you work on a Saturday."

"I don't know. I expect not." Kate smiled. "If you insist, I suppose I could bring myself to attend the dinner. I don't wish to offend your aunt and uncle, who have been so kind to—"

Elsie interrupted with a limp wave of her hand, yawning ferociously this time. "Then it's settled. We'll start work after breakfast. But now I think you'd best help me to my bed before I fall asleep in this chair."

chapter 17

Elsie considered Kate's reflection in the mirror. "You look older."

"That's good, isn't it?" Kate turned her head to get a better view of her upswept hair. "Plaits are very girlish, but they're all I can manage. This is better."

Elsie smiled. Kate was too thin and sharp-featured for conventional beauty, but when dressed in a gown with her hair properly arranged, she no longer looked as though she'd just stepped out of a charity school . . . or a dark alley.

"I like your hair best when it's hanging down around your face, but Aunt would be horrified." She patted Kate's shoulder. "Are you ready?"

The shoulder slumped under her hand. "No."

"Let's get it over with." Elsie laughed lightly. "Aunt's been very patient with us this week. We owe it to her to be punctual tonight."

Kate gathered her skirts to rise, tripping slightly in the process. She glanced at Elsie and sighed. "No one will notice me, anyway—they'll all be looking at you. You are terribly beautiful."

She spoke the words so bluntly that Elsie blushed.

"Much good it's done me," she muttered. When Kate opened her mouth to protest, she took her by the arm. "No more dawdling. I can hear voices downstairs."

As they descended the din grew louder. A man spoke in a booming voice—she couldn't discern the words—and then laughed. Elsie nearly toppled into Kate as the girl came to an abrupt stop on the stair below her.

"What is it?" Elsie whispered.

"That man . . ."

"What about him?"

"I know who it is." Kate turned to Elsie. "I can't go down there. I can't see him."

"Who?"

"He was my mistress's patron. He's . . ." The girl shuddered. "He'll send for the police if he sees me."

"Surely not. My uncle wouldn't allow it."

"He can't know I'm here. Do you hear me? He *can't* know." Kate's hand went to her mouth. "I think I'm going to be ill."

Elsie studied her for a moment. The girl did seem pale in the low light. "You must go upstairs, then. I'll tell Aunt you've taken sick."

Kate nodded, hand still clasped to her mouth, and brushed past Elsie up the stairs.

If Kate hadn't looked so distressed Elsie would have been annoyed. As it stood, she was disappointed. It would have been a comfort to have another girl at the table. One sympathetic soul who didn't give a fig to hear Cambridge Fellows spouting their pompous opinions. So much easier to bear with a kindred spirit. They could have laughed about it later.

Now she must descend the stairs alone and face these strangers, one of whom was so beastly as to send *Kate* into hiding. She was such a fierce little creature, and so independent—could he really have that much power over her? Somehow Elsie had to get to Aunt Helena and explain before she spoke the girl's name aloud.

But when she entered the room the first face she saw stopped her cold in her tracks.

How could it be?

The young man from the British Museum—the one who'd held her in his arms. What on earth was *he* doing here?

He stood with Asher Beale, who spoke to the man in low tones. When Asher turned toward her his eyes widened. The gentleman followed Asher's gaze, also locking eyes with her.

Without thinking, she shook her head. *No.*

The young man blinked.

Heart thudding, she glanced about the room, but everyone else was absorbed in conversation. No one had seen her silencing gesture. And somehow, *he* seemed to have understood.

Clutching her skirt to keep her hands from shaking, she stepped toward her aunt.

"May I speak with you in private, Aunt?"

Aunt Helena frowned. "Pardon?"

"Would you step aside for a moment, please?"

Her aunt complied, though the frown deepened. "What is this about?"

"Kate is ill. She begs you not to mention her absence to the others—she would be quite embarrassed. She is distressed to have inconvenienced you."

"Does she need my assistance?" Aunt Helena touched the lace at her throat with trembling fingers.

"No, I don't think so." Elsie tried to speak soothingly. "I thought, perhaps, we could have some broth sent to her. She seemed to be experiencing severe discomfort—I'm not certain she could have managed to sit at the table for long."

"Well, I'd better find Millie and have her remove the extra place setting from the dinner table. How unfortunate!"

"I can find Millie, Aunt."

"No, there are gentlemen here who are waiting to be introduced to you. They've already met Asher." Aunt Helena guided Elsie toward him. "Mr. Beale, would you do the honor of introducing Mr. Wakeham to my niece? I shall return shortly."

The young man faced her, his grey eyes cool and slightly amused. A tremor coursed through her body. Was it fear or delight? She wasn't certain.

Asher cleared his throat. "Mr. Simon Wakeham, may I please introduce Miss Elsie Atherton?" He shifted his gaze to Elsie. "Mr. Wakeham recently took a first in classics at Trinity College, and your uncle tutored him." Once Aunt Helena was out of hearing, he lowered his voice. "I've begged Mr. Wakeham not to reveal to the Thompsons that he's met us before."

The young man pinioned Asher with his silvery eyes. "And I'm still wondering why."

"Because it was my fault he was there," said Elsie, her pulse leaping as he turned his eyes once more to her. "It's a long story, Mr. Wakeham, but you should know that I went to London without permission, and Mr. Beale followed with the idea of protecting me. As it turned out, that was a good thing."

His eyes narrowed. "You were ill."

"I have a condition, yes. I should have heeded advice and not undertaken the journey."

Mr. Wakeham opened his mouth to ask another question, but he stopped abruptly when another gentleman clapped a broad hand on his shoulder.

"Marshall and I have come to see what you three are murmuring about."

Elsie didn't know this large, barrel-chested man, but she recognized his voice—it was the very one that earlier sent Kate running back up the stairs.

"Ah, Eliot," said Mr. Wakeham. "You have made the acquaintance of our young Mr. Beale, yes? Then let me introduce Thompson's niece, Miss Elsie Atherton. Miss Atherton, may I present Mr. Robert Eliot?"

Mr. Eliot extended a hand. "Such a pleasure to make the acquaintance of Lord Rolleston's daughter."

Elsie had never been quite so grateful for evening gloves as she touched her fingers to his large, damp palm. Thankfully he did not lift them to his large, damp lips.

"Your father never comes to our meetings anymore." Mr. Eliot's left hand covered hers and pulled her a step closer. "How fares he these days?"

No wonder Kate had balked—the man was repugnant. Now the fingers of his left hand were sliding down to caress her wrist.

"My father is very busy, sir." She jerked her hand away. "In fact, he is abroad at the moment."

"I suppose a peer of the realm has many commitments," Mr. Eliot said with a grunt, "and can't be bothered with our Metaphysical Society endeavors. No doubt he wishes to distance himself, lest our reputation sully his own."

"If he did, I wouldn't blame him for it," said the gentleman standing near Eliot.

Eliot frowned. "I say, Marshall! That's a bit rude."

"Eliot, you know better than anyone how I feel about the Society's preoccupation with the spirit world." The words were gruff, but the man's eyes were bright with mischief. Though Elsie guessed him nearer in age to Simon Wakeham than to Eliot, his cunning gaze lent him an air of confidence.

"Miss Atherton, may I present my cousin, Dr. Philip Marshall?" said Mr. Wakeham. "Not only is he the youngest Fellow at Trinity College, but he also devotes his time to medical research at Addenbrooke's Hospital. He loves nothing better than to lord his accomplishments over me."

Dr. Marshall's smile broadened. "You'll be a Fellow soon enough, cousin. It might help if you gave up some of your outlandish notions."

"You speak as though you believe your own research to be nothing less than orthodox," murmured Mr. Wakeham.

"Not orthodox, perhaps, but at the very least *rational*."

Elsie noted their relaxed posture, the humor in their eyes, and knew this was friendly ribbing between cousins. Clearly they enjoyed needling each other.

"Helena is at the door," announced Mr. Thompson from the other side of the room. "We don't stand on ceremony here, of course. Shall we make our way to the table? Wakeham, would you accompany Elsie? I do believe you're seated next to her at the table."

Elsie braced herself as she placed her hand on Mr. Wakeham's sleeve. The last time their bodies touched she had fallen into a spell and seen a dead woman. She'd taken her dose earlier, but a smaller one than usual. She hadn't wished to fall asleep during dinner.

Did she imagine the crackle in the air as Mr. Wakeham placed his hand on hers? She took a deep breath and concentrated on the fabric of his jacket, noting the fine weave. She breathed in his scent of lavender water and shaving soap. It would not happen—she refused to fall to that dark place and embarrass her aunt and uncle. When they reached the dining room, she looked up and met his gaze. His grey eyes were friendly. No ghosts resided there.

Perhaps it *was* possible to control the spells simply by force of will.

❧ ❧ ❧ ❧ ❧

Asher *knew* he would be seated next to the blustering Robert Eliot. The man might be a Fellow in Moral and Political Philosophy at Trinity College, but he was still an ass. To Asher his words fell heavily, uncomfortably—like the clang of a gong. When prompted by Mrs. Thompson to speak about his days as an undergraduate at Trinity, he'd looked as though he could barely contain the urge to stand and strut about the room. What a roaring good time they'd had! As a student and Fellow, he'd never seen a class equal to his own in intelligence, wit, and capacity for carousing.

"I quite miss living in college," said Mr. Eliot, wiping his shiny brow with his napkin. "I have a fine house, but there's nothing quite like dinner at High Table, with the wine flowing just as freely as the conversation. And who could forget our little jaunts after dinner? I think we terrorized the town quite thoroughly." He winked at Asher.

"Trinity is a lively place, to be sure," said Dr. Marshall quickly, "but you'll scare the boy off for good if you continue to characterize it as a den of iniquity." He turned to Asher, his expression earnest. "In fact, I invite you to come stay in college with me, Mr. Beale. Thompson has told me of your interest in becoming a Trinity man. I have spacious rooms, you know, and what better way to get a feel for the place than to spend a couple of days within its walls?"

Asher smiled. "Thank you for the generous offer, Dr. Marshall. I have a mind to accept it."

"Well done, Marshall." Mr. Eliot lifted his wineglass in a salute. "Perhaps you might arrange for a gentlemen's gathering, eh? Show the boy what it takes to be a proper Trinity man?"

Mrs. Thompson cleared her throat.

Dr. Marshall's eyes darted toward her before returning to Mr. Eliot. "Plenty of time for all that," he said evenly. "What we want to know, Eliot, is have you danced with any spirits lately?"

"Good God, Marshall!" cried Mr. Eliot.

Asher cringed. The man was insufferably loud.

Mr. Eliot took a gulp of wine. "Did Thompson and Wakeham tell you already? As a matter of fact, I'm finished with dancing spirits. The medium seems to have packed off to some other town—the house is already up for rent." He raised a napkin to his lips and sighed heavily. "It's a shame, really. I was certain I was close to finding something there. There's no doubt she had a talent. It's too bad she allowed herself to be duped like that. If I could get my hands on the little villain who deceived her, I'd drag her straight to the police."

Asher glanced at Mr. Thompson in time to catch the tightening of the man's mouth. Apparently he was not going to reveal the presence of the "little villain" upstairs.

"Eliot, don't be daft." Mr. Wakeham's tone was mild, almost playful. "She must have hired the girl, for it's the theatrics that bring customers. The more complicated they make these performances, however, the easier it is to spot the frauds."

"They're *all* frauds," muttered Dr. Marshall.

Asher thought of his father. "I hadn't thought exposing frauds was the main business of the Society."

Mr. Wakeham smiled at him. "It's not our intention to

police the world of Spiritualism. It's just that, more often than not, our field research leads us to dens of vulgar tricksters rather than to true mediums, if there is such a thing."

Asher hadn't expected such cynicism from a Society member, especially since his own father had proven such an easy mark. "So, what *is* the business of the Society?"

Mr. Wakeham met his gaze from across the table. "I thought you would know, being the son of Harold Beale."

"I know he is experimenting with thought-transference," Asher said mildly.

"Ah yes, *telepathy,* as Marshall would call it," Mr. Thompson said. "One of many topics of interest to our group."

"I've told Father many times that if telepathy or any other metaphysical phenomena were real, we should be able to establish their existence using the scientific method," Asher said. "But the hypothesis can never be proven because it won't bear up under repeated testing."

"My boy," said Mr. Thompson gently. "The Society members have engaged in this argument many times, and I don't wish to bully you with our notions over dinner. But I must say that excluding from reality anything that can't be proven through the scientific method is closed-minded and prejudicial. Some would say, 'There's so little proof; therefore it must not exist.' But we say, 'There's some proof, so let us investigate thoroughly, from every angle, before we dismiss this as impossible or false.' Most of the scientific community is simply unwilling to fully, rigorously test the realm of the metaphysical."

Mrs. Thompson's eyes were bright with amusement. "Asher, one of my first tasks was to collect all the ghost stories I could find in order to analyze them for common threads—anything concrete to which science could cling for further investigation. I confess to having been quite skeptical at the beginning."

Asher sighed. "But you were convinced to feel otherwise?"

"No indeed. My skepticism increased as I continued to collect data. The stories often were ridiculous. Pure flights of fancy, they seemed to me—nothing logical for any of us to use as a basis for investigation." She paused, her expression softening. "The *witnesses,* however, were credible. They weren't insane or known liars. They didn't seek to profit from their stories. They truly believed they had seen or experienced spirits. And I wanted to know *why.* What makes a person believe beyond the shadow of a doubt that he has seen a ghost? Despite my skepticism, I felt this question warranted investigation."

"I, for one, have had many encounters with spirits," Mr. Eliot said wistfully. "Once one has felt that presence—light as gossamer, at once both warm and cold, sad and hopeful—one can no longer deny that these entities exist."

"Rubbish," said Dr. Marshall under his breath.

Asher glanced at Elsie, but she was staring fixedly at the tablecloth.

"With all due respect to Mr. Eliot," said Mr. Wakeham, "I've long since given up chasing after floating spirit apparitions. I've rarely been convinced by anything encountered during a séance."

"Sometimes I wonder why you even bothered joining the Society," said Mr. Eliot, shaking his head sadly.

Mr. Thompson stroked his beard. "It's because he can't reconcile himself to the idea of extinction."

"Extinction?" Asher asked.

There was a pause as Millie cleared the first course. Then, as though relenting, Mr. Wakeham spoke. "I am convinced that something, some essential piece of us, must endure after death. I don't believe in angels flitting about in heaven, or the bizarre ghostly realm that Spiritualists envision. I do believe, however, that our psyches are too complex, too powerful, for their—shall we call it *energy*—to simply be extinguished upon death."

"Tell him of your theories," Mr. Thompson prompted.

Mr. Wakeham took a swallow of wine before continuing. "Take what Mrs. Thompson said about ghost stories, for instance. So many witnesses, seemingly credible and without ulterior motive, have reported encounters with ghosts, particularly in places where tragic things happened. It has made many of us wonder if something tangible is left behind by extraordinary events. Could a house retain the echo of a violent murder? Could we define ghosts as a manifestation of a persistent energy? And even more interesting—is this energy something we can access and manipulate while we are yet living?" Mr. Wakeham looked at Asher. "This is the sort of thing I wish one day to discuss with your father, for I feel it falls within the category of experimental psychology."

Asher blinked. "I'm afraid I'm not following you exactly. What is this energy? Is it measurable? And how can it survive death?"

"I'm not certain it can. But if it does, it could explain many of the ghostly encounters people have experienced over the centuries." He turned to his cousin. "Philip studies the human mind and has said many times that we only access parts of it on a daily basis. What is that lamp metaphor you use?"

Dr. Marshall leaned forward. "Think of your brain as a house, and in that house some rooms are lighted by lamps, while others remain closed and dark. If we could only open those doors and bring light to those dark spaces, we may discover abilities that we didn't know we had."

"Including the ability to see and communicate with the energy that remains after bodily death," said Mr. Wakeham. "I know you don't agree with me, Philip, but I strongly believe your research could help shine a light on those dark 'between' spaces where the dead linger."

Asher heard a rustle of fabric and turned to see Elsie staring at Simon Wakeham, her eyes glittering.

"The dark between," she said. "I like that."

Simon Wakeham smiled at her in a way that made Asher's fists tighten underneath the table.

"What Miss Atherton terms the dark between, I call the subliminal self," said Dr. Marshall. "You see, all of our ordinary and familiar thought processes I categorize under the supraliminal self—meaning the self 'above the threshold' of our consciousness. But if through exploration we could turn the lights on, so to speak, in the subliminal self—below the threshold of ordinary consciousness—we might be able to access latent capacities."

"What sort of capacities?" Elsie asked.

Dr. Marshall glanced at Mr. Thompson, one eyebrow raised. When Thompson nodded, he continued. "Telepathy, for one thing—the sort of ability that Dr. Harold Beale seems particularly interested in. But also clairvoyance, which, to me, is a different process—more the ability to predict events than to read another's mind. There's also telekinesis, or the ability to move things with your mind." He thumped his wineglass on the table. "Understand that I have absolutely no interest in the dead. I don't care a whit about ghosts, and I'd certainly never wish to converse with one. I'm much more interested in the minds of the living."

Asher found himself liking this brusquely spoken man. There wasn't a hint of romance or sentimentality to him. "Interested how?"

"This notion of latent capacities has consumed me for the past year. I've collected stories of people who suffered physical trauma and nearly died. Upon revival they found themselves gifted with a strange new ability. It's my contention that this brush with death somehow opened a door, helping them access those darkened areas of the subliminal self."

"What abilities have you documented?" asked Elsie, her eyes wide.

Dr. Marshall looked away. "I'm currently locating subjects—people willing to be studied and have their abilities tested—but I'm afraid I'm not at liberty to divulge specific details."

"Oh, of course." Elsie blushed. "I do apologize."

"It is gratifying to see your interest, Miss Atherton," said Wakeham.

The young man was quite freely staring at Elsie, and Asher didn't like it at all. He turned to Dr. Marshall. "Do you believe there is any way to *consciously* access this subliminal self?"

Dr. Marshall nodded, his eyes gleaming. "If there's a way, I am determined to find it."

A silence followed. Mr. Wakeham turned from Elsie to stare instead at his wineglass. He seemed vaguely troubled—certainly not as enthusiastic as Dr. Marshall. Asher opened his mouth to press them further, but Elsie spoke first.

"I'm curious," she said. "If there is an energy left behind by the dead, does that energy have a purpose? Or is it just an echo from the past?"

Asher shifted uncomfortably in his seat.

"I want to believe it is more than an echo," Wakeham said.

"Is there a particular spirit *you* wish to contact?" she asked.

Mrs. Thompson cleared her throat as if in warning, but if Wakeham was offended he did not show it.

"I've scoffed at mediums in the past," he said, "and even ridiculed the gullibility of their sitters, but I've never blamed the sitters for wanting to communicate with a lost loved one. Haven't we all wished to do the same?"

"Whom would you contact?" Elsie pressed.

Asher didn't like this. Elsie pried too closely into the man's privacy, and he knew it had to do with what she'd seen—or *thought* she'd seen—during her seizure at the museum. If she continued in this way she might inadvertently confess something that would compromise them both. She seemed determined, however, to keep Wakeham's attention upon her.

"I'd contact my father, for one," said Wakeham. "He died when I was very young." He lowered his gaze. "And more recently, there was a friend who died tragically. When someone close to us dies suddenly, we are left with so many questions. Unfortunately, mediums capitalize on this very cruelly."

Asher stared at Elsie, willing her to turn from Mr. Wakeham. To see the warning in his eyes.

"I'm sorry for the loss of your friend," Elsie said very gently.

Wakeham met her gaze again. "Her death came as quite a shock."

At that moment Millie bustled in to set plates for the next course, and Asher couldn't have been more grateful. Finally this very public display of private emotion would come to an end. Of course Elsie glanced at him, now that she'd already exposed herself, and it irked him that her expression was triumphant. *Yes, I heard it, Elsie.* Wakeham had said *her* death came as a shock—his friend had been female. Did she think she'd seen this very friend during her spell at the British Museum? It was a coincidence, surely.

Once the second course was served and the wineglasses

refilled, the party occupied themselves once more with the food. Everyone, that is, except Elsie. Asher's heart sank when he looked up from his lamb cutlet to find her staring again at Wakeham.

"Will you continue your studies at Trinity this fall, Mr. Wakeham?" Elsie asked.

"Actually, I leave for the Continent in less than a fortnight."

Elsie's mouth drooped. "How long will you be gone from Cambridge?"

"I'm not certain. Several months, perhaps. No more than a year. I do hope to follow my cousin's lead and read for a Fellowship at Trinity. But, you see, I need to vacate my temporary summer housing before the new tenants arrive."

"Simon has been living at our house on Chesterton Road while we're between tenants," Mrs. Thompson said. "You remember Stonehill, Elsie?"

Elsie smiled. "Oh, I do. We spent several weeks there one summer and had the loveliest time, but that was before . . ." She trailed off, biting her lip.

That was before your accident, thought Asher.

"Yes, child, that was before I took this post as principal of Summerfield," Mrs. Thompson said, rescuing her. "My, what an ordeal it was to get all of Oliver's books and papers moved to this suite! Wasn't it a challenge, my dear?" She turned to her husband, who grinned bashfully.

Asher suddenly wished the meal were over. Elsie stared dreamily into the distance, and he felt quite certain of whom she was thinking. He well remembered how she'd looked at Simon Wakeham at the British Museum, and how she'd later praised him as "gentlemanly." She'd actually predicted they'd see him again.

Did she now think she was clairvoyant?

Chapter 18

Kate returned to her room still shaking at the thought of Eliot being so near. Taking a breath to compose herself, she set about removing Elsie's altered gown, reaching behind her neck and fumbling with the buttons. The gowns of fine ladies were meant to be buttoned and unbuttoned by maids—or by friends, as the case was earlier—and thus it required a series of awkward contortions to divest herself of the garment. With trembling hands she plucked the pins from her hair and brushed it thoroughly before braiding the customary plaits. How grand it felt to be plain Kate again! With that thought she pulled her nightgown over her underpinnings and settled into bed, expecting a knock at the door any moment. Mrs. Thompson was no fool—would she believe in this sudden illness?

She steeled herself at the first knock, but it was only a kitchen girl bringing broth and bread. Once she'd eaten her fill, Kate busied herself by sewing a thick felt sheath into her skirt, perfect for storing Billy's knife. She smiled as she tied off the knot, imagining Mrs. Thompson's expression if she ever learned the fate of her sewing scraps. Surely the lady's eyebrows would climb all the way to her scalp.

More than two hours passed before the second knock roused Kate from her drowsing. Mrs. Thompson came through the door, set her lamp on the desk, and sat on the edge of the bed. "Are you feeling better, my dear?"

Kate nodded. "It was my stomach, ma'am. The broth helped settle it."

Mrs. Thompson smiled gently. "I'm afraid Mr. Thompson and I are at fault. I invited Mr. Eliot because he is a Trinity man, but Oliver neglected to tell me of his involvement in Saturday's séance—the one in which you lost your position. Of course you wouldn't have wanted to see him at the dinner table. But Oliver has been so distracted of late, he must have forgotten."

Kate bit her lip. The last thing she'd expected was an *apology*. "I . . . don't know what to say."

Mrs. Thompson studied her for a moment. "Get some rest, my dear," she finally said, patting her hand as she rose to leave.

Kate watched the clock for half an hour before she slipped out of bed and went to the door. After making certain the corridor was empty, she stepped lightly to the head of the stairs and listened. The strains of conversation came from the sitting room, which meant they'd finished the meal. Her path was clear.

After Mrs. Thompson's kindness, it seemed almost rude to sneak away. But the sound of Eliot's voice had shaken her more than she'd expected. She ached to see Tec, to talk with him about Billy. He needed to know the truth, and she was the best person to deliver it.

Kate returned to her room and dressed quickly in her blouse and skirt, patting her right pocket to make sure Billy's knife was secure. Then she pinned a hat to her head and took the shawl that hung on a peg near the door.

She was accustomed to stealthy movement in darkness, so getting downstairs and out the side door gave her no problem. The iron gate was locked, but even if it hadn't been Kate wouldn't have gone that way. Walking under the street lamps along the avenue in front of the college would have left her too exposed. Instead she would find her way to the southeast corner of the college garden and take side streets to Queen's Road.

During a rare burst of lightheartedness at the library, Freeman had confessed how she and her friends circumvented the wood fence that protected the south border of the college. The solution was simple—they merely lay on the ground and rolled underneath it. Kate had no qualms about rolling on the grass. After slipping out the Gatehouse door, she followed the path behind Summerfield Hall toward the fence.

The path ended in a padlocked gate. On a whim she yanked on the lock . . . and gasped when it came apart with ease. How long had it been broken? Since few girls remained during the long summer holiday, perhaps no one had bothered to check.

This made things much more interesting. If she could walk *through* the gate rather than rolling under it, she could borrow the battered bicycle stored behind Summerfield Hall. She'd been eyeing the contraption ever since the morning she saw Freeman and Barrett lean their own bicycles next to it. Freeman had made a display of turning up her nose at the shabby thing, but to Kate it seemed sturdy enough.

Before long she was pedaling north along the Backs at a steady clip, which was nothing to boast about but definitely faster than walking. She could barely see what lay ahead of her, but even if she'd possessed a match she dared not light the oil bicycle lamp. Anything could have been lurking in the dark shadows—a rabid animal, a footpad lying in wait to rob her, or perhaps something even worse than greedy-fingered Eliot.

She pedaled faster.

Castle End was unusually calm and quiet, but she still took

special care to hide the bicycle in the shadows near the cottage. She had to knock several times on Tec's door before she heard the bar being lifted. The door opened a crack.

"Kate?" Tec whispered.

"Yes. Let me in!"

He opened the door a little wider. "Come in quick." As soon as she'd slipped through he shut the door and locked it again.

She looked around the room, expecting to find the usual collection of boys littering the floor. Just a week ago she would have seen Billy sitting near the stove—on a proper chair, though, as he wouldn't have wanted to crease his suit. But the room was empty. "Where is everyone?"

"Just me now. Martineau has scarpered, and I don't know any other mediums that's needing our kind of talent." He glanced about the room forlornly. "I've done my best to find new places for the boys. It's been a tough few days."

"I have bad news, too, Tec. Terrible news."

"Yeah? What is it?"

"It's Billy." Tears welled in her eyes. "He's dead."

Tec blinked. "He can't be. How could you say such a thing?"

"Because he truly *is* dead, Tec. I saw his poor little body."

Tec stared at her for a long moment. "I . . . I don't know what to say. Was it an accident?"

"There's hardly a mark on him, but I know he was murdered. Problem is, I can't think who would do it. Can you?"

He shook his head slowly. "I figured Billy got wind of Martineau's plans and found a new place for himself. I'd no idea he'd gotten himself into trouble."

"What scheme was he working?"

He looked away. "I don't know a thing about it."

"Really, Tec? You don't have to protect me."

"Honest, Kate—he never told me about no dangerous

scheme. Poor mite must have taken on more than he could handle. Can't believe he's . . . *gone.*"

At the sight of his newly glistening eyes, all the control she'd exerted upon hearing the news of Billy's death, upon seeing his body at the police morgue, vanished. The tears spilled down her cheeks, and she did not bother to wipe them away.

"What are we going to do?" she cried.

Tec placed his hands on her shoulders. "Katie, I'm sorry," he said gently. "I know Billy was like a little brother to you." He brushed at her tears with a calloused finger. "Have you found a new situation?"

She nodded, wishing he would pull her closer. "For now, anyway."

"Good. We're each on our own now—no more little detectives. You've got to be strong, right? And you can't come here no more. There's nothing here for you. It ain't safe."

"It isn't? Why not?"

He glanced at the door. "Whatever happened to Billy . . . I'm afraid the trouble he found might come knocking on my door."

"But how?"

"I don't know," he said gruffly. "But you're better off keeping your distance. You'll be at Summerfield for a few days yet, right? As soon as I get things settled, I'll come find you."

Her heart leapt. "Will you take me with you?"

"You shouldn't take up with a rough boy like me."

"But you'd keep me safe, Tec."

After a moment's hesitation, he pulled her into his arms. "Be strong, Katie. There's a few things that needs figuring out. I'll see you soon enough, but you'd best go for now."

When he let her go, her eyes went again to the chair by the stove.

Tec sighed. "Every time I come in, I expect to find our Billy sitting in that chair. I woke in the wee hours last night, and I felt sure he was sitting there," he continued. "The feeling came over me so powerful-like and so queer, but when I lit the lamp, the chair was empty."

Kate thought of Elsie and that strange photograph she'd taken. "Maybe he *is* here, Tec. Maybe he's come home."

Tec shook his head. "What do you mean?"

"I'm not sure exactly. But I aim to find out."

❊ ❊ ❊ ❊ ❊

Elsie could not sleep.

Images and words flooded her mind, all circling back to Simon Wakeham. She'd hardly taken a bite during the meal, so conscious was she of his proximity. Most of the dinner conversation had floated above her head, but when he'd spoken of persistent energies that transcended death, her flesh had tingled. She'd hung on every word and, strangely enough, it had made sense to her. Everyone had these dark places in their minds, but only a few could access them. It wasn't a curse after all—it was an *ability.*

She thought of her dead grandmother's icy grip and shivered. Maybe for her it *was* a curse.

Elsie shook off the memory and turned her mind back to Simon Wakeham, reliving the conversation they'd shared as the dinner group retired to the sitting room.

"You are looking much better this evening, Miss Atherton," he had murmured.

She'd blushed like the greenest of girls. "Thank you for not revealing our prior acquaintance, Mr. Wakeham."

"I'm still wondering what it was at the British Museum that brought you from Cambridge."

"It was a friend . . . a friendship, I suppose. But it has now ended."

He held her gaze. "I continue to puzzle over the words you spoke that day. Do you remember what you said?"

She wanted to tell him. It would have been such a relief to confess everything. But it was too soon. And far too risky.

"No," she lied. "But Mother always told me I spoke absolute gibberish when I was having a spell. Thank you for staying with me—for making certain I was safe. Many men would have walked away."

Now she again rehearsed the conversation in her head, imagining his reaction if she'd been bold enough to speak the truth. *I do remember what I said, Mr. Wakeham. I was repeating what the dead lady told me. She said she is with you, always watching, and that she is sorry. She loved you very much . . . and I can see why.*

What would he have said to that?

A noise in the corridor startled her—the whisper of boot soles scuffing the wood floor. Elsie threw the covers aside and lighted her lamp. Opening the door, she shone the light in the corridor. Kate froze before her own door, then turned slowly. "Elsie?" she whispered.

"Come in here *now*."

Kate's shoulders sank in submission.

Once Elsie had closed the door and settled Kate in the chair, she sat on the edge of her bed. "Where *were* you?"

Kate stared at her for a moment. "I went to see a boy I used to work with. I needed to tell him about Billy."

"In the middle of the night? What if my aunt had caught you?"

Kate shrugged. "I had to see him. Thought he might know what happened to Billy."

"Well? Did he?"

"No." Kate looked down at her skirt and smoothed it with a trembling hand. "But I had a thought while I was there." She raised her chin and met Elsie's gaze. "Billy used to stay there quite often, you see. In fact, when I walked through the door, I could almost see him sitting by the stove. It was a common sight when he was alive."

Elsie shook her head. "Why are you telling me this?"

"Because . . . I think the three of us need to go to the cottage on Castle End. I think if it's still possible to reach Billy, you could do it there."

Chapter 19

Asher had just reached the second-floor staircase when the girls appeared, as if out of nowhere. Elsie put her finger to her lips as Kate beckoned him into the window alcove.

"Good morning?" he offered tentatively.

"We must go to Castle End," whispered Kate. "As soon as possible."

Elsie nodded. "Kate thinks we might make contact with Billy since he spent so much time there."

"You can't be serious!"

"Lower your voice." Kate left the alcove to glance down the corridor. "We know you don't believe," she said as she rejoined them, "and I told Elsie we should just go without you, but she insisted we ask."

Elsie smiled. "I'd feel safer with you there."

Asher's chest swelled a bit. "Well . . ."

"Kate feels very strongly about this," Elsie continued. "If we learn something, I want you to be there to witness it. Can you please set aside your skepticism . . . just one more time?"

Asher thought for a moment, but he couldn't manufacture a reasonable excuse. In truth, he'd lain awake a long time the previous night, his thoughts alternating between Philip Marshall's theories of the subliminal self and Simon Wakeham's intimate glances at Elsie. She seemed eager to share all the details of her visions with the latter gentleman. Surely it was better for her to explore them under his watch, rather than that of Mr. Wakeham.

"Well?" Kate's eyes flashed with impatience.

He ignored her, turning to Elsie instead. "How will you explain this to Mrs. Thompson?"

"We made a plan already. You tell her that you wish to attend a service at Trinity College Chapel, and Kate and I will chime in that we wish to go, too."

"But what if the Thompsons wish to join us?"

"I doubt they will," said Elsie. "Mama told me they've not been to church for years. I think Aunt Helena might even be an atheist."

"So?" Kate raised an eyebrow. "Are you coming with us or not?"

He looked from her to Elsie, unsettled by the force of their enthusiasm. "Seems I have little choice. I'll go with you as long as the Thompsons give permission."

And, indeed, the Thompsons took kindly to the idea. Mr. Thompson beamed as his wife gushed over their "blossoming friendship," but Asher suspected they were more pleased simply to have a quiet morning to themselves.

Shortly after breakfast Asher led the way to Trinity College Chapel. Having toured it previously, he took the time to point out the statues and tombs in the antechapel. He then steered them into stalls close to the organ to avoid crossing in front of others when they made their early exit. They sat through two hymns and the first reading before Kate tugged at his sleeve and nodded toward the door.

"Such a lovely chapel," Elsie murmured as they walked away. "And nearly everyone wearing surplices. They looked angelic in their white gowns, didn't they?" She turned to Kate. "What if Aunt Helena asks about the sermon?"

"We'll have to make something up," said Kate. "Let's walk quickly, please."

Asher felt a sinking in his stomach as she led them along increasingly filthy streets, lined with increasingly shabby cottages, until she paused before one in desperate need of fresh whitewash and a window cleaning.

"This is it." Kate stepped forward to pound on the door, which opened on its own. "It's not bolted," she said, pushing the door open wide. "Tec?"

No answer came from within.

"Who is this Tec person again?" Asher asked warily.

"He's my friend," Kate said. "You know—the one who managed the little detectives."

"Ah yes, the young spies and thieves." He watched Elsie walk about the room, not touching anything. He didn't blame her. The furniture and the quilts piled in the corner were tattered and grimy. He chuckled at the incongruous sight of an ornate vase sitting high on a shelf. The blue-and-white pattern was familiar. "Did your little detectives steal that as well?" he asked, pointing to it. "If I didn't know better, I'd say it's Wedgwood."

Kate shook her head. "One of the boys found it in a rubbish bin, with a crack and chip on one side. Tec thought it so grand that he built that shelf to show off its good side." She lifted her chin. "And I wouldn't call the boys thieves. If one has thrown papers or fancy vases into the rubbish bin, is it really thievery when another fishes them out?"

"Your Billy was one of these little . . . detectives?"

"He was the best," said Kate. She reached for a leather bundle on the table. "Tec shouldn't have left this sitting out."

"What is it?" Asher asked.

"His tools."

"What sort of tools?"

Kate ran her fingers along the scarred leather. "They're for picking locks," she said quietly. "Anyone could come in and pinch them when they're left out like this. It's not like Tec to be so careless."

Asher studied her as she untied the bundle and inspected the thin implements. She seemed to have forgotten about Elsie in her concern for this Tec fellow. How could she care so much about a boy who lived in filth and ran such a seedy enterprise?

In that moment her eyes lifted to meet his. She rolled the bundle and retied it, glaring back at him. "What?"

"What?"

She lifted an eyebrow and shoved the bundle back into the table's small drawer. When she turned to Elsie, her eyes widened. "That's exactly where Billy used to sit, Elsie. Last night I could see him there so plainly, almost as though *I* were having a vision." Her mouth dropped open. "Elsie?"

Asher's eyes followed Kate's in time to see Elsie rest her fingers on a chair by the potbellied stove. His heart lurched as she began to convulse.

☒ ☒ ☒ ☒ ☒

Elsie clenched her teeth to keep from crying out when she felt the tug of darkness and cold. She was falling into that darkness—the dark between—but knowing what was happening didn't make it any less unsettling. Eyes shut, she prayed for the spinning in her head and stomach to stop.

When the pulling sensation finally ceased, she slowly opened her eyes. She stood next to a chair, upon which sat a boy wearing a smart jacket and full-length trousers. He stared at the stove. She could see nothing but the boy in the chair and the stove—the rest was darkness. The boy did not raise his face to her, nor did he speak.

What should she do? In the past, the spirit had spoken first. She'd never initiated the encounter. "Hello?" she asked tentatively, bracing herself.

The boy looked up. He was hollow-eyed and pale as alabaster, but nothing like the wraith that had once been her grandmother. There was no menace to him. He just looked like an underfed boy who happened to be staring at her in confusion.

"Who are you?" he asked. "Do I know you?"

"I'm Elsie."

He looked past her. "Where is everyone?"

"Who are you looking for?"

He frowned. "Why, Tec, of course. And the other lads. They're usually here."

The poor creature didn't yet know. She willed herself to smile. "I'm sure they'll be here soon. What happened to you, Billy?"

He blinked. "How do you know my name?"

"Kate told me all about you." She took a breath and gentled her tone. "Please tell me what happened."

"You friends with Katie? Well, that's all right, then."

"Somebody hurt you, didn't they, Billy?"

"Oh, that." He rubbed a bruise on his jaw absently. "He caught me in the study pilfering his letters from that Stanton fellow. I waited until the wee hours, but he weren't asleep like I thought."

"What's his name, Billy?"

He frowned. "Why do you want to know that?"

She sensed him pulling away. "Never mind. Did he beat you?"

"Nah, just smacked my face. Said he'd turn me in to the police unless I did him a favor."

"What sort of favor?"

The boy sighed. "He wanted information."

Elsie struggled to keep her voice even. "How curious. What information did he seek?"

Billy stared into the distance, shaking his head. "Curious ain't the half of it. He wanted a tramp from Castle End—a useless drunk—for an experiment that would improve him. All I had to do was give a name and tell him where to find the old waster."

"An experiment that would improve a tramp? What does that mean?"

"I had an idea." He glanced at her. "I found him a proper tramp all right. That's easy enough in Castle End. But I'd read through the gentleman's papers, you see. It put a scheme to my mind, so I stole a few pages—you know, the ones that seemed important. I hid those papers in a special place and searched out the gentleman after the séance."

"How clever. What did he say?" she prompted.

"Thought he'd be angry, but he just asked me to sit and offered me a drink, all friendly-like." He frowned, his hand moving to his chest.

"What is it? What did he do?"

"I remember feeling sleepy . . . and then, when I started to wake up, I was in a different place. There was a pain in my heart, like I'd been stabbed."

"The gentleman stabbed you? Who was it?"

He tilted his head. "You sure ask a lot of questions. Are you thinking to get in on my scheme?"

"Not at all. It's just . . . I'm only . . ." She struggled for a proper response. "Kate is worried about you, Billy. If she could be here, asking these questions herself, she would. I need to know what to tell her."

After a moment he nodded. "All I meant was that it *felt* like I'd been stabbed, but there was no blood." His brow wrinkled. "It were funny what happened then. I saw myself. I saw the man standing over me, and my own body shaking and jerking. It were . . . *horrible*." He shook his head sadly. "I need to find those papers, and then I must find Tec. Can't sit here talking to you."

"No, wait—tell me the name of this man!"

But already she was falling again into darkness.

When the dizziness finally eased and she opened her eyes, Kate's blurry face crowded her vision. Elsie blinked and squirmed. "You needn't get so close—it's hard to breathe."

"How is she?" Asher's voice came from behind her.

Kate backed away. "Are you awake now? Can you sit up?"

"I think so." Elsie grasped the hands Kate offered, allowing the girl to pull her upright. Her head was clear, but a thudding ache threatened to clamp around her temples.

"We shouldn't stay here much longer," said Asher, stepping into view.

Kate's grip on her hands tightened. "What did you see, Elsie?"

"I saw Billy."

"Did he speak to you?"

Elsie stared at her. "I talked to him for a long time. Did you . . . I mean, could you hear any of it? Did you hear *me*, at least?"

Kate shook her head. "You were in a trance. Your mouth didn't even move."

"How odd. I've always wondered, ever since the spell my mother witnessed." Elsie tried to smile. "Billy said he was looking for Tec. He asked me where everyone was."

Kate leaned closer. "Did you ask him how he died? It was murder, wasn't it?"

Elsie closed her eyes again, thinking back through their strange exchange. "He said he was caught in the act of stealing letters from a gentleman's study. The man told him he'd turn him in to the police if he didn't do him a favor." She looked at Kate. "He wanted Billy to find him a tramp."

Kate's eyes widened. "A what?"

Elsie repeated the details Billy had given. "The gentleman wanted a drunkard for an experiment that would *improve* him."

"An experiment to improve a drunkard?"

"That's what I gathered," said Elsie.

"Who was this gentleman?" Kate asked.

Elsie shook her head. "Billy never said. I tried to get the name, but he slipped away. He seemed distracted—said he needed to find Tec."

Kate frowned. "Perhaps he doesn't know he's dead?"

Elsie's head began to throb in earnest. She reached for her bag and fumbled inside for the bottle. When she found it she pulled out the stopper and raised it to her lips.

"Oh, Elsie—not too much or we'll never get you home."

Elsie nodded at Kate and took one swallow. Then she closed her eyes and breathed deeply until the nausea eased and the thudding pain softened to a dull tapping.

"Last time you felt *better* after your seizure," said Asher softly.

She'd almost forgotten he was there. "Something's different," she said. "I provoked this vision, and it's by far the longest I've had. Maybe I stayed too long? I'm not certain."

Kate touched her arm lightly. "Do you think you can stand now? Can you walk?"

"I certainly don't wish to stay *here* any longer."

They each came to her side, placing their hands under her elbows and slowly raising her to her feet. She stood still, taking more deep breaths to steady herself, and nodded.

"Just a short walk back to Summerfield and you can rest," murmured Asher, his expression gentle.

Elsie smiled, for they were trying their best to be kind. Even Asher was curbing his usual skepticism, or at least being polite enough to keep it to himself for the moment. The Chlorodyne had soothed her aches and tremors, but it hadn't sorted the tangle of her nerves. How much of the dose would it take to wash away the memory of Billy's pitiful face as he searched the darkness for Tec?

chapter 20

Asher couldn't help admiring Elsie's determination as they made their way along Queen's Road. She had a great deal more pluck than he'd thought. But he still puzzled over her episode in Castle End. He didn't doubt the reality of her seizures. Never had. It was her interpretation of the visions that provoked his skepticism. The details were always a little too vague. Hints rather than facts. It seemed that a spirit could never give a direct answer to a simple question.

But why would she fabricate this tale of a tramp and an improving experiment?

"Oh," Elsie breathed, her chin lifting. "It's him."

He followed her gaze to find Philip Marshall and Simon Wakeham walking their way. The very sight of Wakeham made his heart plunge.

Dr. Marshall's eyes widened when he recognized them, and he quickly removed his hat. "Good morning, ladies." He nodded at Asher. "Mr. Beale."

"Mr. Wakeham and Dr. Marshall, how good to see you," Elsie said softly. "You've not yet made the acquaintance of our friend." She cleared her throat and turned to Kate. "Miss Poole, allow me to introduce Dr. Philip Marshall, a Fellow at Trinity College, and Mr. Simon Wakeham, a recent Trinity graduate . . . and a member of the Metaphysical Society."

Kate's cheeks flushed a deep red. She opened her mouth to speak but seemed to choke on the words. Asher looked from her to Simon Wakeham, who frowned down at her.

"Ah," said Wakeham, his features relaxing. "I think I've already met your friend. You were the one at Martineau's, weren't you? The spirit apparition?"

Kate hung her head. "Yes."

"Strange sort of work for a young girl," Dr. Marshall said, studying Kate with a raised eyebrow.

"I was only trying to make a living after my mum died."

"You need not explain." Wakeham smiled. "We wouldn't hold *you* accountable for Martineau's deceptions. I suppose softhearted Thompson has taken you in? No doubt he felt guilty for disrupting your livelihood."

Kate straightened up. "Actually, sir, I demanded he make things right for me."

"Did you? I admire your gumption." Wakeham turned to Elsie. "Miss Atherton, what brings you to this part of town on a Sunday morning?"

Asher wondered if he'd suddenly turned invisible.

"We're returning from a service at Trinity," said Elsie, her voice now steady.

Dr. Marshall glanced behind him. "But we just came from there. We are now north of Trinity."

Elsie gulped audibly.

"What she means to say is that we stopped in for a few hymns," said Asher, "and then walked to—"

"We walked to Castle Mound," blurted Kate.

"Yes, we just came from Castle Mound," said Elsie. "You

see, I remember playing there when I was a little girl. I wanted to show them where the Norman castle used to be."

"Of course—it's by the Thompsons' old house, which is where we were walking just now." Wakeham smiled. "Did you enjoy your ramble? More entertaining than a chapel service?"

Elsie started to reply, but Asher cut her off. "It was fine. Unfortunately, Miss Atherton has taken ill, so we must return to Summerfield."

"I *am* improving," said Elsie, returning Wakeham's smile.

"Please, allow me to help." Without waiting for an answer, Wakeham extended his arm to Elsie.

Asher thought the man gave him a reproving look as he tucked Elsie's hand around his arm, and he didn't like it. "We don't wish to keep you from your business," he protested weakly.

"No trouble at all, I assure you," said Wakeham.

They formed an odd group as they walked together, Wakeham and Kate on either side of Elsie, and Asher bringing up the rear with Dr. Marshall. The trio ahead of him chatted pleasantly, but every time Elsie smiled at Simon Wakeham, Asher felt his heart pinch.

"Are you weary yet, Mr. Beale, of being cooped up in that stronghold of lady intellectuals?" Dr. Marshall grinned. "Even Mr. Thompson is a bit of an old hen. You must come to Trinity this week—there are gentlemen to whom I wish to introduce you."

"I should be most grateful," said Asher, keeping his eyes on Elsie. If she continued to look at Wakeham that way, he might go directly to Trinity with the good doctor that afternoon.

Wakeham turned. "Can you believe they've not been out on the Cam yet, Philip?"

"I've only been here a week," said Elsie. "And I wasn't allowed to go when I was a child."

Kate sighed. "I've lived here all my life but never boated on the river."

"We must rectify this alarming gap in your upbringing," said Wakeham. "Shall we all go rowing this week?"

"That's a fine plan for an idler like you, Simon," said Dr. Marshall, "but I have my rounds at Addenbrooke's."

"Do you see patients there?" asked Asher.

"Not exactly, but I do assist another doctor with a . . . unique . . . sort of therapy. I'd be pleased if you would come see our work—perhaps later this week?"

"Ah well, that leaves me to do all the rowing," said Wakeham. "Unless Mr. Beale would agree to take an oar rather than visit a musty old hospital?"

At first Wakeham's challenge seemed kindly meant, but then Asher wondered if the young man was baiting him. Trying to make a fool of him, no doubt. "I'm mightily tempted by Dr. Marshall's offer," he said.

Kate turned her dark eyes to him. "Oh, Asher, what could be nicer than a row on the river?"

Elsie kept her head down, saying nothing. Almost as though she did not care.

"We'll see," he said.

❂ ❂ ❂ ❂ ❂

Kate's knees had very nearly buckled when she recognized Simon Wakeham. Once she recovered, she'd fully expected that shock to boil into anger. In fact, she'd steeled herself for it. The heat had only flamed in her cheeks, however, not her blood.

She should resent him much more, considering how he'd yanked her from Martineau's chair and humiliated her that awful night of the séance. Wakeham was just as guilty as Mr. Thompson for getting her sacked, wasn't he? Yet she felt no overwhelming desire to hold him accountable. Billy's death made her shame seem a small thing.

And if she considered the matter from another angle, Wakeham's actions had set in motion something quite pleasant—several days of good meals and a comfortable bed, not to mention society with people her age who actually spent time outdoors in daylight.

Kate couldn't fail to note the way Elsie's face softened under Wakeham's gaze, how her cheeks dimpled when she smiled at him. Nor could she ignore the glower Asher directed at the handsome pair as they walked arm in arm—like that of a wolf who had failed to defend his territory.

In her mind, Elsie and Asher would each benefit from a swift kick in the rear. Something that would redirect their minds to the matter at hand, anyhow. They needed—well, *she* needed—to find out who killed Billy before the trail ran cold. She owed that to Billy, and she couldn't do it without them.

But rather than kicking, she joined them in waving farewell to Mr. Wakeham and Dr. Marshall at the college gate. Once the two gentlemen were out of hearing, she affected a casual tone. "I suggest we meet in the college garden before supper so we can discuss Elsie's vision in more detail."

Rather than answer, Elsie gazed dreamily into the distance, which only made Asher frown. Keeping a tight rein on her impatience, Kate stood still and waited. The seconds dragged by, but she refused to break the silence herself.

"Fine," Asher said at last. "If Miss Atherton feels up to the task."

Elsie blinked, as if waking out of a dream, and turned to him. "Quite up to it, Mr. Beale."

Kate managed a sober nod and turned away, waiting until

she was a safe distance before she allowed herself to chuckle at their nonsense.

❀ ❀ ❀ ❀ ❀

Later that afternoon, refreshed by luncheon and a nap, Kate borrowed an old quilt from Mrs. Thompson and, with Elsie's help, spread it upon an open patch of grass in the garden. Before long Asher joined them, settling on the grass a few feet away. He pulled a pencil and a battered notebook from his pocket.

"I think it's best to record all the details Elsie can remember."

Kate nodded, strangely cheered by this gesture. For the moment Asher seemed to be taking the spirit encounter seriously. "Elsie, why don't you tell us everything you recall? Don't worry about getting it in order—we can work that out when Asher's written it all down."

Elsie stared into the distance, her brow furrowed. "Billy said he'd been caught pilfering letters from a gentleman's study."

"Good," said Kate, glancing over to see Asher dutifully scratching in his notebook. "Did he say what sort of letters?"

"They were from someone named Stanton."

Kate turned to stare at Elsie. "What?"

"My goodness," Elsie gasped. "It didn't occur to me then, but Stanton was your father, wasn't he?"

"He was." Kate thought for a moment. "Billy was searching out clues for the séance. Martineau was pretending to contact my father, so the man who hurt Billy may also have known him. What else did Billy say?"

"The man told Billy he must provide him with information, or else he'd turn him in to the police. Like I told you before, Billy had to give him the name of a tramp—someone drunk and useless. The man wanted to use this person for an experiment that would improve him."

"What could that possibly mean?" Kate asked. "How do you improve an old drunk?"

Asher tapped his pencil against the notebook. "Clean him up, get him proper clothes, and teach him manners, I suppose. Somehow break his addiction to spirits. But why waste your time? And why would such a do-gooder wish to hurt a young boy?" He turned to Elsie. "All right. Then what?"

"He said it gave him an idea for a scheme—that he took some of the man's papers and hid them. Then he searched him out after the séance."

"He was trying to *blackmail* this man?" Asher looked up from the notebook. "No wonder he was in danger."

Kate flinched. It *was* the scheme that did him in—Billy had taken things too far.

"That narrows it down a bit, too," Asher continued, writing in the notebook again. "This man who hurt Billy knew Stanton *and* was at Saturday's séance."

Kate turned to Elsie. "Did Billy say the gentleman attended the séance?"

Elsie frowned. "I'm not certain, but I clearly remember him saying he met the man *after* the séance."

"Met him where?" Kate asked.

"He didn't say." Elsie paused, her eyes dropping to the ground.

"Still, we have a connection to Stanton and a connection to the séance," Asher said. "I think we should be considering members of the Metaphysical Society. Which Society members were at the séance?"

Kate numbered them on her fingers. "Mr. Thompson, Mr.

Eliot . . . and Simon Wakeham, of course." She dared not look at Elsie.

"So it very well could be Simon Wakeham." Asher's tone was a little too hopeful, to Kate's mind.

Elsie stiffened. "Simon Wakeham wouldn't hurt a child."

"You've only just met him, Elsie," said Asher. "For all you know he's the Ripper of Cambridge, preying on tramps and street urchins rather than prostitutes."

"Oh, Asher!"

"There's no need to be so provoking," Kate said quickly. "I for one don't see how Simon Wakeham could have letters from my father. The man died three years ago. Wakeham would have been a student then, wouldn't he?"

Asher's shoulders sank ever so slightly. "Maybe your father was a mentor of some sort. I don't know."

"What about Dr. Marshall?" asked Elsie.

Kate shook her head. "I don't remember him at the séance."

"*Mr. Eliot* was there," said Elsie. "What about him? He was the one you were running away from last night, wasn't he?"

Kate shuddered. "Yes. He was Martineau's patron."

"So you weren't actually ill," said Asher. "Has that Eliot fellow threatened you?"

Kate thought of his hands groping her during the spirit performances. Martineau knew there was something beastly about him—she *had* to. *Perhaps I* will *allow Mr. Eliot to discipline you,* she'd said that night with a knowing gleam in her eye.

Of course, it wasn't as though Kate had been sitting primly in a chair as he reached for her. She'd been prancing about in her underpinnings, just as Martineau bade her. Her cheeks burned at the thought. A wanton little spirit was asking to be groped, wasn't she?

"Kate?"

She blinked. "I thought if Eliot saw me yesterday evening, he would surely recognize me as the spirit apparition. And yes, he threatened me the night Mr. Thompson and Mr. Wakeham exposed Martineau. Said he'd take me to the police. I feared they might lock me up for defrauding innocent people."

"Not so innocent," said Asher. "Foolish is more like it. I can't imagine any of them stepping forth to press charges. They'd be too ashamed, or at least they ought to be." He looked down at his notes. "So we know three Society members who were at the séance—Thompson, Eliot, and Wakeham. One might argue Mrs. Martineau's primary goal was to impress Mr. Eliot and his friends with specific details, and those details could have been obtained from anyone who knew Stanton well. However, it must be someone who lives in Cambridge, correct? Unless Billy traveled outside the city for his sleuthing."

Kate shook her head. "The little detectives cast a wide net, but I'm certain their targets were all within walking distance. Martineau's funds *were* limited, after all." She sighed. "We've narrowed the suspects, but we still have no idea why a Society member would hurt Billy. And we still don't know *how* it happened. What else, Elsie?"

"Let me think. . . . He said the man treated him kindly. Gave him something to drink. And then Billy felt a pain in his chest, as though he'd been stabbed."

"There was no stab wound on his body," said Kate.

"He didn't say he'd been stabbed. Just that it *felt* as though he'd been."

"A drink followed by a pain in the chest," Asher said. "Do you think Billy's drink could have been poisoned?"

Kate winced. "A poison that makes you feel like you've been stabbed?"

"He felt the pain in his *heart*. And then he saw himself." Elsie frowned in concentration. "Billy saw the man standing over his own body, which was . . . how did he put it? Shaking and jerking."

"The Spiritualists are always going on about 'out-of-body' experiences," Asher said. "They seem fascinated by the idea of one seeing his or her own death."

"I'm just telling you what he told me," Elsie said flatly.

An uncomfortable pause followed. When Kate turned to glare at Asher, he surprised her by nodding thoughtfully.

"It *is* interesting to contemplate," he said. "A poison that stops the heart and makes one convulse. Perhaps I should spend some time in the library tomorrow identifying such a poison?"

Kate shrugged. "I don't see how it would help us find his killer."

"And I don't see how it could hurt. Anything else, Elsie?" Asher looked over his notes. "Something you couldn't remember before?"

"I've told you everything." Elsie frowned. "But I keep thinking of the old lab. This experiment Billy mentioned—what if it involved something more than merely cleaning up an old drunk? I can't think why a boy would be killed over that. If the experiment was something darker, something dangerous . . ." She looked away from Asher, staring into the distance. "Might it have taken place in a disused lab hidden among the trees of a small college? I can't shake this notion that something terrible happened at the old Summerfield laboratory." She lowered her voice. "And that my uncle might know something about it."

"But he said he couldn't find the key," said Kate.

"Perhaps he *won't* find the key—not for you, anyway." Asher scribbled another note on his paper.

Kate studied Elsie. The girl now stared at her hands,

clasping and unclasping them. "Part of me wonders if I should just tell Simon Wakeham what I've seen," Elsie finally said. "This is the very sort of thing he studies—perhaps with his help we could obtain more information?" Her expression brightened.

"I don't think that's a good idea," said Asher. "We can't discount him as a suspect, and therefore it's too dangerous for you to expose yourself in such a way."

Elsie sighed. "Really, Asher, I think you're exaggerating—"

"I just don't think we should trust Wakeham. Not yet, anyway." Asher closed his notebook. "I've written everything down. The question is what do we do next?"

"Perhaps we should return to Castle End and try once more," Kate said. "Elsie may get more details from Billy the second time."

Elsie wrapped her arms around her body. "I don't know. That place gives me the shivers."

"I think Elsie needs a day or two to rest. Perhaps we should revisit the matter tomorrow?" Asher stood. "Mrs. Thompson will expect us for dinner soon enough. See you then?"

Kate smiled. "Yes, of course."

They watched in silence as Asher walked back to the Gatehouse.

"I wish he wasn't so predisposed against Simon Wakeham," said Elsie, once he was out of hearing.

Kate glanced sidelong at her. "It's only natural, Elsie. You must have noticed that he's a bit keen on you."

"Asher, or Mr. Wakeham?"

Kate giggled. "Both, I'm sure."

Elsie lay back on the blanket. "What a muddle. We're hardly any closer to knowing who killed Billy. I'm sorry, Kate." She rubbed her eyes. "I *must* try again, but at the moment the notion overwhelms me."

Kate settled next to her and stared at the cloudy sky. "Mrs. Martineau acted like the spirit world gave her power, but we know she was a fake. What's it really like, Elsie?"

Elsie was quiet for a moment. "I lose control," she finally said. "My body is pulled into a sickening, spiraling fall. It terrifies me. Getting sucked into that dark place—not knowing if I'll be trapped there forever."

"But if you could control it, think of the fortune you might make," Kate said gently.

"I don't *want* to be a medium—you wouldn't wish such a life for me, would you?"

Kate met her gaze. "It might give you independence."

"A precarious sort of independence, I think. The last thing I'd want is to perform for crowds." Elsie looked away. "I just want to better understand it all. Today I learned that, to an outsider, I look to be in a trance. Even if I'm speaking to a spirit in the dark between, you don't hear it, correct?"

Kate nodded. "Your eyes were open, but otherwise you didn't move."

"Well, what if I were in danger? What if a spirit could somehow *harm* me in the dark between? You wouldn't know. There would be no way for you to rescue me."

"All the more reason for you to learn how to control the visions. Isn't that better than taking more and more of the drug to keep them away? That seems far too dangerous."

"I'm sure you're right." Elsie's brow furrowed. "Last night, when Simon Wakeham took my hand, I could almost feel a spell coming on. But I concentrated, breathing deeply to calm myself, and somehow held it off. It would be a relief not to take the dose every day. And yet I feel so ill when I've gone too long without it."

"You could try to wean yourself slowly."

"I know. I want to be strong enough to do that." She took Kate's hand. "You will come rowing with us, won't you?"

"I have work in the library, and I'm afraid your aunt will sack me if I ask for more time away."

"Oh, she'll be pleased you've agreed to accompany us. You know she thinks of you as more than a servant. You're a guest, Kate."

Kate shrugged, secretly pleased by these words.

"I won't be able to go if you don't come, too," added Elsie.

So she was to be the *chaperone*? How tiresome. It was on Kate's lips to decline, to protest that Mrs. Thompson would prefer she keep to her employment, but Elsie's expression was desperate. The girl deserved a pleasant afternoon after the morning's episode. "Fine. You arrange it with Mrs. Thompson and I'll come along. As I said before, in all these years in Cambridge, I've never boated the Cam." Kate took a deep breath. "But you must do something for me in return."

"Absolutely. What can I do?"

"Go with me now to the old laboratory."

"Why?"

"I want to see if we can get in without the key. I know you feel as I do—something happened to Billy in that building."

Elsie nodded slowly. "There may be an unlocked window."

"You'd be surprised by how small a space I can fit through," Kate said with a grin.

Chapter 21

Elsie ran her hand along the old lab's rough brick, trying to sense what had happened inside. How did one access those dark places consciously? She watched her hand skidding along the brick and imagined her mind having similar fingers, reaching out for spirit thoughts, emotions . . . pain. When she closed her eyes she thought something might be there, just out of her reach. A heaviness hung in the air, cold and dark, but it eluded the fingers of her mind.

The sound of Kate's voice dragged her even farther from it.

"The door is still locked, and I can't see. The curtains are drawn."

Elsie blinked, focusing on Kate. "You've checked every window?"

"Yes, but this one tempts me." Kate scrutinized the bottom half of a tall window that extended lower than the others. "Do you see that pane up there by the latch? It's cracked. If I could push that piece through, we might be able to reach inside to unlatch the window." Kate looked about her, then picked up a slim branch that lay near the building.

"I don't know if that's a good idea," said Elsie, but Kate had already poked the small section of pane. Elsie heard the tinkle of glass shattering inside the building.

"Easy enough," said Kate, dropping the branch and wiping her hands on her skirt. "The gardener will think it fell out on its own, if he even sees it. But I can't reach the latch without your help."

"What can I do?"

"Make a step with your hands." Kate bent over and laced her fingers together. "See?"

Elsie knew she could have refused and ended the matter; the girl could not pull herself up to the windowsill. But the vision of Billy's pale face, his pathetic confusion, still haunted her. If something terrible had happened in this building, they might be very close to learning what it was.

She leaned over and made the step. Kate placed her small foot on it and grasped Elsie's shoulder. "Now lift me a few inches," she said. With a groan Elsie hoisted her up, bracing Kate's legs as the girl slipped her thin arm through the hole and reached for the inner latch.

"Young lady, just *what* do you think you are doing?"

Elsie turned to find her uncle standing several feet away, mouth clenched and nostrils flaring. She heard Kate curse softly as she jerked her arm out of the window.

"Come down from there at once!"

"Uncle!" Elsie cried, her knees wobbling. "We were . . . we were just—"

Kate came tumbling down, sending them both to the ground with a thud.

Kate recovered quickly, rising from the overgrown grass to brush leaves from her skirt. "We noticed one of the panes had fallen out, Mr. Thompson," she said, her breath coming fast.

"I was just going to open the window to see if it could be retrieved, but it seems the glass has shattered."

Elsie flinched when Uncle Oliver thumped the ground with his cane. "And now you've no doubt cut your hand in your foolishness. Stand up, Elsie. Both of you come here and let me see if you've hurt yourselves."

"I'm fine, Uncle," Elsie said, awkwardly rising to stand next to Kate. "We were only curious—"

"You had no right to be fooling with those windows. I told you the building is locked and only the gardener has the key. And we keep this *laboratory* locked because there are delicate instruments and specimens in there, flammable chemicals even. Mrs. Thompson doesn't want anything broken, nor does she want anyone messing about and getting hurt." He glowered at each of them in turn. After a moment his face softened. "Am I understood?"

"Yes, Uncle," Elsie said.

"Now come here, Kate, and let me look at your hand."

"It's only a splinter, Mr. Thompson."

He held her hand to his face, lifting his spectacles to peer at it. Then he shook his head. "I can barely see it. Take her to the kitchen, Elsie—Cook should be able to retrieve it. It'll serve you right if it hurts." He released her hand to adjust his spectacles. "After that, I trust you two will find something better to do with your Sunday afternoon than haunt this place."

"Yes, Uncle."

Elsie avoided Kate's gaze as they walked in silence toward the kitchen. She already knew what she would find written in the girl's expression.

Suspicion.

❀ ❀ ❀ ❀ ❀

Asher watched Elsie and Kate out of the corner of his eye the next morning. They sat next to each other at the breakfast table, speaking in low voices. This new intimacy fascinated him, for each of them seemed improved by it. Elsie was more alert and outgoing, while Kate's rough edges had smoothed considerably. Kate was, in fact, looking more human each day.

Just then, Kate turned to look at him. To find him *staring* at her. She grinned before he could turn away.

He quickly focused his attention upon his toast.

Halfway through breakfast, Millie walked in with the morning post for Mrs. Thompson. The girl pointed at the envelope that lay on top. "That one was delivered by hand, ma'am," she said, glancing at Elsie before bobbing a curtsy. Asher thought she might be stifling a giggle.

Mrs. Thompson scanned the envelopes. "Ah, and here's another telegram for you, Asher."

As soon as she handed the thin envelope to him, he stuffed it in his pocket. He might have known Kate wouldn't let that pass without comment.

"Who's it from, Asher?"

"My father," he mumbled. "I'll read it later." He turned from her inquisitive gaze to study Mrs. Thompson as she silently read another note—the very one Millie had singled out.

"My, my," the woman breathed, pushing the note across the table to her husband. "Young Simon Wakeham wishes to invite us on a rowing expedition tomorrow. What do you think of that, Oliver?"

Mr. Thompson spoke from behind his paper. "Too damp for me, I'm afraid. And I've too much work, anyway. Young people seem to have more time for such frivolities."

Mrs. Thompson's smile faded. "You're right, of course. My plate is quite full this entire week, and we have much to do in preparation for the next Society meeting." She glanced at Elsie. "But that doesn't mean the three of you can't enjoy a row on the Cam. Kate, I will inform Miss Barrett that you won't be available that afternoon."

Asher couldn't ignore the triumphant look Elsie gave Kate, and in that moment he hated Simon Wakeham more than his own father. Why was Wakeham the one to make Elsie so giddy? It was Asher who'd followed her to London to make sure she was safe. And when Wakeham departed, Asher had escorted her home and kept her secret from the Thompsons. The only thing Wakeham had done was to be in the wrong place at the wrong time. He was no hero—just a man who happened to bump into Elsie and send her into a seizure.

Why, it was the complete *opposite* of a romantic encounter!

"You seem so gloomy today." Kate's voice roused him from his thoughts. "You will come with us, won't you?"

Asher glanced at Elsie. The sight of her sipping tea and staring dreamily into the distance decided the matter.

"Actually," he said, "I have a mind to accept Dr. Marshall's invitation to visit Trinity."

"Oh, I think you should," said Mr. Thompson, smiling. "Nothing better than an insider's view of the college. No doubt he'll take you on a tour of Addenbrooke's Hospital, too. Marshall lectures on some peculiar aspect of medical research. Can't remember what exactly—electrotherapy or some such."

Asher cast another covert glance at Elsie. She'd not even heard Mr. Thompson, for she still stared like a besotted fool.

"It will be a pleasure to see Dr. Marshall again," he said finally. "In fact, I think I might stay at Trinity for several days."

chapter 22

"I do hope the rain holds off, don't you, Mr. Wakeham?" Elsie twitched her parasol as though to beckon the sun from behind the thickening clouds.

"Indeed." He smiled politely before returning his gaze to the water.

She took in more of the view before trying again. "That chapel is very striking. It would make a lovely photograph, particularly from this angle. Is that King's College?"

This time he only nodded before once again fixing his attention on the oars.

Elsie sighed.

Nearly all the men she had ever encountered felt it their right to stare at her. Some stared openly, while others waited until they thought she wouldn't notice. She'd never sought such attention, nor was she always pleased by it, but she'd grown accustomed nonetheless.

On this morning when she actually would have welcomed it, Simon Wakeham did not stare. In fact, he barely looked her way. He politely met her gaze when she spoke but otherwise was content to look out onto the water as he pulled the oars.

Their conversation continued to lag in the shallows. Kate was no help, for she merely stared into the distance as Elsie and Mr. Wakeham traded bland observations about the scenery. As they glided past Clare College, Mr. Wakeham remarked on the architecture and shared an amusing story of rivalry from his days as a Trinity man. Elsie enjoyed watching his face as he talked, but she wished he would meet her gaze for more than a fleeting moment.

It was then that Kate broke her silence.

"Mr. Wakeham, how old are you?"

"Kate!" Elsie nearly dropped her parasol at the impertinent question. But when she chanced a look at Simon—for she decided now to call him by his Christian name in the privacy of her thoughts—his eyes were merry.

"Why do you wish to know?" he countered.

"I didn't mean to offend," Kate said. "It's just that you seem young to be a member of the Metaphysical Society. Those Society men are all so old."

"I suppose they are," he said, grinning. "But since you ask, Miss Poole, I am twenty-one. I started a little early at Trinity, and perhaps I worked a bit harder than some of my peers." His face grew serious. "I don't say that to boast, mind you. It's just . . . studying was all I had. I cared little about society or sport. I simply couldn't afford to care—they each required more money than I was able to part with."

Kate nodded thoughtfully, and Elsie knew she was calculating Simon's age when her father died. No older than eighteen, she thought. Was it possible for someone so young to be corresponding with a prominent, well-respected gentleman? According to Kate, Frederic Stanton was a man born to wealth who dabbled in many things other than metaphysical research. Why would he bother writing letters to a young student at Trinity College?

"This is my favorite spot for picnics," said Simon, rousing her out of such thoughts.

He moored the boat by a small brick arch and stone staircase on the east side of the river. Keeping one leg inside the boat, he extended his hand to Elsie. It wasn't an elegant disembarkation, but his hand was warm and steady as he pulled her to higher ground. Once she and Kate had climbed the steep bank, they positioned their blanket to enjoy a view of Trinity College and unpacked the picnic basket.

The day had dawned bright with only a few puffy clouds dotting the skies, but now those clouds had gathered into solid grey clumps, and the breeze blew chilly from the river. Elsie did not mind the drop in temperature or the threat of rain, for it meant they were alone in their picnicking. She and Kate laughed with abandon as Simon continued to share anecdotes from his days as a student—more than once poking gentle fun at her uncle and his tendency to stutter, or that odd habit of chewing his long beard when preoccupied. Elsie knew Simon was fond of the man, so she never doubted his teasing was meant affectionately.

When the conversation flagged once again, Elsie reached for her bag and retrieved her camera.

Simon's eyes widened. "You trusted my rowing skills enough to risk your camera?"

"I can hardly bear to be parted from it," she replied, opening the box and clicking the lens into place.

"I'm afraid it's going to rain any minute," said Kate, peering at the sky.

"Then get to your feet and stand so that the college is behind you." She turned to Simon. "What is that building, Mr. Wakeham?"

"New Court," he said. "Built less than a hundred years ago. My cousin Marshall has rooms there."

"It's very grand. Kate, you must pretend you are a princess escaping the tower. Mr. Wakeham, help me pose her."

They laughed so much as they directed the placement of Kate's arms, hands, and head that it took quite a while to arrange an appropriate pose. Afterward Simon consented to be photographed beside the river, and he smiled handsomely when coaxed by Kate. Before they could arrange another pose, it began to drizzle.

Elsie packed her camera away as Simon and Kate pulled the basket and blanket under the canopy of an enormous willow tree. There they settled, listening in silence to the gentle patter of rain. Simon was half sitting and half lying, propped on an elbow. Elsie positioned herself so that she could covertly study the back of his head, his pale neck and wide shoulders. After a moment she leaned against the tree, thinking she'd not felt such contentment in years.

She closed her eyes and imagined walking alone with Simon through the meadow, their arms entwined. She rested her head against the mossy bark, smiling as she envisioned him searching her face, the cool grey of his eyes warming with passion. Yawning contentedly, she settled further into the fantasy.

"Someone is watching us," said Kate.

Elsie opened her eyes to see the girl scrambling to her feet.

Simon jerked upright. "What? Who?"

Elsie leaned forward, peering into the distance, but Simon blocked her view.

"Oh!" Kate cried. "He said he would find me." She glanced back, her expression apologetic. "Please excuse me—I won't be gone long." And with that she was off into the rain, holding the parasol over her head. Her hat lay on the picnic blanket.

"Kate," Elsie cried, "that parasol is not meant for *rain*!"

But Kate was already out of hearing.

"It will be in soggy tatters when she gets back," said Elsie, brushing the grass from her skirt. "I wonder who that was."

"I've no idea," Simon replied, without turning. "Should I go after her?"

"I'm sure she'll be fine. She's very good at taking care of herself."

They sat in silence for a moment. Then he swung around and began tidying the abandoned picnic items.

"Oh, please don't bother with that yet," Elsie said quickly, pushing the items aside and inching toward him. "Let's sit awhile longer. This is such a beautiful place, and I envy you for spending so much time here. Did you say you read classics at Trinity?"

He nodded.

"May I ask, then, what led you to your interest in the metaphysical? Has this always been a passion of yours?"

He smiled. "Would you believe, Miss Atherton, that before coming to Cambridge I fully intended to find my vocation within the church? My father was a vicar, after all."

"He was?"

"Both he and my mother were devout Christians."

"So what changed your mind? Did you lose your faith?"

"Not in a higher power. Just . . . in the church. I couldn't find the answers I sought there. And yet I still yearned for the serenity I'd once found in sermons and hymns."

"And you found it in your research?"

He laughed. "There are many so-called metaphysical researchers, and their studies vary greatly. Some of them seem to make a religion out of it, despite the fact that much of the research has led to disappointment. I'd say most Society members are intrigued by the soul and its afterlife, but for my part I would rather study the matter scientifically than sit through sermons or séances." He paused, his expression hardening. "The

Society members are united, however, in their opposition to the Materialists—those who believe there is no soul, no existence after death. Those who reject metaphysical theories out of hand. They claim to have science on their side but in doing so offer even less comfort."

Elsie knew if she examined her own religious beliefs, she would have little to offer him in the way of comfort. Although she was fond of their handsome village church by the river, she went to services out of duty rather than spiritual zeal. The sermons made her sleepy, but the hymns were beautiful. Sometimes, when the choir was singing, she felt her spirit reaching out to something higher. But overall, religion merely seemed part of the routine of country life.

"I think I know what you mean," she finally said.

"I suppose what drives me to study metaphysical phenomena," Simon continued, "is this certainty I have—or perhaps, if I'm honest with myself, it's really a profound longing—that the life of the mind does not end with death. Corporeal life is over—I understand that." He ran a hand through his hair. "But the idea that I could be completely extinguished, that no part of me would continue to exist and grow . . . well, it's intolerable."

She stared at him. She couldn't help herself.

At that moment she longed to tell him everything. *I have seen the other side. Existence does continue.* But she had only seen the spirit continuing in pain and confusion—there was nothing comforting about that. So she held her tongue, instead reaching out to place her hand on his.

He looked into her eyes for a brief, delicious moment before turning away. "I find it hard to meet your gaze sometimes," he murmured.

She pulled her hand back, inwardly cursing her own boldness. "But why?"

"There's a peculiar light in your eyes. As if you know something about me—something I may not even know about myself." He returned his gaze to her. "It's disconcerting."

She thought of the lady in the dark between. She'd loved him so desperately she could not stay away, not even in death. Did he long to speak with her? Would he even wish to see how desperate she was?

"I think it may be that I can read an old grief in your face," Elsie said.

His eyes widened. "Really?"

"At supper you said you'd lost your father and a close friend. I can see that their deaths still haunt you." She smiled. "I certainly didn't mean to be disconcerting."

He shook his head. "I am behaving like an idiot." He moved closer and took her hand, staring at it for a moment. When he looked up his expression was blandly cheerful. "I invited you to go rowing, but instead of offering you lively conversation I've maundered on about religion and death. And this tree won't protect us from the rain much longer. Can you forgive me?"

Even though he held her hand, she could feel him pulling away. Her mention of grief and loss had made him skittish, as though she'd touched upon something he wished to hold to himself. Of course, this only made her long to delve further into those very secrets he protected.

She wove her fingers through his. "I don't care about the rain, Mr. Wakeham, and I don't desire lively conversation. All I want is for people to talk to me about real things, things that matter, even if they are painful." She sighed. "I wish you weren't leaving Cambridge so soon, for I should like to know you better."

He met her gaze directly, and though his face seemed

haunted, his eyes were wide with surprise . . . and something like yearning.

The rain began to fall with more force, dripping down through the leaves. Simon blinked as a drop splashed his temple. With her free hand Elsie smoothed a lock of hair that had tumbled over his brow and then allowed her fingers to trail down his cheek, following the path of the raindrop. Her heart was pounding, but she no longer felt shame at her boldness. This was innocent. She only meant to comfort him, to put him at ease and encourage his trust in her.

But she also wanted very much to kiss him.

Her fingers trailed by his mouth, and then she let her hand drop to her lap.

He swallowed, his grip tightening on her other hand.

She leaned forward ever so slightly.

And then, finally, his lips were on hers, slightly open and soft as a whisper. She closed her eyes and sank into him. There was nothing frenzied about it—he did not clasp her by the back of the head and crush her mouth with his own . . . as the artist had done. Simon's kiss was so light, like a tentative caress, that she longed to be the aggressor. She pressed against him, imagining herself pushing him to the ground.

A shudder went through her body, but it wasn't a tremble of desire. Rather, it was the sinking feeling that always prefaced a convulsion. She roughly pushed away from Simon, closing her eyes and gasping for air.

"No, no, no," she moaned, willing her body to stop shaking.

"My God, what did I do?"

She lifted her hand to silence him. "Just . . . allow me a moment. Please." She took several deep breaths, willing her pulse to slow. *This will not happen. I do not want this to happen. I control this.*

And somehow . . . as it had the night of the dinner party, her body listened. Only this time the fit had come upon her much more suddenly and powerfully. It had taken all the strength she could muster to push it back. And the only thing that could explain such an onslaught was that *she* was here with him. Simon's lost love.

She opened her eyes.

Simon Wakeham was pale. "I beg your forgiveness. I never intended that to happen."

"You were here with *her*," she whispered.

His eyebrows shot up. "What?"

"I'm sorry," she said, shaking her head. "It was a fleeting thought. The friend you mentioned—it occurred to me that you might have brought her here once. Perhaps for a picnic like this one?"

He narrowed his eyes. "Why would *that* suddenly occur to you?"

"Her memory haunts you. It's . . . holding you back somehow."

"Miss Atherton, when we first met at the British, you spoke words to me. They almost sounded like a message from another person—a person I once knew."

Panic fluttered in her chest. "I hardly remember that day. My condition often leads to gaps in memory." She was stumbling horribly, no doubt sounding like a fool. Asher needn't have worried she would confess everything to Simon, for she was terrified of the havoc her truth might wreak. She was so close to having him.

"What caused your condition, Elsie?" His eyes were gentle, encouraging.

"I was struck by lightning." The words rushed from her

mouth like a sigh she could no longer contain. "I really should be dead."

He stared at her for a long and uncomfortable moment, his eyes steely. She forced herself to return his gaze steadily.

"You are the most unusual person I've ever met," he finally said, his mouth softening into a smile. Then he leaned closer and kissed her again.

Chapter 23

It was Tec who stood in the rain. Kate broke into a run, eager to throw her arms around him. She had so many questions, and so much to tell him.

But when she came within ten paces of him, he turned and stalked away.

"Tec!"

She lowered the parasol and again screamed his name into the rain, but he didn't even glance back.

Heart sinking into her gut, she followed him across the grass and through the gate to Garret Hostel Lane. The rain fell more heavily now—perhaps he meant to find shelter so they could have a proper chat without being soaked. Instead he turned onto Trinity Lane without pausing. She called out again, but he either didn't hear her or was ignoring her. When she stepped up her pace, he did the same. She would have broken into a run but her skirt, heavy with rain, threatened to trip her. The material of Elsie's parasol was so waterlogged that it was tearing from the frame, offering little protection from the drops that splashed her face. She folded it up, praying Elsie wouldn't be too angry when she saw it.

Tec led her on a bewildering chase through the market without once looking back. Each time she thought she'd closed the gap between them, he made an unexpected turn or increased his pace so that she once again found herself far behind. Why had he stood there by the river if he'd not meant to speak to her? And why run away when she called out to him?

On Sidney Street she stumbled on a rock and nearly fell just as a pony cart clattered past, coming within inches of running her over. She dropped the parasol and wrapped her arms around her body, shuddering at the thought of the pony's iron-shod hooves. When she'd caught her breath, she retrieved the parasol and dashed into the alley, giving wide berth to a speeding bicycle . . . and ran headlong into a man.

He grunted at the impact, and she reeled back, apologizing. She tried to edge her way around him, but he grabbed her arm.

"And just where are you going in such a hurry?"

The voice was chillingly familiar.

Lifting her head slowly, she peered at the face.

Robert Eliot.

"You'll cause an accident if you carry on like that."

Kate tried to duck her head as he scrutinized her, but he roughly pulled her chin up.

"There's something familiar about you," he said. "Dark eyes. Pointy chin." One hand gripped her shoulder, but the other ran down her free arm and clenched her wrist like a vise. "It's as though I've seen you before, only you were different."

Kate looked around, hoping for a stranger to see her plight and take pity. But no one bothered to glance toward the muddy alley. The knife was heavy in her pocket, but his iron grip kept her right hand pinned.

He laughed softly. "I know it now. You were the spirit apparition at Martineau's séance." Eliot turned her around, crushing her backside to his body so she could not see him. He twisted her wrist until she squeaked. "You were good, too," he said. "Made fools of us all, didn't you? Working your schemes on the streets now, eh? I should take you to the police this instant."

"Let go or I'll hurt you," Kate growled between clenched teeth, wriggling in his grasp.

He clutched both her wrists in one hand and searched her body with the other. She started to scream, hoarsely, but he only pulled her tighter and moved his free hand to cover her mouth. Better there than in her pockets . . . or under her skirt. She squirmed with all her strength, trying to break his hold on her wrists.

"Strong for such a skinny thing. Must I tie you up?"

He let go of her hands to pull something from his own pocket. Heart thumping in her chest, she fumbled for the knife. As she slipped the blade free of its sheath, he pulled a silk scarf toward her wrists.

Before he could restrain her again, she stabbed at his thigh.

He cried out in pain, finally easing his grip, and she shoved him hard enough to throw him off balance. As he sagged against the wall, whimpering, she leapt toward the street and slogged as fast as she could through the mud and muck toward Trinity Lane, not daring to slow down until she'd reached Garret Hostel Lane.

She leaned against the cold stone of Trinity College and gasped for breath.

What had she done?

Eliot would have the police after her now. She wasn't merely a fraud anymore. Causing bodily harm with a knife would land her in the clink for certain. Eliot didn't know her name, or where she lived, but he could learn it from anyone who used to work for Martineau. It was only a matter of time. She would have to leave Summerfield, never to see the Thompsons or Elsie and Asher again. Seeing Tec there by the river had made her think he'd come for her, that they would leave Cambridge together. And she would have followed him anywhere. But he'd *run* from her. She simply couldn't make sense of it.

She must somehow find a way to leave Cambridge on her own.

For now, however, the rain was easing up, and there was nothing to do but go back to Elsie and Simon Wakeham.

Her first sight of them did nothing to ease her desperation. The two faced each other on the picnic blanket, damp from the rain and sitting too close for casual conversation. Something had happened—they stared at each other without speaking, their expressions grave. As she drew closer, Elsie turned. For a moment the ghost of a frown played at her mouth, stopping Kate in her tracks. Then Elsie seemed to draw herself up, leaning away from Simon Wakeham. She raised her eyebrows in surprise.

"Kate, you're absolutely soaked! Why did you run off like that?"

"I saw a friend. I meant to catch up to him, but the rain . . . it was pouring and I—"

Elsie made shushing noises. "Silly goose. Here—let me wrap this blanket around you. We need to get you home and out of these wet clothes."

As Kate stood still and dumb, shivering under the blanket, the other two worked quickly to pack up the picnic items, all the while averting their eyes from each other. Clearly they must have misbehaved in some way, but Kate didn't care to speculate further. She did note, however, how gently Mr. Wakeham held Elsie's hand as he helped her into the boat. How they shared a glance that seemed heavy with meaning—something deeper than flirtation.

They were a quiet group on the journey back. No one asked her about the boy she'd chased through the rain. They would never guess, of course, that she'd attacked a gentleman in an alley. Alone in her thoughts, Kate focused on the sound of oars slapping the water. She had little time for planning her next move, but she knew her future wouldn't include Summerfield College much longer.

❋ ❋ ❋ ❋ ❋

Asher had warmed to Philip Marshall at the Thompsons' dinner party, but he found him even more interesting in his own element. Self-assured and free with his opinions, Dr. Marshall came across as refreshingly logical.

He also seemed sincere in his desire to open Asher's eyes to the wonders of his alma mater. As they ate a private supper in Dr. Marshall's rooms, Asher listened intently to the man's detailed introduction to the most important people and buildings of the college. Dr. Marshall was an accomplished lecturer, apparently accustomed to speaking for long periods of time without interruption. But he did eventually pause long enough for Asher to pose a question.

"Dr. Marshall, how exactly did you come to know Mr. Thompson? I have trouble seeing you as a member of the Metaphysical Research Society."

Dr. Marshall put his fork down and lifted his napkin to his lips, almost as if to stifle a laugh. "I'm not a member, really. I have spoken at their meetings before, on subjects relating to the mind rather than the soul or spirit. I'll speak at their London meeting this weekend, as a matter of fact. But I keep my distance from their ghost hunting." He set the napkin down, his expression thoughtful. "Once upon a time, Oliver and my father were part of a group called the Ghost Society at Cambridge—they had grand plans to collect true ghost stories and investigate the claims of local mediums and psychics. But nothing much came of it. Oliver was considerably more enthusiastic than my father. Later he did ask me to join the Metaphysical Society, no doubt out of respect to my father, but I declined."

"Because you don't believe in ghosts?"

Dr. Marshall shrugged. "It was more that I had other research interests, and I wished those pursuits to be taken seriously by the scientific and medical community. When I saw how much ridicule was aimed at the Metaphysical Society's efforts, I was relieved I hadn't joined them. I'm not ashamed to confess that. However, I did keep in touch with Oliver and a few others."

A few others. "Did you, um . . . did you count Frederic Stanton among your friends?"

The man's eyes widened in surprise. "Why, yes. Stanton was older, but he supported my work and often mentored me. He had a medical degree, you know, so we had something in common other than an interest in the metaphysical. His death was a blow—in fact, I testified at his inquest." He paused to wipe his mouth again. "He was a good friend to your father as well. Did you ever meet Stanton?"

"No, I didn't." Asher paused, uncertain how to phrase his response. "But Mr. Thompson and my father have spoken of him with great fondness. And Mr. Eliot knew him."

"Eliot?" Dr. Marshall grimaced. "A fool of a man—he's exactly why I don't wish to be a member of the Society. Such a fatuous brute."

"I know you and Simon Wakeham are cousins. Are you good friends as well?"

"Oh yes. We practically grew up together, so we may as well have been brothers. Simon's a bit of a dreamer, I must say. Rather suggestible. I did my best to toughen him up when we were boys, but he's still so damned idealistic." Dr. Marshall grinned. "The ladies love it, of course."

Even as Asher nodded he felt his stomach sink. It would be so easy to put Elsie off Simon Wakeham forever, if he could convince her that Wakeham was the one who hurt Billy. At the same time, he could clearly imagine Kate's penetrating glare if she knew what he was about, and he was ashamed for wishing so desperately to discredit Wakeham just so Elsie would be free of his influence. It smacked of the most cowardly sort of deceit. And the man wasn't even pursuing her, as far as he could tell.

"I'd hope to hear more about your work," Asher said, keen to change the subject. "I confess to finding my father's research rather far-fetched, but your theories on the subliminal self intrigue me."

"It is my dearest hope that you *will* hear more about my theories in the not so distant future—you and everyone in the scientific community." Dr. Marshall smiled. "There's more data to collect, but one day these theories could make my career." He pointed to a handsomely carved file cabinet of oak. "I keep all my notes locked away for now, lest one of my colleagues steals my ideas . . . or, even worse, misunderstands them. I'm afraid it's all a bit unconventional, you see."

"Unconventional how?"

Dr. Marshall crossed his arms. "I feel it's wise to keep those details to myself for the moment. You understand, surely?"

Asher could only nod, for it did seem better to keep unconventional ideas to oneself until sufficient evidence was gathered. Much preferable to spouting baseless theories, as some members of the Metaphysical Society seemed eager to do.

Once the meal was finally cleared away, Dr. Marshall reclined on a lumpy sofa in the sitting room. "I'm just going to close my eyes for a minute or so, and then I'll take you to my favorite pub. Tomorrow we'll dine with a medical friend of mine, and Thursday night we'll sup at High Table—it's not quite so grand out of term, but I've no doubt you'll enjoy it. And at some point you must come by the hospital to see my work with electrotherapy," he said, his eyes closing as he sank farther into the cushions.

That night, as Asher settled into the spare room's narrow bed, he imagined the Thompsons relaxing comfortably in their sitting room with Elsie and Kate. Would the young ladies be talking of their row on the Cam? Had they spared a thought for him at some point during the day?

Somehow, he doubted it.

Chapter 24

The morning after the rowing trip Elsie woke with the feel of Simon's lips on her own. She closed her eyes and snuggled deeper into the pillow, luxuriating in the memory, but the warm sensation soon faded like a dream. Rising from the bed with a sigh, she took her dose—an even smaller spoonful than the day before. Then she dressed and arranged her hair. She wished to develop the previous day's photographs before breakfast.

No one stirred downstairs except for Millie, who smiled and bobbed a curtsy as she opened the door for Elsie. The morning air was cool and fresh after the previous day's rain. As she walked toward the Science Annex, the flesh on her arms prickled again at the memory of Simon's kiss.

Had she confessed too much? He hadn't seemed shocked, nor had she read doubt in his eyes. In fact, her honesty had seemed to draw him to her, and their kiss had consecrated this delicate new bond.

She let herself into the darkroom and smiled as the familiar fumes of developing solution filled her nostrils. To postpone her delight, she first developed the photograph of Kate.

Despite the staged positioning of Kate's limbs and body, the photograph came out beautifully. Kate's pose seemed natural, as though the camera had caught her just as she'd turned around, wide-eyed and mouth slightly open. The pose was a little wild, actually, and Elsie congratulated herself on the composition. She'd had help, though, from Simon.

His photo brought a pang to her heart. He seemed young and unguarded, while at the same time terribly dashing, with his open collar and dark hair ruffled by the breeze. She searched the photograph for any sign of a spirit—she'd sensed his lost lady that day—but found nothing. Clearly he'd been thinking of Elsie at that moment, not *her*.

She shook her head sadly as she loaded clean glass plates in her camera. With Simon due to leave for the Continent, there simply wasn't time for a proper courtship. Not that she had any notion of how to conduct one—her condition had robbed her of that opportunity. At least, she'd always believed it was her condition. Simon didn't seem fazed by it. Neither did Asher, for that matter. She wondered—was it merely her mother's fear that had kept her from joining society and finding a respectable husband?

If only she and Simon had more opportunities to be alone together. If only he weren't leaving in such a short time. Elsie indulged in a fantasy of traveling through Europe with him. Honeymooning in Paris or Venice—places she knew only from books and paintings. When they returned, they could keep house at Stonehill while Simon pursued his master's and, eventually, a fellowship.

Perhaps this needn't remain a fantasy. It would only become reality, however, if she acted quickly. If she confronted Simon and made her feelings clear, wouldn't that help matters along?

The problem was finding the proper setting—a place where they could be alone for more than a few minutes. She would have to be bold, but after that matters would take their course.

It hadn't worked with the artist, but she knew now that he hadn't been worth the effort. She had gotten smarter. And Simon was different.

Elsie raced down the steps of the Science Annex, swept up in an eddy of longing, but she came to a halt when she saw the old laboratory ahead of her. Uncle Oliver's chastising words echoed in her head. His anger had been so uncharacteristic, planting suspicion in her mind even though it shamed her to think ill of him. She shook the memory away. She would not dwell on it this morning. Later she would share her concerns with Simon. He would know what to do.

It was strangely quiet at the breakfast table that morning. Her aunt and uncle ate quickly, each having early appointments. Once Mr. Thompson had departed, Kate took his paper and buried her face in it. Elsie watched her calmly, sipping her cooling tea, but all the while her mind raced.

"Kate," she said.

"Mmmm?" Kate said from behind the paper.

"Tell me—how do you get out of Summerfield at night without being caught?"

❀ ❀ ❀ ❀ ❀

Kate answered Elsie's questions mechanically. On any other day she might have pressed the girl to explain her need for such information, but today all her thoughts focused on how to get safely out of Robert Eliot's reach.

When Elsie finally left the table, Kate turned back to the London paper's listing of vacant situations. She searched for parlor and scullery maids, shop girls—anything that looked remotely suitable. One listing for a photographer's assistant sparked her interest, but that was before she read the requirement that applicants be male. No one needed a library assistant. No one needed a spirit apparition, or they weren't brazen enough to advertise for one anyway. What else was she qualified to do? Factory work? Sewing buttons?

In the old days Tec would have been a great resource, but now he wouldn't even speak to her. In fact, he seemed quite unbalanced. Why seek her out only to run away from her? It hurt to remember, for she'd believed him to be a good friend.

She'd even thought he could be more . . . in time.

Having found nothing ideal among the London employment notices, Kate scribbled the details for two remote possibilities and tucked the scrap of paper in her pocket. What she really needed was enough money and creativity to post her own "situation wanted" advertisement. It was just a matter of choosing which kind of situation, and then manufacturing a character reference that praised her for having the proper skills.

Kate poured herself another cup of tea and picked up the local paper, scanning the city and county news. She wasn't expected at the library for another half hour—one more cup of tea while she perused the local tittle-tattle was preferable to sitting in her room and staring at the walls.

She found little of interest among the announcements. The bishop of the diocese had appointed a new school inspector. A special late train to and from London would begin service on Saturday. The local branch of the Hearts of Oak Benefit Society was having a meeting Thursday next.

She was about to refold the paper when a name caught her eye—*Elizabeth Grove Gardner.* She read the paragraph.

Publicist and Conservative politician William Gardner will appear Thursday evening at the Senate House, where he will lecture on the future of the New Conservative. His wife, Mrs. Elizabeth Grove Gardner, will host a four o'clock tea for ladies sympathetic to the Conservative movement at the Prince Albert Hotel that same day, prior to the lecture.

Kate closed her eyes, considering. Her father's widow was Elizabeth Grove Stanton—was this the same woman?

Kate clutched the paper and made her way to Mr. Thompson's office, clearing her throat when she reached his doorway. "Mr. Thompson, may I ask you a question?"

He looked up, his forehead creased. "I must be out the door this instant, Kate, else I'll be late for my appointment."

"I'll be quick. Did my father's widow remarry a man named Gardner?"

Thompson's face fell. "Have you been reading the paper, my dear?"

"So I'm right—Elizabeth Grove Gardner *is* my father's widow."

"Yes," Thompson said weakly. "And she married a politician. Poor Frederic would be turning in his grave."

"Do you keep in touch with her?"

Mr. Thompson's mouth tightened. "I'm afraid Beth Stanton always resented how much time Frederic devoted to the Society. She had little respect for our work. Oh, she was civil enough in her response to my note of condolence, but she has not been in contact since." He sighed. "A year after his death, she married Gardner, a member of Parliament. She lives an entirely different life now. Much grander than we could imagine, I'm sure."

So there's money, thought Kate. *And the desire to avoid scandal.*

"You're not going to do anything foolish—are you, my girl?"

Kate raised an eyebrow. "Of course not. Just curious, is all. I won't keep you any longer." She smiled. "You'd best leave now if you're to make your appointment, hadn't you?"

Kate's thoughts were a tangle as she made her way to the library. Though she'd never been inside it, she knew the Prince Albert Hotel was located on the northwest edge of Parker's Piece—she and Asher had passed it on their way to the police station. Somehow, before three o'clock the next day, she would come up with a scheme for meeting the former Elizabeth Stanton face to face.

Chapter 25

To Asher it felt quite lordly to reside within the gates of Trinity. The college was older than Summerfield by nearly four hundred years, and though he'd seen the buildings that lay between Trinity Street and the River Cam, he'd since learned that the college spread east to Sidney Street, and beyond the Cam all the way to Grange Road. Trinity was practically a city unto itself. By comparison, Summerfield was but a tiny upstart with little money, land, or tradition.

He said as much to Dr. Marshall.

"I take your meaning," the doctor said as they gazed upon the prospect of the Wren Library from Trinity Bridge. "But even the most revered colleges were ragtag operations in the beginning. It's taken them centuries to build their wealth and adorn their patches of earth with all this"—he waved his hand toward New Court—"ostentation. Perhaps you knew that Trinity originally was two small colleges? Henry VIII compelled the two institutions to surrender everything to him, and he used their revenues, along with the wealth he'd gained by dissolving monasteries, to found Trinity College. It's really quite despotic when you think about it."

Asher nodded thoughtfully.

"The women's colleges have had no such benefactor," Dr. Marshall continued. "In a time when a university education for women is still sneered upon, they've leveraged funds and founded their colleges, and these institutions show no signs of faltering. Honestly, I marvel at their fortitude."

Asher thought of the striking arch of the Summerfield Gatehouse, the handsome Thompson Building, and the small but lavish interior of the new library—all of which made the Thompsons practically weep with pride—and felt a little ashamed of himself.

Dr. Marshall pulled his watch from his pocket. "I am hungry, and Dr. Spring's first-rate hospitality awaits. Shall we make our way? Should be a fine walk this evening. The rain has greened things up quite nicely."

As they walked in comfortable silence, Asher envied Dr. Marshall's relaxed posture and lazy smile. He seemed content—successful as a scholar and fulfilled by his research. He certainly wasn't the sort to lower himself by chasing spirits or seducing mediums.

"Is Dr. Spring a member of the Metaphysical Society?"

"Hardly," said Dr. Marshall with a wink. "His main concern is bodily health in the here and now. The mysteries of the brain hold no interest for him, nor does Spiritualism or any of that rot. He has a lucrative private practice, but in his spare time he developed the electrotherapy wing at Addenbrooke's. I assist him when I can."

"I know little to nothing about electrotherapy. It sounds very forward-thinking."

"If you join me at the hospital tomorrow, you will see it in action. Dr. Spring makes rather conventional use of it, I'm afraid. Many of his techniques were in use over a century ago. I have other ideas, but they're all theoretical at the moment." Dr. Marshall gestured ahead. "We turn right at that street sign, and Dr. Spring's house is the second on the left. By way of warning I should tell you that he's a widower with three daughters and no sons. He is desperate to marry the lasses off to rich young men, and has trained them to that end, so don't be surprised at the frenzied onslaught of feminine charm."

Asher entered the house with some trepidation, imagining maenads or harpies tearing at his clothes. As it turned out, Dr. Spring's daughters were pretty and attentive, but nothing to give fright to a man. If the doctor had indeed trained them, it was to make them biddable. They asked Asher thoughtful questions. They nodded appreciatively as he spoke, even when he struggled to express himself. They laughed prettily when he tried to be witty.

It was nothing like being around Kate and Elsie.

As the main course was cleared, Dr. Spring leaned back and settled his gaze upon Asher. "I always hoped for a son to take over my practice, but alas, I was instead blessed with these three." He waved a hand in the direction of his daughters. "They are good girls, but they have no desire to take on a profession. Not to say there aren't female doctors, but it's a tough row to hoe. Wouldn't wish that on the dears." He wiped his mouth. "Don't suppose *you* have any interest in the medical profession, Mr. Beale?"

The Spring girls leaned forward slightly.

Asher cleared his throat. "Well, I had talked with Dr. Marshall about visiting the hospital."

"He's coming with me tomorrow, as a matter of fact," said Dr. Marshall.

"Splendid, splendid. And yet you must remember that Marshall prefers to research innovative procedures and such—it can get rather grim at times and doesn't bring much in the way of a regular income. I do enjoy my work at the hospital, but I can only afford to visit there because my private practice is so steady, you see. I keep certain hours and tend to maintain the same clientele over time." He lowered his voice, as if sharing a confidence. "And these are all patients of a certain class, if you take my meaning."

"I do, sir."

"Perhaps you might accompany me on my private rounds one afternoon?"

"That's very generous of you, sir," Asher said.

"But tomorrow you must come to Addenbrooke's," said Dr. Marshall, "and see our grim innovations in action."

When Marshall pursued a new topic with Dr. Spring, Asher's mind wandered away from the conversation to consider his host more carefully. Physicians like Spring were respectable and wealthy. They attended well-heeled patients. Medicine was a practical profession, but it also offered opportunities for specialization. Though quacks sometimes infiltrated the ranks, the profession itself wasn't subject to constant ridicule.

He looked about him, admiring the dining room with its elegant chandelier and Baroque paintings in gilded frames. Dr. Spring's entire house was handsome and well appointed. It suited Asher nicely. But did he have a passion for anatomy? For surgery? For curing ills? He didn't think so, but with training he might develop one.

Had he ever *had* a passion?

For too long he'd associated passion with obsession—because of his father. But he'd encountered plenty of people who were keen on their occupation for more reasons than the income or acclaim it brought. Elsie had a passion—he could see it in her eyes when she arranged a scene before photographing it. Kate had a passion for survival. He couldn't help but wonder what she might accomplish if all her energies weren't devoted to something so basic.

He resolved to keep an open mind during his visit to the infirmary with Dr. Marshall. If medicine was to be his passion—and at this point he could neither rule it in nor out—surely he would recognize it tomorrow.

Heavy clouds darkened the sky Thursday afternoon, but no rain fell. Instead a pall of humidity blanketed the city. The oppressive atmosphere worsened inside Addenbrooke's Hospital, as Asher soon discovered. Sweat trickled down his face as Dr. Marshall led him on a tour of the different wards. Even with the windows open the place was stuffy and sour. In every room he found matrons mopping and scrubbing, but the odors of sweat, blood, and urine prevailed.

Dr. Spring had two wards for electrotherapy. The first, a room partitioned into smaller curtained areas, smelled of mildew. Dr. Marshall sidled up to the nearest curtain and spoke. "Mr. Soames, might I trouble you for a moment? A prospective student wishes to see your treatment." Hearing no protest, he pulled the curtain aside to reveal a corpulent bald man lying in a bath, his linen dressing gown floating in the water. The poor fellow seemed to shrink into himself at being thus exposed, but he did not complain.

"I've never seen an electric bath," said Asher wonderingly. "What is this gentleman's ailment?"

"Gout," said Dr. Marshall. "Dr. Spring uses the baths to treat various conditions, including rheumatism, sciatica, and even"—he lowered his voice—"gynecological disorders. The water temperature is kept as close as possible to ninety-three degrees and thus conducts the electricity perfectly. The flow of voltage increases blood circulation in the skin and deep muscle tissue." He recited the details dully, as if by rote. "We've had moderate success with this method. At the moment, however, Dr. Spring is more involved in another sort of electrical therapy. Come, I'll show you."

When Asher entered Dr. Spring's second ward, he was struck by yet another smell. It was acrid, like something burning. Not wood or paper, however.

Flesh.

His stomach heaved even as Dr. Spring bustled into the room.

"Come in, come in!" Dr. Spring's face was pink with enthusiasm. "Come meet young Denny. He served in the Boer War."

Asher nodded at the sullen man sitting on the cot, his trousers rolled up and his socks lying in a bundle next to him.

"He was sent home after a leg injury that resulted in partial paralysis. You can see how the left leg has atrophied."

Marshall brought Dr. Spring a box, which he set next to Denny. Inside was a cylinder with wires and wooden paddles. "This is an induction coil," Spring told Asher, "powered by a dry cell. I apply these electrodes to the affected area to stimulate the muscles."

"And this really works?"

Dr. Spring smiled. "I know what you're thinking. You've heard of electrotherapy for neuralgia and nervous disorders. Heavens, I've even heard of people using it for bowel complaints. All of that is quackery. But using electrical impulses to stimulate atrophied muscles? I've seen it work." He glanced at Dr. Marshall. "My young colleague hopes one day to utilize this technology in his brain and heart research, right, Marshall?"

"In what way?" asked Asher.

Dr. Marshall frowned. "Doctors have applied electrical

current directly to the brain to treat cerebral maladies, but it's time to refine these methods. I'm also interested in the effects of electric shock on the heart. I've worked with others to prove that accidental electrocution deaths result from massive contractions of the heart rather than respiratory paralysis." His eyes brightened. "What preoccupies me most, however, is what happens to the brain and heart of those who *survive* accidental electrocution."

"Whereas I remain content with less complex organs and muscles." Dr. Spring wired the young man's leg and flipped the switch. Denny flinched, his leg jerking twice before settling into a persistent twitch.

"How do they endure it?" Asher asked. "It looks like torture."

"It hurts like hell," muttered Denny.

"Yes, yes, there is pain," the doctor said quickly. "But the muscle responds."

Asher watched Denny's face redden, his leg still twitching, as Dr. Spring continued to apply the current. The longer he watched, the more his scalp prickled. *There's something familiar about this.* He turned away, concentrating on the strange feeling. He'd certainly never seen electrotherapy performed before, and yet he could almost imagine someone describing it to him. Had it been Mr. Thompson? Dr. Marshall had not detailed the process during their prior conversations. But *someone* had told him of a body that trembled and jerked.

It came to him then—Elsie's description of Billy shaking and jerking as a man stood over him. Billy's complaints of a pain in his heart. Asher had seen the burn marks on the boy's chest. Had Billy been electrocuted? He glanced at Dr. Marshall, but the man's expression told him nothing.

When Dr. Marshall left the room to attend the bathing patients, Asher stepped closer to the other doctor. "Dr. Spring, what if you . . ." He trailed off, unsure how to ask the question.

The man turned to look at him. "What if I what?"

"Dr. Marshall spoke of studying deaths by accidental electrocution. Has anyone *purposely* applied an electrical current directly to the heart?"

Dr. Spring blinked. "Yes, it's been done. On animals, anyway. Always made me think of *Frankenstein,* you know? Of course, there's no way to reanimate a corpse that's been dead and buried for so long. That Shelley woman was writing pure fantasy." He turned the machine off and removed the electrodes to massage the leg. "However," he continued, "a pair of Swiss doctors applied electricity to a dog's heart to disrupt the heartbeat—fibrillation is what it's called. After the dog went into cardiac arrest, they applied another shock—defibrillation—to make the heart beat regularly again."

Asher studied the pink marks on the man's leg. "Has this procedure—fibrillation and defibrillation, I mean—been attempted on a living human?"

"If it has, no one would own up to it. Not unless he wished to go to prison," said Dr. Spring with a chuckle. "Far too dangerous."

chapter 26

Kate stood in her chemise before the open wardrobe. After considering her two blouses, she chose the cream one—it was proper enough, but too large and rather frayed at the elbows. It suited her wish to appear needy and tragic, and would pair well with the ugly brown skirt. She brushed out her hair, tying it back with a ribbon instead of making her usual plaits.

She studied her face in the mirror. Her skin was smoother now, not having felt the bite of the luminescent paint for nearly two weeks, but it was still pale. Her face was thin. Despite having enjoyed decent meals for several days, she still looked underfed and sorrowful. It would serve nicely.

That morning she had reported to work in the library as usual.

At two o'clock she'd complained of stomach pains. Miss Freeman glanced at her in annoyance, saying nothing. After her third complaint, Freeman murmured about the evils of indulgent kitchen staff. Miss Barrett, by contrast, offered to make her a cup of tea, which Kate refused as politely as possible. At a quarter of three, Kate rushed to the water closet, slammed the door shut, and made a noisy pretense of heaving her lunch into the modern, shiny toilet. It seemed necessary to make cor-responding splashes with her hand. After a moment she pulled the chain to flush the toilet, washed her hands, and ran cold water over her face to extend the dramatic effect. Clapping a still-wet hand over her mouth, she opened the door.

The two ladies stood a few paces away. Freeman took one look at her and pointed toward the main entrance. "Return to the Gatehouse at once or you'll make us all ill."

"Yes, miss," Kate mumbled from behind her hand, clutch-ing her hat with the other.

She'd returned to the Gatehouse as directed, but slipped si-lently up the stairs to make certain her appearance was perfect for that afternoon's task. Once safely outside again she veered onto a side path and made her way to the unlocked side gate, continuing to Regent Street from there.

The Prince Albert was a stately, sprawling building situated by the lush green grass of Parker's Piece. Kate studied it in si-lence, walking from one end to the other and peering through the windows in the most casual manner she could manage. She noted several windows in a row that seemed to look out from the same elegant room—a ballroom of sorts. This was what she needed.

When she entered the hotel she couldn't help gawking at the massive electric chandelier. A young man in blue-and-gold livery immediately came to her side, his angular face sharpened further by indignation.

"If you're here for work, you should use the side entrance."

Kate drew herself up. "I have a message for one of your guests. She may be in the ballroom at the moment."

"Do you mean the Oak Room?"

"Yes," she said quickly. "I think she's there, preparing for an event later today."

He crossed his arms. "I don't think—"

"I'll find it myself," she said, brushing past him.

He followed, shadowing her just as she'd expected.

The ballroom was at the opposite end of the lobby. In the middle of the grand oak-paneled room, a lady in an elaborate hat pointed at tables and gave orders to two young maids. Kate nodded toward her. "Is that Elizabeth Gardner?"

"That is indeed Mrs. Gardner," the young man said.

"I have a note of introduction."

He looked at her for a moment, rolled his eyes, and took the note from her hand. When Kate gestured once again at Mrs. Gardner, he squared his shoulders and walked toward the lady.

Kate knew this was the moment when matters could go pear-shaped, for her note of introduction was intended to throw the lady off her guard.

> I am Frederic Stanton's natural child. If you wish to avoid a scene—and I am very skilled at making them—you should find time this instant to speak privately with me. I only ask for ten minutes.

Mrs. Gardner opened the note impatiently. She did not frown, but Kate noticed a pucker forming between her eyes. Closing the note, Mrs. Gardner turned to the liveried attendant. "We'd appreciate a little time alone, if you don't mind," she said to him, her voice light and sweet.

He blushed and backed away.

Once he was out of hearing, Mrs. Gardner looked directly at her. Then she gestured for Kate to step closer.

She was the most elegant creature Kate had ever seen. Her suit of soft rose silk, adorned with rows of intricate braid on the bodice and hem, fit as though molded to her broad bosom and tiny waist. Her hat—a towering combination of bows, flowers, and feathers—rested on softly poufed light-brown hair. Her brown eyes were almost inhumanly large in her fashionably pale face. As Kate came to stand before her, she felt dwarfed by the woman's presence.

Mrs. Gardner tilted her head, considering her with a steely expression. "You have the look of my former husband."

Kate couldn't help herself. "Your *late* husband, you mean."

That aristocratic eyebrow quirked. "Shall we sit down?" She gestured toward a table, her eyes fixed on Kate as she sank into her chair. The corners of her mouth lifted, but otherwise her expression was cold. "What is it you want from me, exactly?"

"I am an orphan in need of shelter," Kate replied, not bothering to steady the tremor in her voice. "I've looked for honest work, but there are no suitable positions to be found in Cambridge."

"There are institutions for children like you."

Kate frowned. "I prefer to have my independence."

"Are you asking me for money?"

"I only ask for what is due to me."

Mrs. Gardner's eyes narrowed. "Your father made no provision for you."

"Perhaps he meant to but hadn't the chance. He died rather suddenly."

The woman shook her head. "I can offer you nothing. My husband wouldn't allow it."

Kate clenched and unclenched her hands under the table. She took a breath. "Then you give me no choice."

Mrs. Gardner leaned forward, all trace of politeness gone. "And just how do you plan to blackmail me, you conniving little slut?"

Kate's head snapped back as though she'd been slapped. She'd been called many horrible names, but never *that*. She clenched her fists again, nails biting into her palms. "I will make it public that you've failed in your duty to help your husband's orphaned child. I'm certain many will find my plight newsworthy."

"And I will respond that you are an imposter, for I'm certain you have no proof of your paternity."

"But . . . the scandal?"

"I have weathered many scandals. My *former* husband attracted them like a magnet."

Kate blinked.

"Oh yes, little girl. No doubt you worshipped him as a handsome, heroic sort of *intellectual* man. But his obsessions were bizarre. That book of his—Thompson's idiotic Ghost Society adored him for it, but the scientific community howled in derision. Maybe that's what turned him to narcotics in his quest to lift the veil of the spirit world."

Kate's shoulders sank. "Narcotics?"

Mrs. Gardner waved her hand dismissively. "His young friend Dr. Marshall said he had neuralgic pain, that his death was an *accident,* but *I* knew what was going on."

"What?" Kate knew she was losing her grip on this conversation, but she had to know. "*What* was going on?"

"He and his mad friends were accessing those 'hidden powers of the mind,' as they liked to say. That's what killed him. I know it. His friends *and* enemies know it. It would have been easier to bear if he'd offed himself out of melancholy, but to deliberately overdose in order to reach a higher plane of consciousness? It was downright idiocy. There was a great deal of tongue wagging at the time. . . ." She paused, her gaze distant. "But that sort of thing always runs its course and people forget." She focused again upon Kate. "Try all you like to stir up a little dust, but nothing will come of it. And rest assured that my current husband knows people who can silence naughty black-mailers."

Kate gasped.

"I endured your father's failings for several years. But I have a different life now, and I'm proud to be William Gardner's wife." She grabbed Kate's hand, clutching it so tightly that Kate winced. "There's nothing you can do to hurt me. I'm not some gently born lady who faints and weeps at the first sign of trouble. I was an *actress* before I married your father—I've dealt with much worse than you could ever offer. Do you understand?"

The woman's face was inches from hers, so close Kate could see the flecks of powder on her cheeks. She nodded slowly.

"Now, leave this place quietly." Elizabeth Gardner's sugary voice returned as she released Kate's hand and settled back in her chair. "Or I will have my assistant escort you out the back way." She gestured toward a shadowy man standing in the corner. Kate leapt to her feet, sending the chair screeching backward, and stumbled toward the door. She made it only as far as the lobby before the tears spilled down her cheeks.

❧ ❧ ❧ ❧ ❧

It seemed fitting that she would encounter Mr. Thompson as she approached the Summerfield gate—everything else had gone wrong, why not this? Her face must have been a horror, for he stopped in his tracks.

"Child, whatever is the matter?"

She wiped her face with her sleeve, plundering her mind for a reasonable reply and coming up short.

Mr. Thompson took a step toward her, his eyes searching. "Ah, Kate. You went to see her, didn't you? I could have told you it was a terrible idea."

Kate moaned. "I couldn't help myself."

"I should have taken your query more seriously. Of course you'd wish to see her. She knew your father better than anyone, I suppose. How did she upset you?"

She couldn't tell him the whole truth, for she couldn't bear him knowing the nature of her scheme. "The lady was cold and cruel. She frightened me."

He stepped closer and laid a hand on her shoulder. "There's not a gentle bone in that woman's body." He patted her lightly, an awkward gesture but also sincere. "You should go to your room and rest. I'll have Millie bring up a tray for your supper."

"Please don't tell Mrs. Thompson what I've done! She'll think me so foolish."

"Don't worry a bit about it. I'll explain to Helena and Elsie that you're ill."

Chapter 21

Elsie had lain in the meadow with her art tutor, but never had she been so brazen as to travel across town in the dark of night to knock on a gentleman's door and invite herself in.

But that was only due to lack of imagination.

"Elsie, the school is fenced, but it's not a prison," Kate had told her the day before. "One *can* walk out the door and away from Summerfield without scaling walls or breaking locks."

"How do you manage it without getting caught?"

"You wait until night and you stay in the dark as much as possible."

Elsie had done as Kate described, walking quietly down the two flights of stairs and out the door, taking the garden path through the darkness to the unlocked side gate. She hadn't expected to encounter the bicycle.

So *that* was how Kate had traveled to Castle End so easily. And on this night Kate was ill—Elsie hadn't seen her all day—so she shouldn't mind if Elsie took the contraption out for a spin. It would be a much quicker trip on a bicycle, even one this rickety.

She'd dressed simply in a white muslin blouse and dark

skirt, the plainest petticoat she owned, and a light cloak. She was forced to pull the gown up to her knees to straddle the bicycle, but the cloak hid her display of underclothes. If she kept to the dark she wouldn't call too much attention to herself.

A mixture of excitement and terror at seeing Simon so late at night had numbed her to the dangers of cycling alone in the near darkness. She knew exactly where Stonehill lay, and in her mind she could see that familiar door open and Simon glancing out. Would he smile? Surely he'd be shocked. She'd rehearsed gentle, reassuring words—words that would convince him to let her inside.

As it happened, her head emptied of all these words when she found herself leaning the bicycle against a tree and standing before the front door at her aunt and uncle's former home—a place she'd visited before, but never like this. Through the drawing room window she could see the flickering light of a lamp. He was there.

And yet she was frozen.

She stepped closer. Taking a deep breath, she lifted the knocker and tapped three times.

After an agonizing pause, she heard footsteps. The door opened a few inches, revealing a sliver of Simon's face. He stared through the opening for a moment, frowning in confusion. When she pushed back the hood of her cloak, his eyes widened and he swung the door open.

His face was pale, his usually sleek hair awry. She smiled at the thought of him tearing at it as he'd worked upon some difficult task. He'd not shaved that day. His shirt was rumpled, and he'd shrugged out of his braces, which now hung at his sides. He looked boyish and vulnerable—more frightened to see her on his doorstep than she was to be there.

"Hello," she said softly.

"Elsie?" He smoothed his wild hair. "I mean, Miss Atherton?"

"May I . . . Simon, may I please come in?"

He hesitated, seeming to regain some of his composure. "Your aunt would have my head on a platter if she knew you were here so late. *Alone.*"

"She's asleep. Neither of them knows I'm here, and they never shall. Please don't shut the door on me. I only wish to talk with you."

He stared at her. After a long pause, he finally waved her through the door.

"I've always loved it here," she said softly as he guided her toward the drawing room. She glanced at the desk and the flickering lamp that cast shadows on the books and papers strewn over its surface. This house had not yet been fitted with electricity. The thought of long nights spent working by lamplight made her heart warm even more to him. She loved his grand theories, his determination to know more than it was thought possible to understand.

He gestured at a faded settee, and she let the cloak slide from her shoulders. "If you don't mind, I'd rather not sit. I wish you would instead take me out to the back garden."

"Elsie, this is very strange."

"I'm a strange young lady, remember? But I don't bite. I just want to see the place where I was so happy as a child."

The faintest smile played upon his lips. "Let me get the lamp."

She followed him to the back door. When he opened it for her, she stepped out into the night air. "It's too cloudy to see the stars tonight," she murmured.

"I still can't believe you came so far, and in such darkness, on your own."

"It seems much as I remembered out here. The trees don't

tower quite so much as they did then, but they still make me feel safe." She turned to him. "And I feel safe with you, of course."

"Your reputation won't be safe if anyone learns you've been here."

She waved a hand. "No one will know. Please don't say any more about it."

"But I still want to know *why*."

She stepped closer to him. "I had to see you alone before you left Cambridge. I feared that if I didn't, we'd never have the opportunity to speak about that day by the river."

He looked away. "I owe you an apology. I took liberties."

She laid her hand on his arm. "You didn't. I wanted you to kiss me. Simon, I am no good at being coy and elusive. I felt very close to you that day. I've felt drawn to you since the day we met."

"When you crashed into me at the museum."

"Yes, and I had that horrible seizure. You were kind. You didn't look at me like I was damaged or pitiful."

"You were in distress. And those words you spoke haunt me still. . . . May I ask you about them?"

A flush of heat swelled from Elsie's chest, warming her neck and cheeks. "You may."

"Did you see a spirit that day? A young woman?"

She studied his face. It was open, his eyes trusting. After a moment she nodded.

He sighed deeply. "I have so many questions."

"Take me upstairs." When he opened his mouth to protest, she continued quickly. "I wish to see where my brothers and I used to sleep, and then I will tell you more."

"Of course." His smile tightened.

She followed him up the staircase. At the landing, she

reached for the lamp. "May I?" He handed it to her, his eyes troubled in the flickering light.

She walked down the corridor, past the closed doors. One door was open at the very end. She peered inside, holding the lamp out to illuminate the room. Then she crossed the threshold, setting the lamp on a trunk that sat just inside the door.

"You sleep in the very room that was mine when my family was here," she breathed.

It may have been true. So many years had passed that she couldn't remember exactly which room had been hers. She merely recalled her brothers chasing her in and out of all the rooms on this floor.

The small bed was unmade, the coverlet twisted and the pillow smashed as though Simon writhed during his sleep. Clothes were draped untidily on a chair. Books lay in stacks on the floor. The room smelled like sleep . . . and like him.

Her heart pounded when she felt the heat of his body behind her. He stepped even closer and lightly touched her hair. His hand moved to her shoulder, fingers brushing the side of her neck like a kiss.

She held her breath.

"You shouldn't be here," he murmured at her ear.

"I chose to be here." She turned to face him. "Are you asking me to leave?"

His eyes were wide, the pupils fully dilated in the dimly lit room. "With you standing so near, so warm . . . I don't think I can."

She placed her fingers on his cheeks and stepped forward, closing those final inches between them. Their bodies nearly touched. "Good."

She smiled as he pulled her to him.

Kate woke to darkness and quiet. She lit her study lamp and peered at the small clock on the desk. Nearly eleven o'clock. She'd intended to take a short nap after her early supper, but apparently she'd slept for hours, fully clothed.

As the fog of sleep cleared, Elizabeth Gardner's cruel words came back to her. Had she really deserved to be called a "conniving little slut" and "naughty blackmailer"? The Gardners had riches to spare, and she'd only meant to keep herself clothed and fed without taking charity. As it was, she barely held on to her dignity. Begging would snatch it from her forever. And yet . . . there was poor Billy's example. Blackmail could prove deadly.

Kate shuddered.

The scheme had failed and she couldn't think of another that would fund her escape from Cambridge. If she asked the Thompsons or Elsie, they would bog matters down with their questions and deliberations, giving Eliot enough time to learn her name and report her to the police.

If only Tec hadn't behaved so queerly. Why would he run from *her*? Had someone else been in pursuit? Perhaps he'd been trying to lead Kate away from danger.

She sat up, a strange determination pounding in her blood. She would try one last time with Tec. She would search him out in his Castle End cottage and do her best to convince him they must leave for London together. Immediately.

She rose from the bed, laced on her boots, and walked softly across the floor to collect her wrap. The night air would be damp and the wrap would come in handy for concealment. Once again she placed Billy's knife in her pocket. There was nothing else she wished to take with her.

She crept down the stairs, avoiding the creaky step third

from the bottom. Letting herself out the side door, she walked south, past Summerfield Hall . . . only to find herself staring at an empty patch of grass.

The bicycle was gone.

"Damnation," she muttered.

It would take nearly half an hour to walk to Castle End, and she would have to make her way along the Backs, which she knew were dark and sinister at night. It was bad enough on a bicycle. And yet she had no choice. Eliot could come for her tomorrow.

The night sky was cloudy, but the faint gas lamps gave off just enough light. When a horse approached or a group of men walked in her direction, she stepped into the shadows. Fortunately, few people were on the road this late at night, and those she did encounter took little notice of a small figure wrapped in a shawl, walking in the shadows and doing her best to keep invisible.

More people—men and ragged boys—milled about the cottages on Castle End, muttering and laughing in clusters. She kept her head down and her pace lively. When a boy called out to her, she continued as if she hadn't heard him.

Tec's door was shut but not bolted. She swung the door open and breathed in the fumes of bacon and boiled cod. A lamp and matches stood on a table near the door. Once the flame was lit, she looked about the room. The view did not reassure. Fish-and-chips wrappers, greasy and cold, lay strewn about the floor. Quilts that in the past would have been neatly folded in a corner had been left in rumpled piles near the stove. Tec's wool cap, always on the nail by the door when he was home, was gone.

It looked more like a stranger had been squatting in the cottage. Tec usually kept his living space orderly, if not entirely clean. Perhaps something *was* wrong with him. For whatever reason, he would have to be terribly distracted to allow this disorder. Someone had been in the cottage recently—there were hot coals in the stove. Perhaps if she waited he eventually would come home.

She went to the table and checked the drawer. The bundle of tools still lay there exactly as she'd left them. She looked around the room again before shoving the bundle into her free pocket. It hung awkwardly at her side, overbalancing the pocket with the knife.

She wasn't stealing. She was merely keeping the tools safe until Tec was in his right mind.

Kate glanced at the chair near the stove, where Elsie had the vision of Billy. After a moment she stepped toward the chair and eased herself into it. Could it be possible to fall to that other realm like Elsie? Would she hear Billy's voice? She sat tensely, opening her mind to the possibility.

Nothing happened.

She slumped in the chair. Poor Billy, clever enough to launch a blackmail scheme but still too much of a child to carry it out safely. If only he'd told her more about it, she might have stopped him.

She tried to remember the details Elsie had given. Billy found some papers, and they gave him an idea for a scheme. They must have been incriminating in some way, or why else take them? He'd hidden them, but hadn't said where.

Billy didn't have a home. He didn't have a permanent place to kip other than Tec's house.

Could he have hidden those papers here? Tec hadn't mentioned it, but then again, Billy might have kept it from him. He'd promised to share the proceeds with Kate—no one else. Her gaze moved from the ragged quilts on the floor to the sooty windows. Where would he hide papers so that neither Tec nor the other boys would find them?

She stood and walked about the cottage, imagining possible hidey-holes. The cabinets and larder shelves were rather obvious, but she checked them anyway, to no avail. The walls were bare and smooth—no possible hiding places there. She studied the seams on all the quilts and the undersides of the chairs and table. Plenty of dust and fluff, but no papers. Before she could search the wood floor for loose boards, she had to collect the scattered fish-and-chips wrappers and toss them into the stove. Once the floor was cleared, she walked up and down each board, testing for weak spots. The floor sagged, but the boards were nailed tight. Could Billy have hidden the pages somewhere outdoors? That certainly didn't seem the ideal way to preserve paper for a blackmail scheme.

She stood at the center of the room and swiveled slowly, trying to view each corner, patch of wall, and piece of furniture as a thief might. Where might a precious thing be well hidden? Her eyes alighted on the blue-and-white vase. The shelf was so high that none of the boys could reach it, and how many times had she heard Tec say that he would thrash anyone who dared touch the vase?

She dragged the chair to the wall and climbed up to retrieve it. Once she'd safely brought it down, she sat and peered inside.

A roll of papers was tucked within.

Taking a breath to calm herself, she pulled out the roll. Then she placed the vase on the floor and spread the papers flat on her lap. The top page had been torn from a journal and was covered in neat handwriting.

We have tried everything—dream manipulation, mesmerism, transcendence through meditation, and when that didn't work, transcendence through narcotics. Stanton insisted we always test on ourselves—that we should bear the risk—and it killed him. His death was a terrible tragedy, but we learned from his failings. True progress requires a different sort of sacrifice.

The procedure has worked on animals, but it is time to use human subjects. If we don't make this crucial next step, we may never reach those dark spaces of the mind. I am willing to test on myself—I am willing to die, to be lost to this world forever, just like any explorer on the verge of a breakthrough. But isn't it only logical to choose lesser subjects—the unwanted, the criminal, the burdens on society—to enhance the process first?

Kate released the papers, gasping as they snapped back into their roll and fell to the floor. "Billy, how could you be such a fool?" Tears sprang to her eyes. "You never had a chance."

Chapter 28

Simon's kiss was soft at first, gentle and hesitant, but when Elsie pressed the full length of her body against his, he moaned. The kiss deepened, stealing her breath as it warmed her flesh. Then he was lifting her in his arms and laying her on the bed.

Her pulse was throbbing, but she was not afraid. She was adept at letting her body do the thinking. Her mind had given its permission already, for she knew Simon would not abandon her after such intimacy—not like the artist. Simon was a man of means and would take her to the Continent with him. They would be together always, and she need never see her parents again.

He kissed her neck, his hand sliding down her arm, and she arched her back. With one hand she stroked his hair, but the other guided his fingers to the buttons on her blouse. He worked to undo them, his progress made agonizingly slow by the fact that he used only one hand. She trembled as each button popped free.

She'd worn no corset. When his hand slipped under her chemise, it found bare skin. She gasped, and their eyes met. Then his head ducked, and his lips were on her flesh.

Their movements blurred together. His hand tugged her skirt up to her waist and slid underneath. Her hand reached for the clasp on his trousers. Her body was warm and liquid, aching with need.

"I love you, Simon," she whispered.

He froze above her, his mouth hanging open as he panted for air. Then he crumpled on top of her, gasping into her neck. "I can't."

"Why?"

He rolled onto his side and stared at the wall.

"It's not fair to you."

Elsie bit her lip. "I've been too forward."

"No, it's not that. You are kind and beautiful. It's just . . ." He trailed off, still unable to meet her eyes.

"It's just what?"

"I still think of *her*."

"Oh God," she gasped. "The one who died?"

He raked a hand through his hair. "She still haunts me, even after all this time. I can't do this."

When she reached for him, he flinched. She let her hand drop.

"It's as if she's watching me," he said. "Is she, Elsie?"

"She's not." As she said the words, she realized they were true. She hadn't felt the tingle or seen the aura. The lady had never been to this house.

"Of course," he said, frowning. "It's my own guilt that makes me feel that way." He sat up, swinging his legs over the side of the bed and pulling the braces over his shoulders.

"Guilt?"

"She was the wife of a friend. Part of me feels responsible for what happened to her."

Elsie fumbled at the buttons of her blouse, tears pricking

her eyes. He stood and moved toward the lamp, averting his gaze as she arranged herself with shaking hands.

"I must go," she murmured, wiping at her eyes with her sleeve.

"Not yet," he said. "Could we . . . could *you* possibly contact her?"

She drew back. "How could you ask that?"

He shook his head. "You're right. I'm sorry. But she seems to slip further from me with each passing day. Perhaps another time. Let me walk you back, Elsie."

"I came on my aunt's bicycle."

"Well, let me make you a cup of tea before you go. I can't let you walk away just like that."

She stared up at him. "I *can't* stay here."

His eyes softened. "You shouldn't leave in such a state."

"And why shouldn't I be in a state?" she demanded, cringing even as the words came out. "I've made a fool of myself. You were just using me!"

She pushed past him and ran down the hallway, clutching the banister as she stumbled down the stairs.

He was close on her heels. At the foot of the stairs, he caught her arm. "Elsie, please don't . . . please calm yourself. I am leaving in less than a week. My passage is booked, plans are made. I shouldn't have taken advantage like I did. I never should have kissed you by the river." She flinched as he pushed a strand of hair out of her eyes. "I'm sorry."

She jerked her arm away and, pulling her cloak off the settee, made for the door.

No looking back.

Elsie ran for the bike, clutching the handles and pushing it down the hill into the darkness so he wouldn't see the spectacle of her hitching her skirt and climbing on.

Her head ached and tears blinded her vision. She blinked them away, pedaling wildly until the sobs racked her body. Braking abruptly, she stepped off the bicycle and tipped it onto the grass before falling to her knees.

The dose was what she needed.

The dark oblivion of the dose.

❁ ❁ ❁ ❁ ❁

Kate was sitting in the chair, lost in thought, when the door opened. Tec paused in the doorway, staring at her. She smoothed her skirt and smiled tentatively. His face was curiously expressionless, yet she felt his anger. Literally felt it, as though she stood too close to a raging fire.

"Tec, don't be angry. I know it's dangerous for me to be here."

He continued to stare.

Kate swallowed nervously. "But everything's gone wrong, and I've come to beg you to leave Cambridge." She paused, then added softly, "And to please take me with you."

He held her gaze, still silent.

"Think about it. We could start a new scheme together, working for another medium. Or, or . . ." She paused, her mind racing. "Or *I* could work up an act as a medium. After all those years with Martineau, I know exactly what to do."

He frowned. Then he stepped toward her and knelt to pick up the roll of papers.

"Billy stole those during a detecting job for Martineau," Kate said. "He hid them here and tried to blackmail the man, but ended up getting himself killed. You were right—it's too dangerous to stay here any longer. Come to London with me. We can leave first thing in the morning."

Tec crumpled the papers in his hand, and in one swift movement opened the door to the stove and shoved them inside. The sudden violence of the gesture left her speechless. Smoke billowed, giving way to flames as he shut the door again. He straightened, staring down at her with the same blank expression as before.

Kate cleared her throat. "We might have used those papers, but I suppose it's safer to destroy them if we're off to London." She stood and smoothed her skirt. "You will come with me, won't you?"

His head tilted oddly. He raised a hand, and she leaned in slightly, thinking he might touch her cheek. Instead he shoved her hard. She fell backward onto the rough wooden floor, the impact so jarring that she bit her lip. She stared up at him, the taste of blood bitter in her mouth.

"Tec, what in God's name—"

He stepped toward her, the emptiness in his eyes more menacing than rage. She scrambled backward, then flipped over and pushed herself to her feet. She'd barely cleared the doorway when he slammed the door shut. She heard the bolt slide into place, locking her out.

Kate staggered down the street, her mind reeling. Tec was a gentle boy. He cared about her. He could never hurt her.

And yet he *had*. A sudden, vicious blow from Tec? How could such a transformation be possible? His eyes were vacant as death, but his hands were cruel. Once more the tears welled as she patted her bitten lip. Her sleeve came away marked with blood.

When she finally made it through the back gate at Summerfield she saw the bicycle standing close to its usual place outside the Gatehouse. Who could have taken it out this late at night? Not Mrs. Thompson—surely that was impossible. Kate approached it slowly, considering. And then she knew.

Elsie.

The girl had asked about her nighttime ventures, but Kate hadn't thought she'd actually make use of the information. Where could she possibly have gone?

Kate unlaced her boots and carried them as she padded up the staircase, pausing on the first floor to listen for any disturbance. All seemed clear.

On the second floor she made straight for Elsie's room and knocked lightly on the door.

No answer.

She tried the handle and found it unlocked. Opening the door a few inches, she peered inside . . . into darkness.

"Elsie?"

A sludgy sniffle was the only response.

"Elsie, I have to tell you something—are you awake?"

"Don't turn on the light," a small voice said.

Kate rolled her eyes in the darkness. "Fine. We'll talk in the morning."

"Wait!" The sniffle came again. "Don't leave."

The back of Kate's neck prickled. She set her boots down and felt around for the study lamp that usually rested on the desk. "Sit tight while I light this." Once she got the flame going, she replaced the shade. The soft glow illuminated the room, revealing Elsie curled up on her bed. Her face was wet, her eyes and nose dripping.

Kate stood awkwardly, staring at the girl. "What's wrong?"

Elsie glanced at the bedside table. An open bottle of Chlorodyne sat there. Kate stepped forward and reached for it. She didn't have to shake the bottle to know it was empty. This was familiar . . . all too familiar.

"Elsie, what have you done?"

"I think . . ." The girl licked her lips and swallowed before continuing. "I might have done something very foolish."

Chapter 29

Asher's head spun from too much wine and restless thoughts. He'd managed an hour of slumber, but it had been cruelly punctuated by dreams of limbs covered in electrodes, jerking and flailing . . . then smoldering, blistering. He could almost smell the singed flesh in the air when he woke. He rubbed at his eyes, trying to push the images away. The room was stifling, and the smell of his own sweat was overpowering.

He'd wished to depart from Dr. Marshall's company directly after that alarming visit to the hospital, but the man had invited him to dine with the other Trinity Fellows. It would have been rude—and possibly even suspicious—to refuse. Throughout the seemingly endless meal at High Table he'd avoided Marshall's gaze. He'd sat there, stiff and grim in his boiled shirt and tie, nearly choking on his words whenever Marshall's colleagues tried to engage him in conversation. All the while he'd been preoccupied with wondering. Could Billy have been a part of Marshall's research?

Billy had been tortured, and somehow electricity was involved. At least one other person had died before him—an old vagrant, wasn't it? Had anyone observed the same burn marks on the vagrant's body that he and Kate had seen on Billy's? Dr. Spring had said you could apply electricity to the heart, that it had, in fact, been applied to dogs. But what was the purpose?

He shook his head. He couldn't pull it all together into a theory that made sense and encompassed all the data. Dr. Marshall's research centered on the untapped potential of the human brain, while his daily work at the hospital focused on electrotherapy. How did the two fit together?

In his detective work, Billy had found information that he used to blackmail his killer. Perhaps someone had tortured him in order to find out what he knew. Or had torture never been the goal? Asher shuddered. Perhaps the electric shock had been merely the most expedient way to silence him. What secrets had the boy been hiding?

Kate might know.

If she didn't . . . Elsie could ask Billy.

❖ ❖ ❖ ❖ ❖

Kate raced down the stairs as quietly as she could, all the way to the small basement kitchen.

She's still conscious, still awake. There's a chance.

I couldn't save Mum, but I can save her.

In the dim light of the oil lamp, she fumbled through cabinets until she found the medicine store. After scrutinizing a seemingly endless array of remedies—cod liver oil, dyspepsia powders, paregorics—she finally found what she wanted. Kate plucked the bottle from the shelf and ran back up the stairs, sliding in her stocking feet on each landing.

She'd been gone the lesser part of ten minutes, but already Elsie looked worse. Her head now slumped against the wall, and her color was unnatural. Kate set the bottle on the bedside table, then hefted the porcelain basin from the washstand and placed it on the floor. She sat on the bed and pulled Elsie near. The girl was taller and better fed than she was, not to mention heavy with sleep, and Kate struggled to pull her into a half embrace.

"Wake up, Elsie."

When she slapped her cheek, the girl's eyelids fluttered slightly. With her free hand Kate fetched the bottle from the table, pulling the cork with her teeth. Then she tilted Elsie's head back and forced her mouth open with the bottle.

"Swallow this a little at a time. It's nasty, but drink it like a good girl and you'll feel better."

At least a third of the liquid streamed down either side of Elsie's mouth, but Kate thought she'd swallowed enough. She held her breath . . . and nearly wept with relief when Elsie finally gagged and heaved into the porcelain basin.

Once Elsie's spasms had eased, Kate bunched the pillow and coverlets together, creating a large bolster at the head of the bed. Lifting the girl's light cloak from the floor, she draped it over her legs.

"Good Lord, that was terrible," Elsie gasped. "What *was* that stuff? I've never tasted anything so foul."

"It was ipecac, and it may have saved your life. Thank God your aunt keeps her medicine cabinet well stocked, or I'd have been sticking one of your hat feathers down your throat."

Elsie groaned. "And ruined a damned expensive hat." She squirmed against the makeshift bolster.

Kate's fingers itched to shake the girl's shoulders. "What were you doing? Were you *trying* to kill yourself?"

"I just wanted to sleep. I didn't want to worry about my mistakes anymore. But after two doses my mind was still racing. I wasn't thinking properly." Elsie yawned. "But I think I can sleep now."

"Not likely," Kate snapped. She pulled a chair near and sank into it. "I should fetch your aunt. She'd be horrified to know what you nearly did to yourself tonight, and she would have my hide if she knew I'd kept it secret."

Elsie's eyes widened. "Please don't tell her. I'll be sent away to some horrid sanitarium, perhaps never to come out again. It was just a mistake, Kate! I didn't want to die. I know that now, don't you see?"

"Well, then, I'm going to keep you awake until dawn at least. There's no way to be certain all that filthy drug is out of your system."

Elsie swallowed another yawn. "What if I fall asleep anyway?"

"You won't. I'm going to keep you talking." Kate quietly scooted the chair closer. "You can start by telling me where you went tonight."

Elsie's mouth dropped open. "How did—"

"You took the bicycle."

"Oh."

Kate waited a moment. "Where did you go?"

Elsie opened her mouth to speak, but a strangled sound was all that came out. Finally her face crumpled. "Stonehill. I had to see Simon Wakeham."

"Oh, Elsie. Why would you do that?"

"Because I wanted to make an idiot of myself, apparently."

Kate gentled her tone. "You're in love with him?"

"Yes. And I . . . well, I needed to tell him before he left Cambridge, but it all went horribly wrong."

"How? Surely he didn't hurt you?"

"No, much worse than that. He told me he loves someone else—someone who happens to be dead."

"*That's* why you swallowed too much Chlorodyne?"

"I don't expect you to understand." Elsie turned away and closed her eyes.

Kate looked up at the ceiling and sighed. How to keep the girl talking now? If the conversation weren't steered away from Simon Wakeham, Elsie would be reaching soon for the spare Chlorodyne bottle. Kate looked around the room, desperate for inspiration, until her eyes settled upon Elsie's camera. *Perfect.* A neutral topic, and one that Elsie understood better than anyone she knew. "I want you to tell me everything you know about photography. Starting with all the important parts of the camera. Explain it to me like I'm a child who's never seen or heard of one of these contraptions before."

A faint smile played at Elsie's pale lips.

"Thanks, Kate."

"Just tell me about your camera, Elsie. Start with the lens. I've never understood how it works."

Chapter 30

Asher woke late, having stayed up half the night wondering at the horrors Marshall might have committed. His head and stomach ached, and his mouth tasted sour. He rose from bed and bathed his face at the washstand, then dressed quickly and packed his things.

Marshall's sitting room was quiet, his bedroom door still shut. Asher scribbled a quick note of thanks, making vague mention of a morning appointment, and crept quietly toward the door. It was only once he was past the porter's gate that he could breathe normally.

The Summerfield Gatehouse was a pleasant prospect in the late-morning light—a most welcome sight. When Millie opened the door, her face broke into a broad grin.

"Mr. Beale!"

"Where is Miss Atherton, Millie?"

The grin faltered. "Why, she's in the garden with Miss Poole, sir. Shall I take your bag?"

He wanted nothing more than to go directly to them, but his clothes were sadly rumpled and still reeking from the cloud of cigar smoke in the Senior Common Room. "I fear I must make myself more presentable," he said.

Millie nodded knowingly, and he flashed her a grateful smile before bounding up the stairs to quickly bathe and dress in clean clothes. Before leaving his room, he retrieved the notebook containing their notes from under his mattress.

When he finally saw Elsie and Kate sitting comfortably in the grass near one of the younger trees, the tightness in his chest eased a bit. He took a deep breath, removing his hat as he approached them.

Kate was the first to notice him. "Asher!"

A smile widened her thin face. Asher wasn't sure if her cheeks were flushed from the sun or at the sight of him. Next to her Elsie was pale, her eyes shadowed.

"We've missed you, Asher," said Elsie.

"I've not been gone *that* long." His heart swelled at the greeting, but there was something odd about her manner. She looked beaten down, listless. When she averted her eyes from his, he turned a questioning eyebrow to Kate, but she merely shook her head and frowned.

"May I sit?" he asked.

"Of course." Kate shifted closer to Elsie and patted the blanket. After stifling a yawn, she smiled at him. "How was Trinity?"

"It was fine."

Kate seemed altered, too. Her lip was swollen and her eyes as weary as Elsie's.

"Fine?" Kate's smile faltered. "Is that all you have to say?"

"No, I have plenty to say . . . but not really about Trinity." He paused to take a breath. "It's Billy. I learned something, and I raced back here to tell you."

Kate stiffened at the mention of Billy, but she said nothing.

"Go on," urged Elsie.

Asher turned to Kate. "Do you remember when we saw his body, and he had the red marks on his chest?"

"And the bruise on his face," she said.

"Yes, but no fatal violence to his body, at least as far as the police could tell. Based on what I've learned, however, I think the marks on his chest *were* the evidence of fatal violence."

"How?"

He struggled for the right words. "Well, this is very theoretical, and I confess that my strongest evidence comes from Elsie's conversation with Billy during her spell at the Castle End cottage."

"So you believe her now?" Kate frowned.

"I want to. Certainly more than I did before," he said, glancing quickly at Elsie. "If we take her evidence as fact, we know a man stood over Billy's body while the boy's limbs jerked and flailed. I fear I've seen something frighteningly similar." He explained what he'd encountered at Addenbrooke's Hospital.

As Kate listened, her mouth fell open. "You think someone *electrocuted* Billy? But why?"

He pulled the notebook from his pocket and searched out the correct page. "I do think his killer electrocuted him, but I don't know whether it was part of that 'improving experiment' Billy mentioned, or if it was merely a way to . . . silence him."

Kate narrowed her eyes. "You are quite enthusiastic all of a sudden. You hardly seemed to care about poor Billy before."

Asher closed the notebook. She was right—he'd clung to his doubt so stubbornly. They must have thought him quite beastly at times. But they couldn't understand without knowing about his father . . . and Letty.

"It's true that I never knew Billy," he finally said. "And I've been skeptical about this business of talking to spirits. But in the past two days I've seen things that make all we've discussed more real, more urgent, than it was before. Something terrible has happened, and I . . . I need to understand it if we can hope to stop it."

"I've learned something, too," said Kate softly. "Yesterday was quite the day for dark revelations."

Her voice was uncharacteristically somber—void of teasing or sarcasm. Even Elsie turned worried eyes to her. "What do you mean, Kate?"

"I paid a visit to my father's widow early yesterday evening. She was in Cambridge with her politician husband, and I thought to speak to her at the Prince Albert Hotel." She paused, frowning. "The woman took great pleasure in telling me how much of a disappointment my father was to her. In fact, she characterized him as a fool. But that hasn't anything to do with Billy." She bit her lip.

"Go on," Asher urged.

"She told me that my father and his friends in the Metaphysical Society went to dangerous lengths to—how did she put it—'lift the veil of the spirit world.' Their research involved the use of narcotics. I knew already that my father died from taking too much chloroform, and that it was ruled accidental because he'd been treating his neuralgia. He did have a medical degree, after all. But according to that wretched woman he married, he was using narcotics as part of his research, and in the end it killed him."

Elsie gasped. "Kate, why didn't you tell me any of this?"

"I was distracted," Kate said drily.

"This chloroform . . . is it like Chlorodyne?"

"Actually, it's much less dangerous."

Asher noticed the flush that crept up Elsie's neck. "What

exactly *happened* here?" he asked. "You both look haunted. Is there something you haven't told me?"

"I'm getting to the worst of it," Kate continued. "I was upset after seeing that woman, so when I returned to Summerfield I told Mr. Thompson I was ill and went to bed. But later, long after dark, I left the college again. This time I went to Castle End to find Tec."

"Hold on," said Asher. "You left the college in the middle of the night?"

"There's nothing to it." Kate glanced again at Elsie. "I'm quite used to getting about at night. But that's not important right now. Do you both remember the papers Billy talked about? The ones he found the night he was searching for information on my father?"

"The ones he took for his blackmail scheme," Elsie said.

"Yes. When I went to see Tec he wasn't there. But it occurred to me that the most likely place Billy would hide those papers would be somewhere in that house. Billy didn't have any other home, after all—no permanent place to go anytime he wanted. So I searched Tec's cottage."

Elsie's eyes widened. "Did you find them?"

Kate nodded.

"Did you bring them with you?" Asher asked.

Kate shook her head. "I started to read them, but Tec came back, and he . . . he took them from me and threw them in the fire."

Elsie gasped. "I thought he was your friend, Kate. Yours and Billy's."

"He was different somehow. I can't explain it, but he was quite rough with me." Tears welled in Kate's eyes. "I can't show you what was written on those pages—I don't even know who wrote them because they were torn from a journal and weren't signed—but I remember the most important details. Whoever wrote the notes said that he and my father, and perhaps others, worked together to reach the 'dark spaces of the mind.' They experimented on themselves with mesmerism and narcotics." She frowned. "We know how that ended with my father. But the point of the journal entry was that this person—the very person who must have killed Billy—argued that it was better to experiment on 'lesser' people. Those who are unwanted, who contribute little or nothing to society. I think he meant the poor and those who live outside of the law. The sorts that proper people never see and care nothing about. Who would miss them?"

As a heavy silence fell, Asher felt the last piece of the puzzle clicking into place. "Dark spaces of the mind—are you certain that's what this person wrote?"

Kate nodded.

"Unlocking hidden abilities, accessing the subliminal self— that's Dr. Marshall's line of research. And he knew Frederic Stanton well. He told me he testified at his inquest."

Kate gasped. "I read that in my father's obituary. How could I have forgotten? Do you think *he's* behind all this?"

"I'm certain he's experimenting with electric shock." Asher turned to Elsie. "Didn't he say that the subjects he'd studied— those who had a special ability—only gained that ability after some traumatic event?"

"Yes, he did," said Elsie. "But Kate said he wasn't at the séance."

Kate narrowed her eyes. "Just because Billy met his killer *after* the séance doesn't mean the killer actually attended it.

"Still . . ." Elsie frowned. "He seemed such a gentleman."

Asher nodded. "I found him quite congenial. Billy would have, too . . . perhaps to the point of letting his guard down, or growing too bold."

"I suppose you're right," Elsie murmured.

"I don't understand how applying an electric shock would give someone a special ability," said Kate. "But might this explain Elsie's visions? She *was* struck by lightning."

"Dr. Marshall didn't provide much in the way of details," he said. "But if one did stop the heart, and then start it again with an electric shock—it's been done with animals, I'm told—perhaps it has some altering effect. Perhaps it truly does bring light to those darkened corners of the brain."

"Whatever Dr. Marshall is doing, it can't continue," Kate said fiercely.

"I agree," said Asher. "But we can't rush to the police with a theory like this—they'd laugh us out the door."

"You're right," Elsie murmured. "It would be about as convincing as me accusing my mother of murder because of what my dead grandmother said in a vision."

Asher frowned. "You're not still sore about that, are you? I'm doing my best to put my skepticism aside—you know that, don't you?"

"I know. I'm just agreeing with you, Asher. We need *more*."

He held her gaze for a moment before nodding. "We need tangible evidence. Billy must have somehow broken into Trinity and opened Marshall's research cabinet if he was able to find the notes you described, Kate." Asher paused, thinking. "Marshall told me he'll be at the Metaphysical Society meeting in London tomorrow night. I wonder if I could somehow persuade the porter that I'd left something in his rooms."

"Even if you were let into his rooms, you wouldn't know how to open a locked cabinet," said Kate.

Asher sighed. "I'll have to think of something else. In the meantime, though, we need to get into the old lab. If something happened to Billy there, I want to see if we can find anything. Perhaps Marshall stole the key from Mr. Thompson, and he uses that building because it is so remote."

"Or maybe my uncle *gave* him the key," Elsie said. "How could he not know what's going on right under his nose?"

Kate shook her head. "I can't see sweet old Mr. Thompson being involved. The building is some distance from the Gatehouse, and this time of year the trees provide cover. A colleague of Mr. Thompson's might notice this and take advantage of the setting."

"Perhaps getting into the old lab will clarify matters," Asher said. "The problem is getting in without causing damage or drawing attention."

"I can get us in easy." Kate raised her chin. "I took Tec's lock picks."

"And you know how to use them?"

"Of course I do. Billy taught me. I say we wait until after dark tonight and then meet on the landing by Elsie's room. We'll go down together and make our way to the old lab. I don't need light to pick the lock, but we should have a lamp or electric torch once we're inside. Can you figure that out, Elsie?"

Elsie nodded. "I'll bring my camera, too."

"Wait, now," Asher said. "Tomorrow night might be better—the Thompsons will be in London for the Metaphysical meeting. We'll be less likely to get caught."

"I want to save tomorrow night for breaking into Marshall's rooms at Trinity. If Billy could manage it, I can, too, but it'll take a little planning." Kate's eyes were bold. "Tonight is the old lab, and if that doesn't give us what we need, it's you, me, and Marshall's research cabinet tomorrow night."

Was Kate giving the orders now?

Well . . . she did seem awfully good at it. Asher held her gaze, noting the defiant gleam in her eyes. The girl knew her own mind, much more than he did his own. Those brown eyes challenged him to contradict her—she knew him that well—but he had no challenge of his own to return.

"Fine," he said evenly. "In fact, it sounds like a good plan."

chapter 31

Elsie sat in the darkness, entirely awake. She checked her clock with the electric torch purloined from the hall closet.

Not much longer.

Once the evening's plan had been settled upon, she'd taken half a spoon of Chlorodyne and napped until supper. A headache was forming around her temples now that it was past eleven o'clock, but at least she was alert.

She wasn't afraid, not really. Certainly she'd done wilder things than break into the old lab. And yet this plan was more dangerous than their earlier forays into detecting. At least two people had died, and they knew who'd killed them—now it was a matter of gathering evidence. They had moved past proving Elsie's abilities. Now they were going to prove a murder.

A strange excitement quickened her pulse, but it was nothing like the giddy pleasure of anticipation. Rather, it was a charge to her senses that came from doing something important, taking a risk to achieve a good thing, a *right* thing. She'd never felt this way before. For so long she'd allowed herself to slip into drowsy avoidance whenever conflict reared its head. The only effort she'd made was to attract a man. One who would solve her problems just by loving her. It seemed ridiculous now.

A soft knock came at the door—Kate and Asher were ready for her. She set the clock down and quietly rose from her chair. She could barely see their faces in the hall, but she sensed the tension in their bodies and knew they felt the same excitement. Her heart warmed to them.

No one spoke until they were within sight of the old lab.

"I just need one glimpse of the lock and then I should be able to work it," Kate said. "Elsie, can you shine the light when I tell you to? Asher can stand behind you and provide cover."

Elsie did as told, grateful for Asher's reassuring presence. Kate studied the lock, then slipped a leather-wrapped bundle from her pocket and ran her fingers over each slender tool. "This one should do." She eased one pick into the lock and then inserted a second one over it. "You can shut off the light. I've got the feel of it now."

After a moment Elsie heard a faint click, and Kate grunted in satisfaction.

"Is that all it takes?" Asher whispered.

Kate opened the door. "Nothing to it."

Once the door was shut behind them, Kate and Asher checked that all the drapes were tightly closed. "You can switch the torch back on," Kate whispered.

Elsie pointed the light in the nearest corner. "Let's start here and work our way around."

They scanned shelves, cabinets, and small equipment, none of which looked particularly menacing to Elsie. It was a dusty, stale-smelling building, with a frightful number of cobwebs. Finally the beam of her torch alighted on something that made Asher gasp.

"That's it. I'd wager that box contains an induction coil."

He opened the lid to reveal a substantial metal cylinder. "It's larger than Dr. Spring's." He lifted a paddle that attached to the cylinder with a wire. "If you apply this to the chest and flip the lever, you deliver a shock so powerful that it can stop the heart. But apparently if you shock the heart again, you restart the beating. Dr. Spring told me it had been done on a dog, but I think Marshall's been trying to figure out how to do it on a human."

"And killing old men and children in the process," said Elsie bitterly. "It took lightning to stop my heart. How can they harness that power in such a small apparatus?"

"Can you take a photograph of it?" Kate asked.

"Asher, you take the torch," Elsie said, handing it to him, "and shine it directly on the induction coil. I must hold the camera very steady, or else the photograph will be blurry." She lifted the camera strap over her head, but after a closer look at the coil she couldn't resist reaching toward the metal cylinder—it was simple, and yet so menacing.

The instant her hand touched the cool metal of the coil, the air began to shimmer and contort. A tremendous shudder coursed through her body and the camera fell to the floor.

"Elsie, are you all right?" asked Kate.

Elsie heard the words, but she couldn't answer. Already the pull of the dark between overwhelmed her. All she could do was grit her teeth and endure the fall.

When she felt steady enough to risk opening her eyes, she saw a young man. He stared down at the induction coil, his dark hair flopping into his eyes. His shirt sagged loosely over a thin frame. He lifted his chin and met her gaze. She saw now that he was near her age, and that his blue eyes, framed by dark brows, were handsome. They widened at the sight of her.

"Has he sent you to fetch me?" he asked eagerly.

"What?"

"I'm scared, miss. It's not right me being here. It's too far away, and I'm afraid I'll never get back."

No spirit had ever spoken to her like this. She'd seen confusion and fear—anger even—but not this particular sort of desperation.

"I'm afraid I don't know how to help you. What happened?"

"Same thing as happened to Billy, I think, but Billy's gone for good. The gentleman said it would work this time. But, miss, I fear I'm stuck here."

She took a breath. "Tell me your name."

He frowned. "It's Thomas."

The poor boy didn't understand. She had to tell him, but gently. She took a deep breath. "Thomas, you have died. As soon as you realize that, you will be able to move on."

He shook his head. "But, miss, I ain't dead. And I don't want to be stuck here no longer!"

He lunged forward, forcing her to step back. His urgency was alarming—all she wanted in that moment was to be far away from him. With that thought she felt the familiar pulling, spinning sensation. It was almost a relief to fall.

She woke to find herself on the dusty floor, cradled in Asher's arms. Kate crouched next to them, clutching Elsie's camera.

"Elsie!" Kate laid a cool hand on her forehead. "Are you all right? I never expected another seizure." She turned to Asher, as if seeking confirmation. "The last two times we were near the old lab, nothing happened."

"This is the first time we've been inside it, though," said Asher.

"Did you see Billy?" Kate said.

Elsie allowed Asher to help her sit upright. "No. This vision was . . . so very strange." She shivered. "The spirit I saw seemed unusually aware, and yet more vulnerable than any other I've encountered."

"Another victim of Marshall's experiments?" Asher asked.

"Yes. A recent one, I think. Otherwise I would have felt him before, wouldn't I? He was tall and thin with unruly dark hair. Close to our age, I think. He said his name was Thomas."

"No!"

Elsie turned to Kate. "What is it?"

"I just saw him yesterday," Kate moaned. "He can't be dead."

"Who?"

"Tec. My friend in Castle End—I took you to his house. His real name is Thomas."

"I thought you said he was rough with you." Asher pointed at her lip. "He did that, didn't he?"

"He must have been trying to get me as far away as possible." Kate slumped against the table, her eyes glistening in the torchlight. "Maybe he knew something terrible was going to happen."

Elsie took both her hands. "I'm so sorry, Kate."

"Was he scared?" Kate finally asked. "Did he know what had happened?"

"I don't think so. He said he wasn't dead, and that he thought I was coming to fetch him." Elsie shook her head. "I've seen other spirits who weren't yet aware—Billy was that way— but this boy was different. He said the same thing that happened to Billy happened to him, that Billy was gone for good, but he was stuck. I don't know. I can't quite make sense of it."

"He can't be *gone*," Kate whispered. "I never got to . . . I mean, there never was a chance for me to say . . ."

Kate began to cry, and Elsie pulled her into an embrace, stroking her head until the shuddering and sniffling eased. She'd assumed Kate cared for Tec as a friend, but clearly it ran deeper than that. "I'm sorry," she whispered, drawing a handkerchief from her pocket and gently wiping Kate's face.

Asher stood. "That makes three deaths now." He helped Kate to her feet, holding her until she was steady. When he extended his hand to Elsie, she took it gratefully.

"What do we do?" she asked.

"We break into Dr. Marshall's rooms tomorrow night," said Kate with grim determination.

Elsie looked to Asher, almost wishing he would say no, that after this night, these revelations, he wasn't willing to risk it.

"Tomorrow night, then," he said.

chapter 32

Kate looked up from her sewing to glance at the sitting room clock. "Four more hours."

Since they'd settled on their plan, she'd lost her nerve at least a dozen times. The scheme was preposterous, after all. Breaking into a college? What did they expect to find—a signed confession? But then she remembered Billy's pale corpse, and her last encounter with Tec, and she regained her resolve.

"I hate waiting," Asher muttered. "Wish we could just get it over with."

"It'll come soon enough," said Elsie. "I'll hate staying behind while you two do your sleuthing."

Kate turned to her. "Surely you didn't want to go."

"I *can't*. Millie will be hovering—Aunt has given her orders—and there's no way she'd keep silent if I left the house. I'll have a hard enough time explaining your absence."

"It's difficult imagining two of us sneaking into Trinity," Asher said. "Three is just asking to get caught."

They fell silent again. Kate gave up watching the clock and turned back to the trousers she was hemming. Once worn by the gardener's young assistant, they'd been consigned to the ragbag when he outgrew them. Elsie had fished them out that morning, arguing that Kate couldn't well enter Trinity College wearing a skirt. Kate warmed to this immediately. She rather liked the idea of trousers—much easier to sneak about that way.

All of this would have been much easier had she been a boy.

She'd thought to be gone by now. Gone to London with coins in her pocket from Mrs. Elizabeth Gardner. Gone with Tec to find a new scheme in the biggest city in all of England, far away from Robert Eliot.

Had he learned her name yet? Perhaps he'd already reported her to the police.

"I think I should tell you both something," she said quietly, keeping her head down. She could feel their eyes on her.

Elsie's voice was gentle. "What is it, Kate?"

Kate set the trousers aside. "Do you remember the night I didn't go to dinner because I heard Robert Eliot's voice?"

"Of course. You seemed very frightened of the man."

"I told you he was Martineau's patron. He was her lover, too, I think. His behavior during séances was often . . . unseemly."

"In what way?" asked Asher.

Kate swallowed before answering. "He couldn't keep his hands to himself. There were other male sitters like that, of course, but there was always something especially rough about him. And when I was sacked, Martineau threatened to have him punish me if I didn't leave right away."

"He certainly seemed like a beast that night at dinner," Asher said. "He mentioned you. Not by name, of course, but that he wished the police to get hold of you. Mr. Thompson betrayed nothing, however."

"What is it you wished to tell us, Kate?" Elsie prompted.

"That day by the river—when I said I'd seen someone I knew?"

"And you ran after him in the rain. Yes, I remember."

"It was Tec. I never could catch up to him, but I ran into someone else instead."

"Eliot?" asked Asher.

"Yes. And he threatened to drag me to the police right then and there. He was still angry with me for ruining things with Martineau and making him look a fool. I tried to break away from him, but I couldn't get free. I was frightened, and I didn't want to be locked up as a fraud and a thief. So I . . . well, I had a knife that Billy gave me, and I was just so scared—"

Elsie gasped. "Kate, did you kill him?"

"No! I'm not sure I could have even if I'd wanted to. But . . . I stabbed him." Her voice pitched higher. "Just enough to make him let me go."

"Good Lord," said Asher.

"He never knew my name, but it wouldn't be that hard to discover it. What will happen to me? I'm an orphan, a swindler, and a stabber of gentlemen—for the last few days I've been plotting to run away to London."

"Why didn't you tell us?" asked Elsie.

"Thought I could manage on my own, but I've just made things worse."

Asher straightened in his chair. "Well, no one's going to drag you off to prison. We won't let that happen. We'll get you a lawyer if we must."

"And perhaps Eliot will let the matter drop." Elsie's eyes brightened. "Or we could have Aunt Helena speak to him. I'm certain he's quite intimidated by her."

"If Eliot was fool enough to take a fraudulent medium as mistress, we can figure out some way to get around him," Asher said. "Even if it comes to blackmail."

"Blackmail can prove a deadly scheme," said Kate.

Asher closed his eyes. "Of course. I'm sorry."

"Don't worry about Eliot. We'll get that sorted later." Elsie rose from her seat. "I've finished this jacket, but you'll need braces if you're to keep the trousers up. I'll go poke about in Uncle's things. He's grown so thin he's hardly bigger than you, Kate."

Once Elsie was gone, Kate found it hard to concentrate on sewing, especially with Asher staring at her from across the room.

"What is it?" she finally asked.

"I'm just thinking."

"About?"

He frowned. "Robert Eliot."

"That's a waste of time, unless you've discovered a way to make him vanish from the earth."

"No, I'm thinking of him and Martineau. Wondering why a gentleman would lower himself like that."

"I rather thought of it the other way around. He's a disgusting brute."

"So is Martineau." Asher's voice was harsh. "She's yet another example of why I detest Spiritualism. It's a con game, and half the time the medium uses her beauty to seduce her patrons."

"You talk like someone who's been conned," said Kate.

Asher was silent for a moment. "Not me, exactly."

Kate leaned forward, interested. "Who, then?"

Asher shook his head and picked at his fingernails.

"Does this have something to do with your father? The day we met you mentioned a quarrel, and since then you haven't read any of his telegrams."

Asher stared at the floor in silence.

Kate took a breath, striving to gentle her tone. "Your father was conned by a medium?"

"*Seduced* more than conned," he finally said.

She waited for him to elaborate, but he continued to stare at the floor.

"Tell me, Asher. Unless you wish to hold on to this anger until it burns you up."

He rolled his eyes. "I hate to even think about it . . . much less talk about it. But you deserve to know. Father's been collecting data on a Boston medium for years—a Miss Letitia Smith." He laughed bitterly. "An unassuming name for such an accomplished schemer."

Kate nodded, trying to keep her expression open.

"Father's certain she has legitimate ability, but documenting it has been a trial. He's worked so often and so *closely* with her that even Mother complains."

"So he spends too much time with her?"

He shook his head. "He's in love with the woman. *She* told me so."

She read betrayal in his expression, but not that of a child's disillusionment over a father's failings. Something else fueled this anger, and she'd have to prod him further to learn what exactly.

"Do you feel badly for your mother? Is that why you're so bitter?"

He glanced at her, and she was surprised to see a glaze of tears in his eyes. "I hardly care what Mother thinks. It's a terrible thing to say, but it's true."

And then Kate knew. Strangely enough, it pained her. "This Miss Smith . . . *you* cared for her, didn't you?"

He closed his eyes. "She encouraged it, and I was a fool."

The anguish in his voice took her by surprise. She could think of no appropriate response. He *was* a fool, and yet her heart went out to him.

"As you might imagine, Father proved the worthier target. Once his obsession became apparent, Letty dropped me like a piece of trash. In fact, she mocked my feelings to my face, and I'm sure she made a joke of it to Father." He rubbed his eyes. "I can't believe I'm telling you this."

Kate clenched the hands in her lap. "What a wretched woman. If she were here, I'd . . . I don't know. I'd pull her hair out."

He grinned faintly. "I've no doubt you could do her some damage."

Asher's grin brought a strange flutter to her heart. "Is that why you came to England? To get away from this creature?"

"Yes . . . mostly."

She turned to face him again. "Was there some other reason, Asher?"

He returned her gaze evenly. "You already know Father sent me away—I admitted that our first night here." His tone was light. "He sent me to stay with my uncle in Rye, which is the same thing as being sent to the edge of nowhere, as far as I'm concerned."

"Why was he punishing you?"

He looked away. "I don't want you to think ill of me."

"And yet clearly you wish to speak of this. You've been angry about something ever since I met you. There must be a reason you refuse to read your Father's messages."

After a moment his stony expression crumbled. "I stole from him." He glanced at her. "A great deal of cash. I arranged for passage to England. And do you know why? Even after she betrayed me and made me look an utter fool, I hoped Letty would come away with me . . . if I had enough money."

Kate imagined the beautiful young lady—she rather disliked the way he'd said *Letty*—smiling seductively at him. So seductively that he'd betrayed his own family to have her. It really was very childish. But also bold . . . and strangely passionate from gruff, scornful Asher.

She cleared her throat. "So your father found out and banished you to Rye."

"Without much in the way of funds, as you might imagine. It was my uncle's generosity that enabled this trip to Cambridge. I'm certain he was quite bored with my sulks."

"And this Letty person? What became of her?"

"She's the one who told Father of my theft. As far as I know, she has him under her spell to this day." He turned away, rubbing again at his eyelids.

Kate could think of nothing to say, so she held her tongue.

"Please don't tell Elsie any of this," Asher finally said. "It's so humiliating."

That rankled a bit. Was it better to be the one confided in or the one to be protected? She shrugged the question away, peeved by her own peevishness. "Neither of us has any reason to be proud of our fathers. Yours is in love with a medium. Mine kept a secret mistress and died from taking too much chloroform in some bizarre experiment that I still don't understand."

"We'll learn more tonight, Kate. I fear it won't be pleasant, but at least we'll know. And if all goes as it should, we will find damning evidence."

Kate nodded. That was what she wanted most—to tie everything together, to finally understand. And, of course, to make the villain pay.

chapter 33

The sight of Kate in boys' clothing left Asher speechless. He could only stare as Elsie proudly paraded the girl before him. His disquiet must have been obvious, for as soon as they'd slipped away from Summerfield, Kate laid a hand on his arm.

"Is there something wrong with the clothes? Should I swagger a little more?"

"No, that's not it."

"Then what's the matter?"

How could he say it? In truth, she looked quite fetching in trousers. He'd thought her a rather scrawny girl, but apparently her made-over blouse and skirt had swallowed her form. Now he could see the slimness of her waist, the slight curve of her hips. The unexpected length of her legs. All this added to the way she'd bundled her hair into that cap—so that it drew his eyes to her long neck—left him hardly knowing how to treat her as the same old Kate.

He forced himself to look away. It was nerves, really. He couldn't think why else he'd be distracted by such things. "It's nothing, Kate. I'm just getting accustomed to seeing you in trousers."

She cocked her head. "Don't I make a good boy?"

"To someone who doesn't know you, perhaps."

He knew, however, that seeing her this way only made him more conscious of her being a girl. And if he didn't stop acting like a fool, she would know *exactly* what he was thinking. In fact, she probably already did, for she'd dropped her gaze to the ground.

"Shall we move on?" he finally said.

He kept his eyes focused ahead after that, grateful for the silence that fell between them. When they finally reached the wrought-iron gate at the Queen's Road entrance to Trinity College, he welcomed the strange quivering in his stomach, for it had had nothing to do with Kate.

"Are you certain you're ready for this?" he asked her.

She rolled her eyes. "Of course I am—this was *my* plan, after all."

"You couldn't have managed it without me."

"Don't be so sure of that." She reached out to trace the pattern of the wrought iron. "I've always admired the Queen's Road gate. From this side, the college seems full of mystery and secrets. The Great Gate on the other end looks more like a prison tower."

"This gate will be easier to enter, but not by much." He paced the length of it to study the ditch on either side. The water looked to be several inches deep. "I'll go first. It's going to take quite a leap to get over this." He glanced back at her. "Hope you're not afraid to get those trousers muddy."

"That's why I wore them," she said mildly.

He turned back to the ditch. As far as he could tell in the low light, it was shallowest at the southern end of the gate. As he studied the distance, mentally calculating where to take the leap, he heard Kate yawn. Heat came to his cheeks, and he tensed his muscles in preparation. The leap across was quite bold, but he crumpled to his knees upon landing. By the time he'd scrambled up the hill, his hands and knees were filthy with mud.

"Kate, I'm not sure how you'll manage." He wiped his hands on his trousers. "That was harder than I thought."

"Oh, I'll manage," she said softly.

He turned to find her dragging a small plank toward the ditch. "Where'd you find that?"

"Tucked away under the bridge," she said, gingerly lowering the plank across the ditch. "I figure that's how Billy got across. I'd wager a student stored it there ages ago."

He watched in silence as she neatly stepped sideways across the plank. Once on the other side, she grabbed a low-hanging tree branch and used it to pull herself up the embankment. He offered a hand to ease her final steps toward him.

"Well done," he said. "We should avoid the graveled avenue and take the meadow up to the river instead. It may not be smooth going, but I can't think of any better way in."

"I'll go first."

"Kate, you must be stealthy."

She chuckled. "Getting around in the dark is what I do best, remember?"

As they crossed the meadow, Asher thought back to the day he'd lain there and first realized how much he wanted to be part of Trinity. Matters had become so strangely complicated since then. If they could just make it through this night without being locked up for trespassing, he would give serious thought to what he really wanted to do with his life.

"Stop here," he whispered, pausing by a tree. "We must cross that bridge. Directly across from us is the Wren Library. We need to get into the courtyard next to it."

"New Court," said Kate.

He turned to her. "How did you know?"

"The rowing trip. We had a picnic in the grass over there."

"Of course you did," Asher muttered. "The New Court entrance would be the most direct way to Dr. Marshall's rooms, but the gate is closed and certainly locked. Even if you could unlock it, there's probably a porter just within."

"I don't like the look of that gate," said Kate. "I'm not sure I could manage the lock, and opening that hulking thing would be noisy anyway. If there's a porter in there, he couldn't fail to hear it. Much too risky." She paused, staring at the Wren Library. "What about that entry there?" She pointed at the center of the building. "If we get through there, can we find our way to New Court without crossing the porter's path?"

Asher thought back to the tour Marshall had given him. "Yes. At the eastern end of the cloisters there's a passage that will take us to New Court."

"Let's do that, then. The bridge looks clear, and I don't see anything moving near the library. Follow me."

As they crossed the bridge, Asher noted how noiselessly Kate moved, how still and low she kept her body, and tried to mimic her movements. When they reached the central iron gate, Kate put her hands on the lock and laughed softly. "This one is a cinch. They've added a padlock, but that's no problem at all. Will you hold this?" She opened the tool kit and placed it in his hands. Then she chose a narrow bar and a pick. Within seconds she'd popped the padlock apart and opened the gate.

She waved him through and quietly closed the gate behind him, hanging the padlock back in place without actually locking it. "I'd lock it again," she whispered, "but it'd be the devil to open from the inside. I've no idea where we're going, so I suppose you'd better lead the way now."

He smiled at the reluctance in her voice. How she *hated* to follow.

They stepped lightly along the stone floor of the cloisters. He'd crossed half the distance when he felt Kate's hand on his arm. He turned to find her standing still, finger to her lips. After a moment she gestured frantically behind him.

Now he heard the clattering footfalls . . . and the low murmur of voices.

He glanced around—there was no alcove in which to hide. Perhaps that wall over there? He took Kate's hand and moved quickly, pulling her to him as he flattened himself against the wall. His heart lurched into such a pounding that he wondered if Kate could feel it leaping in his chest.

Two men came into view, their stiff white shirts bright against their dark evening clothes. One, a portly man with his loosened tie flapping, staggered every few steps.

"You'll see I'm correct," he said, his words echoing in the cloisters, "and I'll expect a bottle of the college's finest port to be delivered to my room before tea tomorrow."

"If I'm correct, and I know I am, you'll be delivering that bottle to me." His friend did not slur so noticeably. "Chaucer only mentions Philomene by name in *The Legend of Good Women*. In fact, I'll wager *two* bottles on it."

"No, no, no, I'm quite certain she's named in *Troilus and Criseyde,* book two, when the nightingale sings as Criseyde falls asleep. I know it in my bones."

"In your cups, you mean. You're dead drunk."

"Now that's Cicero. *In thy cups, in the midst of thy revels!*"

Both men guffawed at that. There was a noise of jangling keys and muttered oaths as one unlocked the library door. Soon thereafter the door slammed shut and the corridor fell silent again.

"It's safe enough now," Kate whispered, slipping from his arms. "Do you think they noticed the open padlock?"

"Too drunk, I'm sure."

"Are the Fellows always so jolly?"

"They do like their wine," he said. "Why? Do you fear I'll become a drunkard if I survive this night and become a Trinity man?"

She glanced at him. "You're not that sort of fool."

"What sort of fool am I?"

But she had paused again, this time to stare back at the upper level of the Wren Library. "Good Lord! They keep all the books up there? Look at those gorgeous windows. I thought the new Summerfield library was grand, but this place makes it seem quite ordinary."

"We're almost there—it's just up this staircase. Marshall's room is the first door on the left, so get your tools ready."

Asher meant to keep an eye on the corridor as Kate studied the lock on Marshall's oak door, but he couldn't help admiring her concentration as she selected the proper tools and applied them to the lock. Soon enough he heard the satisfying click as the lock gave way.

Kate stood and opened the door. "What's this?"

He reached for the simple handle of the green baize middle door and pulled it open to reveal the innermost door. "Only the outer door is locked."

"*Three* doors?" She shook her head in amazement. "It's like a fairy tale."

"I'd never seen anything like it before." Once inside he quietly closed all the doors behind them and lit a small study lamp. "Marshall's research cabinet is over there."

Kate stood as if frozen, staring about the sitting room. "Who would have thought a Fellow was allowed so much space? How many rooms are in this apartment?"

"He has two sitting rooms and two bedrooms. Apparently

Fellows are expected to entertain." He pointed at the oak file cabinet. "Shall we get started?"

She glanced sidelong at him. "Marshall is in London, isn't he? We have plenty of time."

"Not enough to waste," Asher said. "If we are caught, my chances of a place at Trinity College are ruined forever, so I say the quicker we're out of here the better."

She held his gaze for a moment. "Don't worry, Asher." After a moment she removed her hat and set it on top of the cabinet. "That thing is making my scalp itch. Shine the light over this, won't you?"

He could see nothing that resembled a lock, but after running her hands over the decorative trimming at each side Kate flipped the panels open to reveal two centrally located keyholes.

"Just as I thought," she said. "Almost as easy to open as a padlock. Gentlemen like Marshall should take more care to protect their secrets."

Chapter 34

Elsie stood at the sitting room window, watching the gas lamps flicker over Summerfield Walk. Asher and Kate had left not quite an hour ago, but already she fidgeted. Each second that ticked on the clock unnerved her. She forced herself to sit, but less than a minute later she was up again, pacing back and forth in front of the window.

What if they didn't return? What was she supposed to do then?

"Miss, can I get you anything?"

Elsie turned to find Millie at the doorway, blinking sleepily.

"I'm fine, Millie. You should go to bed."

"Begging your pardon, miss, but Mrs. Thompson told me not to retire until everyone was settled. You're still up, and I heard Mr. Beale and Miss Poole leave earlier." The girl stifled a yawn. "I don't wish to catch trouble, miss."

"Everything is fine, Millie. You're asleep on your feet, so please don't stay up any longer."

Millie squirmed. "I can't lose this position, miss."

"And you won't. Mr. Beale and Miss Poole will return soon

and we'll all be safe in our beds before midnight. I will assure my aunt that you took wonderful care of us in her absence."

The maid bobbed a curtsy, a grateful look on her face. "Thanks, miss."

Once alone, Elsie turned back to the window with a sigh.

Her thoughts threatened to turn to Simon, but she was doing her best to circumvent them. Only last night she'd resolved to no longer allow her life to revolve around a man's affections. Now that she was alone and listless, her resolve was fading.

That night at Stonehill—had Simon thought of her as he fell asleep? How long after he woke did he remember what had happened? What was his greatest regret—pushing her away, or letting her through the door in the first place? She *knew* he'd desired her. It wasn't just a matter of using her to contact his lost love. Their connection was deeper than that.

Soon he would be gone, and so far out of her reach. He would forget her.

She nudged that thought aside, for she couldn't bear to imagine the days and months that would follow in which she had . . . nothing. No one to love. Nowhere to go. Thoughts like that made her long for the dose.

The clock chimed eleven. The next hour would stretch into eternity if she kept staring into the darkness outside. She settled into a chair and picked up the embroidery she'd pretended to work upon for the past two weeks.

After staring at it for a moment, she tossed the hoop aside.

Throughout the day a possibility had flickered through her mind—a way of passing the time in an active way, but only once Millie had retired for the evening. It was a shameful action she was contemplating, and Elsie cringed at the thought of betraying her family in this manner. And yet she needed to know.

Having grown up in a house of secrets, Elsie well knew how to read the body language of deception. The thought had been niggling at her for days, and now she firmly believed that her uncle was keeping something from them. He'd behaved strangely that day at the old lab, insistent that they not go inside. And earlier he'd been suspiciously vague about the key. Perhaps he had hidden it somewhere in the house. . . . If so, she would do her best to find it tonight.

She'd already looked through his bedroom dresser, but it merely contained clean clothes. Not surprising—her uncle was unlikely to hide anything secret there. So she started with his office, which was in its usual state of disarray. Hiking her skirts, she stepped around the piles of books and papers until she reached the desk. In this part of the house she shouldn't be overheard by Millie, but she still took care to keep quiet.

Her uncle's desk held nothing extraordinary. Inside she found papers, papers, and more papers, as well as pencils, thumbtacks, dusty bits of rubber for erasing, and other things typical to a scholar's desk. Nothing the least bit suspicious. So she turned to the specimen cabinet next to the window. It had a maddening number of shallow drawers, but Elsie was determined to open each one.

Her skin crawled at the thought of tiny mammal skeletons and hairy moths splayed on pincushions. To her surprise, however, her uncle kept more sentimental items in his specimen case. One drawer held a brooch and a watch fob made of human hair. She touched them lightly, marveling at the intricate weaving. Other drawers held pretty rocks, pressed flowers, and folded notes written in French and Latin. She recognized her aunt's handwriting in the latter and was glad she couldn't translate these private messages. She opened another drawer to find a delicate wren's nest, perfectly shaped and holding a tiny papier-mâché egg.

The more drawers she opened, the more she despised herself for invading her uncle's privacy. What had she been thinking? Uncle had bristled and scolded at the old lab because he was worried about their *safety,* not because he was hiding something.

She was close to putting an end to the horrid pillaging of the cabinet when she found the folded handkerchief containing a watch and a key.

The watch was very fine, fashioned of gold and intricately carved. She opened it with trembling fingers. Within she found the inscription she'd been dreading—TO DEAR FRIEND AND PUPIL F. STANTON FROM O. THOMPSON.

Kate had told her of this watch. Frederic Stanton had given it to her, the daughter he could not publicly recognize. Kate had given it to Billy, Billy had given it to his killer, and Uncle had somehow come into its possession after that.

Snapping the watch shut in her left hand, she turned her attention to the key, a clunky thing of dull metal that lay unmarked and untagged. She lifted it out of the drawer. Surely this was the key to the old lab. Why else would her uncle hide it with the watch?

Elsie stared numbly at the items, weighing them against each other as though her flattened palms were the pans of a balance scale.

If Asher and Kate could risk breaking into a Cambridge college, she could at the very least return to the lab and try once more to speak with Tec. This time she would ask him about her uncle and Dr. Marshall. And she wouldn't leave without getting a photograph of that beastly induction coil.

❖ ❖ ❖ ❖ ❖

The files were orderly and well marked—Kate had to give Marshall credit for being a tidy madman, at the very least. "We must be careful to put everything back exactly as we found it," she told Asher. "Someone this organized would notice if anything was amiss, and we don't want him to be suspicious. He might destroy important information if he thought it had been tampered with."

Asher frowned. "But I thought we would take the important evidence with us."

"We can take a piece or two, but not too much. Just enough for the police to take us seriously."

"And how are we to explain how we came upon this evidence?"

She thought for a moment. "I'll tell them Billy stole it and gave it to me for safekeeping."

They found Marshall's files from his student days at the bottom of the cabinet. But when Kate opened the first file, Asher shook his head. "They're just papers written for tutors," he said. "Can't imagine you'll find much there."

Kate moved on to his collection of published articles, carefully dividing them and giving half to Asher before she settled into reading. With all the unfamiliar words and complex sentences, it certainly wasn't easy going. She couldn't contain a gasp, however, when she found an article with *electrotherapy* in the title.

Asher nudged her. "What is it?"

She glanced over the first paragraph. "I can't make much sense of this one, but I think it's about epilepsy." She held up the pages for Asher to see. "Is that similar to Elsie's condition?"

He took the article and paged through it. "This *is* pretty

interesting," he said after a moment. "Marshall writes that epileptic states can be triggered in subjects using a pulsating current of electricity." He paused to read silently.

Kate shifted her feet impatiently. "Well?"

"Hold on. I just to need to make sure I understand this." After another maddening pause, he set the article down and met her gaze. "It's a study on the application of electric shock within a controlled environment. At a certain voltage, the subjects suffered convulsions and stopped breathing. But when the voltage was decreased, respiration was reestablished. At that point the subjects would fall into a profound sleep, proving unresponsive to pain stimulus. When the current was switched off, however, the subjects woke normally."

"My God, that sounds barbaric! Is that what Marshall tried to do to Billy? He must have started the convulsions but failed to bring him back."

Asher handed the article back to her. "I can't say. All these studies were performed on dogs and rabbits. Marshall is just reporting on the work of a French researcher."

Kate slumped. "Still, it's something. Keep looking."

In the uppermost drawer on the right side of the cabinet, she found a plump portfolio marked Research. The first item was an article for the *Metaphysical Society Journal* entitled "Subliminal Self." Following it were dozens of pages of handwritten notes.

"This looks promising." She handed Asher the article.

"Do you recognize the handwriting in those notes?" he asked. "Is it the same from the pages Billy had?"

She studied the neat script. "I only saw those pages for a few minutes, but it *could* be the same hand."

He read the article silently for a moment. "This is the theory Marshall outlined very briefly at the Thompsons' dinner that night—the notion of accessing latent abilities. There's nothing about electric shock here."

"These look to be notes from interviews." Kate scanned the first interview. "Listen to this—this first subject was an ordinary man who never before displayed any musical talent, but after a severe electrical shock he could play the piano as if he'd been trained for years."

"Did Marshall administer the shock?"

Kate read back through the details. "No, it was an accident—the man worked with high-voltage transmission lines. It's a miracle he survived."

"What else is there?"

She paged through. "Here's a woman who was thrown from a horse, struck her head on a tree, and upon recovery found herself able to speak a foreign language." She flipped more pages. "And here's one who claimed the ability to communicate with spirits after a brain injury, but Marshall has written 'known charlatan' at the bottom of the page."

"Can you find any mention of experimentation?"

She continued to flip pages. "It's just a series of interviews. There's nothing about Billy or Tec here. Nothing about the old lab or that vagrant found on the cricket grounds." She sighed. "He's even collected notes from other books—stories of people long dead, but he's noted the details of the 'gift' each person received after a brush with death."

"Search through the rest and let me know what you find." He handed the "Subliminal Self" article back to her. "Return this to the file, and I'll search the next folder."

She did as told, paging carefully through the accounts and pausing to reread when Marshall had penciled margin notes like "plausible" or "story confirmed by medical professional." At the end was a single sheet of paper with a few additional scribbled notes. She took it out and set the folder on the floor. The very first line set her heart racing.

Possible to safely induce mind-altering effects of near-death experience?

Mesmerism disappointing.

Nitrous proves mind-expanding, inspires epiphanies, but effects are temporary and exact nature of epiphany is forgotten.

In small doses, chloroform separates the mind from the body and heightens awareness—

A curious rattling noise drew her eyes from the page. It took her a moment to comprehend the sounds of a key being inserted into a lock and a knob turning. She turned to Asher, whose eyes widened.

"It's the outer door." He scooped up the folder and returned it to the cabinet.

"But I *just* found what we needed!" Kate folded the page and shoved it into her trouser pocket. "What do we do?"

"Lock the cabinet!"

There was no time to extinguish the lamp. No time to hide. All they could do was stand in the center of the room and look foolish as the innermost door opened.

Philip Marshall stood in the entry, eyes wide and mouth gaping.

"What the devil is going on here?"

Chapter 35

Elsie unlocked the side door and slipped out into the darkness, sidestepping the gravel path to run through the soft, damp grass. Her corset pinched her like a vise and the camera thumped against her hip, but she paused only long enough to catch her breath before pressing forward.

She slowed her pace when the white door of the old lab came into view. As she drew near, she studied the windows in the moonlight. All seemed dark and quiet.

She pulled the key from her pocket. Tucking the electric torch under her arm, she felt under the doorknob until she located the keyhole. The key slipped in and turned without effort.

She froze at a sound from within.

A low voice murmured. She couldn't make out the words, but the voice seemed calm. Then it fell silent.

Holding her breath, she slowly turned the key back and pulled it out. She waited to hear movement toward the door, bracing herself for a desperate sprint back to the Gatehouse. The voice came again, still calm. Heart pounding, she took three steps back.

Nothing happened.

Elsie turned around. A light shone in the sitting room window of the Gatehouse, beckoning her toward safety. The prospect of returning to her room and locking the door was tempting, but the thought of Kate and Asher reminded her to be brave.

She stepped softly around the building to the side window Kate had tried to open before Uncle caught them. Elsie had never asked if she'd managed to unlock it. Laying the torch on the ground, she reached up and tentatively pressed on the wood frame until it shifted upward an inch. She applied more pressure, praying for it not to make a sound. Inch by inch she lifted the window.

When she reached in to part the curtain, a sliver of light shone through. Was it enough light for a photograph?

Perhaps not a good one, but if she held the camera perfectly still she might capture the culprit on film. Elsie breathed deeply to steady herself. Asher and Kate were taking a terrible risk this night. She must draw strength from their example. Releasing a final breath of air, she retrieved the camera from the bag and extended the lens as quietly as she could. Then she guided it until the lens barely poked through the curtain. Steadying the camera on the windowsill, she held her breath and activated the shutter.

The click seemed to echo all around her. She steeled herself, but the silence continued. Weak with relief, she slowly slid the camera back through the window and folded it shut. The photograph might turn out dark and blurred, but at least she'd tried. Now she just had to get safely back to her room. She placed the camera back in the bag and gently lowered it to the weeds.

Just as she began to close the window panel, the voice came again. This time she could discern most of the words.

"You must wait exactly one minute . . . before you apply . . . second. Do you understand?

Her pulse leapt. *I know that voice.*

She parted the curtain and peered through. In the flickering lamplight she could see the cabinets of specimens and scientific instruments lining the walls. But a far more arresting sight took away the breath she'd finally managed to control—a bare-chested man lay sideways on a table, propped on an elbow.

Simon Wakeham.

That wasn't the strangest thing. She swallowed a cry when she saw who stood near him, his hand on the induction coil. It was the dark-haired boy from last night's vision—the one who'd said his name was Thomas. The one Kate called Tec.

She'd seen him in the spirit world. He was *dead.* How could he be standing there in the old lab?

Elsie heard a click, then a low whir. She watched as Tec pulled two paddles from the induction coil toward Simon's chest. Then he placed a wooden bar between the young man's teeth and pushed him back until he lay flat upon the table. Simon nodded and closed his eyes.

No.

She knew what Tec was about to do. No matter how Simon had offended her, she couldn't stand by and watch this. She must take Tec by surprise—distract him or throw him off balance somehow.

Elsie snatched the electric torch from the ground and edged around the corner of the building, coming to a halt by the door. She inserted the key and turned it slowly until the bolt retracted. Pocketing the key, she eased the door open and braced herself to rush upon Tec, fully intending to slam the torch at his head with all her might.

But she stopped dead at the sight of Simon's body convulsing as though a puppet string jerked him upward. Elsie could only stare in mute horror as he writhed. Finally Tec pulled the lever and Simon's body ceased its unnatural jerking.

Something in her brain snapped then, and the torch fell from her hand as she stumbled across the room, shoving Tec aside and grasping Simon's arm. He lay utterly still, his lower lip drooping under the bar in his mouth. His chest did not move.

"No, no, no," she groaned, touching his face and feeling the softness of his still-warm flesh. She leaned down, putting her ear by his mouth and then his chest.

He wasn't breathing.

She turned to Tec. "What have you done?"

The strange boy merely lifted a hand, palm facing her, and moved it as though he pushed her. He'd not actually touched her body. Nevertheless, Elsie reeled backward from some invisible force and fell hard to the floor.

Fear and rage battled within her, but Tec's face remained infuriatingly blank as he took a watch from his pocket and studied it. She glanced again at Simon's limp body. His right hand lay palm up, fingers extended.

She crawled toward him.

Let me go there. She reached up to grasp his hand. *Let me be with him.*

I want to fall.

Elsie gasped when that strange thread pulled at her spine and the spasm of nausea gripped her gut. She gave herself to the dark between, falling through the black spiral and the bone-chilling cold without fear. When the spinning, sucking sensation finally came to an end, she opened her eyes.

Simon stood before her, pale and blinking. Tec lingered in the shadows behind him.

Elsie took a step toward him. "Simon?"

He rubbed his eyes. "What's happened?"

"He's killed you."

Simon glanced to the side, as though considering this. "My God, I think he has." His voice registered surprise rather than horror.

"But . . . *why*?"

He looked around him, his eyes wide with wonder, before turning back to her.

"Because I told him to."

Chapter 36

Asher took a breath, thinking to somehow explain, to apologize, to say *something* that would get them away safely, but all that issued from his mouth was a rush of voiceless air.

His paralysis continued until the silence became oppressive, and still Philip Marshall didn't speak. Did he suspect what they were after? Surely he wouldn't do away with them in his own rooms at Trinity. If Kate still had her knife, it was possible they could fend him off—

"Mr. Beale," said Dr. Marshall, "I thought you'd returned to Summerfield, and yet here I find you in my rooms."

Asher swallowed, determined to speak.

No words came.

Marshall's narrow-eyed gaze moved from him to Kate. "And with a girl, I see. Certainly hadn't pegged you for such a precocious fellow. Did you sneak her in here? She's a bit young for this, isn't she?"

Kate stiffened next to him. "I'm his sister."

Marshall grunted. "My dear, you look nothing like him and, moreover, you do not share a surname. We've already met, remember? Last Sunday on Queen's Road. I never forget faces."

He turned to Asher. "And I hope you'd never allow any sister of yours to run about in the dark of night—in a laborer's trousers, no less. Just how did you get in here?"

Asher plundered his imagination for a reasonable answer, but his mind was a vast, empty chamber in which the words *precocious fellow* echoed. So he wiped his sweaty palms on his trousers and put an arm around Kate. "I just wanted time alone with her." He pulled her closer, praying she wouldn't protest. "I wished to impress her with your fine lodgings. It was easy enough to sneak her into the college, and I picked the lock on your door."

He didn't dare look at Kate.

Marshall's gaze was direct and assessing, but Asher refused to waver. After a moment the man's grim mouth softened. "There's more fire in you than I thought. Quite a bold maneuver to impress a girl."

Asher relaxed a fraction. "I never meant for you to find out, of course. I thought you were in London at the Metaphysical Society meeting."

Marshall grimaced. "Wakeham never showed up, and I wasn't about to linger. I usually stay at my club in London, but it seemed easier to take the late train back. My next lecture needs preparing, and all my research is here."

"We'll be on our way, then. I beg your pardon, sir. I do hope you'll forgive this tremendous breach—"

"Yes, yes." Marshall waved away Asher's apologies. "This sort of behavior will stand you in good stead with the Trinity boys next fall, but for your own sake I recommend more self-restraint. Make sure you see her safely to her door, and do not let Helena Thompson find you lurking about together. She'll ship you back to your father before you can take a breath."

"Yes sir. Thank you, sir." Asher steered Kate toward the door.

"Don't forget your lovely adornment, my dear." Marshall

tossed the cap, which Kate neatly caught in one hand. "See you next fall, Beale."

They made their way down the staircase in silence, Asher's heart still thudding at the memory of Marshall's face when he opened the door. He'd never felt so close to danger in his life. What if Marshall hadn't leapt to the wrong conclusion? What if he'd pulled out a knife . . . or a gun? He and Kate were fools for never considering how to protect themselves.

He turned to her. "Are you all right?"

"I think so," she whispered, twisting her hair and stuffing it back in the cap. "That was awfully close."

"You said you found something."

"I kept one page of scribbled notes. You took the folder before I could return it."

His heart leapt again. "Is it enough for the police?"

Kate reached into her pocket and drew out the folded piece of paper. "I didn't have a chance to finish reading, but these are notes about inducing near-death experiences. There's bits about mesmerism, nitrous, and even chloroform—that's what killed my father, you know."

Asher held out his hand. "Let me see."

"But it's dark!"

"I have matches in my pocket. We have good cover here, and no one seems to be about. I need to see this before we leave, Kate."

Once the paper was in his hand, he struck a match on his shoe and read quickly.

Possible to safely induce mind-altering effects of near-death experience?

Mesmerism disappointing.

Nitrous proves mind-expanding, inspires epiphanies, but effects are temporary and exact nature of epiphany is forgotten.

In small doses, chloroform separates the mind from the body and heightens awareness—but larger doses lead to unconsciousness. Overdose is fatal—remember Stanton.

Fibrillation and defibrillation conducted on animals—too dangerous with humans.

Refinement of apparatus possible, but ethical considerations overwhelming.

He reread the last two sentences aloud, tossing the match when it burned his finger. "You didn't read to the end, Kate."

"I didn't have time."

"Well, he seems far too cautious to undertake the kind of experiment we imagined."

"Sounds like he was strongly against *hurting* anybody, much less killing them," Kate muttered.

"All that trouble and we've found absolutely nothing incriminating." He shoved the paper into his pocket. "Come on, we should go."

They walked in dejected silence toward the Wren Library cloisters.

Kate sighed. "I really thought we had something."

"Keep your voice down," he whispered.

"Who's there?"

Asher halted abruptly, pulling Kate behind him. They had turned the corner and were mere yards from the ornamental gate that led to the Backs, but now two men in dinner jackets blocked their path—the same academics they'd encountered before. Judging by their hostile expressions, they'd sobered considerably during the last hour.

"How did you get in?" the stout one barked.

"I'll get the porter this instant," his companion said. "Dixon should ring the police. It seems we have a pair of thieves in our midst."

Asher pulled his hat low over his eyes and did his best to slump like a villain. He didn't remember meeting these two during his time with Marshall, but one couldn't be too careful. Should he reprise the story of impressing his lady friend? Appeal to their manly sensibilities? They'd seemed more interested in fictional ladies than flesh-and-blood ones. And how could he make such a confession without dragging Marshall into it?

Kate poked his back. "We can outrun them," she whispered.

He considered the gentlemen's bulging midsections, made even more prominent by their stiffly boiled shirts. And there was the gate with its open padlock benignly hanging to the side.

"Asher!" Kate hissed.

He squeezed her arm. "Run *now*. I'm right behind you."

Chapter 31

"**I** want to know why *you* are here." Simon's eyes were steely. "Are you . . . dead?"

"No," Elsie whispered. "This is where I go when the dead speak to me."

He looked about him, peering into the darkness. "Have you seen her? Is Amy here?"

"Is that why you did this? To be with her?"

Simon looked behind him, searching the darkness. "Amy, why won't you show yourself?" He turned wild eyes to Elsie. "Where is she? You told me she was with me always. I thought you saw her that day at the British."

She shook her head. "Spirits move on. I barely understand it myself."

Elsie glanced at Tec. He kept to the shadows, his face stricken. Simon did not seem to see him, so she braced herself for the next question. "How did she die, Simon?"

A shadow came over his face. "She took her own life. Her husband was insane, but she couldn't leave him. I loved her so *purely*. In the end it was still too much for her to bear."

"You chose this out of grief, because you wanted to join her in eternity?"

"No. I don't want to die—I just want to open a channel to her." Desperation contorted his features. "Why can't I see her?"

Before she could answer, Simon convulsed again, and she was falling . . . falling back to the hard floor of the old laboratory.

Head pounding, Elsie opened her eyes to see Tec lifting the wires from Simon's chest and helping him to sit upright. Simon coughed and gasped, clutching Tec's shoulder until his breathing calmed. Elsie watched mutely as he ran his hands over his chest, his face, and through his hair. He turned to Tec.

"It wasn't enough time, you fool. I couldn't find her!"

Elsie pushed herself up to her knees. "What have you done?"

"It seems that I've failed," he said softly.

"But . . . you're alive. How?"

"The same jolt that stopped my heart restarted it. It's as simple as that." He eased himself off the table and stepped toward her, offering his hand. "Why are you so shocked? You listened closely to our conversation at the Thompsons' dinner table. When you told me of your gift, I knew I was ready to take the risk."

"It's not a gift, Simon." Ignoring his hand, she shakily rose to her feet. "It's a curse."

"Do you know how long I've worked to achieve what you gained through sheer accident? I tried everything to bridge the divide between life and death—meditation, mesmerism, even mind-altering narcotics." He sighed. "And I've tested the abilities of every known psychic in England. They're all frauds. None of them could find Amy for me. But Marshall . . . he was onto something with his notion of the subliminal self. He'd found anecdotal evidence of people gaining new abilities after a brush with death. But he was too damned obstinate. He wouldn't experiment on himself or anyone else, not after Stanton died. So . . . I had to do it myself."

Elsie shook her head again, this time in disbelief. "How could you be so sure you would come back from death, Simon? How could you take such a risk?"

"I took a risk, yes. But not without testing." He gestured at the equipment. "I learned from Stanton's failings and Marshall's research. It took years to find the right method." He paused to lift one of the wires that had been attached to his chest. "The proper voltage and timing were determined through great sacrifice. Undergoing the process myself seemed the only way to honor those sacrifices."

Sacrifices.

Elsie's stomach convulsed. "Billy?"

"The boy was willing enough. So was Tec, for that matter. And I was willing to pay them quite handsomely for their efforts. They knew the risks."

She glanced at Tec. His expression was eerily blank, but something lurked behind his eyes. Elsie turned to Simon. "But I saw Tec in the dark between."

Simon blinked. "Where?"

"You and I met in a dark place after your heart stopped. I call it the dark between, and yesterday I spoke with Tec there. I thought he was dead, but here he is, and now he can't seem to speak at all. Something is terribly wrong with him. I hardly know how to make sense of it, but a part of him has *died*."

Simon studied the boy. "There's no denying he is altered. Doors to his subliminal mind have opened, just as Marshall theorized. The boy shows signs of telekinesis, but his supraliminal mind is somehow atrophied, or perhaps it's still striving to reconcile this transformation."

"How can you be so detached? Look at him. Look at what you've done! He's barely human anymore."

"Elsie, help me find Amy." Simon stepped closer. "Together we could reach her."

She flinched. "You can't ask me to do that."

"You told me once that you loved me."

He did not touch her, but Elsie could feel his desperation clouding her own mind, and it nearly took her breath away.

"I must reach Amy," he continued. "She was everything that was pure and beautiful in my life, and I failed her. I was selfish and petulant. I must make amends, and you can help me."

Somehow he was in her head—not merely his voice but a tangible sense of his urgency. As she stumbled back he moved with her, taking her face in his hands. Tec stood close behind him, his expression still blank.

Simon's thumbs caressed her cheeks. "You could free me, Elsie."

She searched his eyes and thought she saw a glint of fear . . . or was it madness? He'd killed an old man and a child, and he'd damaged Tec beyond repair. Only a monster could imagine these crimes as something necessary or heroic. What other facts had he twisted in his mind?

Could she trust anything he said?

"Simon . . . did *you* kill Amy?"

The color drained from his face. "Of course not."

"How can I believe you?"

Her heart leapt as his hands slipped down her cheeks to encircle her neck. "I blame myself for her death, I admit that," he said, "but I never touched her." His eyes filled with tears as his thumbs pressed the hollow of her throat. "Help me, Elsie."

"No," she whispered. If she gave in, he would surely silence her afterward. She looked to Tec. "Are you going to let him get away with this? He murdered Billy—your friend!"

Tec blinked.

"Hush, Elsie," Simon murmured. The pressure on her throat intensified.

"Billy was a child," she cried. "This wasn't some venture that turned out badly. He didn't know the risks he was taking. He *couldn't* know. I spoke to his spirit, Tec. He didn't even understand he was dead. All he wanted was to find you—he trusted *you*."

Tec's face contorted, and as it did, sparks flew from the wires attached to the curious cylinder behind him.

Simon shifted his grip to her waist and pulled her close. "Don't listen to her," he said to Tec. "I didn't murder Billy. He was an unfortunate casualty of our research, but an accident nonetheless. Now, we must get her out of here—and *quietly*."

Elsie's mind grappled wildly for another distraction. She stared at Tec, and it came to her. *Kate.* The poor girl had loved him. Had he returned her feelings?

"What about Kate, Tec?"

The wires sparked again, stronger this time. She searched the boy's slack face. Tec couldn't speak, but his mind vented emotion in other ways. She glanced toward the induction coil. It sat near a window . . . quite near the curtains.

"Elsie, we have to leave this building. Come with me to the Continent."

Simon's voice snapped her back to attention. She kept her eyes trained on Tec. "Kate is in danger. Billy found evidence of Simon's intentions to use innocent people for his experiments—he hid that evidence in your house. Kate read every word. She knows what he's done. If you don't stop him, *she* will be his next victim."

The apparatus wires flailed wildly as more sparks showered the room. Specimen jars and vials on nearby shelves began to shake.

"Calm yourself, Tec." Simon spoke soothingly, but Elsie could feel his heart pounding wildly. "We are surrounded by flammable liquids."

He can't control the boy. Hope fluttered in her chest as she appealed again to Tec. "You know he's going to kill us both and leave England entirely."

As Tec's eyes widened, two of the trembling jars tipped over and rolled off the shelf. Elsie heard the crash of glass on the stone floor, and the acrid scent of formaldehyde filled the air.

"Quiet, Elsie!" Simon's voice was husky with panic. "I won't hurt *anyone.* We must leave this place before Tec burns it down."

"Tec," she said in a low, steady voice. "Stop him. Otherwise you and I will both die here. And then he'll go after Kate." She looked him straight in the eye, willing him to remember the life he'd once had. "I can help you, Tec. I'll do everything I can to make you whole again . . . and take you back to Kate."

As Tec returned her stare, his lower lip began to quiver. In one swift motion he pulled Simon's hands from her waist and shoved him hard. Simon stumbled back, careening into a shelf that sent more jars crashing to the floor. Sparks erupted from the apparatus, and suddenly the room was bright with flames that snaked up the nearby curtains. Simon crawled toward the boy, grabbing for his ankles as though to topple him.

Simon looked up at her, his eyes wide with panic. "Elsie, run!"

Elsie stumbled toward the door through the heat and horrible brightness. There was a strange silence, then a deafening bang and whoosh of air. Her body slammed against the wall and she sank into darkness.

chapter 38

As her feet pounded the graveled avenue toward the Queen's Road gate, Kate's heart and lungs pulsed in agony. Her breath swelled and knotted in her throat. She couldn't run like this much longer—something inside her felt ready to explode.

"Don't stop at the gate!" Asher shouted.

"They *can't* still be following!"

"I don't care. Keep running until we reach Clare College."

She ran on, the stitch in her side threatening to break her in half. Finally, mercifully, she lurched into the safety of the Clare College garden, collapsing into the grass and thinking what a blessing it would be to lose consciousness.

"Kate! Are you hurt?"

She coughed into the grass, too choked to speak. Asher knelt beside her, waiting until her spasms eased before he turned her body over and laid his fingers on her throat.

"Your pulse is racing," he said, "but I think you may live. Is anything broken?"

She wiggled her extremities. "Only my spirit?"

Asher smoothed her hair from her eyes. Then he shifted his

body to lie next to her, his head propped on an elbow. After searching her face for a moment, he laughed softly.

Kate squirmed. "What? Is there mud on my face?"

"No, no. It's just . . ." Asher pulled a piece of grass from her hair. "I've never known anyone like you, Kate."

His eyes were so wide and wondering that Kate blushed and looked away.

Asher flopped onto his back. "I'm ruined for Trinity now."

"Dr. Marshall said he'd see you in the fall, didn't he?" she gasped, still trying to catch her breath. "I think our little caper made quite an impression."

He gave her a sidelong glance. "No doubt he found me quite dull before. But now he thinks I'm a rake, and that you're the sort of girl who breaks into college rooms to ruin herself."

"Who says I'm not?"

"Don't provoke me, Kate. Not now."

"I'm not trying to provoke you," she said gently. "We never could have predicted he'd come from London like that, and yet you managed to get us out of there quite nicely."

"At the cost of ten years from my life. Has my hair turned grey?"

She could only giggle.

They lay quietly a few more moments, the silence deepening. With it came a sobering thought. "We still don't know who killed Billy and Tec."

Asher sat up. "We're not done yet," he said briskly. "We've eliminated one possibility. Tomorrow we'll take another look at the suspects."

Once they'd stood and brushed the grass from their clothes, they walked along Queen's Road toward Summerfield, each of them too preoccupied with yawning to speak. Kate didn't mind the silence, for it was a companionable one.

They may have been misguided in their belief about Marshall's evildoings, and she'd led Asher into a ridiculous scheme that had nearly cost him his place at Trinity. But they'd stolen their way into one of the finest colleges in Cambridge, and once caught, had talked their way out of trouble. She couldn't help thinking Billy and Tec would have been proud of their detective work.

And there was that look in Asher's eyes as they'd lain in the grass. Amusement had flickered there, but she'd also seen approval. Fondness, even?

Was she having sentimental feelings for *Asher*? The boy hopelessly besotted with Elsie? She wrinkled her nose. Any hankerings in that direction needed to be quashed immediately. After all, what had her tender feelings for Tec brought her? Nothing more than confusion and pain. She should have learned by now that the entire business of love was outright foolishness and a waste of time.

And yet . . .

The warm glow continued until they crossed the Silver Street Bridge and a sharp odor tickled her nostrils.

"Asher, do you smell smoke?"

They paused on Summerfield Walk.

"I do."

Kate shivered as a clanging sounded in the distance. "The fire brigade?"

"Come on," said Asher, quickening his pace.

When they neared the gate, Kate saw the flames flickering in the distance through the ironwork. Her heart leapt as Asher broke into a run. She followed him to the unlocked gate, scrambling through after him. He paused in front of Summerfield Hall, gasping for breath.

"It's the old lab," Kate said.

He turned to her, his expression dire. "Go to the Gatehouse and make sure Elsie is safe."

"No," she said, her back stiffening. "I'm coming with you."

He gripped her shoulders. "Then stay behind me, and for God's sake be careful."

They tore across the lawn toward the lab. Jagged tongues of fire flicked through the windows, and smoke clouded the building, choking the air. When they drew near enough to feel the heat, Asher jerked her back. "Don't go any closer. There's glass everywhere. The windows must have blown out."

"How could that happen?" she asked, her throat thickened by the smoke.

"An explosion. There's no other explanation." He covered his mouth with his cap. "Chemicals were stored there, weren't they? We should go back to the house, Kate—this smoke is choking me."

Kate stepped back, raising a hand to shield her face from the heat of the flames. The light from the sitting room shone through the window of the Gatehouse. Would Elsie have come out to see what happened, or would she have had the sense to stay safely inside? Perhaps she had been the one to telephone the fire brigade.

As she glanced back at Asher, something at the perimeter of her gaze caught her attention. Turning, she saw a pale shape in the grass. She stepped closer, panic flooding through her as she saw the shape for what it was—a body. A prone form in a long dress, arms and legs splayed.

And golden hair sticking to a face covered in blood.

Chapter 39

Asher's body ached with weariness as he sat in Oliver Thompson's study. Mr. Thompson leaned against his desk, looking far worse than Asher felt. He couldn't help staring at the old man's hands as he spoke, for they trembled so pathetically.

"I come home," said Thompson, "to find one of the college buildings burned—its contents utterly destroyed—and now I've just heard Millie's confession that you and Miss Poole were away from Summerfield when she went to bed."

Asher's heart jerked in his chest.

"I can't fathom why you would leave the Gatehouse in the dark of night," Thompson continued. "What could possibly have prompted such a foolish action?"

"Well . . . Miss Poole craved some fresh air, and it wasn't terribly late—"

"Do *not* pull the wool over my eyes, Mr. Beale. The truth, if you please!"

"Sir, are you certain you don't wish to sit?"

Mr. Thompson submitted to a coughing fit, glaring at Asher all the while. Once recovered, he leaned against his desk almost defiantly. "I'm fine. Now, were you and Kate in the old lab when the fire broke out? Did you mess about with the equipment?"

"No sir, we were nowhere near the lab when the fire started," Asher said, relieved to speak truthfully.

"Where were you, then?"

Asher could think of nothing to say, and the silence weighed heavily upon the room. He was so damnably tired. Then the wisp of an idea tickled his brain—a lie, of course, but one that would serve some good. Strange how it had taken exhaustion and utter confusion for matters to finally fall into place.

"Well, boy?"

"It was Kate, sir. She tried to run away from Summerfield."

Thompson coughed again. "What?"

"She is terrified," Asher continued, emboldened now that he could speak the truth. "Earlier this week she encountered Robert Eliot in town—it was the day she and Elsie went rowing with Simon Wakeham. Mr. Eliot recognized her, and I'm afraid he tried to drag her to the police station."

"The brute! How could he blame her for his own foolishness?"

"It was difficult for Kate to speak of this, but I gather he was rather rough with her. He'd pulled her into an alley to get a better look at her. She was frightened and desperate, so she . . . well, sir, she says she stabbed him in the thigh with a pocketknife."

Mr. Thompson's jaw dropped. "She actually stabbed him?"

"It was by no means a mortal wound, sir. But she's terrified of the police and has been plotting how to run away ever since. Last night I saw her sneaking out. I felt it my duty to follow. When I caught up to her she confessed the whole story."

"Heavens," breathed Thompson. "Of course that's why she

was so keen to see her father's widow. She thought the woman would shelter her."

"She was afraid of disappointing you, and she couldn't imagine you'd wish to house her any longer. Mostly, however, she was afraid of being jailed for attacking a gentleman."

Mr. Thompson's face crumpled. "Why didn't the girl just come to me? I could have settled matters for her."

"Are you at all acquainted with Kate Poole?" Asher suppressed a smile. "You know how independent she is. It was all I could do to convince her to come back to the Gatehouse."

Thompson nodded sadly. "I'll deal with Eliot. Kate need have no fear of him. But what about the old lab?" he asked. "You returned to Summerfield to find it on fire?"

"Yes sir." Asher relaxed a fraction. Everything after their return was easy enough to relate, since he could tell the truth. "As soon as we turned onto Summerfield Walk, we smelled the smoke and heard the fire brigade bell."

"Did you see anyone run from the building? Someone who might have been responsible?"

"No sir."

"A body was found in the lab, burned very badly. They haven't identified him yet, and I'm not certain they ever will." Mr. Thompson slumped forward, rubbing his temples. "I'd lost my own key to the lab ages ago, but I secured the gardener's and made sure the door was kept locked. I even hid the key. Now it's gone—out of my own study." His hands dropped as he looked at Asher. "I can't imagine who would wish to destroy the building. Surely they weren't aware someone was inside?"

Asher sank back in his chair. "It's a mystery, sir."

He wondered what it all meant. Elsie unconscious outside the lab, another person trapped inside and burned beyond recognition. It couldn't have been Dr. Marshall's doing—he would have been on his way home from the train station when the explosion happened. And he seemed to have nothing to do with the old lab anyway.

Mr. Thompson yawned. "We are each lost in our thoughts, and I know you must be exhausted," he said. "Get some rest, and we'll discuss this further tomorrow."

Asher stood, eager to be away so he could share what he'd learned with Kate. But Thompson seemed so shriveled and forlorn. "Can I get you anything?" Asher asked awkwardly. "A cup of tea? I really think you should sit down."

The man sighed and hobbled over to the chair. Asher took his arm, hoping to bear some of the weight as Mr. Thompson eased down. But there was hardly any substance to the man—his bones seemed as light and frail as a bird's. Thompson crumpled into the seat and pushed his beard into his mouth, his expression distracted as he chewed.

Asher lingered, reluctant to leave him.

After a moment Thompson gazed up at him. Smiling feebly, he pulled the beard free, smoothing it against his chest. "Go on now, my boy. I'll be fine."

Still uncertain, Asher made his way up the stairs, checking the corridor on the next floor before walking to Kate's bedchamber. The room was empty, so he returned to the staircase, passing Elsie's door along the way. He heard the murmurs of a deep voice. The police? He had hoped to speak with her first.

Disappointed, he returned to his own room to find Kate sitting on his chair. The packet of his father's telegrams lay in her lap.

"Kate?"

She bit her lip. "They were sitting on your desk for anyone to see. For all you know, he's trying to make amends. Why haven't you opened them?"

"Do we have to talk about this now?" Asher rubbed his burning eyes. He knew Kate was just as weary as he was—certainly weary enough to be scattered and vulnerable—but he couldn't bring himself to engage on *that* issue. "Seems there are more important matters to concern us."

She sighed and placed the packet on his desk. "What did you tell Mr. Thompson?"

"Don't be angry. I told him you'd tried to run away, that I followed you, and that you confessed your troubles with Eliot to me. He's quite upset on your account."

"Really?" Her lower lip trembled. "I hadn't expected that."

"He says he'll deal with Eliot, so put that from your mind. Have you seen Elsie?"

"The doctor's been with her."

He sat on the edge of the bed. "I heard voices and feared it might be the police in her room." He paused, his thoughts racing. "There's something else, Kate."

Her body tensed. "What?" she whispered.

"The police found a dead body in the lab—burned so badly they haven't been able to identify it."

Kate stared at him. "Who could it be?"

"I'm hoping Elsie can tell us."

❈ ❈ ❈ ❈ ❈

"Why would you be so foolish as to go to the old lab?" The question exploded from Aunt Helena's grimly clenched lips. "It was late, and you were alone. What were you thinking?"

If the bed had swallowed her up in that moment, Elsie would have welcomed it. Aunt Helena's face was white with anger. Or perhaps it was fear. Either way, she seemed determined to get answers, and now that the doctor had departed, Elsie could no longer avoid this confrontation. But neither could she tell the truth, not before speaking with Asher and Kate, and Aunt Helena seemed disinclined to wait. Elsie took a breath and met her aunt's gaze. "I saw someone through my bedroom window. I thought it was Asher, and I was curious."

"Did you go inside the lab? Did you see who was there?"

"The last thing I remember is standing outside and looking through the window." The lies tumbled too easily from her lips. "I went to the door and tried to turn the handle, but it was locked. The rest I don't remember. It's this bump on my head—I think it's blotted out my memory."

Aunt Helena stared at her for a long moment, and Elsie returned her gaze without blinking. Finally the woman's shoulders sagged. "Perhaps it will come back to you in time. But in the end, it may be best if it does not."

"Maybe so."

My camera, Elsie thought. *I must ask Kate to retrieve it.*

"You really must rest," her aunt said briskly. "But first there are two people outside who are quite eager to see you. Are you up to it?"

"May I have a moment first?" Elsie reached for the mirror and brush on the bedside table. "I don't want to frighten them with my appearance."

"I'll send them in shortly. You must not let them stay too long, however." Her aunt smiled and withdrew, closing the door softly behind her.

Elsie studied her face in the mirror. The bruise on her forehead was an angry red, the cut just starting to scab. She brushed out her hair and tried to pull a section forward to cover the bruise. Unfortunately, it covered her eye as well. She frowned, rearranging the hair.

The back of her neck prickled.

She turned to the door, expecting to see her aunt. But the door was still closed. There was no one in the room but her.

And yet she felt someone. *Simon.* He was in her head somehow, almost as he had been in the old lab.

"Simon?" she whispered.

She could almost smell him, feel his warmth as though he embraced her. If she opened her mind, would she hear his voice?

A knock at the door made her jump. She set the brush on the table and took a deep breath. "Yes?"

The door opened slowly and Kate peered around the edge. "May we come in?"

Elsie forced a smile. "Of course."

Asher followed Kate through the door and placed a second chair next to Elsie's bed. The two sat, both looking quite pale with weariness. Their bright eyes, however, were expectant.

Asher leaned forward. "How are you feeling?"

"Better than I look," Elsie murmured, lightly touching the bruise on her forehead. "What did you learn in Dr. Marshall's rooms?" She was stalling, but she hardly knew what to say when her thoughts were such a jumble.

"We read through his files," Asher said, glancing at Kate. "It's not him. He's collected a great deal of anecdotal evidence, and he's thought about using electrical shocks to access the subliminal self. But his notes made it clear he'd never put someone's life in danger to do it."

"So it was all for nothing," Elsie said.

"We want to know what happened with *you,*" said Kate impatiently.

Elsie swallowed hard. It would be so easy to tell them what she'd told her aunt, to simply plead that she couldn't remember. Neither of them had especially liked Simon, and she could already imagine Asher's condescending smile when he learned the terrible things the man had done. And then there was Tec—how could she explain his involvement to Kate? She'd already mourned his death.

"I'm sorry . . . my head aches so."

Kate took a breath. "Elsie, they found a body in the old lab."

"What?" Her stomach convulsed. "Who is it?"

"It's burned so badly, we may never know," said Asher.

Elsie pressed a hand to her mouth.

Simon is dead.

Just now . . . had she felt his spirit?

Her other encounters with the dead had been a slow fall into cold, dark terror. This had been different. Warmth and comfort instead of fear.

Was *this* what Simon had felt when haunted by his Amy—an abiding presence so tender and reassuring that he never could forget? Never let go? Elsie's head began to throb. She had prompted his death, she had goaded Tec into setting the lab on fire, and yet Simon's spirit was warm and forgiving. That was what she had felt, wasn't it? A loving presence?

Kate put a hand on her arm. "Elsie?"

"I . . ." Elsie's throat thickened as tears pooled in her eyes.

"Go on." Kate's voice was gentle, trusting.

"The body in the old lab," Elsie sobbed. "It's Simon Wakeham."

They stared at her in pained silence.

Finally Asher spoke. "How?"

"It's my fault. He wanted me to help him contact his lost love. He did so many terrible things, hurt so many people, all because he was trying to find a way to her." Sobs were racking her body, and she could barely draw sufficient air into her lungs. "I found him in the lab—I was terribly afraid. But I can't . . . I mean I don't—" She nearly choked on the words. "I'm sorry . . . I'm so sorry. It's my fault he's dead."

chapter 40

Once Mrs. Thompson was fetched, Kate quietly ushered Asher out of the room. In truth, she was relieved to close the door on the spectacle of Elsie's tears. She could muster no proper response to the girl's confusion, nor any comforting words to soothe her sobbing. Foremost on her mind was the need to understand, but Elsie was in no shape for further questions.

"Come to my room," said Kate. "We need to talk about this."

Asher frowned. "Are you sure?"

"Do you really think anyone cares right now?"

Nevertheless, Kate left the door open a few inches. Indicating the desk chair for him to sit, she perched on the edge of her bed. "You were right about Simon Wakeham."

He shook his head. "There was a time when I wanted to be right, but now . . . I'm not so sure. Elsie could have died."

"It must have been Wakeham who caught Billy searching out details for Martineau's séance. He pressured Billy to find a poor soul for his experiment. But when Billy tried to use this information for blackmail, he silenced him. That's what it looks like, right? And all for the love of a dead woman. It all fits, I suppose. And yet . . . I can't quite believe him capable."

"You know I didn't like him, but it wasn't because I thought him a bad person." The chair creaked as Asher slumped back. "He *was* concerned with what happens to us after death. In fact, he seemed quite keen to prove that something essential remains even when the physical body has died." He paused to rub his eyes. "I suppose that's what these 'experiments' were truly about."

"He was more interested in Dr. Marshall's research than he let on," Kate said. "When my father died and Marshall refused to endanger anyone else's life, Wakeham must have decided to take matters into his own hands."

"And in the end it killed him." Asher sighed. "This isn't going to be easy for Elsie."

"She may remember more in time."

"And how would it help us if she did? Are you prepared to share all this with the Thompsons? With the police? Wakeham is dead. He can't hurt anyone else."

"I still want to know."

"You're torturing yourself, Kate. You already know who killed Billy and Tec. There was nothing you could do to prevent what happened," he added gently.

"Then why do I feel as though I've failed them?"

He studied her for a moment. "You are the most maddeningly independent soul I've ever known. But when you let someone be a friend, you turn fiercely protective." He smiled. "I've seen how you care for Elsie, and I admire it. I know you were loyal to Billy and Tec. But *they* were just as independent as you, Kate, and their choices led them into danger. You can't hold yourself responsible for that."

Kate started to protest, but the shadows under Asher's eyes made her pause. "You look tired."

"I'm exhausted. We both need rest." He stood. "We'll talk more later, but we mustn't push Elsie too hard."

"I know, I know." With a groan Kate rose from the bed to meet him at the door. Without thinking, she reached out to rub a dark smudge from his cheek. He flinched slightly but did not push her hand away.

"Sorry," she murmured. "Just a bit of soot."

He looked down, his lashes hiding his eyes. "Thanks, Kate."

The room felt very empty once he'd gone.

The next morning Mrs. Thompson brought a selection of heavy volumes to Kate's room. "Why don't you read to Elsie? That way you can visit with her in a restful way."

Kate picked Dickens's *Bleak House* because its title page featured a drawing that reminded her of Castle End. She'd hardly made it through the first paragraph, however, before she lost her footing.

London. Michaelmas Term lately over, and the Lord Chancellor sitting in Lincoln's Inn Hall. Implacable November weather. As much mud in the streets, as if the waters had but newly retired from the face of the earth, and it would not be wonderful to meet a Megalosaurus, forty feet long or so, waddling like an elephantine lizard up Holborn Hill.

Kate closed the book. "I won prizes for reading back in school, but this may be too much for me."

"You don't have to read, Kate. We could just talk."

"You're supposed to be resting. I'll push on until we find the house and learn what makes it so bleak. There's a chilling sketch of it opposite the title page."

There was no house, however. Just a lawsuit that apparently had dragged on for centuries. By the fifth page she was sounding out words without comprehending them, but she doggedly pressed on until she reached a dreary woman named Lady Dedlock.

> *"I say I am afraid," says Mr. Tulkinghorn, who has risen hastily, "that Lady Dedlock is ill."*
>
> *"Faint," my Lady murmurs, with white lips, "only that; but it is like the faintness of death. Don't speak to me. Ring, and take me to my room!"*

"Please . . . just stop," Elsie said.

Kate glanced at her over the book. "Are you ill? You've gone pale."

Elsie shook her head, but her eyes filled with tears. Kate pulled a handkerchief from her pocket. "Here. It's clean."

Elsie wiped her eyes. Then she refolded the handkerchief, smoothing the edges carefully. "Thank you."

"Were you thinking of Simon Wakeham?"

Elsie sniffled. "I'm so confused."

"Of course you are." Kate softened her tone. "You have a head injury. And you cared for him, didn't you?"

After a moment Elsie nodded.

"He seemed a fine gentleman . . . at first, anyway. I could see why you might take a shine to him. But I do wonder how you fell so deeply for him, and so quickly."

"My heart acts independently of my head." Elsie turned to stare at the ceiling, her brow furrowed. "I never told you why I ran away to London, although Asher must have guessed it. I'm sure he saw him at the British Museum, before he ran away."

"Before *who* ran away?"

"My art tutor—my only friend at Peverel Place. He was

my . . ." She trailed off, biting her lip. "He's the one who taught me how to use a camera, you see. I thought I loved him, but it was all foolishness. Deep down I knew his passion did not match my own. But as I said, I am led by my heart."

"My mother was the same way, I think," Kate said. "She was a fool about my father. She must have known he wouldn't marry her. I'll never understand why she continued to hope they would be together even after he married that wretched woman." She shook her head. "Why do women think they need a man to be happy? Shouldn't children matter just as much, if not more?"

"Yes. Of course they should," Elsie said. "But the craving for a man's attention can be so strong, no matter how shabbily a woman is treated. Why is that? Why do some men have that power?"

"Is it really about the man?" Kate paused to ponder this. "For some, I think it's more a yearning for escape and independence."

Elsie frowned. "Really?"

"I thought a lot about this that night I sat by your bed. You know, when you went to Wakeham's house and . . . suffered your disappointment."

"Go on, then," Elsie said. "Tell me what else you thought that night."

"Are you certain you're not too tired? I don't want Mrs. Thompson annoyed with me."

"I think I need to hear this, Kate."

"All right." Kate tilted her head, considering Elsie carefully. "From the time of your first seizure, I think you've felt like a changeling in your family. Your father considers you damaged beyond repair. Your mother is deathly afraid of what you know. I imagine it's hard for her to even meet your gaze. Am I correct?"

Elsie nodded slowly.

"But *men*. They notice you, don't they? You're beautiful and they long to protect you. To possess you. And you enjoy their attention. When they offer you love, you're quick to take it because the people who are *supposed* to love you find you threatening." Kate glanced at the bottles on Elsie's desk. "And when that doesn't work, you take Chlorodyne to blot it all out. You nearly blotted yourself out a few days ago."

"That was a horrible night."

"Yes, it was." Kate took a deep breath before continuing. "And then there's Asher. He's obviously smitten with you, but you pretend not to see it. Except when you need him, like that night you invited him to the Fitzwilliam Museum. Did you think I didn't notice how you looked at him? Why do you string him along only to push him away?"

Elsie's face crumpled. "I *don't* string him along."

"Well then, why do you fling yourself at inappropriate men and ignore the worthy ones?" Kate pressed. "Asher can be rude at times, but he's a steady one. He has a good heart."

"I know he does." Elsie wiped her face with the handkerchief and sighed. "I'm not an idiot, after all. I like him awfully, but I just don't have *those* feelings for him."

"Maybe he needs to understand that?"

Elsie nodded slowly, withdrawing once more into herself.

Kate retrieved the book and pretended to find her place. She'd been on comfortable ground discussing Elsie's wayward heart, but once the subject turned to Asher her stomach had soured to the conversation.

A light knock came at the door.

"Yes?" Elsie's voice seemed to come from far away.

The door opened slowly, and Asher peered through.

"Mrs. Thompson said I'd find you both here. May I come in?"

❈ ❈ ❈ ❈ ❈

Asher stood awkwardly in the doorway, unsettled by the distinct impression of having interrupted something.

Kate stood quickly, placing a book on her chair. "I've nearly finished a chapter, and I can't bear another word of *Bleak House* today. Why don't you keep Elsie company for a while?" She swept past him before he could reply.

Asher set the book aside and took Kate's seat. He'd been in Elsie's bedroom before—on the very first day he met her—but this was the first time he'd been alone with her in this private space. She seemed so small in the bed, dwarfed by the jumble of overstuffed pillows. She was pale, bruised . . . diminished.

"How are you feeling?" he finally asked.

"Better."

"I could read to you. Shall I pick up where Kate left off?"

"I'd rather you didn't."

A silence fell. Asher leaned back in the chair and crossed his legs. But that felt too casual, so he uncrossed them and sat forward again. "Were the two of you arguing just now?"

"No . . . not exactly."

He waited for her to elaborate, but she only seemed to sink deeper into her pillow. Clearly he would have to press on without her assistance.

"I told a whopping lie to Mr. Thompson yesterday," he said. "Thought you should know, in case he or Mrs. Thompson asked you about it. I told him Kate tried to run away Saturday night, and that I followed her out of concern for her safety. It was the only thing I could think of at the time, but then I realized it gave me an opportunity to explain her plight—her fear of Eliot and all that—and as it turns out your uncle was quite sympathetic." Asher knew full well he was babbling, but at least it filled the silence. "I'm certain he'll try to convince her to stay at Summerfield. Perhaps you'll be able to help him with that?"

"I'll do my best." Elsie's smile was thin.

"So what *was* going on just now between the two of you?"

"Actually, Kate was lecturing me."

"Lecturing? I asked her not to push you for details on what happened in the old lab."

"She never mentioned that. Instead she seemed more concerned with my heart and how I invite men to abuse it."

Asher cleared his throat. "That wasn't very kind of her."

"She meant it in a helpful way, I think. And perhaps I brought it on myself. I did ask her opinion."

Again he waited in vain for her to elaborate, but the silence thickened instead.

"I won't be able to stay at Summerfield much longer," he finally said. "The students will return soon enough, and the Thompsons will need my room."

"But you can take lodgings in town, can't you?"

Her tone was even, but his heart leapt a little at the words. "I suppose I could. It would be nice to stay close to you."

Her eyes dropped to her hands. "Close to me and Kate. And the Thompsons, of course."

"I once thought I would stay in town to be near *you*." His face burned, but the need for clarity compelled him to press further. When would he have another opportunity to speak to her alone? "Is there any way . . . is there any chance you could feel—"

"No," she said softly. "I cherish you as a dear friend, but no more than that."

"Could it be more someday? I mean, once you've mourned Simon Wakeham?"

His own words echoed in his head, sounding callow and abrupt. Finally she raised her head and met his gaze. Her eyes held kindness and a trace of pity, but nothing more.

"Asher, you fancy the *idea* of me more than the reality."

"I don't even know what that means."

"And I don't know any other way to explain it. We were meant to be friends—good friends—but nothing more."

"Of course," he said quickly. "Please forget I said anything."

"Don't be angry."

"I'm not angry." He tugged at his collar. "It's just blazing hot in here."

Mrs. Thompson came through the door at that moment, her hands full of sewing and more books. She set the items on Elsie's desk and turned to face them. Her searching gaze moved from him to Elsie. "You both look so grim."

Asher took a deep breath and stood. "I was just leaving."

Mrs. Thompson tilted her head. "See you at supper?"

"Of course," he said, making for the door before she could say anything else. He did not look at Elsie.

He dragged himself up the stairs, almost wishing to find Kate in his room again. It was easy enough to imagine her sitting in his chair, rolling her eyes at his stricken face. He would welcome her scorn. He'd suffered a blow to his pride, but the sight of Kate, steady and cynical, would lessen the pain, making it easier to push aside and forget.

His room was empty, however, so he sprawled on the bed and stared at the ceiling. Once his eyes had traveled every snaking crack in the plaster at least twice, he sat up with a sigh and turned to his desk. The bundle of telegrams still lay there. He stood and reached for it, sitting down on his chair to untie the string that bound the envelopes. After studying the first one for a moment, he tore it open.

THOMPSON WIRED TO INFORM OF YOUR ARRIVAL. WRITE TO MOTHER. SHE GRIEVES.

Asher put that one down and opened the next several, quickly scanning each short message.

I WORRY ABOUT YOU. MOTHER MISSES YOU.

THOMPSON WIRES TO SAY YOU HAVE BECOME PART OF THE FAMILY. THIS INTELLIGENCE RECEIVED WITH MIXED FEELINGS. YOUR TRUE FAMILY LONGS TO HEAR FROM YOU.

ASHER, WITH ALL MY HEART I WISH TO CLOSE THIS RIFT BETWEEN US. I CANNOT IF I DON'T HEAR FROM YOU. CAN WE FORGET WHAT HAS PASSED BETWEEN US AND BE FATHER AND SON AGAIN?

He set the messages down and went to the window, thinking of his father before Letty had come between them. They had been friends once, hadn't they? He'd thought Harold Beale the best of men and had been proud to call him Father.

When the sun began to shine in his eyes, he closed the curtains and returned to his desk. Retrieving a blank sheet of Summerfield stationery, thoughtfully provided by Mrs. Thompson days ago, he tested his pen on the blotting pad and began to write.

Chapter 41

Elsie woke late the next morning with the feel of Simon Wakeham's arms around her. Had she dreamed of him? She kept her eyes closed, still feeling his warmth. It was uncanny how close he felt—as though she might reach out and touch him, if she only knew how.

Simon, are you there?

As if in answer, the warmth intensified.

What was she doing? Simon had killed Billy and made a monster of Tec. He may have done it all out of a desperate love; nevertheless, it was madness to allow his spirit to roam through her mind. She betrayed Kate and Asher by even thinking of him.

She tried to blank her thoughts of him, imagining her mind as an unblemished piece of paper. Smooth, white paper—pristine as a meadow blanketed with snow.

The warmth receded . . . leaving her empty and shivering.

She was alone. And quite possibly insane.

Elsie opened her eyes and glanced about the room. She could bear this unvarying landscape no longer. Surely Aunt Helena was taking caution to an extreme by insisting upon three days of uninterrupted rest. Since those uncomfortable conversations with Kate and Asher, each had avoided her. Time had slowed to a glacial pace, and the long silences roared in her ears. All this soothing repose had left her irritable and more than a little unhinged.

She must tell Asher and Kate the whole truth. Perhaps that was the only thing that would free her of Simon's spirit. Kate should know that Tec was in the old lab that night. What if he had escaped and was wandering the streets of Cambridge, bloodied and racked with pain, and Elsie did nothing to help him? Kate might know where to find the boy—somewhere along Castle Street, no doubt—and surely if the three of them worked together they might devise some way to heal him. She'd promised to help him, hadn't she?

She promised him in return for his help in stopping Simon.

Elsie threw back the bedcovers and chose a day dress from her wardrobe. She would leave her room today. Somehow she *would* fix everything. But first she would pay a visit to her uncle's study. Something in her possession needed to be returned to its rightful place.

Part of her hoped he wouldn't be there, that she might slip the key back into the handkerchief and close the specimen cabinet, her uncle never the wiser. But when she saw him at his desk, distractedly chewing his beard as he paged through a textbook, she knew a confession was in order.

He was a dear and patient man, and it pained her that she'd thought ill of him.

At that moment he looked up, his beard falling from his mouth as he smiled. "Elsie? It's wonderful to see you up and about."

"May I come in, Uncle?"

He stood quickly, upsetting a stack of books that had

perched precariously on the edge of his desk. "Oh dear, I'm afraid it's the usual chaos in here. Come sit down." He fluttered his hand toward the chair. "Just push those papers aside. I'll get it all sorted eventually."

"First I must return something to you." Elsie carefully navigated her way toward the desk and withdrew the key from her pocket. "I took this from your specimen cabinet."

He frowned. After an awkward pause, he reached for the key. "But why?"

"You seemed so angry that day Kate and I were poking about the old lab, almost as though you kept something secret in there. My curiosity got the better of me."

"How very Gothic of you." He studied the key thoughtfully. "Is that why you were in the old lab? You were investigating?"

"I suppose you could say that," Elsie said, her voice cracking slightly. "I've no right to ask you this, but please don't tell Aunt Helena. It was wrong of me, and I'm sorry."

He held her gaze. "Well, what did you find? Is there something you haven't told me, Elsie?"

His eyes were kind. So kind that she wished she could tell him everything. What a relief it would be to lift this burden from her own shoulders and pass it to someone wiser and more capable.

But she couldn't bring herself to do it.

"I'm afraid I still don't remember."

He smiled. "Your injury. Of course. It may take a while to recover those memories, if you recover them at all." He looked away. "I don't know what to tell you about the lab. This key is the gardener's, as I said before. I can't think what happened to mine. I may be untidy, but I never lose things."

"Do you think it was stolen?"

"I've wondered that." He looked thoughtful for a moment.

"But the simple truth behind my anger that day outside the lab was that you and Kate *were* behaving in an alarming manner. How would you expect me to react when I saw the two of you? Not only was she breaking a windowpane, but you had propped her up in the most precarious way. And what happened? You both fell, of course. I wasn't just angry—I was afraid!"

Elsie blushed to remember it. "Of course, Uncle. I understand."

"I've been distressed since that first body was found on the Corpus College cricket grounds. The poor boy was found shortly thereafter. Did you know that the police came to Summerfield to question me about it?" He stood and moved to the specimen box, retrieving a familiar handkerchief-wrapped item. "They came because of this. You must have seen it, too, since this was the drawer that held the key. The police found my name inscribed inside, and they thought I might have some connection to the boy." He pulled the watch from the handkerchief and clicked it open. "Has Kate told you she is the daughter of Frederic Stanton?"

Elsie nodded.

"I couldn't imagine why a child of the streets would have the watch I gave him so long ago. Stanton was a dear friend of mine. A pupil first, and then a colleague."

"Was he a good man?"

Her uncle raised an eyebrow. "That's a curious question."

"It's just . . . Kate has become a friend, and I know she wonders about him. She didn't even know he'd died until recently."

His face softened. "I'm afraid I was very vague about him the first day I met her. Frederic was always a moody sort, never satisfied. He had many gifts, and he could have done so much good in this world, but he always grasped for things just out of his reach. Apparently he kept many secrets—having an illegitimate daughter was just the tip of the iceberg, I fear. Still, he would have been devastated to learn how she's survived the years since his death."

"I think she's lost everyone she ever loved." Tears stung Elsie's eyes as she stared at the watch. "I must remember that when she's being tiresome."

"She's certainly dealt with more than her fair share of misfortune."

Elsie wiped at her eyes. "What will you do? I mean, about the lab."

He shrugged. "I've told the police all I know, but I'm certain it won't help them any. They showed little interest in the stolen key, and they've devoted little time to searching the remains of the building. Clearly someone has been making use of it, but I can't imagine for what. Shelter, perhaps?" He tugged at his beard in obvious irritation. "Was there an accident with the equipment, then? Or was this arson?"

Poor man, thought Elsie. But she couldn't tell him. Not until she'd spoken with Kate and Asher.

"I don't remember . . . not yet, anyway," she said aloud.

"Of course. I do apologize." Her uncle shut the watch with a sigh. "Would you do something for me, Elsie? Would you give this to Kate? It will mean a great deal more to her than to me." He placed the watch in her outstretched hand.

She slid the watch in her pocket and smoothed her skirt. "I'm wondering whether you will send me back to Peverel Place now."

Her uncle frowned again. "Why would you ask that?"

"I fear I'm a burden to you—there's been no end of trouble since I arrived."

He waved a hand. "On the contrary, Helena and I welcome you to stay here for as long as you like. You know it is our wish that you might one day study here at Summerfield."

"Oh dear," Elsie gasped. "I'm not nearly clever enough for that."

"You *are* clever, Elsie. The Chlorodyne may have dulled your senses, and it most certainly has compromised your confidence." His eyes softened. "But you have a fine brain, my dear. Any brain needs using, however—the more you exercise it, the stronger it grows. How fortuitous that we live in a city teeming with excellent tutors!"

Elsie opened her mouth to protest, but her uncle held up a hand.

"Perhaps we might prevail upon Kate to join you in this tutoring. What do you think? I've racked my brain trying to think of ways to keep her at Summerfield without injuring her pride."

Elsie considered the notion and found herself warming to it. She and Kate facing this tutor together? It sounded almost companionable. "But how would we convince her?"

"I'll leave that up to you, my dear. Consider it your first assignment."

Elsie found Kate in the library, moving books from a wooden cart to a high shelf. For such a small creature, she heaved each book with great determination.

"Kate?"

The girl whirled around. "You startled me. Everything echoes in this building."

"I've just been with my uncle. He asked me to give you this." She held out the gold watch.

Kate's eyes widened. After a moment she extended a hand and took it. "My father's watch."

"The one you gave Billy. The police must have found it on the boy's body, and they brought it to Uncle when they discovered his name inside."

Kate opened the watch and traced the inscription with her finger. Then she snapped it shut and slipped it into her pocket, raising her chin to meet Elsie's gaze. "Did you tell him everything?"

"It seemed safest to pretend I didn't remember. When, or if, we tell him, we must do it together, don't you think?"

Kate nodded.

Elsie picked at the ruffle on her sleeve as she struggled for the right words. Kate needed to know the truth about Tec, and there was little time for dawdling. But how best to go about it? She would have to revisit that night when she'd seen Tec's spirit in the old lab in order to explain his strange alteration. A spirit divided from a living body—it sounded quite preposterous even now. Would Kate merely stiffen and walk away, thinking her mad? They hadn't spoken intimately since Kate had lectured her. Before Elsie could confide something so bizarre and terrible, she must first break through this wall of politeness that had risen between them.

"I do appreciate what you said to me earlier," she said softly. "I've come to like having you around, even when you're criticizing my faults."

The girl snorted. "Not sure what you'll do without me, then."

"I don't *want* to do without you!"

"The work here is nearly finished," Kate said with a shrug. "I'll be moving on before long."

"Not if I have something to say about it."

"I can't fix things for you any more than your young men could."

"I don't *want* you to fix things. I know I must do that myself. But is it wrong to need your friendship? I need both you and Asher, but he can't stay in a ladies' college. The students will return soon enough."

"*You* should join the college," said Kate. "Then you'll have heaps of friends. Perhaps that's even better than family, at least in your situation."

"I'm considering it. And you could join with me."

Kate dismissed the notion with a wave of her hand. "That's not my sort of thing at all. I'm too young, anyway, and haven't had any schooling for years."

Elsie laughed. "Neither have I, for all practical purposes. We shall need a tutor. By the time you're old enough to enroll, we'll both be ready."

"I can't afford a tutor. I must find a new scheme, and then I won't have time for schooling."

"Let me help."

Kate shook her head. "I appreciate what you're trying to do. I really do. But I refuse to be beholden to you."

"Why? I owe you *my life*," Elsie cried. "How do you think that makes me feel? That debt may never be settled."

Kate opened her mouth . . . and then closed it again.

"Listen," Elsie said breathlessly. "If it's a new scheme you want, I have the perfect one. My parents are always trying to force some sour old spinster on me as a paid companion. *You* can be that companion."

Kate's only reply was another snort.

"No really, Kate, think of the freedom we'll have. We'll serve as each other's chaperone. We've made a good team so far, don't you think?"

Kate held her gaze but did not speak.

"I wouldn't think of you as my servant, if that's what you're afraid of," Elsie said quickly. "I just meant to arrange a salary for you, so you wouldn't feel like you were taking *my* money. When I tell my parents I've arranged for a companion and a tutor, they'll be *grateful* to have me out of the way and doing something meaningful."

The girl still did not speak.

"Kate?"

"It's very decent of you to make the offer," Kate finally said, her tone severe. "I'm inclined to take it, but only if you agree to one condition."

"What is it?"

"Starting tomorrow, we decrease your Chlorodyne dose a little each day until you don't crave it anymore. And together we will work on controlling your episodes so you have some choice whether or not to go to . . . that place. *And* you will not run off in the middle of the night with the next handsome man who smiles at you."

Elsie smiled. "You've given *three* conditions."

Kate raised a threatening eyebrow.

"All right, all right, I agree to your conditions," Elsie said with a smile. "Are you satisfied?"

The corners of Kate's mouth lifted. "I suppose so. For now, anyway."

Elsie thought she might come near—to take her hand or even offer an embrace—but Kate's eyes darted to the shelves instead.

"I must finish my work. There's another cart to shelve, and I'd like to get through the day without Freeman scolding me."

"I could help."

Kate shook her head. "I'd rather do it myself. I'm actually

going to miss this library when I'm done." She trailed her hand along the shelf before turning back to Elsie. "See you this evening?"

"Actually, there was something else—"

"Poole," cried Miss Freeman from across the room. "Are you *quite* done visiting? We still have much to do before we lock up for the day."

Kate grimaced. "I'd better get back to it."

"We'll talk more tonight," said Elsie, ashamed by her own relief.

Tonight, she reassured herself. *I will tell them both tonight.*

Elsie left the library with a lighter heart. The tangled threads of her life *were* sorting themselves out, weren't they? She'd settled matters with her uncle quite satisfactorily. And not only was she on more intimate ground with Kate, but she'd actually convinced the girl to stay at Summerfield.

Asher was another matter. Perhaps she could have handled that conversation more delicately, but the old Elsie would have been so afraid of hurting feelings that she would have let him continue to hope. That was much worse than a blunt refusal, wasn't it? Kate was right—she *had* strung him along. She'd enjoyed the attention, had even encouraged it at times. But now that was over, and he knew it. If it was possible for true friendship to thrive between a woman and a man, she hoped she could have that with Asher.

Once she'd told them everything, once they'd found Tec and somehow helped him, she would be free of Simon. Surely those visitations of warmth and tenderness would fade, and he would haunt her no longer.

She made her way back to the Gatehouse through the garden, pausing to gaze at the blackened shell of the old lab. She'd avoided it for days, but soon she must work up the courage to retrieve her camera. She'd nearly braced herself to do so when she heard someone calling her name.

"There you are, Miss Elsie," Millie said rather breathlessly, withdrawing an envelope from her apron pocket. "You have a telegram. You weren't in your bed, and I've been looking all over for you."

Elsie took the envelope. "I was at the library, talking to Kate."

"Well, I'm glad to have delivered it." Millie eyed the envelope expectantly.

Elsie fought the urge to hide the thing behind her back. "Millie, would you mind bringing tea to Aunt's office? She works such long hours without a break. I'd like to surprise her with some refreshment and company."

"Of course, miss." Millie nodded slowly, making a poor job of hiding her disappointment. "I'll do that now."

Elsie slipped the envelope into her pocket and took her time returning to the Gatehouse. Her heart thudded as she climbed the stairs to her room. Once safely inside with the door shut, she sat in front of the mirror. With trembling hands she applied her penknife to the envelope and pulled out the thin piece of paper.

The telegram was from Paris, dated the day before. The sender's name was left blank, but her heart leapt at the words.

SOMEHOW I FEEL YOU WITH ME.

With great concentration, Elsie returned the paper to the envelope and placed it in the drawer with her unopened bottles of Chlorodyne.

She was not insane.

And Simon was *alive*.

chapter 42

Wednesday morning dawned with the promise of clear skies and a last gasp of summer warmth. Kate settled next to Asher on her favorite garden bench. They basked in the sun, watching Elsie wander in the orchard.

"Hard to believe we could have such a beautiful day after all the recent horrors," Asher murmured. "You'd expect rain and gloom, wouldn't you?"

Kate inhaled deeply. "It's still warm, but you can smell autumn in the air. By next week it'll be raining every day. Soon enough we'll be bundling up against the cold." She turned to Asher. "Did you write to your father?"

"I did."

She waited for him to elaborate, but he held silent. "Well?" she prompted. "Shall you be returning to America or staying with us for a while?"

Asher turned to her, his face solemn. "Neither."

Why does he tease me so? She repressed the urge to stomp on his foot.

A grin spread over his face. "I can see the indignation boiling behind your eyes, Kate. Before you unleash your tongue, let me explain. I'm traveling back to Rye to stay with my uncle for a time. I wired him on Monday and received his reply this morning."

Kate must have done a poor job of masking her dismay, for he nudged her playfully. "You know I can't stay at Summerfield, not once the students return. Since I can't afford to take lodgings in Cambridge indefinitely, it's time I was on my way."

Panic quickened her pulse. "But we *will* see you again, won't we?"

"I'll be back in December for examinations, and in the meantime I won't be that far away."

"You know Rye might as well be the moon to me. I've never left Cambridge," she muttered.

"I suppose it would seem a world away to you, in that case. But I'll return in four months."

"How will you fill your days? Will your uncle tutor you?"

"He's found me a mathematics coach, and I shall study classics on my own, though Uncle says he'll supervise." Asher chuckled. "He's such an old hermit—I think he's afraid I'll trespass on his writing time, and yet he's so keen to do right by his brother's son."

"You'll be near the sea," Kate said wistfully. "You must write and tell us all about it. Do you promise?"

He nodded. "I shall be bored stiff down there. Prepare to receive *stacks* of letters."

When he leaned back and closed his eyes, she took advantage of the opportunity to study his profile. He looked tired and worn, older than when she'd first met him at the Summerfield gate. His hair was in need of trimming, and the recent sun had made his freckles more pronounced. In that moment he seemed steady and wise. And even though he would never be more than a friend—love was for fools, after all—she had to admit he was handsome in a boyish, American way. She wanted to reach up and smooth the furrows from his brow. Instead she savored the friendly warmth of his arm as it casually rested against hers.

It would be lonely at Summerfield—*she* would be lonely—without him.

She turned away reluctantly, spotting Elsie in the orchard. The girl was hurrying along the path to the old lab.

"Elsie, where are you going?" Kate called.

"To look at the ruined building."

"Be careful!" shouted Asher, giving Kate a sidelong glance before closing his eyes again. "It's probably good for her to face it."

"Do you think she's all right? Should I go to her?"

"She needs time to herself, out of her bedchamber," he said, eyes still closed.

"I wonder . . ." Kate trailed off, uncertain.

Asher turned to her, his eyes so blue that her heart contracted. "Go on."

"I wonder if Elsie's not telling us the whole truth."

Kate saw it then—the tightening in his cheek, the shadow that came over his eyes. He still cared for Elsie in *that* way.

"I don't know," he said after a moment. "But I trust her. Still . . . if you need me, send a wire. I'll take the first train back, no matter what."

Kate smiled. "It's a comfort to have you as a friend." She took his hand and squeezed it. They sat quietly for a moment as Kate tried to be content with what Asher had told her. In the end, however, she couldn't help herself. "Were you kind to your father in your letter?"

He held her gaze. "I wasn't unkind."

"You two must learn to forgive each other, you know. What if something were to happen, and you hadn't yet made amends?"

"Don't worry, I was quite civil. In time, he and I may come to an understanding."

"Good," she murmured, settling back against the bench to enjoy the sunshine.

❖ ❖ ❖ ❖ ❖

Elsie slowed her pace as she neared the old lab. The gardener had cleared away most of the broken glass and other rubbish from the front of the building, but it still looked a wreck. Smoke blackened the window casements, and the soot-streaked door barely clung to its hinges.

She had no wish to go inside.

Gingerly, she picked her way through the grass toward the low window at the north side of the structure. Her head throbbed with questions and doubts as she knelt and reached into the overgrown weeds creeping up the brick wall. Her fingers found the hard corner of her camera. It was damp with dew but otherwise seemed none the worse for wear.

Clutching it to her chest, she walked to a nearby tree. Once seated, she studied the compartment that held the single exposed glass plate. She absently tapped the leather case as she struggled to still the noise in her mind.

This was an opportunity to "remember"—to bridge the gap she'd placed between herself and her friends. If she took the camera back and developed the plate, she could confess everything to Asher and Kate. *The photograph has brought it all back,* she might say. *Tec was there, too. It was his body they found in the old lab.*

Kate would be forced to mourn Tec all over again. She

would suffer, and yet she would finally know the entire truth. Elsie owed her that, didn't she?

But Simon . . .

Somehow I feel you with me, he'd written. Their time together in the dark between had forged a link—two minds connected telepathically, just as Marshall had theorized. His feelings could flow through her mind and body, no matter the distance, and his message confirmed that he perceived her presence as well. Could she now betray that connection?

"Simon," she whispered. "Tell me. What should I do?"

She opened her mind and waited.

Nothing.

Closing her eyes, she concentrated on his face, her lips tingling at the memory of his kiss.

Her mind and body stretched to listen, but silence was the only answer. He would not guide her. The decision was hers.

I'm sorry, Kate.

With tears sliding down her cheeks, she pulled the plate holder from the camera and held it up to the bright sunlight, erasing the image forever.

Author's Note

Kate Poole, Asher Beale, and Elsie Atherton are products of my imagination. However, the setting, conflicts, and many of the characters of *The Dark Between* were adapted—with much creative license—from history.

Cambridge, England, is a real and thriving city, and its university, comprising thirty-one colleges, is considered one of the most prestigious institutions of post-secondary education in the world. Summerfield College is based on Newnham, a women's college established in 1871. For more background on Newnham, you might read Ann Phillips's *A Newnham Anthology* or Alice Gardner's *A Short History of Newnham College, Cambridge*. To learn more about daily life in turn-of-the-century Cambridge, read Gwen Raverat's *Period Piece,* a charming memoir of growing up in the quirky Darwin family. (Gwen was granddaughter to Charles himself.) And for a nineteenth-century American perspective on student life at Trinity College and the city of Cambridge, Charles Astor Bristed's *An American in Victorian Cambridge* is sure to inform and entertain.

The Metaphysical Society is based on the very real (and still kicking) Society for Psychical Research, founded in London in 1882 to investigate paranormal phenomena "in the same spirit of exact and unimpassioned enquiry which has enabled Science to solve so many problems" (spr.ac.uk). Frederic Stanton, Oliver and Helena Thompson, Harold Beale, Simon Wakeham, and Philip Marshall are all loosely based on members of the Society.

If you wish to learn more about the real people behind the Society, I enthusiastically recommend Deborah Blum's *Ghost Hunters: William James and the Search for Scientific Proof of Life After Death*. Blum, a Pulitzer Prize–winning journalist, brings these fascinating men and women to life in a carefully researched and meticulously documented book that reads like a novel. (I'm still waiting for HBO to option it for a mini-series.) You would also do well to look at books written by the members themselves, in particular *Phantasms of the Living* (a portion of which is quoted almost verbatim in chapter 10 of *The Dark Between*), by Edmund Gurney, Frederic W. H. Myers, and Frank Podmore, and *Human Personality and Its Survival of Bodily Death,* by Frederic W. H. Myers.

Electricity has been a part of medical treatment since the eighteenth century. If you're keen to know more about induction coils and electrotherapy, an exceptionally detailed overview can be found in *Electricity and Medicine: History of Their Interaction,* by Margaret Rowbottom and Charles Susskind.

For more details about the world of *The Dark Between*, please visit soniagensler.com.

Acknowledgments

Launching a book into the world is a collaborative process, and I was fortunate to have many talented people working with me to make *The Dark Between* the best story it could be.

Michelle Frey and her assistant Kelly Delaney deserve my eternal gratitude (and a lovely afternoon tea on me) for patiently shaping this story with their questions and insights. The copyediting team certainly earned heartfelt thanks for their painstaking work. Art director Isabel Warren-Lynch and designer Melissa Greenberg thrilled me with their beautifully creepy jacket art, and I thank them for that. Hooray for Team Knopf!

Bear hugs to Jennifer Laughran for her wisdom, humor, enthusiasm, and therapeutic skills. It's an honor to work with you, Tenacious J!

Many dear friends were willing to read drafts of *The Dark Between*. L. K. Madigan was an early reader whose love for the story fueled my belief in it. (You are forever in my heart, Lisa, and I miss you so, so much.) Love and gratitude go out to Oklahoma critique buddies Brandi Barnett, Kelly Bristow, Martha Bryant, Dee Dee Chumley, Shel Harrington, and Lisa Marotta—thank you, Inklings, for always being there for me. Diane Bailey, Kim Harrington, Christine Johnson, Lisa Mason, Myra McEntire, Saundra Mitchell, and Natalie Parker also deserve thanks for their support, critical feedback, and all-around adorableness.

Thanks to Deborah Blum for writing *Ghost Hunters: William James and the Search for Scientific Proof of Life After Death*, which captured my imagination and inspired a novel that probably should be subtitled "Children of the Ghost Hunters."

Special thanks also to the porters at Newnham College, Cambridge, for always greeting me with a smile and allowing me to wander around the campus at my leisure. I also should thank a certain Trinity College porter for allowing me a very discreet peek into New Court when the college wasn't officially open to the public.

As ever I wish to give my family and friends grateful squeezes for their love and unfailing support. I'd be lost without you.

And, Steve, my dearest love and bestest friend, thank you for being my everything. Always.

KARAKURIDÔJI
ULTIMO

KARAKURIDÔJI ULTIMO

original concept: **STAN LEE**

story and art by: **HIROYUKI TAKEI**

inker: **DAIGO**

painter: **BOB**

1

KARAKURIDÔJI

ULTIMO 1

CONTENTS

ACT 1   Nanban-Okina Pass   5

ACT 2   Kurenai Dôji   67

ACT 3   A Blaze Surrounds Yamato   113

ACT 4   A Dream of Raseimon   161

BONUS MATERIAL   Karakuri Profiles   205

BONUS MATERIAL   Creator Interview   212

HEART IS WHERE THE *SPIRIT* OF GOOD OR EVIL LIES.

 SUPERIOR STRENGTH IS A *SWORD* THAT MANIFESTS ONE'S WILL.

 **PUPPETS ARE *MIRRORS* THAT REFLECT MORE THAN THEIR HUMAN CREATORS.**

ACT 1 NANBAN-OKINA PASS

ACT 1
NANBAN-OKINA PASS

12th
century

KYOTO
Japan

RATTLE RATTLE RATTLE
RATTLE

RATTLE RATTLE RATTLE

...

WAIT, OLD MAN.

RATTLE

HEH HEH...

DON'T TRY TO RUN IF YOU WANT TO LIVE.

SORRY, OLD MAN. WE'RE GOING TO HAVE YOU LEAVE THOSE WITH US.

RUSTLE

WE WON'T KILL YOU IF YOU DON'T START ANY TROUBLE.

STRANGE BANDITS.

SUCH UNNEC- ESSARY NUMBERS. OLD MEN AND EVEN CHILDREN!

HA!

I HAVE CREATED THEM. THEY ARE EQUAL TO EACH OTHER. NOTHING LIKE THEM HAS EVER EXISTED.

YOU REALLY OUGHT NOT TO TOUCH *THESE*...

THEY ARE *ULTIMATE* MECHANICAL BOYS. FIVE SENSES REACH INTO FIVE DIMENSIONS AND FOUR LIMBS EXTEND INTO FOUR DIMENSIONS. THAT ADDS UP TO THE POWER OF NINE DIMENSIONS.

IF YOU WAKE THEM, YOU *WILL* ALL DIE.

!

OH, REALLY?

SHING

THEIR SHODDY GOVERNMENT HAS COST US OUR HOMES, OUR FAMILIES...

SORRY, BUT I DON'T CARE *WHAT* YOU'VE GOT.

WE HATE THE NOBILITY.

FROM NOW ON, WE'RE TAKING IT ALL BACK.

WE ARE HERE TO MAKE SURE THEY CAN'T HAVE ANYTHING ELSE.

I SEE. YOU'RE *DUTY BANDITS.*

DRIP

BUT THEY ARE *ULTIMATE GOOD* AND *EVIL.*

VICE

ULTIMO

GOOD WON'T FORGIVE YOU. AND NO AMOUNT OF REASONING WILL WORK ON *EVIL*.

AND WHILE DUTY BANDITS MAY IN ESSENCE BE WORKING FOR THE GREATER GOOD, *EVIL* IS *EVIL*.

...IT'S ALL THE MORE REASON YOU SHOULDN'T DO ANYTHING SO FOOLISH AS TO UNDO THE ROPE ON THESE BOXES AND OPEN THE LIDS.

IF YOU WANT TO PROTECT YOURSELVES...

HUBBUB

...Z!

DON'T BE AFRAID!

BOSS...?

YOU AN IDIOT? NOTHING IS *ULTIMATE* OR *GOOD* OR *EVIL.* YOU'VE GOT IT ALL WRONG.

KEH! THE OLD MAN'S BLUFFING!

ULTIMATE GOOD AND *EVIL*?

ALL RIGHT, MEN.

I SAY OPEN UP THE BOXES RIGHT NOW.

BUT YOU TALK SO MUCH... YOU MUST HAVE SOMETHING VALUABLE IN THERE.

SMIRK

SMIRK

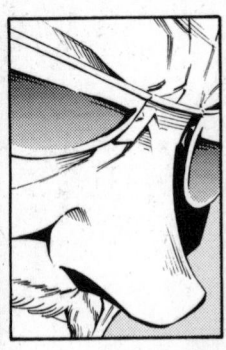

SMIRK

YES!

ONE... TWO...

...

D...

DOLLS
...?

CHATTER

CHATTER

THEY LOOK REAL.

SO PRETTY...

WE COULD GET A GOOD PRICE FOR THESE!

THEY LOOK LIKE THEY'LL START MOVING ON THEIR OWN AT ANY MOMENT!

HA HA HA! WHAT AN HONOR!

HOW NICE, HUH, OLD MAN? YOUR DOLLS HAVE MADE A GOOD IMPRES-SION.

...THEY'RE NOT DOLLS. THEY'RE MECHANICAL BOYS.

HOW-EVER...

ULTIMO...

WELL, YOU'VE GONE AND OPENED THE FORBIDDEN BOXES.

THEY WILL NOW BE AWAKENED AND BEGIN TO FULFILL THEIR DESTINIES.

HUH?

24

UGK...

GASP...

GAH!

I *WILL* STOP YOU.

YOU *WILL* BE PUNISHED.

A CHILD IS NO MATCH FOR ME!

BOSS...

B...

YOU MAY BE A FOOL, BUT YOU ARE NOT A COWARD.

HUH?

YOU SAY THIS EVEN AFTER WATCHING ME WORK?

'CAUSE I OPENED ONE OF THE BOXES.

I'LL FIGHT TOO.

SHING

! WELL, AREN'T YOU ASKING YOURSELF THE SAME THING?

HOW ARE YOU GOING TO FIGHT AGAINST *THAT*?!

HUUH?!

YOU DON'T GO AT THIS ALONE. NOT GONNA HAPPEN.

WE'RE BETTER IF WE ACT TOGETHER!

SHING

WE HAVE NO CHOICE.

I'LL FIGHT TOO.

SIX OF OUR COMRADES ARE DEAD.

THIS IS MY HOME.

...

EVEN IF I RAN, WHERE WOULD I GO?

IT DOESN'T SEEM REAL.

LIVING LIKE THIS EVERY DAY IS MORE TERRIFYING THAN THAT BOY.

IT'S STRANGE, BUT I'M NOT AFRAID!

HEY BOSS, WHAT ABOUT THE AMAZING KARAKURI DŌJI?

YOU FOOLS...

IF WE STOLE THAT ONE FOR OUR SIDE, WE COULD EASILY BEAT THE NOBILITY.

I DON'T KNOW HOW THOSE DOLLS WORK, BUT WE'RE BANDITS, RIGHT?

YOU MUSTN'T...

BLOOP

'CAUSE IT'S PRETTY.

NOD

BESIDES, SHE SAYS SHE WANTS IT.

HEY!

NO! JUST GET OUT OF HERE!

WHUMP

HUMANS, WHICH SHOULD BE THE STRONGEST CREATURES ON EARTH; ARE AT THE MERCY OF THESE TWO CONFLICTING ELEMENTS WITHIN THEM; AND THUS LOSE THEIR STRENGTH.

...EVEN THOUGH TIME OR PLACE TEACH HUMANS DIFFERENTLY AND THERE'S NO CLEAR DEFINITION NOR SHAPE TO GOOD AND EVIL.

BUT THE OBSTACLE TO THAT HAS ALWAYS BEEN... *GOOD* AND *EVIL*.

I AM A SCHOLAR. I'VE LONG SOUGHT THE *ULTIMATE* STRENGTH.

BECAUSE THEY STEAL SEVERAL THOUSAND TIMES MORE FROM PEOPLE IN ORDER TO LINE THEIR OWN POCKETS.

THE WORLD VIEWS THE ACTIONS OF BANDITS AS *EVIL*, BUT TO THE *GOOD* AUTHORITIES THOSE ACTIONS ARE ACTUALLY TRIFLING.

STRANGE, YET FRUSTRATING, EH?

....!

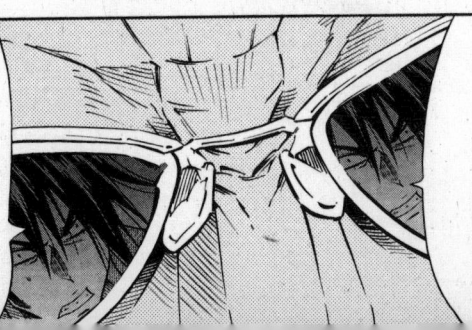

THE ANSWERS TO WHY PEOPLE LIVE IN CHAINS LIE DEEPER WITHIN THEIR HUMAN SOULS.

SO WHAT SEPARATES *GOOD* AND *EVIL*? WHETHER PEOPLE ACCEPT THEM OR NOT? NO.

...ULTIMATE KARAKURI DŌJI, MECHANICAL BOYS POSSESSING BOTH AN UNWAVERING SOUL AND UNYIELDING STRENGTH.

SO I BROKE DOWN A SINGLE SOUL AND SUCCESSFULLY GAVE LIFE TO...

CONTAINED WITHIN IS THE PURE *SPIRIT* OF GOOD OR EVIL.

SUPERIOR STRENGTH IS A *SWORD* THAT MANIFESTS ONE'S WILL.

PUPPETS ARE MIRRORS THAT REFLECT MUCH MORE THAN THEIR HUMAN CREATORS.

ACROSS TIME AND SPACE, THE KARAKURI DŌJI WILL SERVE MANY MASTERS, LEARN THOSE THREE TRUTHS, AND IN DUE COURSE THEY WILL HAVE THEIR FINAL BATTLE.

WHICH WILL WIN, *GOOD* OR *EVIL*? WHAT INFLUENCE WILL THE RESULT HAVE OVER HUMANITY?

...WOULDN'T YOU AGREE?

INTER-ESTING...

THE STRONGEST BEING? WHY WOULD YOU DO THIS?

I DON'T...

...UNDER-STAND!

NOTHING GOOD CAN COME FROM LETTING A CRAZY OLD MAN LIKE YOU LIVE.

I UNDERSTAND ONLY THIS.

HE'S GONE?!

H...

I DO NOT DIE.

I LOOK FORWARD TO SEEING HOW YOU FARE IN ALL THIS-- YOU WHO OPENED THE BOXES!

HA HA HA HA! NOW THEIR TRUE FIGHT BEGINS!

FWSH

DADUM

ULTIMO.

?!!

NO, NO, I'LL BE THERE! I'M JUST NOT A MORNING PERSON!

I HOPE YOU AREN'T SICK. SO YOU CAN COME TO MY PARTY...

SHE'S SO BEAUTIFUL!

S- SAYAMA!

CHAK

YOU'RE WEIRD.

BADUMP

CAN'T WAIT TO SEE WHAT YOU BRING.

BUT I'M GLAD YOU CAN COME.

I HAVE NO IDEA.

WHAT SHOULD I DO? HOW DID I TOTALLY FORGET, RUNE?

UNH, I LIKE HER SO MUCH!

YEAH!

NEITHER DO I!

I'LL TELL YOU RIGHT NOW, I DON'T HAVE ENOUGH MONEY ON ME TO LEND YOU ANY...

SO... WHAT WILL YOU BRING?

HM?

AN ANTIQUE SHOP?

THE KOKUBUNDO SHOPPE...?

I GUESS I JUST HAVE TO PAWN SOMETHING FOR CASH.

YAMATO?!

Excuse me...

YOUR SCHOOL-BAG!

RATTLE RATTLE

ULTIMO?!

古美術 刀剣
国分堂
青童・版画
古物高価買取

ACT 2 KURENAI DÔJI

ULTIMO?

?

ULTIMO?

WHAT...

HEY, WHAT'S GOING ON? YOU'RE REALLY WEIRD TODAY, YAMATO!

IT JUST POPPED OUT OF MY HEAD...

UM, WORDS LIKE THAT DON'T JUST POP OUT OF YOUR HEAD!

I DON'T KNOW!

...IS ULTIMO, RUNE?

DABOOM

ACT 2
KURENAI DÔJI

JUDGING FROM THE CRATER...

...THIS CHILD FELL FROM THE SKY.

NO WAY!

ANYWAY, YOU CAN'T JUST PUT SOMETHING YOU FIND LIKE THAT IN YOUR STORE!

SERIOUS? WOW!

YOU'D UNDERSTAND IF YOU SAW THAT MOUNTAIN.

IT'S COVERED IN TRASH. I'M JUST TRYING TO CLEAN IT UP A LITTLE.

HO HO! WHAT'S WRONG WITH KEEPING WHAT I FIND?

ONLY LAWS *ARE* GETTING STRICTER. FOOLS THINK AS LONG AS NO ONE FINDS OUT, IT DOESN'T MATTER WHAT THEY DO.

PEOPLE TODAY DON'T TAKE CARE OF ANYTHING.

LOOK AT THIS SHOP.

I PICKED OUT ALL THESE TREASURES WITH MY OWN EYES AND GATHERED THEM ALL HERE ON MY OWN.

YOU SHOULDN'T RELY ON OTHERS TO HELP YOU DETERMINE WHAT'S *GOOD* AND WHAT'S *BAD*.

IN NO TIME AT ALL, YOU'LL SIMPLY BE UNDER SOMEONE ELSE'S CONTROL.

WHY WOULDN'T THE NEWS REPORT SOMETHING SO CRAZY?

YOU'RE NOT EVEN LISTENING!

FELL FROM THE SKY! THAT'S REALLY SOMETHING!

GRAMPS...

BLINK

MASTER...

BLOOP

ULTIMO MISSED YOU VERY MUCH!

GLASS! SHNK

IT MOVED!

IT TALKED!

WHY'S THIS KID IN A GLASS CASE?!

WAP

!

WHO ARE YOU?!

DID YOU FORGET THE DAY WE BOUND OURSELVES TOGETHER? WHEN YOU BECAME ULTI'S MASTER AND ULTI BECAME YOUR SERVANT?

...

DID MASTER FORGET ABOUT ULTI?

BLOOP HUH...?

HOW LONG HAVE YOU KNOWN ME, RUNE?!

YOU THINK I HAVE ANY IDEA?!

YAMATO, WHAT'S HE TALKING ABOUT...?

WHOA...

...WHO IS THIS BOY?

THEN...

IT WOULD HAVE BEEN A MIRACLE FOR YOU TO BE REINCARNATED AND STILL REMEMBER ULTI'S NAME.

I UNDERSTAND.

SHUMP

WHO IS THIS BOY?!

WHO'S THIS BOY?!

YES.

WITHOUT A DOUBT YOU ARE THE YAMATO WHO I MET IN THE 12TH CENTURY.

REINCARNATED?!

HE FLED FOR HIS LIFE ACROSS TIME AND SPACE, AND YOU FOLLOWED. NOW WITH YOU REINCARNATED IN THE HERE AND NOW, WITHOUT A DOUBT, HE WILL COME FOR YOU.

YAMATO-SAMA'S ORDERS DROVE VICE AWAY. THE GRUDGE HE BEARS KNOWS NO END.

HE WILL INDEED BE HIDING SOMEWHERE NEARBY ALREADY.

...YAMATO-SAMA AND THIS ENTIRE WORLD WILL MEET A TERRIBLE FATE.

IF WE DON'T FIND AND DEFEAT HIM BEFORE HE FINDS A MASTER AND REGAINS HIS POWER...

YOU'RE CAUSING TROUBLE. YOU'RE DRESSED FUNNY...

I DON'T KNOW WHAT KIND OF GAME THIS KARAWHATSIT DOSOMETHING IS, BUT YOU SHOULDN'T BREAK GLASS.

YAMATO-SAMA...

RIGHT?

REALLY...

...I JUST FOUND HIM ON THE GROUND.

WHROOSH

AND YOU, GRAMPS!

WHAT ARE YOU THINKING?!

HUHN

BEFORE YOU PLAY WITH YOUR GRANDCHILD, GET YOUR *OWN* ACT TOGETHER!

EVERY TIME I RUSH SOMETHING IT'S ALWAYS A DISASTER.

WHAT A WASTE OF TIME!

SIGH

SHEESH! THAT WAS A MESSED-UP ANTIQUE SHOP!

UH... YAMATO?

SOMETHING WAS WEIRD ABOUT THAT BOY.

AW, MAN! WHAT SHOULD I DO ABOUT SAYAMA'S PRESENT? AM I GONNA HAVE TO BLACKMAIL SOMEBODY FOR CASH OR WHAT?

...AND *YOU* SAID ULTIMO, BUT THAT'S NOT EVEN THE WEIRDEST THING.

SURE, WHEN WE WENT IN I SAID YOUR NAME...

...BUT AFTER HE HUGGED YOU, HE WAS ALL CLEAN AND SHINY...

FIRST HE WAS ALL BEAT-UP AND DIRTY...

DID YOU SEE?

AND MOST OF ALL...

NO, IT WAS MORE THAN A WOW FACTOR!

UM, IT'S JUST YOUR IMAGINATION. THERE WASN'T ANY WOW FACTOR TO THAT GUY AT ALL.

...HE WAS ONLY A PUPPET WHEN WE WERE LOOKING AT HIM. NO WAY HE WAS A REAL KID.

...

MAYBE.

...I KNEW NOTHING GOOD WAS GOING TO COME OF IT.

AS SOON AS I LOOKED AT HIM...

BUT, YAMATO...

...

AND SAYAMA HAS NOTHING TO DO WITH THIS MESS EITHER.

I MEAN, I'M NOT REINCARNATED. COME ON. BUT I STILL DON'T WANT ANYTHING TO DO WITH HIM.

...BECAUSE I KNOW BETTER THAN ANYONE ELSE HOW, IF SOMETHING HAPPENED, YOU'RE THE TYPE WHO COULDN'T LET IT ALONE.

...I'M WORRIED...

TOO BAD.

YOU'RE ALREADY INVOLVED...

OH, GENERAL.

IT'S TOO LATE TO PLEDGE YOUR DEVOTION.

WHAT ARE YOU DOING, YAMATO?! IT'S DANGEROUS TO STAND THERE!

HW000

KREAK

BE QUIET AND WATCH CLOSELY AS I BREAK MY ENEMY.

IN THE BATTLE BETWEEN GOOD AND EVIL, I'VE GOT CHECKMATE.

AND THEN WATCH ME COME FOR YOU AND YOURS!

I WON'T LET YOU.

ACT 3
A BLAZE SURROUNDS YAMATO

VROOM!!

FWOOSH

...

EEK! AAGH!

AN EXPLOSION?!

CHATTER

WHOA!

TERRORISTS!

田茄子駅
北口

SFX: FWOOSH
SFX: FWOOSH

ULTIMO!

!

HUNH?!

...

HEY!
YOU
OKAY?!

HEY!!!

YAMATO!

OH
NO!

ULTIMO
...?

AND HE LOOKS BROKEN.

HE'S LIKE A PUPPET AGAIN. HE CAN'T MOVE.

WEIRD...

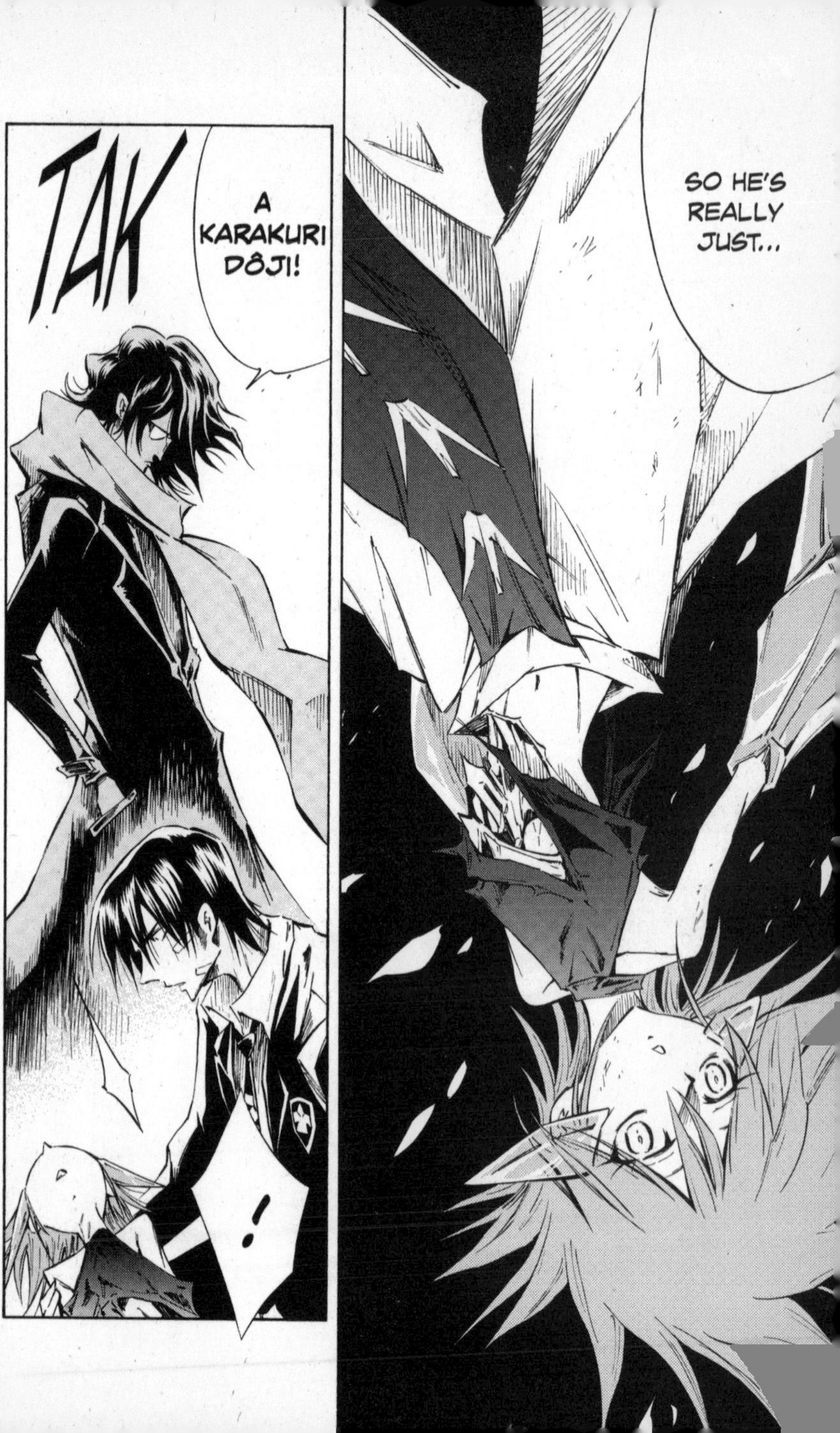
SO HE'S REALLY JUST...
TAK
A KARAKURI DÔJI!
!

ONCE THAT HAPPENS, THERE'S LITTLE HOPE OF RECOVERY.

HIS SPIRIT SPHERE IS BROKEN.

DON'T EXPECT MUCH.

WHO ARE YOU?

HUH?

I ENCOUNTERED THE KARAKURI DÔJI EXACTLY ONE YEAR AGO IN THIS VERY TOWN.

K.

I FOUND ONE ON THE VERGE OF DEATH. AND I FIXED HIM.

...

HIS NAME'S WRITTEN ON HIS COAT...

AFTER ALL I'VE DONE, HOW COULD I *NOT* KNOW THEM?

NOT VERY BRIGHT, ARE YOU?

YOU KNOW THESE TWO?!

VICE MASTER ?!

AFTER I WENT TO ALL THE TROUBLE OF FIXING IT, YOU RUINED IT AGAIN.

I DON'T NEED TO TELL YOU ANY MORE THAN THAT.

HUH?!

THIS JERK...

NOTHING COULD STOP ME!

I QUIT MY JOB AND RENTED A ROOM.

WITH VICE IN MY POWER, I NEVER WOULD HAVE HAD TO WORK AGAIN!

IF WE TALK TO THEM, WE CAN CLEAR UP EVERYTHING, ALL THIS MECHANICAL BOY BUSINESS.

BUT THIS IS GOOD.

GASP

WAAAH! WHAT DO WE DO, YAMATO? THE POLICE ARE HERE!

NNK...

I TRIED TO CATCH HIM, BUT HE BEAT ME UP AND TOOK ME HOSTAGE...

HELP ME, INSPECTOR. THIS GUY BLEW UP THE BUS.

NNGH...

...GGHH...

HEY! LIAR!

WHAAAAT?!!

DON'T MOVE!!!

WHOOSH

I'M ARRESTING YOU FOR ASSAULT AND BATTERY.

WE'LL TALK OVER THE DETAILS AT THE STATION.

KSHAK

WHAT DON'T YOU GET?

WHAD-DAYA MEAN, HUH?

HUH?

ANYWAY, ISN'T TODAY SAYAMA'S BIRTHDAY?

OH, RIGHT! EVERYONE'S GOING TO THE PARTY, RIGHT?

AH HA HA! OH, NOTHING! IT WAS NOTHING!

I HOPE HE'S ALL RIGHT.

...I SAW YAMATO COMING TO SCHOOL LIKE NORMAL.

BUT...

HA HA
HA HA HA

WHEN VICE MORPHED, WE TOOK OUR CHANCE AND GOT AWAY!

IT'S NOT GOOD AT ALL!!!

HUFF

HUFF

HUFF

WE SHOULD HAVE GONE WITH THE POLICE!

YAMATO, THIS IS SERIOUS!

GOOD, RIGHT? NO ONE WILL FIND US HERE.

AND WE EVEN BROUGHT THAT BOY!

NOW IT'S EVEN WORSE!

HE TRIED TO HELP US.

WE COULDN'T JUST LEAVE HIM.

THAT COP LOOKED DIRTY. YOU WANT HIM TO HAVE ULTIMO?

WHAT ARE YOU GONNA DO?!!!

SO WHAT?

...TO FIX HIM.

I'M GOING...

YOU'RE GOING TO REPAIR A ROBOT? THIS IS RIDICULOUS!

WHAT, YOU DON'T THINK I CAN?

I THINK HE HAS A HEART.

HE'S NOT JUST A ROBOT.

RUNE.

...

YAMATO...

SO DON'T CALL IT REPAIR.

...YOU'RE RIGHT.

I MEAN, YOU'RE PROBABLY RIGHT. IT MIGHT BE TRUE.

...GOT TO GO TO SCHOOL.

I'VE...

I DON'T WANT TO GET INVOLVED EITHER. BUT I THINK I'M ALREADY IN TOO DEEP TO GET AWAY FROM IT NOW.

I'M SORRY, RUNE!

...SIMPLY BY PRETENDING TO FORGET ABOUT THAT OLD GUY DUNSTAN, THAT DIRTY COP, K, AND-- MOST OF ALL-- THE MECHANICAL BOYS... THE...THE KARAKURI DŌJI!

THIS WON'T END...

THE FIRST THING TO DO IS FIX ULTIMO.

AND I HAVE AN IDEA HOW TO DO THAT.

I GOT HOME BY THE BACK ROADS.

47

ALL RIGHT.

NOW I JUST HAVE TO MAKE IT TO MY ROOM WITHOUT LETTING ANYONE SEE ME.

RUSTLE

I DON'T THINK ANYTHING WILL HAPPEN, BUT I GOTTA BE SUPER CAREFUL!

HEH HEH HEH

YAMATO?

149

I'VE ALWAYS TAKEN CARE OF YOU... AND BY MYSELF I MIGHT ADD. SO THE VERY LEAST YOU CAN DO IS NOT WASTE WHAT I'VE PAID TO YOUR SCHOOL.

FINE.

IF I DON'T GET ARRESTED...

PROBABLY.

...DON'T BRING YOUR WEIRD FRIENDS INTO YOUR ROOM.

And don't go number two outside...

AND...

I'LL BE LATE AGAIN TONIGHT, SO EAT WHATEVER YOU LIKE FOR DINNER.

47-402

東 AGARI

THAT WAS CLOSE! I DIDN'T EXPECT TO BUMP INTO MOM!

IF SHE'D BEEN IN A BAD MOOD, SHE'D HAVE KICKED MY BUTT!

SURE...

WHEW, I GOT LUCKY!

Well, yeah, about that number two thing...

SO,
ULTI...

OKAY,
I'M
IN MY
ROOM.

ULTIMO...

SO HE'S
NOT DEAD.

UH-OH,
THESE
INJURIES
ARE
REALLY
BAD.

BUT WHEN
WE WERE
OUT IN THE
DARK ALLEYS,
I COULD SEE
HIS SPIRIT
SPHERE
SHINING
FAINTLY.

...BUT AFTER HE HUGGED YOU, HE WAS ALL CLEAN AND SHINY...

FIRST HE WAS ALL BEAT-UP AND DIRTY...

DID YOU SEE?

ULTI WOKE UP BECAUSE YOU CAME WITHIN HIS RANGE.

DON'T EXPECT MUCH.

ONCE THAT HAPPENS, THERE'S LITTLE HOPE OF RECOVERY.

...ONCE I DO SOME SPECIFIC THING, YOU WILL RECOVER ON YOUR OWN.

WHICH MEANS...

...WAIT, IS THAT REALLY WHAT I'M SUPPOSED TO DO?

YOU WAKE UP A SLEEPING PRINCESS...

...HOW DO I MAKE THIS WORK?

UNH...

A KISS SEEMS CRAZY... BUT WHATEVER. I DON'T HAVE TIME TO THINK OF ANYTHING ELSE!!!

FWIK

WAP

I'M SORRY, SAYAMA!!!

MASTER ...

...YOU'RE TRYING TO HELP ULTI?

BLOOP

I WAS WORRIED, SO I SKIPPED OUT OF SCHOOL TO COME SEE...

YAMATO?

KACHAK

N.OK N.OK

...YOU.

HUFF HUFF

DIE

HEH...

THUD—

AGH!

SAYAMA...

KLIK

YAAAAAHHHHH!!!

ACT 4
A DREAM OF RASEIMON

AS THE NOBILITY GROWS MORE CORRUPT...

...MORE PEOPLE OPPOSE THEM.

AND NOW...

RAAAAAH AAH

YAAH

YAAAH

YEAH. IN THREE YEARS...

HA HA! CHIEF BOSS DID GOOD.

...OUR SMALL BAND HAS GROWN TO AN ARMY!

...WE HAVE *HIM*.

THAT OLD MAN LEFT US SOMETHING INCREDIBLE.

ULTIMO.

TODAY IS THE BATTLE, CORRECT?

SORRY, ULTI. I WASN'T CALLING YOU.

MASTER!

IT IS.

HA HA HA! YOU'RE JOINED AT THE HIP!

BUT MANY WILL DIE TODAY.

I WOULD UNDERSTAND IF TODAY YOU WISHED TO LEAVE.

YOU HAVE BEEN LOYAL.

DISTINGUISHING BETWEEN GOOD AND EVIL IS NOT SO SIMPLE TO DETERMINE.

THUS, THE KARAKURI DŌJI MUST SERVE UNDER MASTERS.

FWUMP

!

THE PALACES OF THE NOBILITY LIE BEYOND.

RASEIMON GATE.

ONCE THIS WAS THE CAPITAL'S GLORIOUS MAIN GATE.

IT'S ABANDONED AND ROTTING. VICTIMS OF PLAGUE LIE EVERYWHERE.

WHAT A WRECK.

HOWEVER DESOLATE THE LAND IS, DON'T DROP YOUR GUARD.

ULTI AND I WILL BREAK THROUGH.

NOBLES HAVE A KARAKURI DÔJI?!

NEWEST CREATION?!

MURMUR MURMUR MURMUR

DON'T RECOGNIZE HIM!

MUTTER

A NOBLE!

CHATTER

MUMBLE

A NOBLE?!

CHATTER

MUMBLE

MUTTER

WHO *IS* THAT?!

MUMBLE

MUTTER

YOU SEEM TO HAVE NO IDEA HOW TO USE A KARAKURI DÔJI!

IF I WERE YOU I'D RETREAT RATHER THAN CALM DOWN.

HEY!

BE CALM!

176

A DÔJI IS STRONGEST WHEN CLOSE TO HIS MASTER, BUT ALSO MORE DANGEROUS.

THE DÔJI MUST THEN HOLD BACK. AND YOU LOOK RIDICULOUS JOINED AT THE HIP, BY THE WAY.

JEALOUSY.

YOU'RE ARROGANT FOR SOME- ONE SO STUPID!

WHAT?!

...SEVERAL NEW DÔJI AND DISTRIBUTED THEM THROUGH- OUT TIME.

JUMP

WITH UNCOMMON SKILL AND UNCEASING EXPERIMENTATION, DR. DUNSTAN HAS CREATED...

BEFORE WE EVEN FIGHT, YOU ARE ALREADY OBSOLETE...

...MY *BROTHER.*

AND THAT LEGEND WILL PROPEL ME INTO THE RULING CLASS.

AN UNKNOWN NOBLE OF LOW RANK WILL STAND ALONE AGAINST THE BANDITS. AND HE WILL DEFEAT THEM.

!

...UNSCRUPULOUS.

YOU ARE...

MAYBE. BUT THE PEOPLE...

...WILL CALL ME **GOOD.**

Iruma Tomomitsu (48) Unscrupulous noble

HUH
?!

DIE

DIE

WHOOSH

...

A DREAM?

THEY
DO!

KARAKURI
DŌJI
DON'T
EXIST...

HA HA...
OF COURSE
IT WAS...

WHOOSH

THAT MUST MEAN SAYAMA REALLY DID--

...AND IT WASN'T!!!

IT WAS A DREAM...

!!!

SAYAMA...

From Sayama

...so...

BADUMP BADUMP

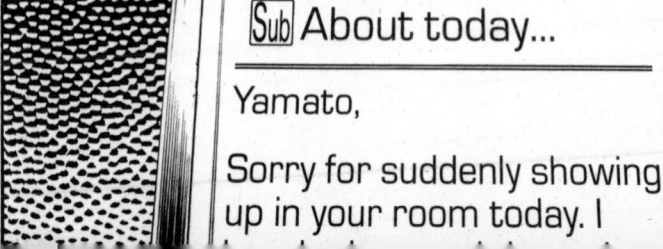

From Sayama ♥
Sub About today...

Yamato,

Sorry for suddenly showing up in your room today. I

Yamato,

Sorry for suddenly showing up in your room today. I knocked several times, but you didn't answer, so I opened the door.

It looked like you were going to kiss that puppet doll thing...?

I won't tell anyone about this, but it'd probably be best if you don't come to the party tonight.

191

MASTER...

BLOOP

HWOOO—

THE WINDOW...

ACHOO

KRASSHH

ULTIMO IS SORRY, YAMATO-SAMA!!

THAT'S STRANGE...

THERE'S NO INFORMATION ON THE ATTACK THIS MORNING.

BUT IT ISN'T ANYWHERE ON TV OR THE NET.

MECHANICAL PUPPETS HAVE A STREETFIGHT. NO WAY THAT DIDN'T MAKE THE NEWS!

"WHY WOULDN'T THE NEWS REPORT SOMETHING SO CRAZY?"

THIS MORNING YAMATO SAID...

IF WHAT THAT OLD ANTIQUES DEALER SAID IS TRUE...

THIS CHILD FELL FROM THE SKY.

...SOMEONE IS COVERING THIS UP!!

...BUT IF I'M RIGHT, YAMATO IS IN DANGER!!!

I COULD JUST BE PARANOID...

WHO MADE THIS?

WAIT!

IT'S SIMPLE, BUT THE CHEF HAS SKILLFULLY DRAWN FORTH THE FLAVOR OF THE INGREDIENTS FOR AN INCOMPARABLE SAVORY EXPERIENCE!

TASTES SOOOOO GOOOD--

THIS TASTES AWE-SOME !!!

NOM NOM NOM NOM

IT MUST HAVE BEEN *HIM!*

MOM'S COOKING ISN'T THIS GOOD.

WOOOOooo

HEY, ULTI--

WHOOSH!

AW, MAN...

...SO OF COURSE HE'S NOT HERE.

I KICKED HIM OUT...

SIGH

THUD

LIKE HOW HE CAN COOK WITH THOSE GAUNTLETS. AND WITHOUT HIM, I CAN'T STOP VICE AND K.

THERE'S SO MUCH I WANT TO ASK HIM.

...I WANT TO KNOW IF THAT DREAM WAS REAL.

AND MORE THAN ANYTHING...

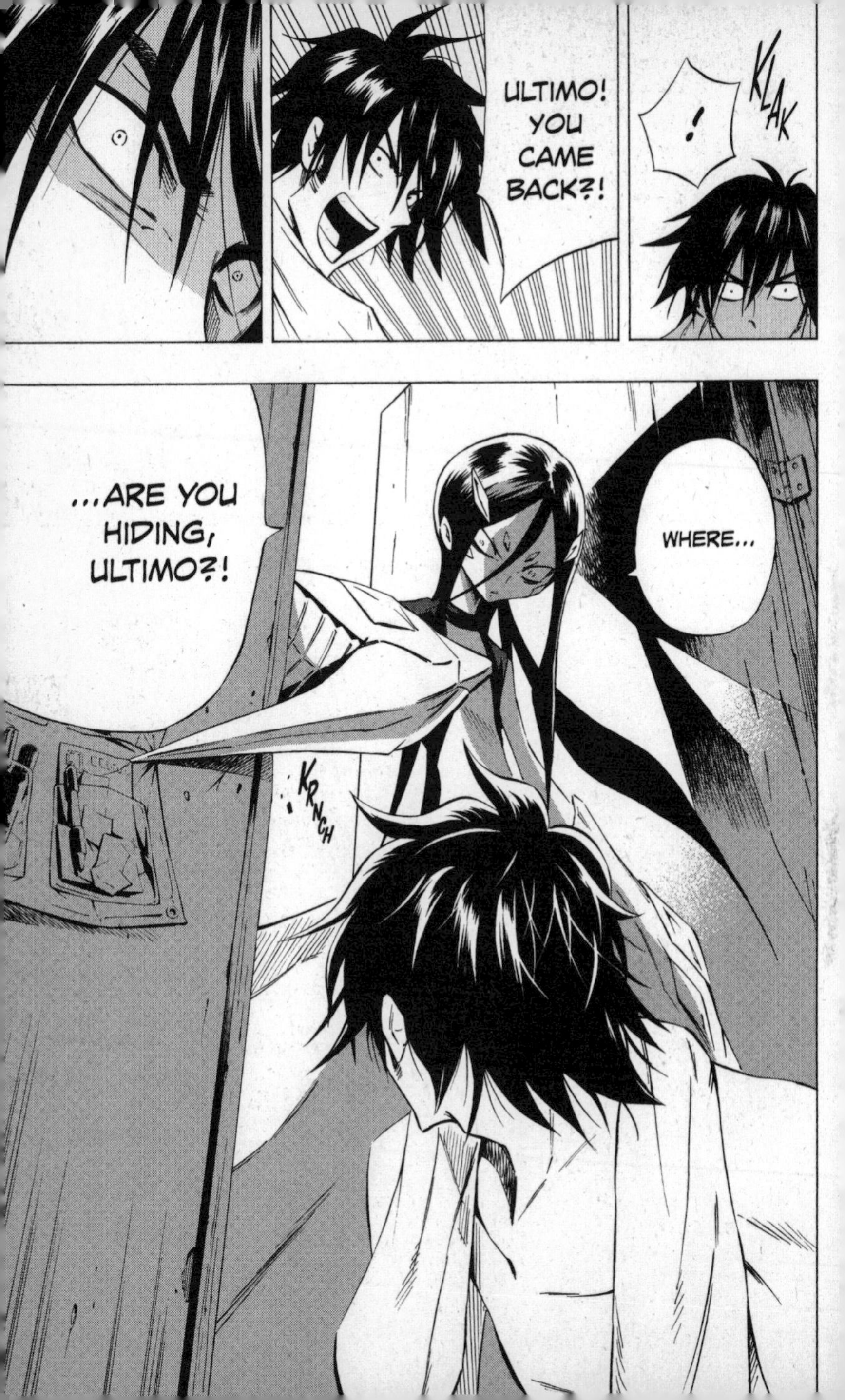
KLAK
!
ULTIMO! YOU CAME BACK?!
WHERE...
...ARE YOU HIDING, ULTIMO?!
KRNCH

YOU REMEMBER ME?

...

HM

...JEALOUSY!!!

Y-YOU'RE...

WHOOSH

YOU'VE REUNITED WITH ULTIMO. WHERE IS HE?

VEEN

IT DOESN'T MATTER.

I KICKED HIM OUT A LONG TIME AGO!

NOT HERE!

WHAT?!!

I SHOULD KILL YOU...

...AND SEARCH AT MY LEISURE.

I'VE GOT A DEAL FOR YOU.

YOU MUST BE SICK OF ALL THIS TROUBLE BY NOW.

WHAT?!

!

SELL ME ULTIMO!

THERE'S A HUNDRED MILLION IN THE CASE.

CHARACTER DATA COMPILATION
KARAKURI ILLUSTRATED PROFILES
1

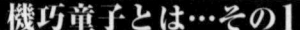

機巧童子とは…その１

機巧童子は人間の「善」と「悪」、そしてそのどちらが
強いのかを知るためにダンスタン博士によって開発された
童子型の機巧人形である。

童子は無垢な者の象徴であり、これが彼らが
純粋な「善」と「悪」であることを示している。これは
同時に彼らが学習型のロボットであることも意味する。

彼らは未完成であり、「殿」と呼ばれる人間を
任意に選出することで共に行動し、時代と地域を
越えたあらゆる人間の「善」と「悪」を学んでいくのだ。

…続く

What is a Karakuri Dôji? Part 1

Mechanical dolls that look like children, the Karakuri Dôji
were designed by Dr. Dunstan to find out about good and evil
from humans—and to discover which is stronger.

Dôji are untainted beings. They can be either pure good or
pure evil. They are robots designed to learn.

But Dôji are incomplete. They must choose a human master
to accompany, in order to acquire the human traits of good
and evil that transcend time and space.

To be continued...

 機巧童子 ARAKURI DŌJI

ULTIMO

ウルティモ

The first Karakuri Dōji of Good that Dr. Dunstan created. His actions are based on Dunstan's idea of "good," but exactly what that means is unclear. Just as his name implies, he is top class in everything from appearance to functions. However, precisely because he is perfect in some ways, he is lacking in many others. He is currently gathering information about goodness with Yamato as his master.

His theme color is scarlet.

His Karakuri Henge are based on cranes and lions.

VICE

バイス

The first Karakuri Dōji of Evil, created together with Ultimo. He is a clone possessing the exact same capabilities as Ultimo, but his purpose is the exact opposite. Thus, he bears a name meaning evil. He serves his master in order to learn about evil and gain evil energy, and otherwise acts only under a variety of evil impulses.

His theme color is that of iron. [Usually Vice is associated with green, but here it says his theme color is "iron(or steel)-color."]

His Karakuri Henge are based on turtles and demons.

YAMATO

AGARI YAMATO 東大和

Born Nov. 15, Scorpio, Blood type O, 16 years old

The main hero. He is immensely enthusiastic and kind, but always gets himself into trouble. He currently lives with his mother in public housing.

His favorite thing is Sayama.

RUNE

小平 ルネ **KODAIRA RUNE**

Born Feb. 4, Aquarius, Blood type AB, 16 years old

A boy in glasses who adores Yamato. His family is rich and he's an excellent student. He's extremely serious, but a little too inflexible. Later on, his character will develop in a surprising way.

His favorite thing is sweets with whipped cream on top.

SAYAMA SAN

狭山 真琴 **SAYAMA MAKOTO**

Born May 5, Taurus, Blood type A, 17 years old

A cool and mysterious high school girl who always keeps her head about her. Capable of taking bold action, she has rescued Yamato from crises many times in the past, but her cold reactions deliver even deeper psychological damage.

Her favorite things are mushrooms and cheese.

K

ケー

Born May 31, Gemini, Blood type A, 31 years old

A man in glasses who dreams of being evil. A short-tempered person of low caliber, when he gets flustered he doesn't know what's happening and starts trembling.

His favorite things are motorcycles and heavy metal. He feeds the sparrows on his veranda.

DUNSTAN

ダンスタン

Born Dec. 28, Capricorn, Blood type O, ? years old

Another man in glasses, unidentified and shrouded in mystery. He is a joker-type character who created the Karakuri Dōji, thus giving to the series a wide variety of characters.

His favorite thing is…a secret.

ULTIMO
Volume 1

Original Concept: Stan Lee
Story and Art by: Hiroyuki Takei

SHONEN JUMP Manga Edition

This graphic novel contains material
that was originally published in English
in SHONEN JUMP #79-82
Artwork in the magazine may have been
slightly altered from that presented here.

Translation | John Werry
Series Touch-up Art & Lettering | James Gaubatz
Design | Fawn Lau
Series Editor | Joel Enos
Graphic Novel Editor | Jann Jones

VP, Production | Alvin Lu
VP, Sales & Product Marketing | Gonzalo Ferreyra
VP, Creative | Linda Espinosa
Publisher | Hyoe Narita

Printed in the U.S.A.

Published by VIZ Media, LLC
P.O. Box 77010
San Francisco, CA 94107

10 9 8 7 6 5 4 3 2 1
First printing, February 2010

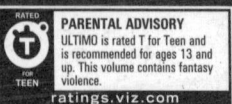

VIZ
MEDIA
www.viz.com

www.shonenjump.com

STAN LEE

As a kid, Stanley Martin Lieber spent a lot of time dreaming up wild adventures. By the time he got to high school, he was putting his imagination to work writing stories at Timely, a publishing company that went on to become the legendary Marvel Comics. Starting with the *Fantastic Four*, Lee and his partner Jack Kirby created just about every superhero you can think of, including *Spider-Man*, the *X-Men*, the *Hulk*, *Iron Man*, *Daredevil* and *Thor*. Along the way, he wrote under a lot of pen names, but the one that stuck was Stan Lee.

HIROYUKI TAKEI

Unconventional author/artist Hiroyuki Takei began his career by winning the coveted Hop Step Award (for new manga artists) and the Osamu Tezuka Cultural Prize (named after the famous artist of the same name). After working as an assistant to famed artist Nobuhiro Watsuki, Takei debuted in *Weekly Shonen Jump* in 1997 with *Butsu Zone*, an action series based on Buddhist mythology. His multicultural adventure manga *Shaman King*, which debuted in 1998, became a hit and was adapted into an anime TV series. Takei lists Osamu Tezuka, American comics and robot anime among his many influences.

HIROYUKI TAKEI   **STAN LEE**

CREATOR INTERVIEW

HIROYUKI TAKEI: How did you come up with the ideas for Ultimo?

STAN LEE: I don't know. I was trying to do something that would be good for the Japanese audience as well as an American audience. There aren't too many robots here in America. I didn't know if they had a good robot fighting the bad ones in Japan and thought maybe this idea would be good for both countries. So I said, "Well, why not? I'll write it, and we'll see what they say." When I saw your first drawings, they made me think of many new things. I got so excited about them that I was really thrilled to be working with an artist like you.

HK: What made you want to collaborate with a Japanese manga and comic artist?

SL: I love Japanese manga, and I know how popular it is, certainly in Japan, but even in America. I've never done anything with manga. I don't like to think there is anything that I haven't done, so I was really eager to do something, and to do it with the best artist possible. That was, you know, something I couldn't resist.

HK: You have the rough page layouts. What did you think when you first saw them?

SL: It's very hard for me to understand them because storyboards in America look a little different. They're tighter and they're more complete. The Japanese layouts are very rough, so it's gonna take me a while to get used to looking at that type of storyboard. Of course, I need English to understand what I'm looking at. It's a little hard to tell because I don't read Japanese as well as I used to. [*Laughter*]

HK: Stick figures are actually what it comes down to because we have to produce 19 pages a week.

SL: That's a tremendous amount. I mean, when I was doing comic books years ago, our books were originally 64 pages in the 1930s. Then they got whittled down to 48 pages, and finally by the 60s they were only 32 pages. Now, of the 32 pages, 8 or so were ads. There ended up being about 20 or 22 pages of actual comics, and we had to do that in a month. For you people to do all of this in one week, I think that is absolutely amazing. And to have it turn out as good as it does, I think you're all geniuses.

HK: Everyone does it in Japan.

SL: No wonder you always look so tired. The difference is, we only did 20 pages a month, but I was writing between 12 and 20 comic books a month. So we did quite a lot, too. You know, there was Spider-Man, The Hulk, The X-Men and so on.

HK: What do you think of Japanese manga?

SL: I love it! That's why I wanted to do this. I love the way the stories flow. I love the characters. I love everything about it. I just hope that I can write it as well as what I've read in Japanese manga. But I'm gonna do my best.

HK: Lastly, do you have a message for SHONEN JUMP readers?

SL: Oh, absolutely. Save your money and go out there and buy as many copies of *Ultimo* as you possibly can. Don't just buy one, because they're gonna be worth a lot of money in the future. So buy a lot of them and save them. Now, I have a question for you. Why are you sitting here wasting all this time when you should be working on *Ultimo* and getting that out as fast as possible?! [*Laughter*]

IN THE NEXT VOLUME...

Things just keep getting more complicated for Yamato since Ultimo showed up. Now Yamato and Ultimo must face new Dôji and deal with people whose intentions aren't always so clear. Can Yamato find the strength to meet these challenges and solve the mysteries of the Karakuri Dôji?

AVAILABLE AUGUST 2010!
Read it first in SHONEN JUMP magazine!

A BRUSH WITH THE AFTERLIFE

All Colour But The Black
THE ART OF BLEACH
By Tite Kubo, creator of *ZOMBIEPOWDER.*

EXPLORE THE WORL
OF *BLEACH* **THROUGH TH**
HIGH-QUALITY ART BOC
SHOWCASING ARTWOF
FROM TITE KUBO'
POPULAR MANGA SERIE
WHICH INCLUDES:

- Vibrant illustrations, includir art from volumes 1-19
- An annotated art guide
- Extra character information

PLUS, AN EXCLUSIVE POSTE

COMPLETE YOUI
BLEACH COLLECTION WIT
THE ART OF BLEACH
ALL COLOUR BUT THE BLACK—
GET YOURS TODAY

On sale at
www.shonenjump.co
Also available at your loc
bookstore and comic sto